SISTAHGIRL
PUBLISHING CO.

Sonia Caulton

No More LoveMaking

A Novel

A SistahGirl Publishing

No More
LoveMaking

Publisher's Note
This is a work of fiction. Names, characters, places and incidents either
are the product of the author's imagination or are used fictiously, and any resemblance to
actual person, living or dead, events or locals is entirely coincidental.

Library of Congress Cataloging-in Publication Data
2001118972

No More LoveMaking: a novel/Sonia Caulton.-1st SistahGirl ed.
ISBN 0-9655545-2-X
I. Title
Printed in the United States of America
SistahGirl 2001

God's Praise

For I know the thoughts and plans that I have for you, says the Lord, thoughts and plans for welfare and peace and not for evil, to give you hope in your final outcome. Then you will call upon Me, and you will come and pray to Me, and I will hear and heed you. Then you will seek Me, inquire for, and require Me and find Me when you search for Me with all your heart. I will be found by you, says the Lord... (Jer: 29:11-14 AMP).

In spite of the letters and reviews that advised me to give-up writing, for the errors that were made in my novel Voodoo Love after I entrusted a so-called professional editor to edit it for me, God had already chosen the path I would take to reach my destiny, before I was conceived. He never told me it would be easy nor did I think it would be without me making mistakes that would cause me humiliation and people to not understand. However my faith in God, caused me to hold my head up high and continue my journey toward my foreordained destiny to be a writer. For there is never a journey worth traveling, without rocks, mountains, storms and people with criticizing and judgmental opinions that made me want to give-up and head back home to comfort. I've come to realize without those obstacles, I would have never known the determination I have to weather the storms and continue on with my journey.

Allow this to be the encouragement you need to keep going when you feel like giving up.

Acknowledgements

Thank you Gary A. Wallace and your family for your time and dedication in editing No More LoveMaking to perfection. Because you were a reader, a friendship was established.

1

It was said that there is always one person in the relationship that loved more than the other and that one person ruled the relationship. DeDe was now beginning to believe she loved Stephan more than he could ever love her, and because of that, he had her just where he wanted her. He had her praying for him to love her just as much as she loved him. Coming to that conclusion was a very hard pill for her to swallow, but all the signs point to it. After an argument, it was she who would apologize first whether she was wrong or not. She considered him in all of her plans, but he considered his friends and daughter in his. She called him much more than he called her. When she walked through the door after work, he's the first person she calls if she's not heading to his house and when she headed there she calls him to see if he needs anything before she comes. Sorry to say, he doesn't do the same. If she doesn't call, most likely they will not talk that night. He claims to not be a phone person except for if and when he calls his mother. DeDe had taken him to meet her parents six months after they had been dating. She met his parents four months ago, after three years of them being together. He claimed he doesn't believe in introducing every woman he meets to his mother, unless she's someone special. Being together for three years meant she was more than someone special; she should have been the woman he wanted to marry. The long anticipated wait for her to finally meet his family turned out to be a nightmare along with the truth of why she hadn't met them before four months ago. His mother was very anti-social toward her and she asked about Shannon and Alexis every couple of minutes. After being so angry, Stephan later told her that his mother doesn't care to meet any woman who isn't Shannon, because she preferred they get married and raise their child in a two parent home.

DeDe was happy about their relationship. They hadn't had an argument within a month and she's been spending every night of the week at his house. Stephan had even made plans for them to fly to Miami for the Memorial Day weekend on Friday evening. Since she's taken a new job at Stein & Stockton Public Relations firm, she and Stephan haven't spent much time together lately because she's been working twelve-hour days. DeDe took off work earlier than usual, so that she could cook dinner for Stephan at his place. Her sister and brother were living with her for the time being and there was no privacy at her place. She was cooking all of Stephan's favorites: fried chicken, macaroni and cheese, greens and yams. She hated that everything had to be from a box or a can, but that is all she had time for. The oil was now getting hot enough for the chicken, as she seasoned and battered it in buttermilk and flour. The phone rang and DeDe looked at the caller ID before answering. She sighed and had made up her mind to not answer and let the machine answer. But then again, she should let Shannon know she was there and Stephan was not. In other words; to let Shannon know she had a key.

"Hello."

"Let me speak with Stephan."

"He hasn't made it home yet."

"Then what are you doing over there answering the phone?"

DeDe's point accomplished, she thought but she chose to act as if she had ignored her question. "Would you like for me to tell 'im you called?"

"No, I don't need you to tell him anything. I'll call back."

"Fine."

"You know I don't like you," Shannon made it a point to tell her.

"Shannon, feelings are mutual."

"You actually think he's going to marry you. Don't wait on it. He can see right through you DeDe."

"Shannon I know he's going to marry me and you know it also, that's why you are so angry. And what concern is it of yours if he does? I thought you told him you had somebody; so don't be bitter because he has someone."

"I can have him if I want him. I'm his child's mother."

DeDe's rare tan peach-bronze complexion had turned beet purple, because she had always felt Shannon could have Stephan back if she really tried.

"Haven't you heard? There's going to always be a bond between Stephan and I?"

"He doesn't want you so I'm not worried," she said, as she tried to show her confidence through her insecurity.

"Don't be bitch!"

"You're the bitch!"

"You think you have Stephan fooled. You're over there cooking him dinner every night, decorating his apartment, helping pay his rent and that damn car note, all for a ring that you are not going to get. You are so low; you would even use my daughter by trying to buy her to get to her daddy."

"I care for Alexis," she said, and ran her fingers through her very short hair that was cut close to her scalp. After seeing Nia Long's hair in a magazine, she took the picture to her beautician Roberta and made her promise she would give her the same exact cut.

"Like hell. She doesn't need you to care for her, she has a mother."

"And I wouldn't try to come between a mother and child, Shannon."

"Don't." *Click*

DeDe took the phone away from her ear and stared at it long and hard before hanging it up. She took a sip of her wine and slowly walked over to the stove and turned off all of the pots, before pouring her another glass of wine and walking into the living room and sitting down on the sofa. Once again, like always, Shannon had ruined her mood. Stephan walked in and threw his keys on the table in the foyer.

"What's up baby," he asked as he kicked off his shoes at the door before walking on his pure white carpet. "What 'cha cook?"

"Nothing."

"Why, I thought that you were?" He walked over to her and engulfed her thin lips with his thick wet ones.

"Well, I was until that bitch called."

"Who, Shannon? What did she want?" He asked, as he walked into the kitchen and DeDe followed.

"You, and I mean, literally. She said you'd always want her. You two have a bond together." No matter how much she tried to tell Shannon and herself that wasn't true, she was beginning to believe that it was. They did have a six-year-old child together and they had been together for eight years before walking away from each other.

"Why do you let Shannon get to you like that? She does it because she knows she can get up under your skin."

"No, she does it because she knows you are not going to say anything. She called me a bitch."

Stephan was in the kitchen searching for food, as he looked under the lid of each pot on the stove. "Why didn't you cook? You told me you were going to cook. Damn, I'm hungry."

She sighed, rolled her eyes up to the ceiling, and placed the glass on the counter. "I'm leaving."

"Where are you going?"

"Home."

"Home," he repeated. "And why?"

"It's obvious you're just going to let her run all over me," she said, looking him in the eyes as they stood toe to toe. She was 5'3", petite with nothing big on her but her size 36c bouncy round breasts and Stephan was 5'9" with a slim, muscular build. He was shorter than any man she had ever dated and he was sure as hell not the richest, but none of that mattered to DeDe. Stephan had other things working in his favor. He was funny, he allowed her to be herself around him and his lovemaking was the bomb. He had the perfect size sex for a man his height and he knew all the right spots to hit for her to climb the walls.

"No, you are going to let her run all over you. I'm not going to get in the middle of that shit you and Shannon are doing, and neither is my daughter. You and Shannon have to learn to get along. You are wrong DeDe, for thinking that I should take sides. I have to deal with her for the next twelve years, until Alexis is eighteen. I'm not trying to fuck up my relationship with her for something that might not even last. Niggahs do it all the time and regret it later. Once you mess up shit between you and the woman you have a child with, your life is living hell. Ask Melvin if you don't believe me."

She didn't give a damn about asking Melvin's tired ass anything. "What do you mean, might not even last? We've been together for three years Stephan." She raised her eyebrow and put her hands on her hipless shape. "If this isn't going to last, let me know now. However, after three years, that shouldn't have even come out of your mouth. You should know this is going to last, because I should be the one you want to marry right?"

"DeDe you are getting into something totally different. Marriage has nothing to do with this."

"Yes the hell it does," she assured him by stretching her small hazel eyes wider through, her thin wire frame glasses.

He slipped on his shoes, grabbed his keys and walked toward the front door. "I'm going to get me something to eat, do you want to come?"

Although she really wanted to go with him, her anger made her say, "No, I'm going home." She grabbed her purse and briefcase and followed him to the door.

"Fine." They both walked outside to their cars.

"She told me you would never marry me," she said, as she followed him down the stairs. "And, I'm just here to help you out when you need it."

"DeDe, you know why you and I can never be married, you listen to everything someone tells you about me and you believe it. You know why I know you believe it, because you repeat it." He jumped into his car and started it up. "Shannon has her life and she's miserable with it, so she wants to see everyone else miserable. Drive safe."

DeDe jumped into her car and sped off. She hated Shannon for knowing just the right things to say to piss her off. She hated Shannon for having all the power she does over Stephan, because she is his child's mother. There were so many things that she wanted to say to Shannon. But she was concerned about what would Stephan say, if she repeated some of the things he had told her about Shannon. Ever since she and Stephan have been dating, Shannon has given her pure hell. She disliked her for no reason other than she and Stephan were together and in love. DeDe wasn't trying to take her place with Alexis, as Shannon claimed. Alexis had the sense of a twenty year old at the age of six, so that wasn't hardly happening. She told DeDe everything Shannon had said about her. Maybe there's some truth to her being able to have Stephan back anytime she wants. He has never defended DeDe, when they argue. In addition, he and Shannon are always laughing and talking about more than Alexis. DeDe didn't understand their relationship. She has known babymama's and daddies to hate each other. When Shannon and Stephan argue, he's a lot more respectful to Shannon than he is to DeDe when they argue. DeDe feels because he's never cursed her out, she's welcomed to the house any damn time she feels like dropping Alexis off unannounced, and since they still do Christmas shopping for Alexis together there might just be some feelings lingering there on both of their parts. Not just on Shannon's part like Stephan tells her. For her to have hurt Stephan the way he said she did when she left him and took Alexis, he seems to have forgiven her. When DeDe's sister Kendra argues with those two jackasses, she has children by, they cut her down so low in front of their girlfriends, showing her very little respect; she doesn't even care to deal with the children basically because of their fathers. DeDe had told herself she would never date a man with a child, because of the drama of dealing with the bitter mothers, who are angry they have to be single parents and the father has moved on with his life with another woman.

WHEN SHE FINALLY got home, there was Melvin's black V12 Mercedes parked in her driveway blocking the entrance to her garage. Melvin was Kendra's ex-husband and DeDe couldn't stand him, although he was Stephan's best friend and he had introduced them. DeDe couldn't believe Kendra had him sitting up in her house, after what he had done. It was obvious she had lost her damn mind. DeDe threw her car in park and jumped out in a fury. He was going to get the hell out of her house and if Kendra wanted to go with him, she could. He had mistreated her, by beating her every time he felt the urge, and not wanting anything to do with her children and he had even hit DeDe. She sure as hell didn't want to have anything to do with Melvin after that. She was trying to stop him from beating Kendra to a pulp, when he hauled off and slapped her to the ground. On top of that, her own man, his best friend just stood there and did nothing. Stephan talked her into not pressing charges, because the media would catch wind of it and ruin Melvin's career. DeDe stormed toward the door and shoved her key into the lock. She walked into the house and slammed the door behind her. There was Kendra and Melvin sitting on the sofa laughing like the best of friends. DeDe meant to make her stare noticeable as she walked into the room. Melvin looked at her, smiled and turned his head to watch television.

"I thought you were at Stephan's; what are you doing home?" Kendra asked.

"Don't I live here?" She snapped, as she threw her mail on the table.

"You damn sure do. But don't come in here with an attitude, because the muthafucka pissed you off."

"My boy is in the doghouse again DeDe?" Melvin asked and laughed.

"What are you doing in my house?" DeDe asked Melvin.

"He's here to see me."

"Then you and him get the hell out. This low-life isn't thinking about you. He married you and divorced you within a year, he beats your ass for the hell of it and he doesn't want anything to do with your kids."

"DeDe shut up," Kendra told her.

7

"Why should I? I'm telling the truth aren't I?"

"DeDe," he said, as he sat on the edge of the sofa. "I'm sorry about what happened between you and I. I had no business hitting you, while you were trying to protect your sister, but I was high. Since then, I've gotten help. I love Kendra."

DeDe looked at Kendra and said, "If you believe that shit you are stupid." She rolled her eyes, walked to her bedroom, and slammed the door behind her.

A minute later Kendra barged into her room. "What is your damn problem?"

"What is he doing here?"

"Like I said, to see me... you had no right."

"You're stupid."

"Just as stupid as you are over Stephan, so bitch let's not start trying to act like your shit is so much together. You're mad with that niggah tonight and you'll be back with him tomorrow. Now what's wrong?"

"Nothing. Is he spending the night or are y'all going to the damn mansion he somehow won in the divorce?"

"DeDe, I don't want to talk to you right now."

"Good. Now close my door and get out." DeDe felt she was far from stupid, when it came to her and Stephan. They had their arguments, but she had no doubt in her mind that he loved her. That's more than she could say for Melvin. Kendra had a habit of wanting everyone else to be in the same fucked up situation as she was, when it came to Melvin.

DeDe turned on the television and jumped into the shower. As the warm water ran down her short petite body, she thought about how stupid she acted for leaving. She had let Shannon win again. She turned off the water jumped out of the shower and ran to call Stephan to let him know she was on her way back over, but there was no answer. She didn't bother to leave a message. She threw on some sweats and tried calling for the next hour and a half. It was understood during the beginning of their relationship that she is not to just pop-up unannounced, even if she just happened to be in the neighborhood.

However, he did promise to let her in. But even if he didn't let her in, she had a key.

She finally grew tired of calling and getting no answer. She then put on her nightgown and jumped into bed.

2

$\mathcal{AT}$ seven-thirty this morning, DeDe woke up out of her sleep dialing Stephan's number. Before she could wash her face or brush her teeth, she was reaching for the phone, but still there was no answer. She knew he was there with an attitude. Another woman had never crossed her mind. Not answering the phone was one of the games he would play, when they were angry at each other. He would see her name come up on the caller ID and he wouldn't answer, until he's heard enough of her pleas for him to call her back. They had each other figured out. Almost.

ON HER WAY to work, she drove by his apartment and she didn't see his car. Her heart began to pound. For the first time, since she hadn't been able to get in contact with him, another woman came to the forefront of her mind. It was eight-thirty and he would just be getting up to get dressed for work so he should be there, she thought. She threw her car in park and apprehensively walked up the stairs to his apartment. She knocked twice before taking her key and going in. There was an empty beer bottle and container on the countertop from where he had gone to get Chinese for dinner last night. The living room still looked like it did, after she had cleaned it. As she looked down the hall to his bedroom, she whispered his name before approaching the closed bedroom door. Nervously her hand gripped the doorknob and she took one deep breath, before pushing the door open. His bed was still made-up from the morning before. His underwear and sock drawer was halfway opened and his toothbrush was gone, and so was his overnight bag. She stormed over to the telephone, called his cell phone, and pressed #2, the prompt to page him. With advanced technology, the phone repeated and displayed his home telephone number where she was calling from. Then she called him back and left a voice message. "I see you didn't sleep at home last night."

When she got to her office, she tried calling him again, but still no answer.

She slammed the phone down and fell back in her chair and before a tear could fall, Dionne walked into her huge spacious cubicle and noticed her frustration.

"What's up girlfriend?" She asked, as she sat down and crossed her long tan legs. Everything on her body was long: her feet, her head, her hair, her nose, her arms, and her fingers. Her long wavy hair was pulled back tightly into a ponytail, as it always is. She was tall, big boned with a huge wide mouth that stretched clean across her face when she smiled or talked. Sistah's with mouths that wide like Millie Jackson, Stephanie Mills, MiMi from Brownstone, Rachelle Ferrell and Erma Andrews who sings in DeDe's church choir usually can sing their asses off, but she didn't know about that in Dionne's case. She had never heard her but what DeDe did know she talked too damn much at times. She could go for a half-breed, but she was fully black and didn't mind acting it, if she was caught on a bad day. She had all the White people in the office afraid of her; at least that's what she thought. She was thirty-something maybe a year or two from forty, but she looked good for her age. She could pass for a model, but she wasn't as shallow as some of them could be. She was a very direct woman and sometimes came off as rude and bitter to people who didn't know her personality. DeDe had to learn it quick in order for her to tolerate Dionne. DeDe, Dionne, and Starla were the only three Blacks in the company of all Whites. DeDe and Starla sat in cubicles opposite each other. Dionne had her own office; she's been there since the company started ten years ago. Starla had been there for five years and she was well favored among the big wigs of the company, because she knew how to kiss their asses and rub her nose all up in it at the same time. She was a half-breed who wished she had been born completely White. If it wasn't for her mustard color that looked more like a high-yellow Black, she would be White just like her best friend and husband she talked so much about. Dionne looked more of the mulatto breed than she did. Starla hardly talked to them, mainly because she and Dionne didn't get along. Dionne got a kick out of pulling Starla's chain, by making sure she pointed out her African features such as, her long kinky hair that she permed every six weeks and her big ass that verified she was a Black woman.

"Why are you looking like that? What's on your mind?" Dionne asked her.

"Nothing," DeDe said, as she jumped up from her chair and pulled note binders out of her overhead.

"My nephew, AJ was over last night and I rented the Green Mile for us to watch and girl I actually cried," she said, and laughed but seeming a bit embarrassed. "That was a really good movie. You should rent it."

DeDe paid her no attention, as she stared out into the aisles of the office.

"Girl what is on your mind? I know you're not letting the Erika St. James people get to you? I told that damn Vanessa back when I tried to get them as a client that she better start learning how to talk to people, before she mouths off to the wrong person and they curse her out something deadly. She's only a secretary over there at Element Records, but you would think she's an executive."

"Her and Gina Hairston, the chief-editor of Cultured Pearl do not know how to talk to people, but I have them under control. I made a couple of phone calls and Erika is on the cover of every magazine on the market, including Cultured Pearl for next month and I had a five city radio interview lined up for her, but she thinks she's too good to pump her own album. She's Erika St. James."

"Girl please, somebody better tell her she's only as good as the last album she puts out and that was—"

"Four or five years ago. I got her on the Tavis Smilie, Jay Leno, and the Oprah show also."

"You go girl, but how are you going to do her album release party and Cultured Pearl magazine release party at the same time? Isn't it also in two weeks?"

"Yeah, I'm going to tie them in together. Charva and Jeremiah thought it would be a good idea for her to perform and kill two birds with one stone."

"So, Jeremiah gave Charva Cultured Pearl to make her feel like she was something more than a baby factory." Dionne asked, and began laughing at her own sarcasm. DeDe looked at her and rolled her eyes at her as true as she knew that it was, but she doesn't talk about her best friend to anyone not like Dionne talks about Charlotte and how stupid she is for putting up with Ian. DeDe hoped she didn't talk about her the way she talked about her other girlfriends, but DeDe felt she did because she was that type of person.

"Seven hundred to a thousand invitations were sent out two and a half weeks ago. Everyone in the industry is supposed to be there." She flopped down in her chair and sighed. "I spoke with Danny the Senior Artist Marketer at Element and he's saying this is one of Erika's best albums yet."

"Have you heard it?"

"Hell no. I don't like her music. She tries to sound too sexy on top of looking it."

"I heard this is the one that tells all. She really went through some shit, after the break-up with that basketball player, Juan Barkley."

"Nothing no other woman hasn't gone through." DeDe could testify to that with all the shit she's been going through with Stephan. She didn't care about any other woman and her woes.

"Yeah, you're right. But I learned a long time ago that I can't tolerate shit from a man."

DeDe wished she could say the same for herself. Then maybe Stephan wouldn't be taking her through the shit he does every other month. As far as she knew, Dionne was single and proud of it. There weren't too many women she knew that didn't have a man and they were happy about it. Listening to the women at the beauty salon wishing they had a date for the weekend and the financial security of a man DeDe dreaded being single again. She never heard Dionne wish or talk about anything such as the likes of a man. She always talked about what she could do for herself. Stephan had DeDe believing Dionne could be gay. Because she always talked about her girlfriend Charlotte, and how through she was with her every other day for the shit she was putting up with from her man Ian, her five-year-old nephew AJ, and her 2001 black BMW utility vehicle, which she had personalized on the licensed plate to say, "myblkmn." DeDe liked her from the first day they met. She seemed down to earth and very cool although she was very opinionated, loud and bossy. But she's from New York, what else could DeDe expect? DeDe had often found herself wanting to have the same independent take-no-shit from a man backbone when she confided in her regarding Stephan.

"I guess that's why you're single because you don't. Maybe I need to adopt that philosophy."

"Single," she replied. "Where did you get that from? I'm not single. Byron and I have been together for six months now. He's a sweetheart and my best friend. I let him know from the beginning that I wasn't going to tolerate any bull and I wasn't going to date him five years, before he decides if he wants to marry me or not."

So she's not a dyke, DeDe thought. She couldn't wait to tell Stephan that he was wrong if he would ever call her back. He was so sure she was a dyke he had DeDe believing it too, and had even described the type of women she dated. Stephan hated her, because DeDe had made the mistake of telling him some of the advice Dionne had given her, during one of their arguments and the advice wasn't in Stephan's favor. DeDe had known Dionne for the last four months and she felt they were close. Close enough for her to feel she could confide in her and Dionne could have mentioned she had a man before now even if he is married; which would be the only legitimate excuse DeDe could conjure up as to why Dionne had never mentioned Byron. She probably felt DeDe would judge her and try to persuade her to leave him alone or maybe she thought she might know him or his wife.

"So is this Byron married?" DeDe blurted out.

"Hell no, why do you ask that?"

DeDe shrugged her shoulders and smiled. "You just never mentioned him before."

So if he's not married, he must not be shit or he's ugly as hell and Dionne's just embarrassed about letting people know she's dating him, DeDe thought, and she could understand that. None of her friends thought Stephan was amongst the top ten in nice looks. They thought she was crazy for leaving Waymon, a handsome tall conservative educated Black man who was sure to give her the life of an up and coming middle class Black American for a hip-hop, Urban clothes wearing, collection manager with the nickname "Sporty", which she never called Stephan. Stephan is short with dark thick lips, a small but noticeable gap in the middle of his front teeth, slightly slanted eyes, baldhead, with a defined thick goatee and eyebrows. His looks weren't all that and they didn't keep him from getting women. To be short he was fine and no one could deny that. Women were attracted to him by his personality and confidence that he was the cutest brother alive. That's what drew DeDe to fall in love with him with the addition to how he made her feel in bed. However, Dionne didn't seem like the type who would date a man less than a ten. She thought she was cute and perfect and she seemed like she wanted her men that way also. Maybe that's the big to-do with her not having any friends; she's insecure about her man and her girlfriends being around each other. The strongest women are always the most insecure. That's why she has never invited DeDe over to her house. She's also never accepted DeDe's invitation to come over to hers, and she's invited her over on several occasions.

"So you have a boyfriend and his name is Byron?" DeDe was surprised and it showed on her face.

"Yeah, why are you looking like it's so hard to believe?"

"Because you never talk about him. I talk about Stephan all day long and you never say anything about Byron."

"I have nothing to say about him. I give him enough attention when I'm at home with him," she said and chuckled. "We were friends for three months and we've been a couple for four. I'm happy with him."

"That's good." So why didn't you mention him before now? DeDe could not get pass the big secret. "I was happy with Stephan in the beginning of our relationship too and I'm still happy, but sometimes I could kill him. We had an argument last night; well it wasn't even an argument. It was his babymama."

"Child's mother," Dionne corrected her.

"Whatever. I hate her. I know babymama seems ghetto, but that's exactly what this bitch is."

"Why? What has she done to you; got you scared that Stephan might go back?"

That was it exactly; but DeDe would not let her know that. "No. She just keeps up a lot of problems."

"For him or you?"

"For both of us. She called last night, I answered the phone, and she had this attitude."

Dionne began to laugh. "You wanted her to know you could answer his phone. You thought you were running shit, huh bitch?"

"No. But I am and that's why she started acting crazy. She called me a bitch for no reason. This woman just doesn't like me. Stephan tells me all the things she says about me to him."

"He does what? Girl, he's playing games."

"Why do you say that?"

"He tells you what she says?"

"Yeah, and so does his little girl. She talks about me to the child."

"I understand why a child might repeat something, but a grown-ass man. I can't stomach it. He's keeping up drama between you and that woman. I bet he tells her what you say. That's why she can't stand your ass. How old is he? Are you sure you want to marry him? He seems childish."

"No, he's not. He just had a baby by the wrong woman. He said she trapped him."

"He said, she what? Girl, how old are you because I know you don't believe that mess. If she didn't pour the sperm out of the condom into her stuff, she didn't trap him. All sane men should know by now, birth controls are not one hundred percent and neither are condoms. A man will always scream a woman trapped him when he doesn't want to take care of his responsibilities. Entrapment is supposed to justify why he acts the way he acts."

"He takes good care of Alexis. She holds the child over his head. He can't even get Alexis without her bitching about something."

"From my experience women don't bitch unless there's a reason given. Have you ever thought that maybe Stephan is giving her a reason to bitch? After all, they do have a child together and she's pretty confident that she can have him anytime she's ready. There's a bond there and I'm sure you know that."

"But it doesn't mean anything."

"That's what you think."

"I know it doesn't."

"Then you go girl."

"I love Stephan, Dionne, and I know he loves me. When we're together, we have a good time. We laugh and joke. The only time we're stressing and there is drama between us is when it comes to that bitch Shannon. I've done a lot for Stephan and he's done a lot for me. I know I shouldn't be letting Shannon get to me; but if she makes him mad and it affects our relationship, I'm going to develop my own feelings for the bitch. And right now I don't like her."

"Well maybe you are developing these feelings toward her because deep down inside you believe he might go back to her or he has some feelings for her. You have some insecurities you need to work out."

Who did she think she was, Oprah? "No, that's not it. He tells me that he hates her and he hates that he has a child with her. I know she wants him. That's what's wrong with these damn babymamas. They have babies by these men and when the relationship is over and the men move on with their lives, the babymamas become bitches because they don't know how to move on."

"And you believe that shit? Like I said, they have a child together and they have a bond. She's now a single parent and no woman wants to be a single parent. They want the love and the relationship that is supposed to exist between a man and woman when there is a child. When and if he thinks of that child he thinks of her-believe that. And if he has a heart he thinks of that child every day." She was trying to make her feel as stupid as she sounded for believing Stephan had to choose between her and the woman he has a child with. "Yeah, they didn't work out and you two are together now and will be getting married someday. But what he has for her is different from what he has for you, if he's a man with a conscience and a heart. She had his child. Have you ever sat down and talked to this woman before without the attitude?"

"No and don't want to. She's a bitch."

"That's what Stephan has you believing. Why haven't you met her? Out of the three years, you and this man have been together and discussing marriage, you've never sat down with this woman? Her child is around you; she needs to find out if you're crazy since you believe she is. Have y'all ever talked civilized, when she's called the house?"

"No, I just hand the phone to Stephan," she said, looking at her watch and the clock. "He should be at work now."

"You don't say hello to her?"

"No, she doesn't say hello to me." She picked up the phone and dialed Stephan's work number, but hung up before his voice-mail came on. "He must be in a meeting," she said, as she hung up the phone.

"Have you ever gone over to her house with him to pick up his child?"

"Hell no. She would break fool."

"Good, because if she hasn't invited you over there don't go. I was dating this man once and he thought he would take me with him to pick up his son and that woman acted a fool on both of us," Dionne chuckled, as she reminisced. "Do you hear me girl, she broke fool. He couldn't understand why, but me being a woman I could. She wanted the man that would make her family complete."

"For you not to have any children you know a lot about what the other woman is feeling."

"I'm a woman and if I was in her situation I would want the same thing. We are all alike in many ways, as far as our feelings are concerned. How do you feel about his child or are you pretending, until you get the ring? A lot of women do that you know. Are you one of them?" She asked and chuckled.

"No, silly. I like Alexis, but she's too damn grown. Stephan will kill for that little girl." She picked up the phone and dialed his office again. There was no answer so she left a message. "If Shannon told him he couldn't see that child, that man will probably kill her. He loves his child."

"Do you?"

"She's too damn grown and he sees no wrong in her."

"Why would you want him to, she's only a child. *His* child. If it were *your* child, would you want him to see any wrong in her?"

"She just tells her mother everything that goes on in our house."

"She's a child and children talk. When you marry him that child is going to become a part of you as well as he is."

"I know, but he's going to have to start to discipline her more."

"You can't dictate that to him and if he lets you, he's a fool. One thing about women who date men with children..."

"I always told myself that I would never date a man with children."

Dionne ignored her as she sighed and continued to talk. "Finding a brotha, who is single, not previously or recently involved, divorced without issues, or doesn't have any children; is like looking for a needle in the dark. It's difficult. If they don't have the drama and insecurity with the child's mother, the other woman finds fault with the child. Two people that were there before you and will be there after you're gone; you shouldn't get involved with what they go through. Don't mess up his relationship with his child. You obviously see the relationship with the mother is already fucked up. And believe it or not, you might have had something to do with that."

DeDe felt delighted in knowing she did, because they didn't need to be together anyway. Shannon was crazy. She hated the fact they were together and she would show it by starting senseless arguments with Stephan and DeDe's name would always end up in the middle. "I'm not going to come between him and his child, but I had nothing to do with him and Shannon. She left him for another man and now that she and the man have split up, she wants Stephan back. She will stop at nothing, until she gets him. Because of her, I walked out on Stephan last night. I'm tired of him not defending me against her. I'm tired of her shit."

Dionne laughed. "So how is he supposed to defend you against her; curse her out in front of you or beat her up?"

"Well, don't let her curse me out." She picked up the phone again, dialed Stephan's number, and then paged him, when he didn't answer.

"Only a coward would play his child's mother against his girlfriend and it seems like that's what Stephan is doing. He should want you two to get along if he's planning on having his daughter and you in his life. But if he's still trying to fuck you and what's-her-name, he would have to keep you two at odds."

DeDe had never thought of it that way.

"It's Thursday and no work tomorrow, are you all packed for Miami?"

"No," DeDe snapped, as she rolled her eyes at the thought.

"Well, go get packed, he'll call," Dionne told her knowing that he wasn't. "I hear there's live jazz at ElBuddha's café tonight. I guess I'll go there. "

"Girl, I'm just going home. I'm not packing shit." DeDe knowing the way Stephan acts; she thought that he was probably already in Miami, sunning it up without her.

"Don't you dare go home moping like some sad, ailing puppy."

DeDe got up out of the chair.

"I'm not. I have so much cleaning to do, with my sorry brother and crazy sister living with me. They're both nasty as hell. I can't wait until their condominium is ready next month, and they can move out and nasty-up their own place."

"Girl, I know how family is. They'll take advantage if you let 'em," she chuckled. "Well, I'll see you later," She couldn't understand why DeDe was putting herself through the stress with Stephan. She had seen him before and he didn't look like all that. Whether he was or not, DeDe had no business crying over the bastard, she thought. From the stories DeDe had told her, she had no logical reason for being with him as far as she was concerned.

3

$\mathcal{AS}$ long as Stephan had been playing the game of building DeDe up
to feel comfortable with their relationship and then snatching the rug from
underneath her, she still had not prepared herself for the fall. It was Thursday;
two days after she walked out on him, and a day before they are supposed to
fly to Miami and she still hadn't been able to get in contact with him. She had
cried for the last three days and she had even called up some of her girlfriends
she hadn't talked to in months crying to them, but nobody could give her
comforting words to console her hurt. She wanted Stephan back, which was
the only thing that could console her broken heart. Every hour on the hour, she
had called his voice-mail pleading with him to call her back and checking her
voice-mail to see if he had called and left a message, but he had not. On her
way home from work last night, she drove by his apartment, he wasn't there,
and she let herself in. She could tell he had been home. The empty beer bottle
and Chinese container was in the trash. She walked to his bedroom and there
was a note posted up on his mirror that said, "If you are in my apartment
snooping around, get the hell out. The locks will be changed." She left.

WHEN SHE TRIED to open the door with her key this morning, the key
didn't fit. The locks were changed. With fury and velocity, she did what she
should have done yesterday morning when she had gone by his apartment and

he wasn't there. She immediately called the airline to cancel the tickets to Miami, because it was evident that he wasn't taking her and she wasn't going to let him take some other woman. Not on the tickets she had purchased. The airline representative explained to her that she couldn't cancel the tickets, because the charge was placed on Stephan's credit card and only he could authorize the cancellation of the tickets. Without realizing it, she had explained to the representative how she made the monthly payment by phone to his credit card company so he could have enough money to purchase the tickets for both of them to take a vacation, because he said they needed to get away. Therefore, in reality, she had purchased the tickets and she should have the right to cancel them. The representative apologized one last time and told her there was still nothing she could do.

JUST BEFORE SHE got off the exit to the beauty salon, she called her voice-mail at work and home. There was a message from Stephan on her home phone. Her heart sank deep into her stomach, as she tried to prepare herself for another fall as he told her that he was going to Miami without her. With her heart pounding, she waited for it to play.

"What's up? I decided to leave this message at this point and time, because I knew it would be after work and if you started that crying shit, that damn nosey Dionne wouldn't be asking you what's wrong. But knowing you, you told her anyway. That's another reason why I don't like to go around your friends. Besides them being messy married women, who are unhappy in their lives, you tell them too much of our business and you got them thinking I'm the bad guy in all of this, when I've tried to end this before but you keep calling me crying. I got your messages, I saw where you kept calling on the caller ID the other night after *you* walked out, and you have even gone in my house snooping around. Let me tell you I didn't appreciate that shit, so as you probably know the locks are changed. Before your little narrow mind begins to think I was with another woman last night, I had gone over to Dedrick's to play some pool. I knew we were going to be up drinking all night, so I packed my bags to stay the night there; but I don't have to explain shit to you. You don't need to call me anymore for any reason, because we have nothing to talk about. You walked out for no damn reason. Everything had been going fine between us DeDe, so why would you leave? You know me by now, I'm not going to jump through hoops and run after you. I love you, but I would rather love you from a distance because I don't want to keep hurting you like you keep saying. I knew it was a mistake for you and I to carry on as long as we did, but I thought some things would change and they haven't."

His time for leaving the long message was cut-off. Tears began to swell up in DeDe's eyes. She pressed the number one to get her second message. It was a conclusion to Stephan's first.

"You want marriage and kids and I don't. I would be wrong to make you think I do. You are a beautiful woman and I'm sure in time you'll forget about me and move on with your life. Some other man will take my place, as much as it hurts me to think that, but I know it will happen. You are jealous of the relationship I have with Shannon and your jealousy is causing problems. Not only between you and I, but also between Shannon and I. We have a child together."

"Fuck her," she screamed, as she hung up the phone before listening to the full message. She paged Stephan 911 and then called his voice-mail.

"Stephan, I have two things to say to you, fuck her and fuck you! Send me my damn tickets that *I* bought and *I'll* go to Miami by my damn self. I don't care if you never would have left me a message. My friends don't like you either, because you *are* the bad guy. They think I'm stupid as hell for dealing with yo' ass. You want to call them messy, because they are trying to hip me to your game which is very messy." She slammed the phone down and began beating the steering wheel. She was so angry she just felt like canceling her appointment at the beauty salon and going home. Maybe she would cry or just watch television, but she didn't feel like being bothered. To cancel meant, she would have to reschedule for Saturday and she could find a thousand and one things to do with her time than to spend it in a beauty salon. But she and Stephan weren't together anymore. He was in Miami on her tickets with some other woman. What else did she have to do but sit at home and cry? Before going into the beauty salon, she sat outside in her car trying to pull herself together. She was the type of woman that carried her worries on her face and she didn't want Roberta, her nosey beautician asking any questions. Because Roberta was her best friend's older sister, she knew of some of the problems she had with Stephan. DeDe put on her mask of joy and walked into the beauty salon smiling.

"Hey girl!" Roberta yelled from the back, as she slapped mounds of white perm to a woman's head.

DeDe waved at her and sat down. The receptionist, Wendy, handed her two magazines and a complimentary glass of wine. DeDe couldn't even say thank you before her lips embraced the rim of the glass to sip the white wine she loved so much. She needed a drink with all the drama Stephan was taking her through. She noticed a couple of women she had met by coming to the beauty salon every week for the last five years staring at her, wondering if she was going to speak to them as she did to Roberta. So she waved, sat down and began flipping through the pages of the magazine. She wasn't up for talking today. The full service spa and beauty salon was crowded as usual. Friday's after work are her usual days to come, but since she thought she was going to Miami, she scheduled an appointment for today. The beauty salon was to women, what a single man's bachelor pad is to a married man and the sports bar is to him on Sundays. This salon was a place of peace, pampering, bonding and healing for many of the sistahs that hardly missed an appointment. The neutral colors and the contemporary decor of the upscale beauty salon screamed out elegance for everyone who came to Matthew's. Darinda, the owner, named the shop after her son, whom she considered a good luck charm. The salon mostly catered to the professional women who didn't mind paying fifty for a wash and blow-dry, thirty-five for a cut, eighty-five for a perm and one hundred-fifty to be pampered for an hour or two. Matthew's was the talk of the town. To get an appointment with one of the platform artist, when they weren't traveling around the world teaching their skills to those who wanted to be just like them, was like standing in line to purchase a Luther Vandross, Patti Labelle, and Frankie Beverly and Maze concert ticket that sold out ten minutes after they had gone on sale. DeDe noticed many of the women waiting. She hoped they weren't waiting to sit in Roberta's chair. She had a habit of over booking and DeDe was in nobody's mood to be waiting all damn night. She had the urge to ask them who were they waiting for and how long they had been waiting, because if it was for Roberta she was going to get up and walk out. She already didn't want to be there, but she knew she needed her hair done. She would rather be at home crying and feeling sorry for herself than to be around women who seemed like they had it all together. There were some with their office work covering their laps and others planned weekends with their boyfriends and families, and those who boasted and bragged about having it all.

DeDe continued to flip through the magazine, until she came across an article that captured all of her attention, <u>Women CEO's of the Future</u>. The women in pictures were all white, but the article still seemed like it would be motivational. She crossed her legs and glued her eyes to the small print on the paper that motivated her to move on with her life and aim for something more besides Stephan's love. Whenever she and Stephan would break-up she always searched to reconnect with her spirit. It was like shedding layers of dead skin so that her new skin could breath and heal. The process was painful, but it always made her see life without him in a different manner. She began to read the four-page article line by line and she became excited about starting her own PR firm and being the CEO of her own company. She didn't need Stephan or any man for that matter. Through her pain, she tried to make herself feel good about being single again. She continued to read the article, while getting inspired at the same time. She knew how she was going to get over Stephan this time; she was going to occupy her mind with starting her own business. She was going to sit down, do a five-year plan for her life, and start working toward it. She stuck out her chest, and reached into her brief-case for her legal pad and began to write non-stop until Toni Braxton's *'Just Be A Man About It'* came on the radio. DeDe's heart sank and she nearly fell apart in tears that she fought so hard to hold back. She tried to think of something else, but the reason Stephan had broken up with her this time wasn't adding up and he wasn't man enough to tell her the truth. It wasn't because she was insecure about him and Shannon's relationship, or she wanted to be under him 24/7 and wanted to get married and he didn't. It was because there was another woman. Even if he had told her the truth, he had still broken up with her.

"Just be a man about it, no you just be a woman about it. What he's trying to do is protect your feelings, but he is damned if he do and damned if he don't." Candace, one of the beauticians in the shop said, as she helped one of her clients up from the dryer. "'Cause if he did call and tell her he didn't want her anymore because he's in love with some other woman, the song would have been called *Why Her and Not Me*."

Some of the women chuckled. Candace could be a clown when she wanted to.

"Sad but true." Katina, another beautician chimed in.

"No, y'all are missing the point of the song. She's saying, he said that he loved her, so be a man about it and mean what you say. Don't be calling me talking about you need your space, if you love me so much. Girl, I have the CD and I listen to it all day everyday," Dawn Winters said. She and her husband owned the only black Acura and Lexus car dealership in Houston. They lived in Camden Estates, a rich suburb of Houston to prove just how rich they were. DeDe couldn't imagine her listening to Toni Braxton, she seemed too damn snooty.

"You too," another woman agreed.

"If my man calls me talking about he needs space, that's exactly what he's going to get. Space is only time for another woman and for him to see if it's going to work between them. Donnell Jones said it best," Candace said. And just as she said that, the song came on the radio. *Donnell Jones, 'Where I Want To Be.'*

DeDe held her breath and wished she could just disappear or die. One of her close guy friends told her the best way to get over someone you love is to not listen to any slow songs, because they make getting on with life hell. She got up and walked to the ladies room hoping no one noticed the sadden look on her face, because the man she loved had broken up with her. She walked into a stall and stood up against the door crying silently, while still hearing the words to the depressing song. Why is it so easy for a man to break a woman's heart and walk away without looking back, she thought? She hated that she had not hurt Stephan before he had hurt her. But how could she when she couldn't see life without him? When she walked back out to the salon that was precisely the point of discussion; women moving on with life, after the thrill is gone. Someone else was going through exactly what she was going through. Today was just like every Friday when the women used the salon to vent and receive advice. DeDe had never told any of them her business, but she always listened and learned from others.

"Are women stupid for crying when a man leaves or are they stupid for letting him come back?" Tanisha Willis asked. She was married with three children and she used her visits to the salon as a vacation get-away.

"I'm ready when you are ma'am," Roberta said, as she tapped the cream colored swiveled plush chair. DeDe sat and became all ears.

"A man breaks a woman's heart, because she lets him. He shows all the signs in the beginning that he's not there for the long haul and he's not there to love her. Now, that chick on that video let him come back, after he talked about needing his space. We as women are buying into this thing of men being so scarce, so we have to put up with their bullshit." Laverne Butler said, as she looked around to make sure there were no children in the room that had wandered in from the children's room located in the left rear section of the salon. There was even a closed circuit television monitor, where the patrons could see their children playing. The salon had it all for the women. "I'm not, because I don't need a man that bad. My grandmamma didn't, my mamma didn't and neither am I."

"Were they happy?" Dr. Betty Atkins asked, in her calm professional voice. She was smart, intelligent, and always got to the root of a person's hurt or way of thinking, by associating it with how they were raised and taught. She needs to be on Oprah, when she has those so-called self-healing people on her show. She always made sense of the situation. She was a therapist who dug deep into the human spirit and mind to unfold where a woman had come from to make her think and react to situations the way she does. That was another reason DeDe never took part in any of the conversations about life and love, she didn't want Dr. Atkins to discover she was empty about it all.

"Yes. My grandmamma took care of six children by herself and my mamma took care of five," Stacy boasted proudly. She was one of the new beauticians in the salon.

"You have to learn how to love yourself, before any man could love you," Laverne said.

"What makes you think women don't love themselves?" Dr. Atkins asked, not giving her time to answer before she began to speak again. "Low self-esteem on a woman's part isn't the reason why a marriage doesn't work or why a man takes her through pure hell. Of course she might allow it, because she doesn't know any better or she feels she doesn't deserve better."

DeDe had always had better before she got together with Stephan, but it was her choice to let them go.

"A marriage not working believe it or not, takes two people not knowing anything about compromising, sacrifice or no spiritual base."

"Wait a minute," Candace interrupted. "Lord don't strike me down but I know a lot of people in the church that are getting a divorce, and sometimes it's the preacher. Everyone chuckled and agreed. "So I don't know about spiritual base."

"Low self-esteem comes from what a woman perceives herself to be in her own mind. And what we as women perceive ourselves to be, is what we were taught and told by others. Some of my patients have low self-esteem and their husband's haven't left them yet. As a matter of fact, they love the ground they walk on and even come to some of the sessions to help them get through whatever they are going through. I discovered that Black men don't or won't love us, because we don't give a sense of urgency for love. Most of us come from single parent homes or if we did have fathers in the household, we didn't see him loving and kissing our mothers like the men did on television. And our mothers didn't stress about not being shown affection and that has left us to say, 'Hey, my mother got by without love, then so can I.' We've perceived love as; having a man in the household, helping out with the bills, disciplining the children, and satisfying those sexual needs whenever they come, because that's what we as women have seen our mothers do and they seemed to be happy with that definition of love. Some of us have never really seen a man love our mothers. She had a boyfriend here and there, but not one that loved her enough to marry her or even help her provide for her children; and she made it. Her children never went without and she was content without him marrying her, just as long as he was there. So, a lot of us have adopted that subconsciously and pull it out verbally when we need it to justify 'I can do bad by myself or I'm my own man.' We play a major part in the reason why so many of us are single today."

No one said a word, whether they agreed or not.

"And Black men, they've never seen a man love their mothers enough to learn from that man how a woman is supposed to be reverenced, cherished or revered; so that's why it's so easy for them to *not* be a man about it. They simply do not know what it takes to commit, stick around when things are rough, be fathers or show the affection that we as women need, so we can't be mad at them. This thing goes way beyond what we are experiencing to-day."

4

ELBUDDHA'S was crowded for a Thursday evening 'happy hour', but since no one downtown had to go to work tomorrow that explained the crowd. Dionne was on her second apple martini sitting in her usual seat at the bar, taking in the atmosphere and the vibe from the jazz band. She kept watch at the door for her girlfriend Charlotte, who promised her she would come and join her right after work. Dionne didn't know why she believed her, because she had promised to meet her several times for drinks after work, but always reneged without calling to let Dionne know she wasn't coming. She just wouldn't show. Dionne wasn't sure if she'd been reneged on again, since she got off work thirty minutes ago, but she still held a seat for her just in case. Charlotte was the owner and editor-in-chief of the popular weekly entertainment newspaper The Rapture that circulated throughout Houston and five other major cites. It featured the up-coming events from week-to-week throughout the greater Houston area, and the other five major cities it circulated in which people of color would most likely visit. It also featured the hotspots for clubs and restaurants, the black 'who's who' in the entertainment world, celebrity gossip, interviews from the stars and pages of advertisement, which paid for the free public newspaper. She believed in her idea for the paper so much, she quit her job as a commercial realtor/broker earning four hundred thousand a year. She took all of her savings and invested it into the start-up of the paper.

A tall cinnamon-brown complexioned, handsome man in about his late forties walked over to Dionne and the stool on which she had her right foot perched. "Are you holding this chair for me," he asked and smiled.

She sized him up from his feet to his eyes and smiled. "No, my girlfriend."

"Where is she?" He asked, as he looked around.

"She's around."

"Well, why don't I buy you another drink and keep you company, until she comes?"

Normally, Dionne would not have to ponder before taking a handsome man up on his offer to buy her a drink, but she had invited Byron to meet her also and although he said he had to work late; today would be the day he decides to bring his work home for the weekend and show up. "No thanks."

"Okay," he said and smiled at her. "But I'm sorry that I couldn't persuade you. Maybe some other time. Good-bye."

She began cursing Charlotte out for being late, reneging and not calling her, when she walked in smiling like she was on time.

"Hey girl," she said, as she placed her purse on the bar and hopped up into the chair. "I bet you thought I wasn't coming." She asked, and chuckled as Dionne presented an attitude while looking straight ahead. "We had some new sales for advertising to come in and you know advertising is money and time is money."

"Well, I was just about to give the chair to someone else, because I thought you were going to do that renege thing you normally do when I ask you to meet me somewhere."

She laughed and leaned over and kissed Dionne on the cheek. "I love you. What are you drinking, an apple martini?"

"And you know it."

She ordered a glass of wine and Dionne another martini. "The paper is doing so well girl, I can't keep up. Everyone thought I was crazy when I said let's tack on the charge of twenty-five cents for the paper. The retailers are saying they can't keep it in the stores and our advertisers are saying they are getting more business than they can handle, so now we are selling more ad space than ever."

"So what happened so different from two months ago to this month?"

"I gave people something to talk about." She held her glass up for a toast. "I have a reason to celebrate."

"Here's a toast to The Rapture and you and all of your hard work." Dionne said as the rims of their glass touched.

"I've never been happier Dionne. You would think my husband would be happy for me also. All he does is tell me what a big mistake I made to quit my job to start the paper. He doesn't even read the paper and when he does, he gives me nothing but criticism and it ain't constructive either. Have you ever met someone who's too afraid to fly, so he says anything that might keep you from going out there testing your wings?"

Dionne nodded and took a sip of her drink. Her father was like that and he still is, but he's her father and he's in New York. She can choose when she wants to talk to him and if he starts downing her, she just hangs up on him and does not talk to him for another six months.

"Have you ever met anyone who's so unhappy in their life that they want to make anyone who's around them just as unhappy? That's Ian."

He had been that way as long as Dionne could remember. They were high school and college sweethearts and they had been married for twenty years. He's made her into what she is today, because he's dictated to her what she will and will not do. Now that she has deviated from his plan to no longer be his robot, he criticizes everything she tries to do without getting his approval.

"I realize nothing I do will make him happy. Could you imagine being married to a man that you can count on one hand the number of times y'all have made love in a year?" She asked, and forced herself to chuckle about the situation. "We sleep in the same bed, but he doesn't touch me and I dare not touch him. He says there's more to a marriage than sex. Can you imagine a man believing in such bullshit?"

Only if he was cheating, and Dionne knew he was. But Charlotte was in denial just as DeDe was about Stephan. Ian looked like the type. He wasn't all that bad looking for a forty-three year old with long dreadlocks. He's always in the gym trying to stay in shape and every time Dionne sees him, he's looking at another woman. And she didn't have to be a patient lying on his examination table at his Ob-Gyn clinic either.

"I'm forty-one and I've reached my sexual peak and there's a dildo that gives me better pleasure than my sorry excuse for a husband. If I didn't know any better, I would think he's turned gay on me," she laughed.

"What? Gay? Wouldn't you think he would try cheating with a radiologist or nurse first?" Dionne asked because she always thought there was another woman.

"There's no other woman that's going to put up with Ian and his crazy ass. Every nurse he hires in his office leaves within a month, because he's a bitch and he's that way around the house with me. Iyana, he doesn't mess with, she's perfect."

Why don't you leave 'im, Dionne wanted to ask her. How many times had Charlotte told her that leaving Ian would mean she would be alone and she was afraid of being alone. Ian is the only man she has known who has shown her love and affection, since high school. She knows there's something wrong with how Ian treats her, but then again she's not sure. She never had a father or a brother to model her ideal man after, but neither did Dionne. Dionne's brothers are younger than she is, her father came around every blue moon and her mother's boyfriends were few and far between. She could never keep a guy long enough for Dionne to understand the relationship between a man and a woman other than lying down with one and two months later hearing her mother cursing because, she missed her period.

"Girl, Byron stands behind me with everything I want to do, because that's what makes me happy. You would think Ian would do the same, but no two men are alike."

"After Iyana graduates and goes off to college, I'm going to divorce 'im."

Dionne didn't even bother to comment, because she could not understand why then and not right now.

"Sometimes I just wish he would find some woman that he really wants, because I'm not her and I can't make him happy."

"You don't want your man to go to another woman. You'll be like that fool I work with; insecure and crying every other day."

"DeDe, what's wrong with her?"

"Other than crazy? I don't know. She's a cute girl and can get any man she wants without trying, but she's just crazy about that damn Stephan and all the shit he takes her through. Some women I'll never understand."

WHEN DEDE GOT home, she headed straight for the kitchen to pour herself a glass of wine. She looked beautiful with no man and with no place to go. She learned from her visit at the beauty salon that it was alright for her to feel like she was done wrong, and it was alright for her to be called weak and stupid for still loving Stephan, and it was also alright for her to cry. And she did just that her whole drive home and she hated Stephan for making her cry time after time. Crying used to be a cleansing therapy for her, but for some reason, tonight it wasn't working. She had cried so many times and gone back to him; even her convincing herself that she had had enough wasn't working. She couldn't stop crying, she didn't feel rejuvenated like she had tried to make herself feel in the salon, and she didn't have the desire to move on with her life. The man she loved was gone. She threw her mail on the kitchen countertop, grabbed the bottle of wine and a glass and walked into the living room. She put on all five of her Will Downing CD's, flopped down on the sofa and cried for the next three hours while consuming half the bottle.

It was pitch dark in the house and she liked it that way. She felt dark, gloomy, betrayed and fucked. What had she done in her life to deserve this? She got up and lit two candles, then flopped right back down in the same warm spot. Her soul ached, as she listened to the words of Will Downing's rendition of '*I Can't Make You Love Me.*' She cried for every word he sang, because she knew there was no way in hell Stephan truly loved her. She also realized that the way she was feeling, there was no way in hell she could ever make him love her. She needed someone to talk to, so she picked up the phone to do something she hasn't done in a while. She called her girlfriends.

She only had two and both of them were married with children. A family was something she felt she should have had by now. When she first met Stephan, he wanted to get married and he told her she would be the one he'd marry, and now it's a totally different story. She called Bridget first.

"Hey, Jerome,"

"DeDe, what have we done to be blessed with a phone call from you?" he asked and chuckled.

"Jerome, don't be funny. Where is your wife?"

"She took the kids over to her mother's house. She and I are hanging out this weekend. Why didn't you come by last weekend? Everyone was asking about you."

"Everyone like who? Bridget didn't invite me over. I didn't know that y'all were having a get together last weekend. Who was over there?"

"Yolanda and Emmett, Calvin and Jennifer, Robert and Eunice, and Waymon."

"Waymon who?"

"There's only one Waymon." He began to laugh.

"You tell your wife to call me when she gets home."

"Will do."

"Was he there with someone?" She asked, just before they hung up.

"Yeah, he brought his fiancée."

She didn't want to seem surprised or shocked. She knew eventually he would find someone and move on with his life. "Tell Bridget to call me, as soon as she gets in." She hung up the phone and sat there in a daze, while staring at the flickering candlelight.

The man she should have married was about to marry someone else, and she had no one. Now her life was really in a crisis. And she deserved it and everything Stephan was putting her through. The word she could use to best describe it was pure hell. She was wrong for how she had done Waymon and she desperately wanted to apologize. But his heart was so cold toward her; he wouldn't let her speak without hanging up first. She loved him, but not enough to live the rest of her life with him and his logical way of thinking everything through and his financial strategies for them to be debt free by the age of thirty-five. She thought there was more to life, so now what. She spent three years of her life with a man who has her credit totally fucked up and the only logical thing he thinks is if the car doesn't start; it must be the battery. She and Waymon had dated for four years and they were going to be married. She tried to overlook their differences and she had, until she met Stephan. He was all the reason she needed to walk away. The phone rang and she jumped out of her daze to answer it on the first rang. It was Stephan finally returning one of her many phone calls and pages.

"What's up?"

"Where are you?" She asked.

"You paged me?"

"Where are you? I want my damn tickets, the six hundred dollars I loaned you, and the six hundred you owe me on my furniture that is in your apartment. I'm going to get my name off of those damn credit cards you are behind on, and I want my television."

"You gave me that television. Why are you trippin'?"

"I didn't give you shit Stephan and you know it. I let you borrow that television, because you didn't have one."

"Whatever. I'm going to give you back the money and I'm going to pay you back for the tickets, when I get back on Tuesday."

"Where are you?"

"Miami."

"Miami," she replied. "We were supposed to go together. I bought those tickets."

"Yeah, we were but DeDe—"

"Who are you with Stephan; Shannon?"

"Don't concern yourself with that. Why did you page me?"

"Who are you with dammit?" She asked, through clenched teeth.

"Me and Dedrick. What's up? Why did you page me?"

"We were supposed to go together. You haven't returned any of my phone calls. I had the nerve to meet you at that airport, because I knew you were going to pull some shit like this."

"I knew you would have done something like that, that's why I left today instead of tomorrow. DeDe we're no longer together. Didn't you get my message? I wasn't going to bring you with me and have you down here walking around with your lip poked out, if Shannon just happened to page me. I'm on vacation and I don't want to argue. Like I told you the other day, it's best you go your way and I go mine. It's not working."

"Because you don't want it to work. Stephan, you know I love you."

"And I love you too, but the way that you love me and the way we love each other isn't healthy. We've been at this relationship for three years. You and I don't want the same things and you know that. I don't want to hurt you. You're over there crying, and for what? I've been telling you that you love too hard."

"What other way am I supposed to love you Stephan?" She asked him through her tears.

"DeDe I have to go now."

"No, talk to me."

"Bye." He hung up the phone and she buried her face into the plush pillow on the sofa where she cried out loud. She didn't believe he was in Miami with Dedrick for one second. To her that was all a lie to keep her from believing he had taken Shannon. It was Shannon, who was in Miami with him, along with Alexis. They were all being a happy family on her tickets. She wanted to make sure her intuition was correct, so she picked up the phone and pressed *67 to block her name and number from coming up on Shannon's caller ID, as she dialed her number to see if she would answer. She memorized her number from Stephan's caller ID. Within two rings, Shannon answered the phone and DeDe hung up. She felt relieved that he hadn't taken Shannon, but she still didn't believe he had taken Dedrick either. Dedrick lived with his girlfriend Carla and she was five months pregnant. There was no way in hell she let him leave for five days with Stephan, whom she could hardly stomach. DeDe began calling Dedrick's house by punching in *67, but she quickly hung up when she heard Kendra and Kendall at the door. She managed to jump up, turn off the stereo, blow out the candles and run to her bedroom. She couldn't dare let them see her face and notice she had been crying. They were the last two people she wanted to see her cry, especially over Stephan.

She lay across her bed and closed her eyes to sleep through her depression instead of crying. It always worked. When she heard the loud music blasting from the living room, she jumped up. Her eyes were puffy and swollen from weeping, so she ran into the bathroom and wiped her face with a wet towel before going out of her room to turn the music down. She hated letting them move with her. DeDe only did it because her mother was so worried about where they were going to stay, when they got evicted two months ago. Neither one of them believed in paying rent; thus they were frequent nomads. Since DeDe's parents were already saddled with the burden of taking care of Kendra's two children; DeDe decided to give her folks a break and let these two full-grown, irresponsible twin siblings move in with her on a very temporary basis. When she stormed into the living room, Kendra was sitting on her brand new cream-colored sofa smoking a joint.

She startled her, as she came around the corner. "What did I tell y'all about smoking in my house?"

"I thought you would be in Miami," she said, as she tried to put the joint out. "What are you still doing here?" She walked over to the patio door to let the smoke escape.

"Don't worry about Miami. Why are you smoking in here Kendra, after I told you not to? See that's your problem."

"What's my problem?"

"What's up DeDe?" Kendall asked her, as he walked out of the kitchen with a sandwich and one of DeDe's wine coolers. "I thought you and Stephan would be lying on South Beach by now. I know I definitely would be letting it all hang out, if I was there." He placed the sandwich and the bottle on the table, flopped down on the sofa, crossed his legs and placed his manicured hand over his knee. "Why are you still here?"

"Don't ask her that. She'll be too embarrassed to tell us," Kendra chuckled.

"Is everything going alright with the condo? Because at the end of next month y'all have to go."

"Yes, it is thank God. Don't worry; we'll be out of here. We want to go as badly as you want us to."

"So the niggah went to Miami without you, and now you want us out?"

"Kendall, don't talk to me. I've wanted you two out of here the same day I let you move in."

"Why are you jumping all over him, he's telling the truth. When Stephan pisses you off, you take it out on the world."

It seemed that way, but Stephan had nothing to do with it. She was angry with them for how they were living their lives; irresponsibly and carefree and her parents had to suffer the consequences. They aren't able to enjoy their retirement, because they have to raise Kendra's two children, while she's out pretending they don't exist but yet and still collecting ten-thousand dollars a month in child support. On the strength of a dollar, she laid down with each child's father with the intent to get a guaranteed ticket to never have to do for herself or work again. She was a trifling groupie and she thought like one too. She had tricked men into getting her pregnant. She had even bragged about it to DeDe. She would straddle over them rocking her knees backwards and forwards and continue to ask them if they were about the cum, and just before they did, she would jump up off of them, snatch off the condom and push them back inside her for their seed to meet her eggs. Three months later, she would tell them she was pregnant. She hardly ever visits the kids just as their fathers don't. Out of the ten-thousand dollars a month in child support, she doesn't send her parents a penny to help take care of the boys. Also, she doesn't have a penny or anything tangible at the end of each month to show for the amount of money she initially received.

Kendall was in and out of drug rehabs and their parents were taking all of their retirement money to pay for his rehab, only for him to get out and get back on drugs three months later. She looked at both of them and rolled her eyes, as she walked into the kitchen. They were truly twins, who were a lot alike in more than just looks.

"I hope you two plan to help me clean-up behind y'all nasty asses? There are dishes in the sink that I haven't used, because I haven't been here. Y'all are the only ones here during the day, because you don't work like normal people."

"Jamal Raspberry, who plays for the Dallas Wranglers is having a party."

"And."

"We're going so we can't help you clean-up anything tonight. You know how you get when Stephan pulls one of his numbers on you. You find comfort in cleaning up all damn night. When I get my check next week, I'll hire a maid for a day."

DeDe rolled her eyes and sighed. She didn't need Kendra to hire a maid or anything else for her, she just wanted her out of her house. "Who's fucking 'im you or him?" They both looked at each other and laughed. Kendall was a gay groupie with plenty of rich, nice-looking bi-sexual men that didn't mind taking care of him, as long as he kept their secret. He is single at this moment, as he mourns the death of his off and on lover, who was killed in a car accident three months ago. DeDe was not aware that men who looked like men that she would be very attracted to were gay, until meeting Kendall's ex-lover who was a basketball player, married with two kids. He had just come from seeing Kendall, when a drunk driver going down the wrong side of the road caused him to run into a tree. The sad thing about his second life is that his wife never knew her husband preferred men and she did not know he had just come from seeing one, when he was killed. DeDe was sure the poor woman still didn't know. For as long as DeDe could remember, Kendall had feminine ways, even as a kid. He would rather play dress-up dolls than play with trucks. He wasn't a flamboyant faggot who wore women's clothing or lipstick. He was a handsome, nice-looking man who made women do a double take, until his masculinity transformed into femininity. When this occurred, he began to talk and his lips smacked, as his eyes rolled and his wrist flew all over the place to show expression with every word he'd say. He had never laid with a woman, though he could have. Women were always approaching him, as if they could not see his femininity lurking behind his masculine physique. Kendall wore short twist in his hair and diamond studs in each ear just like heterosexual men who thought they had it going on. He couldn't get into women, because he wanted the same thing they thought he was; a man with a hard dick.

"I'm fuckin' him silly," Kendra answered, as she walked into the kitchen and began packing the dishwasher. She and Kendall were almost the same height. They towered over DeDe. If no one knew, they would assume they were no kin to her. Kendra and Kendall had tight slanted eyes, long narrow faces, high cheekbones, almost flat noses and a nut-brown complexion. They had always teased DeDe by telling her she was adopted, because she looked like no one in the family. DeDe poured herself another glass of wine, gulped it down within a few seconds, and poured herself a refill, not noticing Kendra staring at her.

"You don't have to go to work tomorrow, why don't you come and go with us."

"Hell no! I'm not a groupie. I have my own. They'll be intimidated by me, because I don't have to sleep with them on the strength of a dollar or a pair or Dolce & Gabbana jeans," she said and chuckled. She hoped Kendra got the hint.

"But you sleep with Stephan and you help him pay his rent, car note and you get nothing from him, but a hard dick and bubble gum. I don't see him coming over here helping you cut the grass or paint your room. You've been screaming you want that room painted for three months now."

"What in the hell are you talking about?"

"She is telling the truth, sis." Kendall said, as he walked in and got another wine cooler. "I guess Stephan's broke ass isn't intimidated by you, because he knows you'll write him a check any day. For the life of me, I can't understand what in the hell you want with him anyway. He's broke and not that attractive."

"Pretty girls always want someone uglier than them," Kendra said and laughed.

"So that's why you are with Melvin, because he's ugly as hell."

"But he's paid," Kendall and Kendra said in unison.

"Stephan is a bill collector and you are a publicist making a hundred grand a year," Kendall told her.

"He's not just a collector; he's the supervisor of the collection department at the bank."

"He still makes seventy-thousand less than you," Kendall said.

"Money isn't everything Kendall," she thought about what she had said. "But I'm sorry, I'm talking to the man who loves money, but doesn't work to make any."

"But I have it though." He and Kendra gave each other a high-five and chuckled.

"On the real tip DeDe, you should consider going with us. You don't need to sit around here crying over him. He's in Miami living it up and you are sitting here crying poor DeDe. Get off it. Have a good time. Stop letting him control your happiness. You don't have any friends, because you spend all your time in Stephan's ass."

"I have friends; they know my number. They are the ones that stopped calling me."

"Yeah, they got tired of you crying on their shoulders one week, and the next week you were back with the niggah."

"I don't need a man, I just need to get my life together right now."

"You're not going to the party looking for a man, you're just getting out of the house. If you sit in this house listening to that lonely-hearts music, you will make yourself crazy. You know how I got over Melvin? I went out and partied. He thought I would be calling him and begging him to come back although I wanted to, but a sistah got pride like a mutha. The mistake you always make is that you cry and beg him to come back."

She thought about it and Kendra was right. All she ever does is cry and beg while Stephan moves on with his life. "I can't help it. I love him, but tonight I'm in there. Let's party."

"You go girl!" She and Kendra gave each other high-fives. She had never gone out with Kendra before and she couldn't believe she was going to do it tonight. No doubt, the wine helped alter her decision. She walked to her room to find something to wear.

"And don't wear that shit you be wearing to work," Kendra told her. "We are around ballers so play the part sistah."

She stuck her head out of her bedroom door. "Then what do I wear?"

"You better help her on that one," Kendall said, as he gulped down his wine cooler. "She can't be coming behind me looking like a schoolmarm."

"And you're right. I have a pair of those Dolce & Gabbana's that you were talking about, that will look good on you, girl."

5

THE huge brick mansion was overflowing with people. Mostly women. Expensive cars with tinted windows and souped-up rims were lined-up and down the street. Although Kendra and Kendall had been around celebrities with money, they still acted as if it was their first time. They were genuinely groupies. DeDe was almost afraid to go inside, there were so many people. She did not like crowds, especially crowds of groupies and ballplayers. The two just didn't mix. They were both bound to do something stupid in order to be seen. It was a meat market in there and she really wasn't trying to find the catch of the day, although she was dressed like she was. Kendra had let her borrow her royal blue Dolce and Gabanna leather jeans, and her powder blue sheer shirt with the word Moschino written all over it. She was defiantly playing the part of a high maintenance groupie. Every man she's ever met was always in an unexpected place such as at a red light, grocery store and through a blind date. That's how she met Stephan; through a blind date set up by Melvin and Kendra, while she was on her last nerve of boredom with Waymon. She could count on her right hand the number of men she's seriously dated in her life time; one, two, three, four. Stephan makes the fourth. All her relationships lasted from three to five years.

Although she looked like all the other women dressed in expensive de-
signer clothes, they didn't have the same motive that DeDe had for being
there. DeDe knew it and walked with a different type of confidence. She had
her own money and she didn't give a damn about a man with a couple of
million. She could get her own hair done, the clothes she had on belonged to
her sister, but if she wanted to go out tomorrow and buy her own leather
jeans, she could. Men grabbed at her, but she ignored them as she followed
Kendra with her head high.

"Kendall, what's up man?" An attractive, huge, muscular guy standing at
about 6'3" walked up to him and asked.

"Can't call it dude," he said, as they did the Blackman handshake, inter-
locking their hands and forearms together, then pulled each other close. "Dog,
let me introduce you to my sister DeDe. You know Kendra already."

"Yeah I know her ass. She's old news. What's up Kendra? Hi, DeDe."
"Hi."

"DeDe," Kendall said with bass in his voice. "This is Rick Tatum, he plays
for the 59ers. DeDe is a publicist, so if you need one she's the best."

"Cool, I'll keep that in mind. Let me talk to you outside for a second."

DeDe stood in shock. Kendall looked and sounded like a full-fledged
man. She had never seen him like that before. She didn't think he knew he
was a man after playing the woman's role to so many bi-sexual men. DeDe
couldn't wait to tell her mother.

"Girl, don't look now, but there goes Melvin. Shit." Kendra noticed the
puzzled look on DeDe's face. "Why are you looking like that?"

"I almost thought Kendall was a man."

"He is. He can't come up in here flaming like a faggot and expect anyone
to talk to him."

"Kendra," Melvin called out once he realized it was her.

"Shit," she said, as she tried to hide her face from him. "I thought he would
be in Denver visiting his kids."

"There goes the party. Don't you two start that shit in here tonight," DeDe
warned her.

"What are you doing here?" Melvin asked Kendra, as he bent down nose-to-nose in her face to frighten and intimidate her into giving him the answer he wanted to hear.

"Melvin, don't start," Kendra, begged him.

"Yes I am," he said, grabbing her by the arm. "DeDe, what are you doing here? I know Stephan doesn't know that you're here."

"He's not her daddy."

"See there you go trying to influence the girl by the way you think. I'm yo' daddy," he said, and grabbed her ass. "DeDe, knows Stephan don't play that. Where is my dog anyway?"

"Miami," she said, and rolled her eyes.

"But you're looking good though. I gotta give you that. The niggah would be proud." He grabbed Kendra's face with a firm grip. "And if I find out you're messing with anyone up in here, I'm going to be all over your ass," he told her.

"We're divorced, remember?" she said, and rolled her eyes at him as she snatched her face away from his hand.

"So what? You didn't say that when you asked me to pay the deposit on that damn condo."

Kendra smacked her lips and rolled her eyes.

"So don't say shit now," he said, and dragged her outside by her arm without warning.

DeDe stood by her lonesome hoping none of the men that were eyeballing her from head to toe would come over. They were cute, but they were also football players and too flashy. She liked ordinary men; men that she could be herself around. Not that she didn't have a wild side to her, but she enjoyed being laid-back and conservative. She enjoyed wearing her small wire frame glasses and her Donna Karan Signature suits. She didn't need a man trying to transform her into a so-called hot girl or video queen like Kendra. The most makeup she wore is lipstick and foundation. Stephan tried to get her to wear more, but she wasn't with it. She wished he could see her tonight. There's no doubt in her mind that Melvin was wrong. Stephan would not be proud, because she was looking too good and other men were checking her out. Stephan was a very jealous individual, when it came to DeDe.

What's up?" A light-skinned, tall brotha asked, as he walked toward her. "You're wearing that leather."

"Thank you."

"What's your name?"

"DeDe," she said, as she unfolded her arms and slid her hands into her back pockets.

"DeDe, that's a nickname for what?"

"Nothing, just DeDe."

"You're cute DeDe," he said, as he looked her over, while he smiled and licked his lips. "And I got to say once again you are seriously wearing that leather." His eyes rested on her large, round, shapely breasts that had the word Moschino stretched across them. "Who do you know here?"

"No one. I'm here with my sister and brother." She noticed his eyes were not looking at her but directly at her breasts. She's always had large breast and men have noticed them all of her life, but this guy's glaring was embarrassing. Her blouse was a bit too tight and her breast stood out. Kendra and the wine had convinced her that it was a perfect fit.

"Is your brother a player?" He asked, while his eyes remained fixated on her Moschino billboard chest.

"No, he's not."

"What's up cutie?" Another tall, light-skinned, medium-build brotha asked, as he walked over and stood to the right of her. The two men were friends.

"Hi," she said, franticly looking up at him and his buddy. They both soared over her.

"So what are you getting into tonight DeDe?"

"DeDe," the man standing to the right of her smiled and stated, "That name fits you." He too was looking down at her breasts. "I used to date a girl in college name Dee. DeDe what?"

"Wilson," she answered skeptically. She felt closed in by both men as they surrounded her. She hoped they didn't think she was a groupie who was trying to be seen by wearing a tight shirt that emphasized her ample breasts to solicit lustful attention and get picked-up. She couldn't bear the thought of them getting the wrong idea about her and trying to double-team and rape her.

"Are you okay? You seem to be a little tense."

"I'm fine. I'm just out of my element."

"What do you mean? Out of your element?" One of them asked, as they looked at each other and smiled.

"So would you like to step outside or go for a ride with me and my boy here?" The man to the left of her asked as he looked at her and licked his lips with expectation of a positive reply.

"No," she snapped, as she stepped backwards, while looking up at both of them.

"Well, you said you were out of your element," the man on her right said. "I thought you maybe wanted to escape this scene."

"I'm not a groupie like most of these women that are here. I have my own. I'm a publicist for Stein and Stockton Public Relations firm. Have you ever heard of them?"

They looked at each other smiling and shook their heads no.

"I'm not impressed by a man and how much money he makes. I work and earn my own money."

"That's good sistah," the man formerly on the left of her, but now on the right of her said, as he chuckled. "Nice talking to you." They both walked off laughing and shaking their heads.

She spotted Kendra, as she walked back into the house. She rushed over to her. "Where is Kendall, I'm ready to go?"

"He's gone for the night and I'm not ready to go. We just got here."

"So what?"

"If I would have known you were ready to go, I would have let Melvin take you home. Thank God that damn nut is gone."

"The men here are intimidated by me."

"And why is that; when they make millions more than you?"

"I'm not their ordinary woman. They are looking for women that are going to show them a good time and who they can take care of."

"Then where are those men, because I need somebody that's willing to take care of me," she said, as she looked around the room spotting someone she knew. "I know that nigga ain't talking to that bitch in my face. Excuse me." She walked off. "Jamal Raspberry, I know you ain't."

"Hello DeDe," a coca brown, medium height man wearing black oval wire frame glasses said, as he approached her. "I thought it was you. What are you doing here? This doesn't seem like your kind of crowd."

"It's not, but I needed to get out of the house." He was nice looking with a sexy smile and his faded sideburns were very becoming.

"I'm glad you did or I wouldn't have had the pleasure of talking to you and maybe exchanging numbers."

"Do I know you?" She asked, as she tried to figure out how he knew her and where she may have encountered him. He wasn't one of her clients.

"I'm Elliott Anderson, the owner of ElBuddha's where you and Dionne sometimes have lunch and bring your clients."

"Hi," she said, as she extended her hand out to him. She still didn't know who he was. "I've never met you before."

"No you haven't. I'm normally in the kitchen helping with the orders."

"So how do you know my name?"

He chuckled. "Now I'm not some crazy man, so don't think it, but I remembered your name from your credit card."

"My credit card," she chuckled. "Had it ever declined?" She only asked because she had been letting Stephan use one of her cards from time to time and he never paid the bill. Thus, she had been embarrassed because her card was declined a couple of times, due to Stephan's delinquency.

"No, I was telling one of my waitresses how sexy I thought you were; so when you paid with your credit card she told me your name. I noticed you the very first day you walked into the restaurant and that was four months ago."

"Yeah, that's when I started at the firm."

"I thought you to be a very unique woman and I wanted to come and introduce myself, but during lunch time we are always so busy and I never had the chance."

DeDe was flattered about her new admirer.

"Would you like a glass of wine?" he asked her, as he motioned for a waiter.

"Yes."

"Chardonnay, White Zinfandel or Merlot?"

She smiled. "White Zinfandel."

"Forgive me, I still think I'm at the restaurant." He handed her a glass of wine and looked down into her eyes. "You look nice tonight. I almost didn't recognize you without your glasses and the organizer tucked under your arm, and your conservative suits."

"Well, my sister made sure I didn't wear any of those things here tonight."

"Why? I love to see you in them. You're so sexy when you're conservative."

She blushed with delight and thought to herself, he thinks I'm sexy. Stephan had always told her she looked like a bookworm and a nerd and here was this handsome man telling her she looked sexy. "Thank you," she said, looking up at him.

"My pleasure."

DeDe took a sip of her wine and looked around the crowded room, as she tried to think of something to say to keep the conversation rolling. He was handsome and he admired her, so she didn't want to turn him off by saying something stupid. She had no idea how to flirt with a man and she sure as hell didn't think she had sex appeal. She was short with a flat ass and no noticeable hips; but she was cute. She's made a couple of heads turn, but never from any of the men she would be interested in dating. All the men she had dated were intellectuals just like her, so they didn't care if she didn't have a bodacious ass. However, they loved her breasts, the fact that she was bright and had a good job as they did. Stephan was the only man she dated who wasn't well versed on a multitude of subjects. He was someone different from her norm, and she was hooked on him. She couldn't believe she was meeting a man so soon. Before, when she and Stephan broke-up; it was always so hard for her to get over him. Either there were no men for her to meet or the men she did meet were men she had no attraction to whatsoever. She was going to give Elliott her number and hoped he would call. He reminded her of one of the men she had seen in a Hennessey or Courvoisier ad.

Out of the corner of her eye, she sized him up and felt very thrilled he had approached her. He was the cutest and the sexiest man in the entire room. He was only wearing gray slacks and a navy blue sweater shirt, unlike all the other men who were dressed in neon silk or satin Crayola colored shirts with the pants and gator shoes to match.

"Would you like to go downstairs to dance?" DeDe asked.

"I'm not a dancer. I'm your first and only Black man you might meet without rhythm."

She smiled seductively. "But I'm sure you have rhythm in other ways." They both smiled.

"Would you like to go outside?" He asked, and made a gesture toward the door. "I've seen enough of this circus."

She looked at him skeptically. "As long as you don't have a friend out there, waiting to pounce on me."

He chuckled. "I don't want to share you with anyone."

They walked through the crowd to the patio. There were naked people in the hot tub including Kendra and Jamal. DeDe was embarrassed.

"Hey cuz, why don't you and shorty com' on in? The water is just right."

"That's okay Dog."

"Everyone in here is cool people," Jamal told him.

"Hey DeDe, girl." Kendra yelled, while holding up her champagne glass. DeDe reluctantly waved back.

"Do you know her?" Elliott asked.

"Unfortunately, yes. We came together. She's my sister."

"I've seen her over here a couple of times. Jamal is my lil' cousin."

"Little," she replied, glancing at him from his waist to chest, as he stood up out of the water and walked over to them. He was huge and his body reminded her of black shinny steel. Her eyes bulged and her mouth dropped open without anyone noticing once she laid her eyes on his swinging limp dick that came halfway down his inner thigh. She turned her head out of embarrassment. She had never seen anything like it. She thought Stephan was big, but Jamal sure as hell had him out numbered and gunned. She wondered if Elliott was working with such a gift, since they were cousins. She slowly moved her eyes down below Elliott's waist to see if there was such a bulge.

"Cuz," Jamal slurred, with his hand on Elliott's shoulder. "Why don't you take shorty across the lake to the gazebo. Things are about to get heated up in here," he said and smiled as if Elliott knew what he was talking about.

DeDe looked at Kendra and rolled her eyes. She knew what type of heat was about to generate between three men and five women. She became sick. Her sister really was a trifling slut.

"But if y'all want to stay you can," he said, looking down at DeDe and smiling.

"Jamal," Kendra yelled, as she stood up, just as nude. "Niggah don't you even try it. That is my sister and we don't get down like that."

"Ain't nobody trying to do nothing, so sit yo' ass down."

"You feel like the walk baby?" Elliott asked.

The word baby sounded so good coming from him. "Sure."

Elliott grabbed her by the hand and led her down the stairs through the path to the bridge leading over to the gazebo on the other side of the lake. She was quiet with a number of things going through her mind like was Kendra actually letting Jamal put all that inside of her. Was Kendra now dyking and had Elliott ever been a part of one of the orgies?

"So do they always get heated at parties like this? If he was talking about what I think, they're about to have an orgy."

"I couldn't tell you baby-girl, but my cousin is off the hook."

"You said you've seen Kendra over here a couple of times, while you've been here, right?"

"I guess I come over when it's quiet. I'm Jamal's financial adviser. I watch his money and I invest it. I drop by every now and again to talk to him about his investments and Kendra is sometimes here cooking dinner."

"Cooking dinner?" DeDe replied.

"Yeah,"

"So what are you doing here tonight?"

"Like you, I needed to get out of the house. I was tired of the norm. You know, how does it go? All work and no play. So, I had never come to one of Jamal's parties and I thought I would come to this one, and I'm glad I did."

DeDe looked at him, as she sat down.

"Or I never would have met you. So, tell me some things about yourself. What do you like to do in your spare time? You know life can be boring if you don't have a little fun. Or are you seeing someone?"

"I don't do much of anything besides work and now that I'm not with my boyfriend anymore; I'll be working."

"So you just broke up, is that why you're here, to get over him? Getting over someone is hard."

"Not if there's someone to help you get over them." She looked at Elliott and smiled. "Are you seeing anyone?"

"No, I'm single. Women can't understand my schedule. I work long hours."

"So do I. I believe that was one of the problems with Stephan and I, as well as the situation with his child's mother. Do you have any children?"

"No, but I would like one someday."

" How old are you?"

"What does that mean? Do you associate a man's age with whether he should have kids or not? I'm thirty-eight and before you ask, no, I've never been married, but I would like to do that one day too. And now I believe I will."

They heard screaming. Elliott grabbed DeDe's hand and pulled her along as if she was a rag doll as they ran back toward the house. The commotion had gotten louder, as they approached. DeDe heard Kendra scream and she began to panic. "Oh my God it's Kendra," she shouted.

When they finally got to the patio door, Elliott busted through the door dragging DeDe behind him. They froze in their tracks, as they saw Melvin pointing two guns. One was aimed at Kendra and the other at Jamal.

"DeDe." Kendra cried, as she stood with a towel covering her naked body and shaking like a wet, cold puppy. She looked terrified, along with everyone else who stood around wondering if Melvin was crazy enough to shoot Kendra and Jamal in front of so many witnesses. DeDe knew he wasn't going to. It was all a part of the 'jealous wife and husband' game he and Kendra played, every time they would go out together. It would take nothing for one of them to be carrying on a casual conversation with someone and the other takes it as lustful flirting. They would shove, curse and slap each other; then leave and go home and fuck like animals. Kendra had always loved to fight with every man she had ever dated. It was her way of knowing they cared. Even if he did catch Kendra sitting on the lap of another man rocking backwards and forwards, Melvin was not going to kill her or anyone else.

"I told you bitch that I was going to kill you if you were fucking around with someone up in here, didn't I? But what I didn't tell you was, that I was going to kill the niggah too. And I'm about to kill this niggah?"

"Dog." Jamal said, as he stood up out of the water with his arms open wide. DeDe hoped Melvin didn't look down and see the size of the branch Kendra had been sitting, rocking and twisting on, or he might just kill him for that alone.

"Naw, Dog. How you gon' fuck my wife?"

"She told me y'all were divorced. You know I wouldn't have fucked with her, if I knew y'all were married. You're my Dog."

"Melvin don't do this," DeDe calmly told him knowing he wasn't going to do anything but take Kendra home, beat her ass and then screw her silly. DeDe wasn't even going to try to intervene. That's how she had gotten the shit slapped out of her the last time, because she didn't know her sister flirted on purpose to get a reaction out of her husband who was leaving her for another woman. DeDe pondered whether Kendra knew that Melvin was still around here somewhere or that he might come back. "You have too much to lose."

"I don't have shit to lose. I got the nerve to kill everybody up in here, because of this trifling bitch."

The other women in the tub began to scream and cry.

"Dog, why don't you just take her and y'all leave? Somebody has called the police by now anyway. You shouldn't let your career go down over some trifling bitch like her. You got my word man, I don't want shit to do with her after this."

Melvin looked Kendra up and down, as he thought. "If anyone tries anything stupid, I won't hesitate to shoot." He stuffed one of the guns in his waist while still pointing the other one, as he walked over to Kendra and snatched her by her thin arm.

"I don't want to go with you. We're divorced and you can't control my life. DeDe, tell him," she cried. DeDe looked at them both and rolled her eyes, as she turned around and walked outside. As far as she was concerned, Kendra had no business marrying him in the first damn place. But she was so fascinated with being an NFL player's wife, who did Saturday shopping sprees, Sunday brunches and weekly visits to the spa. She said yes, to his proposal and quickly shipped her kids off to Ohio for good to live with their parents. He wanted them to start their own family, which they never did, because they didn't stay married but a damn year and a half. But DeDe couldn't blame it all on him for her not being a decent mother. She wasn't before she married him and she damn for certain isn't one now!

He snatched her out of the house and no one else moved until they were gone.

6

"I didn't think you would be comfortable with him and her there," Bridget told DeDe.

"So why didn't you just not invite *them*? I am your best friend, aren't I?" DeDe asked, as she sprayed lemon Pledge all over the wooden coffee table.

"You probably never would have come anyway. You hardly come to anything we have. Marie and Wayne had lil' Caitlin's birthday party and they invited you, and you didn't show up. Need I say that Marie was pissed about that?"

"I didn't want to be around all of the happily married couples," she told her but the truth was Stephan didn't want to go and she didn't want to go without him. "and besides; I don't have children. She just wanted to make sure Caitlin had lots of presents. You know Marie."

"Girl, do I ever. She was looking cross-eyed when Patrice brought her child and didn't bring a present."

"I could imagine. So what does she look like?"

"Who?"

"Waymon's fiancée."

"She looks okay. She's a little bit taller than you, medium length hair, and caramel complexion. She's cute and she's an ophthalmologist. She talks a lot though, but so does Waymon."

"Are they talking about going into practice together?"

"Eventually."

"Is he happy?" Her heart began to pound, as she waited for Bridget to tell her the answer.

"Yeah, he seems to be. They met a year and a half ago in California when he was there visiting his brother, and she moved here five months later. They have a house together."

"So he's serious. Out of curiosity, did he ask about me?"

"No, he hasn't asked about you in a while, but your name did come up and he seemed a little uncomfortable."

"What was said and who brought it up?"

"Mr. Mouth All Mighty, Jerome. He was telling Yolanda and Eunice about your new job and how you work with the big stars and all of the money you're making doing so."

"So what did Waymon do?" She asked, in all her glory.

"He walked out of the room. Your name is the last name he wants to hear. Remember when you were trying to call him to smooth things over? He was threatening to get his number changed, if you didn't stop calling. He was angry and he still is. I can tell."

"With me? It's been three years." She walked into the kitchen and began unpacking the dishwasher.

"That man loved you and you really hurt him, when you left him for that bastard Stephan. Speaking of him, where is he anyway? When Jerome told me you called, I kinda figured either he was out of town and you were bored or you two broke-up again and you needed a shoulder to cry on. For me to be your best friend, you know I don't hear from you, until either one of those circumstances occurs."

"You know how to dial my number also. It's not like you don't have a way to reach me Bridget. When I do call you, you're never at home."

"Don't try it bitch. I'm always here. This house is my life," Bridget laughed.

"Stephan and I broke-up four or five days ago." She was keeping count.

"I don't even keep up with the days anymore."

"For good this time, or until he finds out this new woman isn't as big as a fool as you are?"

"Bitch, and you call yourself my friend."

"I am. Only a friend can tell you the truth. Someone in the street will tell you what you want to hear and at the same time talk about how stupid you are for falling for it."

"Yeah, it's over for good," she said with solemness but the minute she thought of Elliott her attitude changed to vibrant and cheerful. "But I met someone new last night. His name is Elliott, he owns a restaurant downtown, and he has no children. Now, someone like him is a rare commodity these days."

"Where'd you meet him?"

"At a house party last night."

"That's the best place to meet a man if not at the grocery store, church or even at the stop light. Do you like him or are you just going to use him, until you get over Stephan. God knows how long that will take, but maybe you'll start liking him in the process."

"I'm serious, it's over between Stephan and I. I'm tired of the drama with Shannon."

"His babymama, right?"

"Yeah, and him not wanting to marry me. We've been together for three years and no wedding plans or ring."

"And the other women."

"What other women? To be truthful Bridget, I don't think he's fooling around. Stephan loved me, but we just didn't want the same things. When I used to be at his house, I would answer his phone, I had a key to his apartment and I was always over there. How could there be another woman?"

Bridget sighed, "If you don't know neither do I."

And DeDe truly didn't know. Out of the three years she and Stephan had been together, she never caught him with another woman. She accused him of still messing with Shannon, because of the kind of relationship they had for two people who couldn't make it while they were together. They were friends instead of enemies and they had a child together; she thought there had to be some feelings between them. In the beginning of the relationship, DeDe and Stephan broke-up several times, because they weren't spending enough time together. He worked long hours and so did she, and what she didn't complete at work she brought home. That's why she had to find her a new job, before she lost him to Shannon. She wasn't worried about any other woman. When she and Waymon were together, there was no big deal made about them not seeing each other. It was a part of the sacrifice plan Waymon had pitched to her, in order for them to be financially secure, when they got married.

She knew of other women wanting Stephan. He had told her about the one woman who worked with him and liked him; but he assured her it was nothing and she believed him. He had even introduced DeDe to the woman at his company's Christmas party as his fiancée. He said that for DeDe to make assumptions about him fooling around with other women and questioning him about those assumptions meant there was no trust. Also, in order for their relationship to work there had to be trust between them. He assured her that she could trust him enough to tell her that he was fooling around. He also stated that he had nothing to hide and he didn't want to hurt her by her finding out from someone in the streets or from the other woman. DeDe couldn't understand why Bridget along with Marie and Dionne wanted her to believe that, when she and Stephan break-up for a day or two that he's automatically fooling around. DeDe didn't think so. She knew of him to be moody and at times not wanting to be bothered with not even her. That's why she didn't agree with Candace, when she said, "A man needing his space, is a man trying to decide between the woman he's with and the other woman who he thinks he wants to be with." Being in a relationship takes a lot of energy and sometimes people can lose themselves, and sometimes space is needed. Unfortunately, it's always the men who lose themselves; so they are the first in the relationship to cry for space. Stephan of course needs it more than other men. Now when they break-up, it's because they argue too much about Shannon and her drama. DeDe looks at arguing as being a part of the relationship and he looks at it as mental drainage. Therefore, he feels he needs his space to regroup.

Stephan wasn't a total ex-factor of DeDe's life, because their break-up was still fresh and new, so she thought about him from time to time and he wasn't a major factor either. She wasn't crying her eyes out all day and night like she usually does. She wasn't paging him around the clock, and she wasn't calling his voice-mail cursing him and his mother for allowing him to be born and in the same voice begging him to call her back, so that they could talk and work things out. But she still jumped to answer her phone when it rang, hoping it was him. It was crazy, but they had been together for three years and he was the man she wanted to spend the rest of her life with. It was going to take more than a couple of days to get over him, even if he was the one to call it off for the fifth time in seven months. They were together three years and she loved him enough to want to marry him and have his children. She hoped by her meeting Elliott last night she could get over Stephan and move on with her life for good, because she was tired of Stephan putting her through the pain of breaking up.

LAST NIGHT SHE and Elliott sat in his car outside her house talking nonstop for two hours realizing they have a lot in common. They both have crazy relatives. He had Jamal his cousin, whom his mother raised and she had Kendra and Kendall. They had both just gotten out of relationships and they loved to bowl. She was glad to hear from him when he called.

"What's up pretty lady?"

"Elliott, hiiiii. . . how are you?" She asked, as she sat down and slid the silk scarf from her head as if he could see it.

"I would be doing better if I could get some work done, but I keep thinking about you."

She smiled. She can't remember ever having a man to flatter her so freely.

"I wanted to hear your voice," he told her.

"That was nice."

"So is your voice."

"I was thinking about you too, while I was cleaning." She couldn't wait to see him again. They were supposed to go to dinner and the movies tonight, after he gets off work. "Are we still on for tonight?"

"Oh yes. I can't wait to see you. I was telling my frat brother about you. He's my partner here at the restaurant."

"What did you tell 'im?"

He chuckled. "It's a secret and you wouldn't understand man talk."

"Try me."

"I'll tell you, when I see you."

DeDe's heart sank, when Kendra walked in with her lip swollen and her left eye closed shut. "Let me call you back."

"Sure."

She hung up the phone and stood staring at Kendra's face. "So are you going to press charges or is this just his way of showing you that he still cares?"

"Not now DeDe," Kendra said, as she threw her hand up to stop the questions and DeDe's antagonizing stares.

"He's changed and he's gotten help, huh? That lousy bastard! And you're just going to let him get away with it aren't you? Did he fuck you good afterwards? Did he tell you how much he loved you and how sorry he was, but you made him do it or did you enjoy having your ass beat?"

"Fuck you DeDe," she tried screaming, but it hurt to move her lips.

"You nearly got everybody killed last night including yourself, just so you could get fucked by a raging bull. Elliott had to bring me home last night, because you left with the keys."

"Bitch, you didn't try to help me. You just stood there looking like some damn fool who didn't care that her sister was leaving with some crazy asshole that might kill her. You see what he did to me?"

DeDe's eyes moved around Kendra's face feeling the pain she must have felt with each punch, but she was too angry to allow her to know she felt any sympathy for her. "You like that type of shit Kendra. Didn't it prove to you that he loved you? While you were married to him, he used to do it all the time and I used to tell you to leave him. But you thought it was cute, because he showed how jealous he was with a fist upside your damn head. Now you two are divorced, because he wanted it and he's still beating your ass. There's a price you pay for being greedy for money."

"You think you know everything don't you bitch?" She asked, as she slowly walked toward her bedroom.

"Well, I do know he gave you the deposit for that condo, so you and your lil' queen brother will be out of here at the end of the month."

Kendra rolled her eyes to high heaven, walked into her bedroom, and slammed the door.

DeDe was too upset to do anymore cleaning. Her mood was ruined. It was only once every other week she gets the urge to clean and now she couldn't do anything. She wished she had Melvin's number to call and curse him out, but she figured what would be the use; if Kendra was only going to go back to him even before her face heals. DeDe left everything just where it was. The household cleansers on the kitchen counter, the vacuum in the middle of the living room floor and a neat pile of trash in the middle of the kitchen floor, and headed straight for the shower. She was going to hit the malls. She felt a funk coming on, and whenever she gets depressed she has to shop. She thought about how stupid Kendra was and how stupid she was for loving men who couldn't possibly love them, which was displayed by their actions. And to top it off, she let a good man like Waymon go, because she was too stupid to realize she had a good man with a plan that included her. A funk was the last thing she wanted to get into today, because she wouldn't be able to shake it and it was sure to ruin her whole weekend. She dried her body and oiled it down with Royal African Oil. Stephan was heavily on her mind. She thought about how he had sold her a sack of false dreams, regarding them spending the rest of their lives together and she became angry with him. He made her think they were going to be married a year after they started dating, and here it is three whole years later. She put on her orange linen short set, combed out her short wrapped hair, put on her make-up and headed straight for the garage.

AS SHE DROVE down the street, Deborah Cox and RL's *'We Can't*

Be Friends' began to play. She immediately changed the station. She didn't understand how her radio was on when she never listened to it. On any given day, she would rather listen to her CD's instead of the radio. She didn't know all the words to the song, but to just think she and Stephan would walk pass each other one day and act like they never knew each other would surely hurt. She had never seen Waymon out in public, after they broke-up. But if she did, she would surely speak to him with no hesitations. But of course, she had done him wrong; so there were no hard feelings on her part. When she changed the station form 104.5 to H-103 there was Brain McKnight's *'Back At One'*. It took everything in her not to cry, but the tears came anyway. Damn, another sad slow song to add more misery to her life. She scanned through the many stations looking for a more upbeat tune, but she couldn't find any. She grabbed her CD case, and with one hand on the steering wheel she flipped through the CD's and came across one of Stephan's rap CD's and pushed it into the player and tried her damnest to fall in love with rap, as she tried bobbing her head to the beat and voice of Jay-Z. This quickly became an exercise in futility.

SHE HAD CHANGED her mind about going to the mall. She didn't want to go there and see happy couples laughing and holding hands like she should be doing with a man. She didn't want to be alone. She needed a man to comfort her from her wail of pain, as she thought about Stephan. She drove downtown to Elliott's restaurant. He was standing at the host station, when she walked into the door.

He noticed her and smiled. "Hey, what's up?" He asked, as he hugged her. "What are you doing here?"

"Well, I finished cleaning and I got a little hungry, so I thought I would stop by for some lunch. You don't mind do you?"

"No, I have the perfect seat for you." He took her by the hand and led her up three stairs to a platform of tables overlooking the restaurant. His cologne smelled of masculinity and strength. She inhaled it deep into her nostrils, so that it would always remind her of him. He pulled out her chair. "A special seat in the VIP section, for a beautiful young lady."

"VIP? In a restaurant?" She asked, as she looked around at the elegant décor.

"Yeah, all of the big wigs sit up here." The area was crowded with what looked like people with money and plenty of it. DeDe felt privileged. Elliott sat across from her leaning toward her with his elbows on the table smiling. She stared at him, as if she was looking at him for the first time. He had a beautiful smile and sleepy bedroom eyes. She didn't realize how handsome he really was. She was attracted to him, without a doubt.

"So did your sister make it home?"

DeDe's smile turned into a solemn frown. "Yes."

"Was everything okay?"

"Sure." She couldn't dare tell him that Kendra came home looking like the elephant man and have him go back and tell Jamal, so she lied. She kept staring at him trying to figure out what was so different about him from last night. "You look different. Did you shave your mustache?"

"I never had one. Facial hair doesn't grow right on me. It grows in patches."

She smiled, as she figured it out. "Where are your glasses?"

"At home I decided to wear my contacts today."

"I could never get into wearing contacts. "

"You shouldn't; you're beautiful in your glasses."

She smiled at his compliment that lifted her to the ceiling.

A waitress wearing all black came over and introduced herself, as she brought DeDe a menu and a glass of water. Elliott viewed the waitress and was very pleased at how professional she looked and sounded.

"Bring her a glass of the best RH Phillips' White Zinfandel from my private stock." Elliott told the waitress and smiled at DeDe.

"Thank you," DeDe said, as she opened the menu. There were so many things to choose from, she became indecisive and it showed.

"I recommend the Rosemary lemon chicken, steamed asparagus and garlic mashed potatoes."

"Rosemary chicken? I was thinking of having the seafood angel hair pasta with the Alfredo sauce."

"That's good too; both of them were originated out of my kitchen."

"Really."

"Not only am I an ex-Wall Street investment broker, I'm also a self-taught chef. Cooking is a hobby of mine. Especially breakfast."

"Is it?" She asked, as they looked at each other smiling. "So how did you come up with the name ElBuddha for this place? When Dionne told me the name of the restaurant, I thought it was an East Indian type of establishment. "

"It's a combination of Elliott and my frat brother's name Buddha. Once you meet him, you'll see why we call him Buddha," he said, as he waved his hand over his stomach to make a round gesture. "In a few minutes, I'll bring him over and introduce you."

The waitress brought over her wine. "Would you like to order now?" She asked.

"Yes, I'll have the Rosemary lemon chicken, Mr. Anderson's suggestion," she said, looking at Elliott and smiling.

"Good choice," he said, as he got up from the table.

"You're not going to join me?"

"Unfortunately I can't, but I might be able to sneak out with you afterwards and hang with you for the rest of the day."

"That's even better." They looked into each other eyes and smiled, before he walked away.

DeDe watched him, as he showed customers to their seats. She couldn't wait for Bridget and Marie to meet him. She knew they would like him, because she sure did and she had only known him for a day. After she finished with her meal, she pushed her plate away, wiped the corners of her mouth and sat watching his every move. When he noticed, he walked over to her in a serious sexy stride. "So are you going to be able to sneak out of here with me?"

"Sure. Are you ready?" He asked, as he took off his reddish and black jacket and silk tie that matched his jacket, threw it over his arm, and loosened the first two buttons of his crisp red shirt.

She left the waitress a very good tip and they headed out of the door.

7

IT was Elliott's idea to go bowling, after they left the restaurant and walked around the park. They stopped by the nearest Wal-Mart and grabbed a pair of socks and they bowled for three straight hours. DeDe was having the best time of her life. They talked in between games about silly stuff and they innocently made fun of people. Elliott had even felt comfortable enough to kiss her on the cheek. Bridget was right when she said the only way she was going to get over Stephan was having another man to help her. Right now, Stephan and the thought of him was the farthest thing from her mind.

After they left the bowling alley, they decided to check out a movie so they went by Elliott's house to look through the newspaper to see what was playing and at what theater. His house was beautiful and lavished. It was a three story, contemporary European Stucco, decorated in a Japanese motif. He grabbed DeDe by the hand and showed her around the huge four-bedroom house, as he educated her on the expensive Japanese sculptures and paintings. DeDe was impressed with his knowledge of the Japanese culture. She was really digging on him, but she felt he was way out of her league, although he had told her how much he admired her. He was the type of man she felt she could love unconditionally and that was scary. She just knew for a man with his gifts, there had to be something wrong with him. He was cute, successful, funny, and he came into her life too soon after Stephan. She realized she had better slow up on what she was feeling. He showed her downstairs where he had a home theater with ten theater chairs bolted to the floor, a huge screen covering the wall, a full bar, a popcorn machine and DVD's for days.

She walked over to the alphabetized racks of DVD titles. "We don't need to go to the movies. We can stay right here."

"If you would like," he said, smiling as he stood back watching her amazement.

"You have every movie that has come out in the last seven years."

"I have a little something." He walked over to the bar. "Would you like a glass of wine?"

"Sure."

Elliott handed her a glass of Zinfandel, took the movie section of the newspaper back from DeDe, and flopped down on the red, contemporary, butter soft, leather sofa that accented the funky yellow, blue and green décor. DeDe knew he had style.

"What are you in the mood for?" Elliott asked. He liked action, but DeDe's mind was somewhere else. She looked at him, he looked at her, and they both smiled.

"I'm talking about movie selections," he said and smiled. "You have drama, action, and romance to choose from." He said with much sex appeal.

"Whatever, like I said, we don't have to go to the movies you have everything here. The way this room is set-up; it's just like a movie theater. I love it."

"Well, pick out a movie," he said, as he got up from the sofa and walked over to the small refrigerator behind the bar. "And I'll pop us some snacks in the toaster-oven. Unless you're hungry, then I can go upstairs and work my magic in the kitchen."

"Magic," she repeated. "That Rosemary chicken was alright."

"It was better than alright," he laughed. "Give a brotha his props."

"Not just yet," she said, as she gave him a sexy but devilish smirk.

The toaster-oven's bell rang, which meant the hors d'oeuvres were ready.

Good. DeDe had grown hungry, after two glasses of wine. Elliott neatly arranged the cheese sticks, chicken fingers and diced fruit on a plate. DeDe wondered how often he did this type of entertaining, because he had diced apples, oranges, grapes and strawberry in separate zip lock bags. She sat down on the sofa with the stack of movies she had chosen. He placed the food on the coffee table, dumped more ice into the bucket of wine and grabbed napkins, just before he sat down beside her. With the remote, he turned off the radio, lights and started the movie. DeDe was interested in seeing the Green Mile, but she would much rather talk to him. She hoped he didn't mind her talking, during the movie. "You know what? I've told you everything about me, but I don't feel that I know enough about you," she said, as she dipped a cheese stick into the red marinara sauce and pulled it apart with her teeth. "I know that you grew up in Philadelphia, you're an only child, you graduated from Morehouse and got your graduate degree from Harvard; and one day you would like to get married. But being thirty-eight, why haven't you gotten married before now?"

"I don't look at my age to dictate that I should be married. I was into my career. I've only been in love twice in my life and those were the two women I would have loved to marry, but the timing wasn't right. My life and time was devoted to my career and now that I'm secure financially, I'm ready." He noticed her glass was soon to be empty. "Would you like another glass of wine?"

She handed him her glass. Last night he had mentioned a woman he seemed fond of, as he spoke about her. DeDe noticed him smiling as he talked. She wondered if Stephan would ever reminisce about her to another woman and smile while doing so. "The woman you talked about last night, who just picked up and moved to Indiana without telling you, are you trying to get over her? How long ago did she leave? We're you in love with her? Was she one of the women you wanted to marry?"

"So many questions at once," he said and smiled. "No, she left six months ago. Yeah, I was beginning to love her and no she wasn't one of the women I wanted to marry. Why all of those specific questions?"

"Curious."

"Those are things I should be asking you about Stephan." They looked at each other as he handed her the refilled wine-flute. "So you're in the mood for crying?"

She gave him a puzzled look.

"The movie. Most women cry while viewing this film." He placed his hand on top of hers. "But you can use my shoulder," he said and smiled.

Three glasses of wine and two hours later, DeDe had fallen asleep on Elliott's shoulder halfway through the movie. He woke her after the movie was over and the credits were rolling. "What time is it?" She asked, through her yawns while looking around the room for a clock. "I missed the movie and all of the hoop-la about it," she said, sarcastically and chuckled.

"You would've had to stay awake and watch it through to understand the hoop-la. It's a good movie, believe me." He stood up, stretched, and looked at his watch. "It's ten o'clock. I can take you to get your car or you're more than welcome to sleep in one of the guest bedrooms."

The guest bedroom, she thought. She knew from when she first met him where she wanted to sleep; and it wasn't in his guest bedroom. That's why she put on her favorite matching pink, lace panties and bra set.

"And I'll just take you in the morning to get your car. I have an extra pair of pajamas or t-shirt for you."

"A t-shirt will be fine." But the guest bedroom, she thought again.

He turned off the lights downstairs and she followed him upstairs to his bedroom to get a t-shirt. His bed was neatly made and it sat high off the plush carpeted floor. It looked very comfortable and masculine, along with the Japanese décor of his room. He handed her the shirt and she was hoping he would kiss her again or perhaps try to convince her to sleep in his bed, if he promised to sleep on his side and not touch her.

"I'm going to need some towels so that I can take a shower," she told him, while sizing him up.

"There are some in the guest bathroom."

"Thank you." She turned around hoping he was staring, but she didn't feel like he was.

She took her shower, slipped on the white and maroon alumni t-shirt and laid up under the covers sleepless. She kept the light on hoping he would knock on her door to talk. That would be his way of trying to make love to her. She felt an attraction to him and part of it was sexual, which she wasn't embarrassed about at all. She knew she wanted to have sex with him the first night they met. He said nothing mesmerizing to sweep her off her feet for her to arrive at that decision. There was something else about him that had her wonder how he was in bed, because she wouldn't mind sleeping with him. It takes a special man with extreme powers of sexiness and charisma to conquer a woman's way of thinking; to seduce and woo her without dinners, movies, and countless phone calls. Normally it takes a month or two of him convincing her he's there for the long haul, before she decides to have sex with him. DeDe had gone through this process with every man she's dated, because her mother and father had always taught her not to give it up easily. At thirty-four she was truly behind in the times. DeDe had never come on to a man before, and she had never slept with a man on the first date or even spent the night in his guest room wishing she were in bed with him. She didn't even know how to flirt. But tonight, she wouldn't mind it being her coming out party; to be a woman who goes after what she wants. She desired Elliott like no other man, and she had only known him a day. She made Stephan wait two weeks before they slept together, although he tried to seduce her sooner. Waymon, poor Waymon waited a month.

She tossed and turned, as she tried to think of something to get Elliott's attention. It hit her, she would ask for a glass of water. She jumped out of bed and slowly opened her door. His light was on and his door was closed. She took a deep breath, before she tiptoed across the hall and gently knocked on his door. He answered on her second knock.

"What's up?" He asked, as he looked down into her eyes. Not once did he look at her standing in his t-shirt with no bra or panties on.

"Do you have any lotion or oil?" Asking for water seemed like a come on.

"I have some Lubriderm."

"That's fine."

He walked into his bathroom and she nearly fainted. He was wearing silk pajama pants with no shirt. He was shaped like a genie: small waist, perfect round ass, firm chest and broad shoulders. She walked into his room and the covers on his bed were pulled back.

"What are you doing?" She asked him, as he handed her the lotion.

"Reading."

"I wish I had something to read because I can't sleep." She bent over and began to lotion her legs very enticingly.

"Yeah, it's kinda hard trying to sleep in a bed that's not yours; so if you need for me to take you to your car, I can."

"No, I don't. I'm fine. I can wait until tomorrow morning."

"Are you sure? Because I want you to be comfortable." He tried not to look at her but it was hard not to.

"Your bed looks comfortable," she said, as she jumped up on it and grabbed the book he was reading and read the title aloud. "Staying a Successful Millionaire. Are you a millionaire?"

"Yes, but do I have a million in the bank? No, I'm a millionaire on paper with my stocks and bonds and mutual funds. I'm working on getting the million in the bank," he said, as he leaned up against the wall while staring at her and she staring at him. There was silence between them.

"Are you shy?" She asked.

"No, I don't think so."

"I am."

He chuckled. "I can tell."

"Are you used to a woman initiating the first move?"

"If that's what she wants."

"I want it, but I don't know how. I'm not good at initiating the first move."

"And that's what makes you so sexy." He walked toward her, placing his hands on her face and locking her bottom lip between his two. They kissed with a burning desire for one another. He straddled over her and gently laid her back on the bed. Her legs opened so she could feel him through the silk pants. She was much too shy to take her hand and rub him there. He lifted her shirt once he realized she didn't have on any panties. Then he pulled it over her head and stared at her body in amazement, before kissing her burnished pink, erect nipples. He grabbed a condom from his nightstand and pulled down his pants that had her wetness covering the front of them. He was definitely Jamal's cousin. It was obvious that size runs in the family. She laid there slightly embarrassed. He touched her clitoris just before gently sliding inside of her. DeDe felt the walls of her vagina expanding, making her ovaries feel as if they were going to burst. She held on to his arms and sank her teeth into one of them, as he slid in and out of her. The feeling for her was overwhelming. She had never known love to feel this way before. She didn't have a clue on how to move to his movement of lovemaking, and she was embarrassed. She's never been with anyone that required her to get into the lovemaking. She was sure he thought she was the worst woman he had ever made love to, because he had to lead her to the thousand and one positions he had put her in.

"What are you doing to me?" she moaned, as he kissed her and she exploded for what must have been the tenth time.

WHEN SHE AWOKE, she lay in bed with her legs stretched wide open, as she could still feel the friction of him going in and out of her from last night, and she became moist all over again. She hoped he would come back to bed and do it to her again and again. She wouldn't complain.

She followed the wonderful aromas downstairs and discovered Elliott in the kitchen cooking breakfast.

"What's up sleepy head?" He asked, and kissed her on the forehead.

"Good morning."

"Would you like some juice and breakfast?"

She nodded, as she sat down on the barstool.

"I was going to serve you in bed, but here you are with those beautiful breasts and all of your loveliness in my kitchen."

She smiled. "I can go back." Maybe he didn't think she was that bad after all or he wouldn't be trying to serve her breakfast in bed. He would probably be trying to get her to her car instead.

"Please," he said, and smacked her on the behind.

Just before she walked out of the kitchen, there was something on her mind she just had to ask him. He was too perfect. "What's wrong with you?"

"What do you mean?'

"You're perfect."

He chuckled. "Not at all. I have my issues."

"What are they?"

"I'm never on time, I can't read a woman's mind, and sometimes I tend to care."

"I can live with that."

"Yeah, you say that now, but you'll find out later that's not what you want."

"Please, try me."

8

THERE was an undeniable gleam on DeDe's face, as she told Starla all about Elliott. Dionne hadn't made it into the office yet for DeDe to give her the 411. So when Starla made the mistake of asking her about her weekend, she held her in the break room for over thirty minutes letting her in on every detail about Elliott. DeDe was proud to tell Starla about Elliott, because she's heard her crying and arguing with Stephan over the phone several times, but she's never said anything. And truly DeDe didn't care if she did. Stephan was her man, they were going to argue and Starla was no one she cared to impress. DeDe was surprised when Starla spoke to her, but she didn't get an attitude and not speak back. Dionne had made her believe Starla wasn't to be trusted, because she wanted to be White and all her friends in the office were White.

Starla made it a point to let DeDe know she was not fully Black, when they first met. Her mother was White and her father was, "One of you people," she said and laughed, but DeDe didn't find it amusing. Out of the four months they've been working together, they've never really said more than hello and goodbye, and if Dionne is walking with her they don't even say that. Starla held most of her conversation with the White people in the office, as she tried to fit in with them. She would incessantly talk about her White husband Todd, the summer home they're having built in Florida, his wealthy family in Virginia and their dog Mr. Peter's. DeDe overheard several of her conversations and became sick with her struggle to be accepted, as she always spoke over properly in an aristocratic manner. If DeDe hadn't seen her face to know she was Black, she would have thought she was one of those so-called 'blue-blooded' White women.

"He's very intelligent. He used to work on Wall Street and he owns Elbuddha's down the street. The first night we met we talked for hours. He's so funny he had me dying laughing. He's a pro at bowling and I love to bowl."

"Where'd you meet?"

"At a house party. I wasn't going to go, but my sister kept bugging me to get out of the house, and I'm so glad I did. Girl, he's God sent. "

"That's how I felt about my Todd when I first met him. Other men were trying to talk to me, but I kept looking at Todd and we were married eight months later."

If Elliott had asked DeDe to marry him right now; with them only knowing each other for six days, she would with no hesitation. He was very much marriage material and he had no drama, games or children.

Dionne walked around the corner and noticed them talking. She looked at both of them and turned up her nose with no discretion. She walked past them to get coffee without saying a word. DeDe knew she had an attitude. Dionne didn't like Starla and thought DeDe shouldn't like her either. She's gotten an attitude even when she saw DeDe laughing and talking with some of the White girls around the office. She always had something negative about each of them unless they were kissing her ass.

"Good morning Ms. Scales," DeDe said. Starla rolled her eyes.

"Don't good morning me," she snapped.

DeDe turned around and snapped back, "And what is your problem?"

DeDe's response shocked her into changing her whole attitude. "Girl, I'm just trippin'," she chuckled. "Good morning Starla."

Starla looked at her and rolled her eyes to the back of her head, before walking off.

"See if I ever speak to that bitch again. How was your Memorial Day weekend?" Before DeDe could tell her, she began talking about hers. "Chile, Byron and I had a night on the town Saturday night. He rented us a limo and inside, it had roses, wine and chocolates. He noticed the look on my face when he handed me the chocolates and he said I don't have to wait until Valentine to give you chocolate do I? He's so wonderful but I'm taking my time. We had gone to see the play, 'Mama I Love That Man'...a really good play, you should go and see it. And after that we went to dinner at Lexington's, what a great steak house and they give you so much food. I guess I don't have to tell you what we did after dinner, when we got back to his place. Yesterday we grilled. He's a master at barbecuing. He's just wonderful. He wants me to go to Dallas with him to meet his parents."

"After six months?" DeDe asked, with a shocked and envious look on her face, because she had waited three years to meet Stephan's parents.

Dionne continued to gloat. "Yup, six months. But that's nothing. Men who are really serious about 'cha; they'll introduce you to their family sooner than that. He said the reason I haven't met them before now is because he hasn't had any time off from work. He's crazy about me girl! He said it was a hypothetical question, but I knew he was talking about us. He said, what if a man asks a woman to marry him within six months of meeting her; is he moving too fast or is he on point?"

DeDe's heart boiled with envy, although she had just met a great man who seemed like he was crazy about her, but she had been with a man for three years who wasn't.

"Girl, that man wants to marry me," she screamed with excitement. "And I believe he's going to propose, when we go to visit his parents in four weeks."

DeDe thought and internally said to herself, 'He must be ugly as hell and Dionne is the 'prettiest thang' he's dated and he doesn't want to lose her, because there's no way in hell that after only six months he's taking her to meet his parents and proposing. I was with Stephan for three years and he ain't thought nothin' about marriage.'

"What did you put on him to get a marriage proposal after six months?" DeDe asked, and forced herself to chuckle.

"Nothing. All men are not dogs."

DeDe could not believe her ears. Now that she's got a man and is in love, men are good.

"So true." DeDe had to be happy for her, although there was some envy. Finally at forty she was getting married to a man she had only been dating for six months. Normally after the first three months of wining, dining, phone calls at work just to hear each other's voices and spontaneous, frequent sex, making the good impression is over. Many times, when a man has felt he's already won the prize; things can either go down hill or just stay where they are, with no growth. But this man seems like he's in love with Dionne. For three years DeDe had no growth or love as far as she was concerned in her relationship to Stephan; and she stayed. To listen to Dionne brag about her weekend with so much excitement showed DeDe why she doesn't want Stephan back. He wasted her life. In three years, they've never had a weekend she could brag about with any excitement. He's never rented a limo or given her roses or wine for the hell of it. The only time he kinda makes an effort is for Valentines Day. Them going to a play, was out of the question. He said, "Only stuck-up wannabe types go to see a play." And going to an expensive restaurant like the Lexington for dinner, never. Yeah, they've gone out to eat on occasions only if she paid for it, because he claimed to never have any money. And because she wanted to go out to dinner and have dinner with him, she paid for it without complaining. She couldn't let Dionne rub her good man and her possibility of marriage all in her face. "I had a great weekend also, I met this guy name Elliott."

"Elliott, who?" She asked, as if she was trying to see if she knew him.

"Anderson, you might know him, he's the owner of Elbuddha's."

"Yeah, he's one of the owners," she said, as she took a sip of her black coffee.

"I know that," DeDe told her to let her know she wasn't telling her anything Elliott hadn't already told her. "I met his partner, Buddha when I had lunch there on Friday. Is there anything else you want to tell me?"

"No, I was just saying…"

DeDe didn't know what she was saying, but she knew what she was trying to do and that was to hate, as she does on anyone that might be happy.

"You know how men lie and I didn't want him making you think he owns the whole restaurant, while trying to make himself look good." They began to walk toward Dionne's office. "So I take it you didn't go to Miami?"

"Nope, and I'm glad." DeDe stopped walking. "If I had gone, I never would have met Elliott. Have you ever talked to him before; he's so intelligent and funny? He had me dying laughing. We met at his cousin's house party. You've probably heard of him, Jamal Raspberry, who plays for the Dallas Wranglers. My sister's screwing him and nearly got everyone in the house killed, when her crazy ex-husband snapped. My brother ran off with some football player, I forget his name, but I believe he's married."

"You are kidding me, right?"

"Nope. There were a lot of men there, but they wanted groupies and Elliott wanted me. He told me how much he admired me from the first day I had gone into Elbuddha's for lunch."

"Yeah, he's asked me about you a couple of times," Dionne told her.

"Why didn't you tell me?"

"Because you were so in love with Stephan and I didn't think he was your type."

DeDe looked at her and shook her head. "You should have told me what he said and what you were thinking; and I would have told you if he was or wasn't my type."

"It's no big deal DeDe. Let's be happy that fate brought you two together, but for how long? Maybe just until Stephan decides to come back, she chuckled. "Girl, you don't want any other man, other than Stephan. For what, I don't know. I've talked to Elliott before and he seems like a cool brotha."

"He is. I'm so crazy about him." DeDe gleamed with excitement. "Hopefully he'll go to New York with me for Erika's album release party. I haven't asked him yet, but I know he'll go."

"If y'all are together by then. That's two weeks away."

"We will be. We have so much in common and he doesn't have any babymamas. This man is simply perfect."

"There's no perfect man."

No man, so neither is Byron. DeDe didn't understand how she could say that, when she was just bragging about how great her man is and now there are no great men. "In my sight he is."

"Yeah, until Stephan tries to come back, then you'll find every damn thing wrong with the man. I'd hate to be around when that happens. Who are you kidding, you are not over Stephan and dating another man isn't going to help you get over him either."

"And I never said it would. But right now and never do I want Stephan back."

"He hasn't called to beg you back either," she chuckled. "But if he does, don't go back. You'll be a lot better off without him."

And I don't need you to tell me that, DeDe thought. Her joy had turned into sadness and she hated she had even opened her mouth to Dionne. DeDe didn't know the whole issue with her and men, but whatever it was, it had made her bitter or maybe she was just that way with everybody else's men. "Girl let me go, I have so much work on my desk I need to be doing. I'll talk to you later." DeDe didn't want to hear another negative word come out of her mouth.

DeDe was on her way back to her desk, when Chris Shultz's secretary approached her. Chris Shultz is the CEO of the organization. "Hello DeDe, I tried calling you at your desk, but you didn't answer and I didn't want to have you paged because of the stares. But Mr. Shultz would like to see you in his office."

DeDe's heart sank and her peachy bronze complexion had turned red with nervousness. "Sure." DeDe followed her to the elevator to the second floor where all the chief executives sat. She led her to his office. It was DeDe's first time ever seeing the inside of his office and it was as exquisite, as Dionne had described.

"Hi," he said, as he stood up to greet her with a handshake.

"Hello," DeDe smiled, while trying not to shake with nervousness.

"Have a seat." They looked at each other before he began to speak. "I understand you came up with the Bowl and Win project for FantastiCola and you also went to Bushel and Coleman Tobacco Company with the buy back program. They'll exchange with the consumer a two week supply of Quiterspatches for two packs of cigarettes, for those who want to stop smoking," he chuckled. "Where did you get the nerve? That is a tobacco company, that's how they make their money by people smoking."

"I understand that Mr. Shultz, but they're facing a large law suit right now and it looks like the judge might rule in favor the Cayman family on this one. I figured why not show the judge and the public although they were found guilty for using addictive chemicals to enhance the tobacco, there was still no intention to harm their customers. So, the offer to take back the two packs of cigarettes customers might smoke in a day for the exchange of the Quiterspatches is remorseful. Bushel and Coleman is the sister company to Lovelace and Lovelace produces the patches; so they are not losing any money."

"The public doesn't know that."

"I know."

"Are those your accounts?"

"No, Dionne's, she asked me to help her while she worked on the United Way project and the Mayor's fundraiser."

" Well, it's yours now. You're the only person they'll work with. They love your idea. Bret Johnson, the CEO of Bushel called me personally to tell me how brilliant the idea was. He loved it."

DeDe was flattered they loved her work but she couldn't take the account. "I can't. Bushel and Coleman is one of Dionne's largest accounts along with FantastiCola. I only worked on those projects because she was in over her head with her other assignments."

"I'll talk to her, she'll understand. DeDe we make our clients happy. That's why we are where we are today; one of the top Fortune 500 companies in

America. We give our clients what they want and Bushel and Coleman wants you on this campaign. It was you who came up with the idea."

"But it's not my account."

"I understand your loyalty, but our clients come first. The campaign starts here in Houston and will travel to four other cities within a month on a trial basis to see how the public responds and they want you there with the media." He noticed the twiddling of her thumbs and that the view through the huge window behind him had most of DeDe's attention. "So what do you think?" What damn difference does it make, she thought. You don't care about anything but making the client happy and getting paid. You couldn't possibly understand my loyalty. You don't think Black people have loyalty to one another, when it comes to money and promotions. If it was a White girl's account, it wouldn't matter one iota, if the President of the United States had asked for me personally; you wouldn't give me her account. It would have then been unheard of and against company policy. She finally snapped out of her semi-daze and looked him straight in his eyes.

"Dionne will understand you don't have to worry about that," he tried to assure her and the skeptical look on her face. "This will be a great project for you to work on. If all goes well, it will bring you great recognition and a bonus. I'll see to that, I promise." He walked over to her and shook her hand.

DeDe didn't give a damn about his promise; she just didn't want the account. She wasn't hungry enough for success to climb the company's ladder for recognition or money, by stabbing Dionne in the back and taking one of her larger accounts. She would not only be taking her account she would also be taking seven thousand dollars in commission out of her pocket. DeDe had gotten sick all over again. She stood up and gave him a firm handshake, while looking him straight in his eyes and trying to think of another way to explain to him her loyalty to Dionne. She liked her, she's a sistah and they're friends.

She walked out of the office to the elevator down the hall. She wasn't going to wait for him to tell Dionne, she was going to tell her herself. She walked back to her department with all the stares of her colleagues following her. She was sure they knew what was going on. She walked over to the empty conference room, closed the door behind her, let out a long sigh, and rushed over to the phone on the coffee table in the corner to call her girlfriend Bridget. She needed her advice.

DeDe saw Dionne emerge from her office through the glass wall of the conference room. DeDe froze and hung up the phone on the second ring. She then thought, telling Dionne wasn't a good idea. She had only told her a thousand times, how she didn't have any friends, because they were messy and she didn't trust them. DeDe was sure she would think the same about her, if she told her Mr. Shultz had given her one of her top accounts. She wouldn't dare blame Mr. Shultz or Bushel and Coleman, for wanting DeDe on the account. She would blame DeDe even if she had no choice in the matter. As Dionne headed down to DeDe's cubicle, she looked through the glass wall and saw DeDe lounging by herself in the conference room near the phone and walked in. "Why are you in here by yourself? What's going on? I heard Shultz called you in his office," she asked, in a singsong voice.

"Yeah, he did and I'm in here making a personal call, because I do not have any privacy in my cubicle with Starla all up in my business." DeDe said, as she tried to look Dionne in the face.

"Okay, to hell with Starla. But why did Schultz call you; for what? Did you do something?"

"No, he just wanted to know how my ninety days has been."

"What? He's the CEO of the company, what does he care?"

"Yeah, I was thinking the same thing, but I guess he's trying to get involved."

"What'd you tell him?"

"I told 'im, it was going great and I love it here."

"You do?" Dionne asked, as she sat in the chair opposite DeDe.

"Yeah, don't you? You've been here ten years."

"But I hate it. I hate working for people who care more about their damn clients than their employees."

DeDe's heart began to race with nervousness. The clients were important.

"You'll see, they don't give a damn about you around here. That's why I trip off of Starla, who breaks her neck to be just like them. To them she's Black. They don't give a damn that her mother and husband are White. I've been here ten years and she's been here five and neither one of us have made Senior Publicist. The only thing they've given me is an office with a view and some of the company's big accounts. Don't get too comfortable here."

"I'm not. I'm working on a plan to start my own firm within the next year."

"That's great."

"With my experience and your experience we could really make it."

"Girl, I'm not trying to do that. Owning your own business is a big responsibility I don't want. The monthly bills that I have to pay and my family is the only responsibilities I'm able to deal with right now. It's time for me to leave here, because there's no growth. But I haven't found anything better as of yet."

"Well, would you come and work for me, if you don't want to be partners?"

"Don't take it personally, but no. When I first graduated from college, I moved to D.C., I worked for a Black owned PR firm there, and I hated it. The women there were messy. The company was unorganized and every two weeks they had a problem with payroll. Girl, I don't want to go through that anymore. I like to know I'm getting paid for the work I do. You and I seem cool for now, but if we start having to work together in an employer/employee capacity we might not be able to make it," she chuckled.

AFTER LUNCH, DEDE had no words to say to Dionne. She was pissed with her to the point of no return and she didn't give a damn if it showed. As a matter of fact, she wanted it to really show. First of all, DeDe didn't even invite her to Elliott's for lunch. Dionne had invited herself only to be nosey. She had already tried to put doubt in DeDe's mind about him, and then she wanted to drill him about his life. She was treating Elliott as if he was a criminal, and acting like she was DeDe's mother. The entire time during lunch she complained about everything; the salmon was too dry, the waitress had an attitude, when actually she was the one who had the attitude. DeDe had seen her occasionally pull her 'unsatisfied customer' act, when they've gone out to lunch in the past. But when she did it to Elliott and he gave her her meal free, DeDe felt like cursing her out, which she probably needed anyway. DeDe was hoping Elliott would have snapped from his cool, laid-back self and cursed her out, for asking him a thousand questions, as if he was a fugitive from America's Most Wanted. He just smiled and entertained her by answering her stupid questions. If DeDe wasn't concerned about his intentions for her, Dionne shouldn't have been. DeDe didn't even invite her to go to lunch in the first place. It looked like Dionne was trying to mess things up for her.

The truth of the matter was, it wasn't the women who were messy, it wasn't the White people who weren't to be trusted and it wasn't the job Dionne didn't like. It was her who was just crazy as hell. At this point, it wasn't too hard for DeDe to figure out the reason Dionne didn't have friends. She was too damn messy and no one with any sense could stand to be around her, once they realized what type of person she was. Dionne was angry at the world and all the Black men in it, because one or two had hurt her. Even after she had bragged about how great Byron was she still tried to recruit DeDe to join her women against men bandwagon after seeing how much DeDe liked Elliott, but DeDe didn't fall for it. She didn't hate men in spite of the drama Stephan had taken her through with his quest for space. She'd heard about the dirt some men do, with their cheating, lying and abuse but she had never experienced it, so she couldn't dislike them enough to say, 'all men aren't shit.' For the most part, her experience with men had been good. Every man she'd dated cared for her and loved her. It was her who got tired of them for various reasons. Either they were boring or not much of a challenge.

Later, DeDe called and apologized to Elliott for Dionne's behavior. He said, "Babydoll, forget about it."

9

CHARLOTTE was shaped like an hourglass, which was the perfect shape in most men's eyes, and envied by many women. She had nice size breasts, a small waistline, wide hips and a protruding round butt. It was a hereditary blessing in her family to have such a figure. Dionne couldn't understand why Ian had called her fat and she was on a diet. "Girl, she looked so surprised the other day, when I told her I had a man."

"She did, why?" Charlotte asked, as she dipped the wooden spoon into the pot of spaghetti sauce for the fifth time in three minutes and allowed her lips to suction the sauce from it, until it was clean and dry.

"Because I don't tell her my business." Because, she didn't trust DeDe or any woman other than Charlotte. "Today she was so happy about this new man she met at a party over the weekend. His name is Elliott, he co-owns ElBuddha's. Can you believe she's already crazy about him? She said the reason she and Stephan broke-up this time is because of his child's mother, who he's still very much in love and sleeping with if you ask me. From what I can tell, he let's her run shit between him and DeDe."

"Yeah, he's still sleeping with her, if she's running thangs?"

"Of course, because DeDe spends her nights at that damn office instead of at home with him. The love affair between me the job and all the paperwork is ancient history. I don't even bring my work home anymore, now that Byron is there all the time. DeDe doesn't leave out of that office some nights until eight-thirty, even then she takes work home. That job is her life. She thinks she's going to move up over those young White girls, but I told her to think again. They ain't about to give no Black bitch shit at Stockton's. I've been there for ten years and they haven't given me shit. They only hired her because they needed another mocha face to offset mine. Starla wasn't chocolate enough; she's too busy screaming she's White."

"How does this Elliott man look?"

"Oh, very handsome as a matter of fact. We had lunch at his restaurant today and she hung onto his every word." Dionne said, smiling at Byron as he entered the kitchen to get a beer for him and Ian. She couldn't wait for them to go home, so he could make love to her like he did this morning. "Baby, are you guys watching the game downstairs?" She asked and noticed his zipper was undone. She pointed down and he took the hint and zipped his pants, without Charlotte noticing, because she was busy at the sink.

"Yeah," he said, as he winked at her, threw the beer bottle to his lips, and walked out of the kitchen with her eyes and a smile following him. Byron was just her type, handsome, tall, slim, sexy, beautiful smile and a sharp dresser. A man that could dress was all that she needed. Damn the physical characteristics, they were only a plus.

"Girl, if you were at home you would eat that man up whole," Charlotte said and laughed.

"He's so sexy. You see that shirt he's wearing; I was with him when he picked it out. Isn't it sharp? It's been six months; he's the one."

"Six months already. Damn how time flies. I remember when you first met him coming out of Ian's office building. What was he doing there again?"

"Visting a friend I believe. I don't know. But yup, he's the one that made me love again."

"Do you love him already?"

"No, but I'm damn near close." They both laughed. "Thank you for inviting us over," Dionne told her and took a sip of her wine.

"Girl, don't mention it but I didn't invite you Ian did. He wanted Byron to help him put the speakers in the wall downstairs in the den. I'm glad he told me to call you because I needed to talk to you anyway. Since Byron is over your place all the time and Ian wants dinner cooked during the weekdays; which makes it impossible for you and me to meet during the week, his suggestion was perfect."

"Well, I'll thank Ian later. He knows how much I love your cooking." The lasagna was in the oven, the corn on the cob was boiling and the salad sat in the middle of the table along with a bottle of red wine.

"So what did you want to talk about anyway? When you called me at work saying you needed to talk to me, I prayed nothing was seriously wrong. By the way you sounded, I wasn't sure."

"No, everything is fine." She gulped her wine down and began loading the dishwasher. "So she didn't go to Miami I take it?"

"Hell no, I told you that! He wouldn't even call her back on Thursday. They were supposed to leave on Friday. I felt sorry for her, but then again I didn't. The man doesn't want her and he's not going to marry her like she keeps hoping for. She needs to just move on."

"It's hard according to what some women are saying. There are women that sympathize with DeDe and there are some women who understand your frustration."

"My frustration," Dionne replied and chuckled. "About what? I'm just tired of her being used as the fool and I'm tired of hearing about it. Hell, but I guess if she likes it, I should love it. I'm not frustrated, I'm more like tired." Just as she was with Charlotte and her damn crying, every damn time Ian hurts her feelings.

"Have you been reading The Rapture lately?" Charlotte asked her.

"No," Dionne answered skeptically, because she didn't want to hear Charlotte's mouth because she hadn't.

"I'm not going to even ask why," Charlotte said, while cutting her eyes over at Dionne expecting her to give her a reason anyway.

"I don't have time to read anything, except the shit on my desk. I'm swamped with work."

Charlotte didn't say anything, but Dionne knew she wanted to. She took pride in her paper and the articles she wrote for it; and if her own husband wasn't going to support her she thought at least her best friend would. She closed the dishwasher door, walked over to her briefcase, and handed Dionne the folded newspaper from Friday. "Read that." She then grabbed her a small saucer, dumped four spoonfuls of sauce onto it with a piece of Italian bread, and sat down at the table across from Dionne.

Ian walked into the kitchen looking crazy, after he noticed the small plate of sauce and bread in front of Charlotte. "Are you eating already?"

"No, this is Dionne's. It's just sitting in front of me, until she finishes reading the paper."

Dionne looked at her and rolled her eyes for not standing up to him and saying, 'Hell yeah, I'm eating and I'm going to eat some more, as soon as the lasagna comes out of the oven.'

He grabbed a can of peanuts from the cabinet and two more beers from the refrigerator. Dionne couldn't wait for him to walk out of the kitchen, before she began cursing him out for being an asshole that enjoyed controlling her best friend.

"Who in the hell does he think he is?" She whispered. "There's nothing wrong with you. Your weight is perfect."

"Girl, forget him," she said, as she waved her hand. "Read."

What makes her think I want to listen to her go on and on for two hours straight talking about this man, who could give less than a damn about her. He's a dog and she's a fool. I picked that up just in a couple of minutes of listening to Angelic talk about their relationship. Whenever he needs space, he breaks up with her. Whenever he decides to come back, she takes him with open arms. I think he's fooling around and so does she, but she talks about him like he's the perfect man and every man in the world should model themselves after him. Like hell! I know the scoop on Tibias and so does she, but she's too in love to realize the situation isn't as good as she wants me to believe it is. That's the funny thing about Angelic, she won't admit that her s#*t is kind of raggedy.

He calls her and tells her he's on his way and he never shows up and she lets him get away with it! What a fool! I keep telling her there's an-

other woman, but she doesn't think so. She actually thinks she's the only one. They fuss every other week when he tries to think of a way to break-up with her for the weekend, so he can take some other woman out. One week he gives her hope for the future and the next he's missing in action. However, she still wants to marry that fool. Does that sound like another woman or someone on crack too strung out to find his way back home?

Tibias had even tried to get her to have his baby a couple of months ago and she said no. I'm glad she had that much sense. But she had considered it, when they broke-up two weeks ago. I guess she thinks a baby will give their relationship some stability. If she thinks that, she better learn from the babymama she hates so much. She was probably thinking the same thing and how that girl is a single parent going through hell to get that dog to give her child support.

If Angelic doesn't wake up and see that he doesn't want her, I might just have to tell her. I can't take it anymore. I don't want to hurt her feelings and tell her to wake up and stop being so gullible, but if she continues, I just might have to. That's what girlfriends are for, right? Angelic sees no wrong in this man, even when others around her do. Angelic forgives him for all the wrong he's done, without making him suffer a little. A real woman doesn't give in to a man because he apologizes. She makes him beg a little and kiss her ass a lot.

They are back together now and there's no pulling them apart. But if he finds something stupid to break-up with her about before they go on their trip and she doesn't go, I'm going to have to sit the sistah down and give her the "When a man doesn't want you" speech.

Dionne stopped in the middle of the article and peeked over the newspaper at Charlotte, who didn't look up from the saucer and bread she stuffed her face with. Dionne sat speechless and in shock. She let the paper slide out of her hands onto the table. "Girl, what is this, and what have you done?"

"What do you mean?" She asked, as if she didn't know what she was talking about.

"Is this supposed to be DeDe and Stephan?"

Charlotte smiled innocently through her devilment of betrayal. "It's hot, isn't it? The women love it. It's healing for them."

"Healing," Dionne replied.

"They now want to know who is this damn Angelic and Tibias and who are you; the 'Frustrated Friend'. Everyone thinks it's either them or someone they know."

"You fell in the shower and bumped your head, haven't you?"

Charlotte laughed. "I know they've been going strong for the last month or so until now. So what I did was this; I took last month's break-up when you told me that he didn't call her for four days and when she finally hears from him, it's in the form of a voice-mail message to tell her it was over. Girl, I took her drama and your gossip and turned it into this column I call 'No More LoveMaking'. Isn't it awesome? But now they've broken-up for real which makes things perfect." She gleamed with excitement not paying any attention to the disappointed and confused look on Dionne's face.

"This is everything I've told you about her, Charlotte. So today while I was talking to you about the new man in her life and her brother sleeping with the football player what did you do?"

"It's not everything you've told me Dionne, I added some of my own drama."

"Like what, different names? Why Charlotte? How long have you been doing this?"

"For three weeks."

Dionne could have fallen out of her chair. Three weeks, she thought.

"The people love it; Atlanta, Dallas, Philly, New York and D.C."

"So you are running her business in all of those cities?"

She continued to ignore Dionne's interrogation "I sent it to a couple of the radio stations. They pumped it for about two weeks, and then people started fighting to get their hands on a copy. Honey, advertising sales are up!"

"Three weeks." She replied. "I told you those things in confidence. You can't do this, it's wrong. What if she finds out?"

"She won't, the story is written under Celeste Biggs, she's fictitious, and the names and places are changed. Girl, women can't wait to read this column every week. Men are even getting into it also. Yeah right now, everything between them is cool, but three weeks ago when he broke-up with her and she was crying and trying to figure out what was wrong; sistahs were showing sympathy for her. But now that they are back together, sistahs are not feeling her. They think she's stupid."

Dionne became disgusted with Charlotte's childish excitement. She thought she knew her and could trust her. "I can't believe you."

"What is there to believe? There are so many women feeling like you are and there are so many women doing exactly what DeDe does. She's playing the fool and crying on everyone's shoulder, but they have no intentions of leaving the men or taking anyone's advice."

"But I tell you these things not for you to put them in your newspaper and make a spectacle of her, or me for that matter."

"A spectacle," Charlotte replied. "That's a little harsh. She began laughing, but quickly shut-up, when she noticed Dionne wasn't laughing.

"Dammit Charlotte!" Dionne yelled, as she jumped up from the table and walked out of the kitchen.

"Don't go anywhere finish reading."

She flopped down on the sofa and sighed out of betrayal and frustration, and she was angry on top of that. She felt used, because Charlotte didn't even have the decency to tell her what she was doing until now, three whole weeks later.

"Girl, women can relate to DeDe and women can relate to you the 'Frustrated Friend'. Who gives a damn about her men problems, because she's stupid like that? But then again, there are women who do care, because they've been through it."

"You had no right, how in the hell am I supposed to look that girl in her face?"

"It's not even that serious Dionne. It seems to me that, you don't like her anyway, so why are you trippin'? You don't even know her good enough to get upset about this. She's only been working there for four months. Y'all are not friends and you talk about her."

"And."

"You don't talk about me."

I do as a matter of fact, Dionne thought, as she looked at her and rolled her eyes. "That's besides the point Charlotte. I do like her. I just don't trust her or any other woman besides you; there's a difference. When I tell you things about people, I don't mean for you to make fun of them in that damn newspaper. I told you Jessica Perkins lies all the time about stupid shit, you didn't write about her."

"She's crazy and she needs help for the things she lies about. That bitch lies about being a vegetarian and she has a freezer packed with meat. No one wants to read about her and her sickness to lie."

"I told you about Starla, who thinks she's White just because one of her parents is. Why didn't you write about her?"

"She's a screwed up nut. Who cares if she doesn't want to be Black even though she is?"

"Well what makes you think they want to read about DeDe and her stupid ass? That's her business and she feels like she can talk to me about it and I feel like I can talk to you about it, because you are about the only damn friend I have besides my mother and Byron." She couldn't wait to tell him what her so-called best friend had done.

"I'm not making fun of her, I'm just helping other women deal with the same situation she's going through." She sat down beside her. "It's not that serious Dionne"

"Yes the hell it is! I brag about how I can talk to you about any damn thing, because you're supposed to be my best friend, and you turn around and do something like this for three weeks. You didn't even tell me. This is something a messy, untrustworthy bitch would do."

"Whatever." Charlotte said, and fanned her off.

"When I tell you things about my family, are you going to write about it in your little column or do I need to not tell you shit else?"

"Yeah, don't tell me shit. Your family is different Dionne. DeDe is a very stupid woman, who doesn't know when to let go. She'll never find out."

"But why did you do it?"

"The paper needed a twist and some spice. When I wrote it three weeks ago, hell, I was just joking and then the response from the women and the radio stations started pumping it. Girl, it's hot. They love it"

"I don't understand this."

"The articles I was writing weren't hitting on shit and I had no other place to turn. Ads stopped selling and our clients weren't getting the response from our readers like I had promised. Also, people stopped picking up the paper, and it was free. I couldn't let Ian know that I had failed at this, when he told me not to go into it in the first place."

"So it's about him?"

"No, he doesn't know. You venting to me about the love DeDe wasn't getting made me start the column. Stephan doesn't love her, but she's too stupid to realize it and there are women just like her."

Like you for instance, Dionne thought, and turned her head away from her.

"The women of Houston love this column."

"I don't care."

"Listen," she said, as she ran over to the radio and pressed the play button to the tape player. "Women called into the 'Casey Jenkins and Sylvia Reed Morning Show' absolutely going off."

"They did what?"

She smiled. "'No More LoveMaking' is the new thing of the future. These days the networks follow people around, with cameras all day and call it 'Reality TV'. Talk shows have folks face to face and they can never get their point across with both parties yelling and acting stupid. But this column allows *you* to vent, with her not knowing it's about her. Other women are learning from it and the readers are getting emotionally involved. It's a new way to let off some steam. But with this, they are listening to this one woman who vents about the girlfriend, who is stupid over a man who doesn't want her. That one woman they listen to is actually you Dionne. When I say there are women just like you, there are, and they don't know how not to listen to the mess of a stupid girlfriend. Listen to this."

"Caller, now you say, you have a girlfriend just like Angelic? Is it really frustrating to you that she's being played and she doesn't see it?"

"Yes, and no."

"Yes and no?" Sylvia replied. "Would you talk about her by writing into The

Rapture like this 'Frustrated Friend' or would you tell her? But first of all, before you answer those questions, what do you mean when you say yes and no?"

"I'll just give her time to burn herself out from crying and being hurt," the caller said. "Every fool gets tired of playing one."

"So true," Sylvia agreed.

"And while she's being burned out she's going to burn him out and then I'll be there with my arms open wide."

"You will what?"

"For her or him?" Casey asked.

"For him silly; I don't roll like that. I believe that's what her so-called girlfriend is waiting for also. You go girllll..."

Charlotte chuckled.

"I don't want to hear anymore of this." Dionne jumped up and turned off the tape.

"What's wrong?" Charlotte asked, as if she didn't know.

"This is wrong," Dionne said, pointing at the tape in the tape recorder. "I can't stand by you on this one."

"But I'm your best friend since grammar school, and she's just someone you just met," she proclaimed.

"Again, that's beside the point. It's not right. She confides in me."

Charlotte sighed, while trying to understand Dionne's gripe. No matter how hard she tried, she couldn't. She talks about DeDe like a dog. She was no friend of hers. She couldn't be, the way she carries on about her. "I understand. If you want me to pull the column, I will after Thursday's run, when she and Stephan breaks-up and she meets Elliott. It will hit the stands on Thursday afternoon, the radio will talk about it on Friday morning, and if it hits the stands on Friday afternoon, they'll talk about it on Monday morning. Sometimes I don't get everything to the printer on time, because I try to sell ad space at the last minute."

"So, when I was talking to you today over the phone, you were writing it down and getting it ready for print?"

She dropped her head, as her long bouncy hair fell forward in her face when she nodded, but not feeling as ashamed as she wanted Dionne to believe.

"Charlotte."

"I don't want to make you uncomfortable Dionne. You're my best friend, don't worry, I'll pull it."

"Thank you." Dionne said, as she got up from the sofa and walked back into the kitchen to pull the lasagna out of the oven. "Now let's eat."

10

$\mathcal{SO}$ this is how it feels to be treated like a queen, DeDe thought. She couldn't wait to get to work tomorrow and tell Dionne she had gotten roses and a card after knowing Elliott for only six days. This wasn't for a Hallmark occasion and for no special reason, other than she was beautiful. He had cooked dinner for her and had it waiting on the table, when she walked in, after *he* had worked all day. Then he had drawn her a warm bubble bath with lavender scented lit candles to serenade her soul. She sank deep into the warm water to rinse the apricot and tangerine scrub from her body, to later emerge from the water with soft, baby smooth skin. She rubbed her hands over her leg and arms imagining her touch to be Elliott's. She watched and hoped for him to walk through the bathroom door to wash her back. He was the perfect man and there was nothing for her to be afraid of, because she always knew a man like him existed. What she was experiencing at this moment and time wasn't a dream. She had pinched herself several times and she was still lying in his tub.

There was a soft knock at the door. "Are you okay?" Elliott asked, as he walked into the huge bathroom the size of a master bedroom. "You've been in here for about an hour I'm getting lonely out there."

"Why don't you join me?"

He smiled and knelt down beside her. "I'm a lot of things, but I'm not selfish. You seem like you're enjoying yourself and I don't want to mess that up." He took the half lit joint out of the ashtray, took a long drag from it to rekindle the flame, and passed it to her.

"I'm in heaven," she said, as she took a long drag from the joint and passed it back to him and began laughing. She felt good. She hadn't smoked weed in a year. That's when she stopped, to get Stephan from smoking it so much. He smoked it everyday and she began to smoke it with him, but it had gotten old, after he would spend his last dollar to buy it before buying anything else. She hoped Elliott wasn't a person who got high before he brushed his teeth in the morning. "I have to say it again, you are the perfect man. There are not too many men that are like you, so why don't you have a girlfriend again?"

He chuckled, took a quick puff, and passed the joint back to her. "I just haven't found the woman that's for Elliott."

She took a sip of her wine. "What are you looking for? I know women pretty much want and like the same things as the next woman, when it comes to a man? You're good in bed, you seem like you don't play games, and you know how to make a woman feel like a queen."

He agreed by nodding his head and he took a sip of her wine.

"I believe you have someone special, Elliott. Everyone has someone."

He didn't respond, as his half closed glassy eyes pierced through the deteriorating bubbles to gaze at her peach thigh. To say yes, she might just perceive him as a playa and he doesn't want her to form that opinion, because with that only comes problems. And to disagree and say he doesn't have anyone special, she might perceive him as being gay. Since he hears that so many brothers are living alternative lifestyles these days, he damn sure can't have her thinking like that.

"How important is she?" DeDe probed. "I haven't heard your phone ring since I've been here; not tonight or any other night."

"No, you haven't."

"Why, what do you have to hide? You said you're not in a relationship."

"And I'm not, but I'm not only Jamal's financial advisor, I advise a couple of his buddies who call me just to hear me tell them they have five to fifteen million in the bank and what stocks they should sell or buy." He felt he needed to tell her, since she was inquiring. If he didn't, he would be playing games. "I do have a couple of lady friends. You don't want them to call while you're here and neither do I."

DeDe felt like sliding under the water and drowning. She knew a man that perfect had women lined up and down the street, waiting their turn to be with him. If he didn't, she would think he was gay.

He noticed the disappointed look on DeDe's face. "Everyone might not have someone special, but what I do know is everyone has friends."

"Friends that you are sleeping with?" She asked, but already knowing the answer.

"Yes."

She mentally had gone under the water and drowned. He had women, he was thirty-eight, love had only visited him twice and DeDe didn't think she was the goddess he would experience it with for the third time. She didn't feel she was that special. So marrying for the convenience of sex when he wanted it, companionship or anything else people might marry for other than love, was not going to get him to walk down the aisle. Therefore, she had nothing to brag to Dionne about after all. She sure as hell knew he wasn't going to be introducing her to his parents and she didn't want him to either, with all the women she bet he had. She thought of Stephan and she hated him for wasting three years of her life and making her have to start over.

"But DeDe, I'm willing to let all of them go for you."

Her heart began to beat again, as he pulled her out of the water and resuscitated her back to life.

"You are the woman that's right for Elliott. I like everything about you, from your beautiful eyes to your ugly little pinky toe." She began to laugh through her solemnity, as he laughed.

"Is it that ugly?" she asked.

"It's very ugly," he said, and kissed her on her lips. "I would be lying if I told you I didn't worry about you going back to Stephan, but I have to take your word for it when you say you're through with him."

And she was. With someone like Elliott treating her like she knew she deserved to be treated, she wasn't going back to Stephan. He had broken her heart and seen her cry for the last time.

Elliott helped her out of the tub and he dried her body while kissing every part of her the towel touched. He led her into his candle lit bedroom, pulled his comforter back, laid her down on his bed, and began oiling her body. She lay lifeless with her eyes closed, as his hands and lips worked magic on her shoulders, breast, stomach, thighs and toes. Tingly sensations trembled her body, as she let out quiet passionate moans of seventh heaven. He took off his shirt and pants with gracefulness and laid on top of her to kiss her neck, her face and lips for just being there and being beautiful. She was ready for him to be inside her, as she reached down to pull down his silk underwear. He stopped her and whispered, "Not just yet." He rolled her over on her stomach and began oiling her back and arms while still kissing her. She wondered in her mind what was he doing to her, because she had never felt the touch of a man that had left her powerless. He massaged and oiled her small flat ass, as if it was a handful to shape and mold round. He then placed his forearm under her stomach, while gently pulling her up and pushing her thighs and legs forward causing her ass to arch in the air. He stood on his knees watching her in all of her beauty as he kissed each peach cheek of her behind. Although she felt completely awkward in the ass-up position, while he stood up staring at her, she was enjoying every minute of it. He thought that she was even sexier and more beautiful than the day he first noticed her. He stepped out of his underwear with sensuality and rubbed his hands down her back, over her ass and thighs and followed with kisses from his wet lips. She closed her eyes and laid her head down on the bed feeling utterly gratified. But what he did to her next made her grip the sheets and tear them from the mattress as she screamed out in passion, "Oh shit."

THE ALARM CLOCK had awakened her. As she fought to move her weak, drained body to turn it off, Elliott sat up awake reading the newspaper, while drinking a cup of coffee. She looked up at him and he looked down at her and smiled with the pleasure of knowing he had satisfied her and had put her to sleep, during the first round.

"Good morning," he said, and rubbed his hands over her hair that stood straight up on her head. "How did you sleep?"

She sat on the edge of the bed looking down at her feet and the plush carpet floor before answering. "The bed was a little lumpy," she grumbled.

"Really," he said and smiled. "You could have fooled me, I heard you snoring the whole night and you didn't move; not once out of that fetal position."

She looked back at him, got up, and walked into the bathroom feeling slightly embarrassed that he noticed. He chuckled at her, for not wanting to give him his props for making her sleep like a baby.

She sat on the toilet with her chin in her hand, staring at the wine colored wall thinking about how he had made her feel last night. He deserved a standing ovation, two thumbs up, a ten circle snap, a smile, a stomp your feet, clap your hands, shake your hips, and a "Will you be my man?" She wanted to be with him, and she wanted to know if he was telling the truth about letting all of his lady friends go in order to be with her.

"There's coffee if you would like a cup," he yelled through the bathroom door. She quickly wiped, jumped up off the toilet, washed her hands, dashed to the door and snatched it open.

"What's up?" he chuckled, as she looked up into his face and they stood looking into each other's eyes.

"Can we do it again, before we get dressed for work?" She asked.

He smiled and kissed her on her lips. "Yes, if you would like."

DEDE SAT AT her desk waiting for Dionne to come out of her meeting, so she could tell her about the roses and the dinner Elliott had cooked for her last night. She was so excited to now have a man she could brag about to her girlfriends without wondering if she was going to have to eat those words later, after he decides he needs his space. Marie and Bridget couldn't wait to meet him. While DeDe sat in la-la land, she noticed Dionne flying pass her desk.

"Hey girl." She whispered, while trying to flag her down as she rolled her chair out into the aisle. "Come here."

Dionne took a deep breath before turning around. She was nervous about seeing DeDe after learning what Charlotte had done. When she told Byron on their way home, he had jumped down her throat, as if she had put Charlotte up to it. He made her feel as low as possible for telling Charlotte DeDe's business. She didn't tell him that she had told DeDe, Charlotte's also. He compared her to the gossiping vultures in his father's church he hated so much. After he finished blasting Dionne out, she regretted she had ever told him, but then she had to admit what he had said was right. She was messy. "Hey girl, I thought you weren't coming in today." She was really hoping that DeDe wouldn't. "I walked past your desk at nine-thirty this morning to go to my meeting and you hadn't made it in yet."

"I was running late," DeDe said and smiled. "Elliott and I had a long night last night. He is so sweet. He cooked me dinner last night and he gave me roses and a card that said 'I'm so happy we met.' And he ran me a warm bubble bath and he bought me this tangerine body scrub that leaves your body so silky soft. You should try it. And he dried my body off and oiled me down with this scented oil, and it was on." She said, as she began giggling and reminiscing. "That man is powerful. I think we're going to work on a relationship." DeDe gleamed with excitement. She was hoping for Dionne to show her the same exact excitement she had shown her, when she bragged about the great weekend Byron had shown her. But she just stood there nodding her head looking off. DeDe became offended. Why couldn't she be happy for her and her newfound love? She had always told her she needed to find her someone else to get over Stephan and now that she has, DeDe can't talk to her about him. But DeDe knew how to fix her. The next time she comes talking about Byron, DeDe was going to ignore her and jump to another subject.

Dionne hoped DeDe didn't think she wasn't happy for her, although she knew Elliott wasn't going to be around long, once Stephan calls her back begging, but she was having a hard time looking her in her face. "Oh my God girl," she said, as she tapped DeDe's desk to get her attention from the bemused look on her face. "Look at the time. I need to be going. I have so much work I have to do, I can't see straight," as she waved good-bye.

DeDe had an attitude and she didn't bother to say a word as Dionne walked off. She just wanted her gone.

11

FRIDAY had come around once again and Charlotte called Dionne first thing this morning for her to turn on her radio to listen to Casey and Sylvia talk about her column. Dionne wasn't interested in listening, but as eight-thirty drew near she became curious about what Charlotte had written and what the callers response would be. Charlotte had given her a copy of The Rapture, when they met for lunch yesterday and begged Dionne to read it right then and there, but Dionne refused. She was still having a hard time accepting what her best friend had done. After having to face DeDe on Wednesday, Dionne avoided her for rest of the week, by staying locked in her office and in the field visiting her clients.

Dionne poured herself a cup of coffee and waited for Byron to leave for work, before running over to the radio and turning it on. She had come in on the middle; Sylvia was already reading.

Three is truly a crowd and Tibias knew it would be crowded in New York. So, he had to pull one of his most famous stunts and manufactured an argument with Angelic and ended their relationship two days before they were supposed to fly out. I knew he wasn't going to take her, when she kept bragging about the fun they were going to have. There's another woman who wouldn't dare let him. Not while she's spending the

Memorial Day weekend alone and her mind tells her that they are mak-
ing passionate love all over the hotel suite. I didn't tell Angelic any of my
intuitions regarding the sudden argument he created about her leaving
the cap off of the toothpaste. That mere oversight later materialized into
him stating that she doesn't respect him enough, and he doesn't think
they should be together. All this foolishness and drama, just two days
before their trip. Once again, I just let her cry on my shoulder and watch-
ing her cry was sad. Just when she thinks everything is going well, he
sucker punches her and leaves her to deal with her own wounds of hurt.
It's like a job to him. Two weeks on and two weeks off. But who is there
to blame if she allows it? Hopefully, the doors to her heart are closed
and there is no more work for him to do. Tibias is now without a job.

Angelic has found a new man, and her heart is under a new manage-
ment of loving. There was no daily crying during this split between she
and Tibias; I was happy for her. Instead, she got out and partied at the
mansion with the stars where she met Jasper, a very handsome realtor-
broker. She and he hit it off great, while her groupie girlfriend nearly got
everyone killed in the party by her ex-husband; once he discovered her
participating in an orgy with one of his close friends. Also, her brother
who is gay left with a well-known baseball player to go park at
ButterMeNot Lane. Women beware! Even the most masculine looking
men, can also be gay. A week has gone by and she hasn't shed so much as
a single tear and she damn sure hasn't brought up Tibias' name. I bet he
thought when he broke-up with her this time she would be calling him
begging him back. That's not gonna happen, while Jasper has all of her
attention." Sylvia read. *"I'm happy to see she's moved on with her life.*
Now that she doesn't have Tibias to talk about, she's talking about Jas-
per every minute, but I don't mind. She asked him to go with her to a
party in Miami for one of her clients, and I believe she's paying his way.
Hasn't she learned from dealing with Tibias that men don't care how
much money you make and what you can buy them. If they don't want
you, they just don't want you.

"That is so true girlfriend. Angelic doesn't mind taking care of a man does she?" Sylvia commented.

"You women should learn from Angelic," Casey chimed in. "Ain't nothing wrong with taking care of your man in every aspect. And believe me, Angelic isn't the only woman out there taking care of her man."

Sylvia chuckled and continued to read.

Jasper is a good guy. I met him and he's smart. Angelic describes him as a unique and rare commodity, because he doesn't have any children and that means no babymama drama. I just believe it's too soon for her to go away with him for the weekend and pay for it. But if she likes it, I love it. I'm not giving a man a dime.

"And that's probably why you are alone and all in Angelic's business," Casey said. "It's always the lonely girlfriend who has so much to say."

But if she feels complete with taking care of Jasper she can continue as long as she doesn't go running back to Tibias whenever he calls crying, because God knows he will. A man can't let his fool stray too far for too long. And Angelic was truly his fool. Believing she was the only woman, helping take care of him and his child, if he needed her to. I hope her eyes are finally open about him. He was a user and she was being used. But if she takes him back, I won't be surprised. She loves him and no matter how good of a man Jasper is, she'll drop him so fast he won't even realize he hit the ground, until he sees her walk past him holding hands with Tibias. Angelic is like many women. A good man who cares about them, isn't what they truly want. They like to cry in self-pity, because the man who doesn't love them has shattered their heart. Women like her love being in love with men who do not love them back.

"Man, every time I read these articles I'm just baffled that someone so close to you can be such a backstabber. You confide in them and they tell the world about it and you know nothing about it. Like my mama has always told me; keep your enemies close and your friends closer. The friend even writes about Angelic's groupie friends. But is she telling the truth about women being in love with men who are not in love with them?" Casey asked and chuckled.

"The best-friend's brotha is gay and he sleeps with professional football, baseball and basketball players. So all of you groupies out there be careful, because it might not be what it looks like," Sylvia said and Casey laughed.

"And the best friend dates a lot of the ballplayers also?" Casey asked.

"Yeah, they are both groupies. It's scary to think there are so many brothas living this extra dual-type life, and us women not know anything about it. The column says the gay guy is handsome. Is he all gay or bi?"

"Damn, ladies y'all got it bad. But you got a brotha right here who ain't never been with a man, never will be, and has never thought about it! Do you hear me?"

"That's good to know, but what about the other brothas we don't know about?"

"What about 'em?"

"They could be gay."

"I believe if someone invented a device that could detect the guys that were taking it up the hershey highway, they would be billionaires because you women would buy it."

They laughed.

"But on a serious tip, I think I just may know who this Angelic is. But she has a brother and a sister; not a best girlfriend and her brother... and they are groupies. There is also a Tibias in her life, whom she won't let go of," Casey said.

"Every woman at some point has had a Tibias in her life and at some point she gets fed-up, but she always finds herself going back. It's sort of like that book 'VooDoo Love'. Remember when we had the author on the show about a month ago? That book was very good in pointing out some very powerful truths. Y'all should read it, because it talks about how there are strongholds that keep pulling us back to where we never should have been in the first place. I'm kinda on the same wavelength with the 'Frustrated Friend'. I believe if he calls her back, she's going to take him back and Jasper is history."

"I don't think so," Casey said. "I think it's over and she's moved on with her life. A fool gets tired of being a fool. If this Tibias guy was dogging her the way the 'Frustrated Friend' says he was, and she's found this new guy whom she's just crazy about; I think she'll stay. She even likes the way he sexes her better than Tibias."

"That could say a lot," Sylvia chuckled. "Ladies call us up and tell us what you think 555-WHEE, your breakfast-jam station. Here's Joe with, '*I Wanna Know*.'"

Dionne turned down the radio and poured herself a second cup of coffee. She was nervous and upset. Her phone rang. It was Charlotte laughing.

"Did you hear it?"

"None of this is funny Charlotte."

"No, it's interesting and a great conversation piece. Like I told you, it's not that serious and she'll never find out. Dionne, this column is helping people."

"Once again I ask you, how do you figure Charlotte? Everyone is in her business and they are calling in commenting. How is that helping people?"

"The groupies know that there are a lot of bi-sexual men out there, so they need to beware." She chuckled.

Dionne let out a loud frustrated sigh and hung up the phone in her ear.

"Good morning Houston!" Sylvia sang, as she came back on the air. "For those of you who are just now joining us, we are talking about the 'No More Lovemaking' column in The Rapture weekly entertainment guide. It hits the stands between Thursday and Friday afternoons of every week, and people are getting addicted to this column. My girlfriend has gone to three convenience stores looking for this once free, now 25 cents newspaper and they were sold out. People are not getting this newspaper because they want to read the interviews of the celebrities or find out what entertainment is happening in the city through the week. Folks want to know what's going on with Angelic and her drama-filled life. I was at Matthew's beauty salon on Wednesday and that's all we talked about."

Dionne's heart sank. "That's the beauty salon DeDe goes to also." She rushed over to the phone to call Charlotte, but there was no answer. "Damn." She left a message. "Dammit Charlotte! Sylvia, goes to the same damn beauty salon as DeDe. What if they run into each other?" So what, they didn't know each other, Dionne thought. "But what if they start talking about the column in there? As stupid as you think DeDe is, she could figure out that you are talking about her."

"Everyone feels like they know these people personally or they have a friend in the same situation. WHEE, caller you're on the air. Do you think she'll take him back again, if Tibias calls her begging and asking forgiveness?"

"Yes, I do. She loves him. It's hard to let go of someone you love. I don't care how good the other man's sex is. I'm glad she's with Jasper, but I don't think it's going to last."

"Neither do I," Sylvia agreed, and went to the next caller.

"And I don't like that backstabbing b#%*h!"

BLEEP.

" Lady this is a family show, please watch what you say," Casey advised her.

"I'm sorry. I'm just upset about this woman who is writing all of this and Angelic has no idea. That no good b#%*h!"

BLEEP.

"Shouldn't be putting her business in the street like this. I would never pick up that newspaper, it's garbage and so is the b#%*h."

BLEEP.

"Of a so-called friend who's writing it?"

"Some people just have to be so ignorant." Sylvia said, as she disconnected the call. "WHEE, caller you're on the air."

"I don't know anything about what Angelic is going through with Tibias, because I've never been in that situation. However, what I do know about is her girlfriend and her brother. My boyfriend plays for the Dallas Wranglers."

"Who is he?" Casey asked.

"That's neither here nor there," the caller replied. "But look, he's had several parties and I've seen them there cozying-up to ballplayers who are married. They always seem to get lost and disappear with some sex-hungry baller."

Dionne nearly stopped breathing. Her stomach bubbled with nervousness. It wasn't hard to decipher who the column was talking about, if DeDe's friends or herself was listening. All that Charlotte did was change DeDe's brother and sister to her best friend and her best friend's brother. This minor alteration couldn't conceal whom she was really talking about, if someone smart read the column and put two and two together.

"But the people I know are White. Are these people White or Black?" The caller asked.

"What difference does it make caller?" Sylvia asked.

"Because I believe I know them. The friend used to be married to a player that used to beat her silly and her brother is a gay makeup artist. They need to do an article just on the sister and the brother. Their lives are more interesting than Angelic's life."

"Have you been following the article, do you think Angelic will go back?"

"She shouldn't, but she seems to be stupid so she might."

"Why do you call her stupid?" Casey asked.

"It seems that she takes care of men. I wouldn't be flying Jasper or any-body else anywhere. If he wants to go, he would pay his own way and mine."

"See that's the skewed and twisted attitude of the new millennium Black woman. Caller you have a nice day," Casey said, just before he disconnected the line. "And she calls Angelic stupid."

"WHEE, caller you're on the air."

"I've been in Angelic's situation. After being with a man that treated me like a queen without drama and him not breaking my heart, I didn't want anything else. My ex tried coming back, but I wouldn't take him back. I thought about all the grief and garbage he had put me through and I told him to go straight to hell."

"Good for you," Sylvia chuckled.

"I don't think she'll take Tibias back. The way the friend talks about Jas-per, I think he might just be the one."

"So do I," Casey said. "WHEE, caller you're on the air."

"I'm glad she found someone else. She's better off without Tibias," the caller said. "I knew he would take someone else to New York and I bet it was his babymama. He'll get his, one of these days; all dogs do."

"Do I hear some bitterness caller?" Casey asked and chuckled. "You haven't gotten over it yet, have you?

She hung up and Casey and Sylvia began to laugh.

"Now that was wrong Casey. When someone hurts you, it's very hard to get over it."

"It's not that hard. It's a mind thing."

"Okay, I comprehend." Sylvia said, as she somewhat agreed. "WHEE, caller you're on the air."

Dionne ran into the den to turn the stereo on full blast, as she went upstairs to get dressed for work. She continued to pray DeDe or no one she knew was listening.

"The so-called friend who's writing these articles; she needs to go get a life of her own and stay out of Angelic's. She's like that old Ojays song, she's a 'Backstabber'. I think Angelic and Jasper are going to work. I don't care what the friend thinks."

"Thank you. WHEE, caller you're on the air."

"Who was the athlete that left with the best-friend's brother?" The caller asked.

"How do you think *we* know his name, they didn't say it in the article did they? We don't know these people just like you don't," Sylvia said, with annoyance in her tone followed by a sarcastic chuckle.

"I know a couple of football players that are bi-sexual and some are married. Whose party were they at?" The caller then asked.

Sylvia hung up the line and sighed. "Give me a break. WHEE, caller you're on the air."

"I hope Angelic didn't buy the tickets for she and Tibias to go to New York. If so, she needs to make sure she gets her money back from him or she needs to take it out of his a#$."

Bleep.

"I believe he took his child's mother, and he's a dog if he did. That's why women shouldn't date men with children."

"Why is that?" Casey asked.

"They are still connected to that woman, because of the child. I don't blame her for hating his babymama. They keep up a lot of drama and nine times out of ten they are still sleeping together."

"Has that ever happened to you?" Sylvia asked.

"Yes. He and I are married now, but I still believe he loves that woman."

"Alrighty then." Sylvia hung up the line. "The lines are ringing off the hook, which means the women of Houston have something to say, but now we have to pay the bills around this place by breaking for commercials. If you haven't been following this story, you need to. Because it is hot, juicy gossip and it might just be you or someone you know that has Houston caught up in the Rapture."

"I have one question to ask our listeners. If you are not making love on this beautiful, sunny Friday morning, what in the hell are you doing?" Casey asked.

"I hope they have their radios locked in to WHEE your breakfast-jam morning show station. Call us up and tell us what you think about Angelic, Tibias, her best friend, the gay groupie brother, and the backstabbing 'Frustrated Friend' who's writing all of this." Sylvia chimed in, just before going to a commercial.

12

$\mathcal{DIONNE}$ stayed in her office for the most part of the morning to avoid running into DeDe. She just couldn't look her in the face. She prayed DeDe wouldn't knock on her door to talk. If she did, she wasn't going to answer. When she pulled into the parking garage this morning, she let out a sigh of relief that she and DeDe didn't pull in together. She took the stairs instead of the elevator, just in case DeDe was already on it. When she had to go to the ladies room she took the long way, so she wouldn't have to walk past DeDe's desk. She was too nervous to even think about doing any work. She just wanted the day to be over and the people of Houston to forget about the article. If DeDe hadn't read it by now, she probably was never going to read it and that made Dionne feel a little at ease; but Charlotte still had to pull it.

She began calling on a couple of her important accounts, since she had neglected them while she worked on the Mayor's fundraiser. Her first account to call was Bushel and Coleman. She had them as a client for the last nine years and they were very important to her.

"Hello Bushel and Coleman."

"Hello, Rachel." After all these years she knew her voice by heart. She had been answering the phone as long as Dionne has had the account.

"Dionne, how are you doing, girl?" She asked with a syrupy Texas drawl.

"Great, and yourself?"

"Couldn't be better. My little Chelsea is walking now and she's trying to talk. My mother-in-law thinks she's trying to move out of the way for another one. But I don't think so, 'my friend' came on just last week."

"You can still be pregnant and still have a period you know?" Dionne laughed. "Has it been that long since I've seen you? Your little girl is talking already?"

"Well, I've been out on leave with her, up until she was twelve months."

"Yeah, it has been that long. Is Patsy in?"

"Yeah, but she's in a meeting. She's going to be in meetings all morning, as a matter of fact. She just got out of a meeting thirty minutes ago with some really sweet, pretty girl from your office. She's a tiny little something. What size does she wear, a four?"

"From *my* office?"

"I believe Caroline checked her in." She held the phone away from her ear, "Caroline who was the girl that came in from Stockton, this is Dionne."

"Hi Dionne," Caroline yelled across the room.

"Tell her I said hello."

"She said hi."

"DeDe Wilson, tell her she's really sweet."

"What was she doing there?" Dionne asked.

"She's working on the QuittersPatch campaign."

I know the hell this bitch didn't, Dionne thought. "She's doing what? That's my account."

"I don't know; she's been here several times. I thought you knew. I hope I didn't get anyone in trouble."

"No... you didn't." Dionne was pissed. "Let me find out what's going on and I'll call you back later. Thank you Rachel."

"You're welcome and I'll have Patsy call you, as soon as she gets out of her meeting."

"Thank you."

She hung up the phone with fire spewing through her nostrils, with every angry curse word she pulled from the pit of her stomach. She couldn't believe it. She was unexpectedly backstabbed again. That's why she didn't have women as friends, because of shit like this! Backstabbing Black bitches weren't to be trusted. Now she knows why she didn't let her guard down with DeDe, when she tried to act like she was so different. She was a friend to be trusted, right. Dionne expected Starla to steal accounts, because she was a wannabe White bitch. That's how they survive in corporate America, by backstabbing and fucking their way to the top. But DeDe was the last person she expected, although she really didn't trust her. For no particular reason, other than she was Black and it was Black women who had betrayed and hurt her in the past. She never got over it and she thought them all to be the same; messy, jealous-hearted, cut-throat backstabbers. She felt they always came after her and she didn't really have shit and sure as hell didn't put up a front like she did. Nevertheless, every woman she had tried to befriend had lied on her or done her in. She was happy being the only Black woman at Stockton before they hired Starla and DeDe, because there was no drama to be kept up and no lying gossip. Of course that went on amongst her White colleagues too, but they didn't have her in the middle of it. She had them too afraid to ever consider stealing one of her accounts. And if they lied on her, she abruptly cursed them out and went on about her business.

She jumped up from her desk and stormed down the hall looking for DeDe, because she was about to do the same to her and take her account back. Bushel and Coleman earned her seven thousand a month in commission. This bitch was now fucking with her money and livelihood. Dionne hoped that she didn't have to kick her ass, but she was so angry she just might on 'GP'. DeDe wasn't in her cubicle. "Shit!" She then stormed down to the office of Brad Michaels, their manager. She went right past his secretary and barged into his office without knocking. He was on the phone.

"She stole my account and I don't appreciate it," she screamed as she slammed the door behind her.

"Excuse, me," he told the person on the phone. "I will have to get back with you later on this; there's a situation that's developed that I must take care of."

"I tried to stop her, but she just flew right past me," Helen, the secretary said as she stormed in behind Dionne.

"Listen Helen, you don't have to give me permission to talk to Brad," Dionne said while pointing her right index finger with her left hand on her hip and her neck slightly rolling. "He and I go way back. When I have a problem, I can't wait on you to open the door for me to talk to him. I'm sorry for walking over you, but I need to talk to him right now."

Helen looked at him to intervene and correct her by giving her the correct procedure on how they do things, but he didn't. "Helen, I'll handle this."

She huffed and puffed as she rolled her eyes and stormed out of the office.

"Dionne, is everything okay?"

She flew into a rage while pacing the floor. "She stole one of my biggest accounts. I knew I couldn't trust her. The company policy was explained to her in the beginning. I don't understand. I asked her to help me with an idea and she did that and stole the account. "

He sighed and leaned forward placing his elbows on the desk as his green eyes followed her agitated fast pace. "Calm down Dionne and have a seat."

"I'm too pissed to sit down," she snapped and rolled her eyes at him and the thought.

"No you're not."

Dionne looked at him and continued to pace. "She stole my account. I just so happened to call to schedule a meeting with Patsy and I was told DeDe had been there for a meeting with her earlier this morning."

"Dionne," he said, as he slightly raised his voice to show her he was the authoritarian. "I'm going to have to ask you to have a seat; this pacing is making me nervous. Please, sit down."

She stopped and flopped down in the closest chair to him and sighed. "I tried to see her about it, but she wasn't at her desk. She better thank God for that, because when I do see her I'm going to curse her ass out and take my account back."

"You'll do no such thing."

"Excuse me Brad, she stole my account. It's against company policy! Isn't she supposed to be put on some type of disciplinary sanction if not fired for stealing accounts?

"She didn't steal the account. Bushel and Coleman asked for her specifically."

"So you knew about this?"

"They liked her idea. She did come up with the QuitersPatch Campaign didn't she?"

"Yes, but she was only helping me, because I was swamped with the Mayor's fundraiser."

"I understand that, but they still asked for her and it's company policy to keep our clients happy. It's in our best interest. They really like her. Also, you and Patsy have had several misunderstandings in the past."

"That's in the past! We are in the present now. And right now, I can't believe you're telling me I just have to give her my account. She hasn't been here five months and she's stealing accounts already. Brad, I remember when you were just a publicist with no experience and no knowledge. Do you recall when you would come to me with a bevy of questions, and I answered them with no problem? Maybe if I would have stolen your accounts, you might just understand what I'm feeling about company policy."

"Is it the money Dionne?"

"Hell yeah, and the fuckin' principle of the whole matter! Brad you are not giving me the answer I need so I think I'm wasting my time talking to you. I need to be in Chris Shultz's office talking to him," she said, as she jumped up out of her chair and walked toward the door.

He chuckled, fell back in his chair and sighed. "He's the one that okayed the whole deal. Patsy called him asking if DeDe could handle their account."

Dionne's heart sank. She felt helpless and it showed on her face. There was nothing she could do. They were all in on it.

"Dionne, it's not that serious."

"It's not that serious?" she replied. "I'm tired of people telling me what's not that serious." She immediately thought about Charlotte and her response to how she reacted about the column.

"It's only an account."

"If it were your money or one of your friends, maybe you would think it was serious!" She didn't come right out and say it, but she was speaking of her White colleagues. "It wouldn't be just an account." She walked out of his office, slammed the door behind her and rolled her eyes as hard as she could at Helen. She stormed back down the hall to her office, wishing she could just pack the few things she had in there and walk out without even telling anyone she quit. That's how angry she was. She's been in similar situations before and she's done just that. But now, it wasn't that easy. She had a brand new house, car, and bills that needed to be paid. Quitting her job would simply be stupid. She flopped down at her desk and let out a sigh of frustration, as she ran her hands across her slick wavy hair. "Company policy my ass! It's also against company policy for her to have clients outside of work." She thought about what she had said and smiled. Vengeance was all hers and there was something she could do. Having outside clients is grounds for termination, if the company ever found out about it. Today they were going to find out DeDe was on the payroll of Element Records and Cultured Pearl magazine. Dionne jumped up from her desk and ran back down to Brad's office to tell him. She was going to get her account back after all, and then some.

"Helen, I need to see Brad."

"He's not in," she snapped and continued to type what looked like 75wpm. Dionne sighed. "I just left him."

"And he just left. Now I can schedule you to see him when he gets back after 1:30p.m.

"Yes, do that."

"That's more like it." They looked at each other and rolled their eyes.

Dionne walked back to her office feeling great. She called her mother to tell her what DeDe had done. Her mother had always told her not to have too many friends, because "too many bitches spoil the brew". Her mother wasn't in, so she then called Byron. He answered in his sexy baritone professional voice.

"Byron Upchurch, how may I help you?"

"Hey,"

"Hey, baby what's up?"

She sighed. "Let me tell you what that backstabbing bitch did."

"Who, Starla?"

"Hell no, the other one, DeDe." She became angry all over again as she told him. "The bitch stole the Bushel and Coleman account from me and she's been sitting up here laughing in my face, knowing she stole my account."

"How did you find out?"

"I just so happen to call them and one of the girls over there told me she had been meeting with Patsy in Human Resources and the Director of Operations. A while back, I asked her to help me on the account, because I was tied up with the Mayor's fundraising party. She helped me alright; she helped remove that account right from underneath me."

"Damn, she's sneaky."

"I knew I couldn't trust her." But deep in her heart she had hoped that DeDe could be trusted.

"Stealing accounts are grounds for termination. Did you tell Brad?"

"Hell yeah, but he did everything but laugh in my face. He and Chris Schultz gave her the okay, because somebody had told them she had come up with the QuitersPatch campaign. He couldn't understand why I was so upset. I told him that he couldn't understand it because she didn't steal his damn money; she stole mine. The bastard! I'm so angry, I just might go off on her and without words."

"Calm down baby," he told her because he knew her temper, he knew her mouth, and she couldn't control either one of them.

"Calm down," she screamed. "Byron she stabbed me in the back. I've been working that account for nine years. I can't calm down. That's seven thousand dollars in commission stolen from me and there ain't shit I can do about it." She jumped up from her desk with her bottom lip trembling and her heart racing with anger. She felt like crying she was so angry, but she wouldn't allow herself to. She noticed DeDe pulling into the parking lot, as she was staring out of the window. "There goes that bitch. I'll call you back," she told Byron. "I'm going to wait for her at the door."

"Dionne, no. Don't do that. Just calm down and think." Now he was becoming angry with her foolishness. "It's not worth it and she's not worth it. Baby, I know you know how to handle this situation without out acting a fool."

A tear fell from her eye. He was right, but right now acting a fool was the only way she felt she was going to get justice. She was so tired of being done wrong and not being able to do anything about it, but get angry and walk away. "I don't understand Byron, why?"

"People are just low-down baby. You know how people smile in your face, but really hate you deep down inside? DeDe's one of them. She wants to pour out all of her business to you because you are sweet, loving and about the only fool that will listen to that shit."

She thought about the column Charlotte wrote and it was no longer wrong, it was justice for the knife DeDe had jabbed in her back. "Baby, I'll call you back."

"No, don't do anything stupid Dionne."

"I'm not. I'm cool, I just have to call you back." She hung up the phone and hit the speed dial button for Charlotte's office.

"Run it."

"Who is this?"

"Me silly."

"Hey girl, I didn't like the way you hung up on me this morning."

"I'm sorry. You can continue to run that column as long as she keeps running her damn mouth to me. I don't owe her shit."

"I'm glad you finally realized that."

She hung up the phone with no remorse about what she had told Charlotte to do. She felt just as justified as a vengeful waitress, who might bring up some mucous from the bottom of her throat and spit it all over the food and in the tea of an annoying, obnoxious, complaining customer. She had done that once when she was working as a waitress, while in college. She had a flashback and remembered the justified euphoria she felt, as she stood by and watched the asshole customer dine and drink with delight.

DeDe knocked on her door and walked into her office smiling. "Hey girl, what's going on wit'cha?"

Dionne looked up from her note pad into DeDe's eyes and thought, what a bitch. You come in here smiling, as if you ain't done shit by stealing my account. Bitch, I don't have two words to say to you even if you were on your dying bed, she thought as she went back to writing.

DeDe noticed the solemn look on her face, which only meant one thing as it does every other day. Dionne was in one of her moods and couldn't be dealt with today. "What's wrong with you?"

"Nothing," she snapped and rolled her eyes.

DeDe could have slapped her. "Well, I just thought I would come by and say good morning. Come by my desk when you find time."

"I don't think so," she bluntly replied. "I have a lot to do here."

"Okay," DeDe sighed. "I'll let you get back to your work and I'll talk to you later. Bye," she said, just before she walked out of her office.

Dionne didn't even bother to look up.

13

THE salon was as quiet as DeDe could never remember it to be. There was no gossip, no talk about men, the children, current affairs or venting going on. Everyone was in their own world either flipping through a magazine, typing away on their laptops or staring into space. DeDe was fighting to stay awake as she yawned, after her second glass of wine and her handful of crackers. She lived for her routine Friday visits to the salon, just to hear the discussions. But today, no one was talking. Not even Roberta nor Darinda's talking ass was talking; and they were always up for a good knockdown, drag-out discussion about anything. DeDe eagerly waited her turn to sit in Roberta's chair to have her hair done, but as slow as she was walking around taking her time; it probably won't come until tomorrow morning. That's simply not going to work, because DeDe and Elliott needed to be on their way to New York first thing in the morning. DeDe hadn't packed one thing mainly because she didn't have anything to wear. She had a list of last minute arrangements and things she had to do for the double release party. She still felt there was something she had neglected. She wished Roberta would put fire under her ass and move a little faster than the way she was proceeding, because DeDe didn't want to be in there all night. Time was tighter than tight. She had to steal time this past Wednesday from other things she should have been doing so she and

Elliott could go shopping for something swanky and new for her to wear at the party. DeDe was excited about him going to New York with her. She had tried to get Cultured Pearl to pay for his ticket, but they refused. She would pay for it herself, because she was the one asking him to go. She didn't care how stupid Dionne thought she was, but Elliott being the man he is, wouldn't dare let her spend a penny on him. DeDe wished she was at Elliott's right now making love to him instead of falling into everyone else's funk, while inhaling the toxic smell of no-lye relaxer, burning hair, hair shine, and waiting her turn to be called to the shampoo bowl.

DeDe couldn't understand the change in the weather from earlier in the day when it was sunny and beautiful to now torrential rain. The rainy weather was perfect for cuddling and lovemaking, but it also made it a waste of time for her to have her hair done in such weather. Her curls wouldn't last from the time she walked out of the salon, until the time she gets to her car. It would puff like an afro and then after she and Elliott sweat it out tonight, it's going to look like she had never paid ninety-five dollars to have it done. They hadn't seen each other in the last two nights, because both of them had been working late. She couldn't wait to see and kiss him. It was going to be great having her man travel with her. Although he's not officially her man even though they act like he is. He hasn't asked her as of yet. To keep from being tight-faced and assuming, she decided to wait on him to ask her to be his lady. It was back in the 90's when a woman would assume she and the man she was sleeping with on a regular basis were a couple, but not in the new millennium. She was missing him and she was going crazy. She enjoyed being with him and he was also occupying her mind from thinking about Stephan. Not that she was thinking of him as if she missed him and wished they were still together; but she had noticed that he hasn't called her either. This probably meant he wasn't missing her and he hadn't experienced the pain from their break-up like she had in the past. Normally, after a week or two after being broken-up, he would call asking if he could make love to her and she would give in to him without a fight. Their break-ups never lasted over three weeks. He would eventually miss her or get tired of her calling him crying and they would find themselves back together. Making-up never happened by him seeing his inappropriate-ness and apologizing. He never thought he was ever wrong; at least he never admitted to it.

"The next job application I fill out, I'm going to check other." Everyone stopped what they were doing and looked at Dorothy Phillips, as if she was crazy. Not for the statement she had just made, but for the loud outburst. She stuffed the newspaper she was reading into the pocket of her leather briefcase and fell back in her chair in frustration. She was one of Houston's top female attorneys so she wouldn't be filling out any job application. She was in prac-tice with four other women who often visited the salon also. They were all alike; loud with always something to say.

"What's going on girl?" Tamia, her beautician asked, as she roller-set one of her other clients. "That's why I don't read the papers or watch the news. It ain't healthy if it makes you scream out like that," she said and laughed.

"Girl, I'm sorry, I just don't want to be Black anymore. Hell, it's embar-rassing. Some of the things we do are just embarrassing," Dorothy said and the whole beauty salon began to speak. There were several issues that were never agreed upon in the beauty salon and sometimes it just got down right ugly. The verbal sparring erupted whenever they brought up topics like reli-gion, women and married men, White women and Black men, or just Black folks period.

"Embarrassing? How?" Darinda said, as she stopped what she was doing. "What do we do that's so embarrassing from what any other race of people do?" DeDe knew it was about to get 'crunk', as soon as Darinda stepped-up on her soapbox. She was very pro-Black and she believed there were rea-sons that caused Blacks to find themselves in certain situations. And they were situations beyond their control.

"Are you talking about that councilwoman that stole the ninety-three thou-sand dollars, took lavish vacations and had her house remodeled? I saw that this morning on the news," Roberta said, while shaking her head and combing out the curls of one of her clients. "I felt sorry for her, because they are trying to put her in jail."

"Bump that, I didn't." a woman said, as she rolled her eyes in disgust. "She had no business taking the money."

DeDe didn't know what they were talking about. She hadn't heard anything about a sistah stealing ninety-three thousand dollars. But, of course she wouldn't. She doesn't read the newspaper, because she doesn't have time and she's never at home in time to watch the five and six o'clock news. By the time it comes on again at ten and eleven at night, she's in bed with her head up under the covers in a deep sleep. It was sad, but she got her update on current affairs from the women in the salon.

"White people embezzle money all the time. Hell, they created it. They embezzle enough money to make the whole damn company fold," Linda Roper said. "I worked for a company that went under, because the Chief Financial Officer stole over four hundred thousand dollars. The company knew about it, but they were giving him a chance to stop and return the money on his own." She began to laugh.

"And I bet he just got a tap on the hand and allowed to resign from the company with benefits," Darinda said and chuckled.

"She had no business taking that money y'all," Dorothy simply put it as she flipped through her magazine. "I don't care who has embezzled money before and gotten away with it. She was a sistah, making us all look bad. You know they don't want us in high positions anyway and she goes and does something like that."

"So true," several women agreed in unison while shaking their heads and smacking their lips.

"No it's not," Roberta disagreed. "She didn't make me look bad. I don't know her. She's not my child nor my sister or mother. Those are the only people that have an affect on my life like that."

"Out of all the city council's women and men that are crooked, why did they decide to probe into her business?" Timothy, the best damn male beautician in Houston who wasn't even gay, asked. "Because she was Black," he answered in a matter of fact fashion, as he led his client to the shampoo bowl.

"No, because she was stupid," Dorothy blurted out. "That money didn't belong to her and she didn't have to take it. She didn't take it to feed her children, but she stole it to take vacations in the islands and to remodel her house. I don't feel sorry for her."

Neither did DeDe as she listened and formed her opinion of the whole situation in her mind. She had learned from working in corporate America, voicing her opinion on certain issues that did not pertain to anything that couldn't make a difference wasn't always necessary. So, she didn't bother to tell anyone what she thought. No matter what any of the women thought, the reason for the government to have probed into her business was that they had to think for some reason or another she had taken the money. The proof lies in the vacations and the remodeled house. Obviously, those two things are enough for any jealous-hearted person to bring it to the attention of the authorities and the press. Whomever that person was that 'dropped a dime' on the councilwoman could be Black, White, or even green. Green with envy, because they were wondering why she was living the good life and they weren't.

"I'm not going to stand behind nobody in the wrong, be it my son or another damn Black person that I don't know," Katina said. And I'm not going to let each Black person that does something stupid in life define me. I'm Black and I'm proud of it. Can't no other Black, Hispanic, Asian or White person make me embarrassed to be Black. Yeah, we do stupid things and make wrong decisions, but who doesn't? It has nothing to do with being Black. It's about being just human and all the frailties that goes along with it."

DeDe didn't remember them getting this rowdy even when O.J. was on trial. They didn't buy into the conspiracy spiel about the LA police trying to frame him. They didn't give a damn. All they knew was that he loved White women and had taken care of Nicole and her entire family, while turning his back on his own. They figured he would get what he deserved, if he had to spend the rest of his life in jail. So, in their minds there was nothing to get rowdy about.

DeDe had tuned the women out as she continued to flip through her magazine hoping they would just shut-up or go to another subject. She had heard enough of everyone screaming out their opinions about this woman who didn't give a damn about Black women, when she stole the money. Not once did DeDe believe she asked herself, 'if I steal this money and get caught, would it make Black women look bad?' The whole race of African American women had nothing to do with why she stole the money and why she wouldn't steal it, if she had a chance to do it over again. So why were the women carrying on like nuts? Greed was her main motivation and reason for taking money that didn't belong to her.

Tuning people out was a mental process DeDe had learned from watching her mother do it to her father. Earlier today she was just about to tune Dionne out for good. If she didn't change her attitude and stop acting as if DeDe was a nuisance; she was going to simply leave Dionne alone. She didn't mind not having her as a friend anymore. She was too damn moody and DeDe was tired of not knowing whether today was a good day or what tomorrow might bring. She has an attitude about something every other day and today when she snapped on DeDe, she had had enough. She was just about to go off on her like an alarm clock to let her know the world doesn't revolve around her and her damn attitudes. DeDe had made up her mind to never talk to her again to show her that when she deals with co-workers and friends with a funky, foul attitude, she doesn't want to be bothered with her. So that explains why she doesn't have any friends and no one besides DeDe talking to her in the office. Strangely enough, by the end of the day, she was back to normal and she was talking as if everything was fine.

The bell on the salon door sounded. DeDe along with everyone else looked to see who in the world was coming for a hair appointment at six-thirty in the evening. Out of all the people in Houston that could walk into the beauty salon, why did it have to be Waymon. Her heart began to pound with nervousness. Her mouth flew open and her eyes had looked him over twice, then a third time for good measure. He looked different from three years ago; he looked even more handsome. She scanned the room wondering which one of the women was his fiancée.

"Hey baby," a woman sitting under the dryer tried to whisper, but it still came out loud. "Give me another twenty minutes. I'm almost dry." She was cute and she seemed like his type. She was quiet and conservative. DeDe stared at her just long enough for a bit of jealousy to come to the forefront, although she felt she looked better and she had a better man. Waymon walked back toward her, counted out some money, and handed it to her. He was still a gentleman in spite of how DeDe had done him. After three years of her not seeing him, she still wasn't ready to run into him. She felt ashamed for breaking such a good man's heart and she couldn't look him in the face. Nevertheless, she didn't drop her head to keep him from noticing her. As he walked toward the door, he felt DeDe's stare and their eyes met. She didn't expect him to speak and he didn't. She wanted to speak, but she was too embarrassed at the thought of him not reciprocating. She could see the anger in his eyes as they stared at one another without blinking an eye. She looked away, but figured this would be her last time to apologize and give him time to bring closure to the anger and resentment he has toward her. She grabbed her umbrella and ran out of the door behind him.

"Waymon," she called out, and ran behind him as he walked towards his car. "Waymon please, I need to talk to you."

He turned around and snapped. "About what DeDe, it's raining like hell out here!"

"Please talk to me."

"About what? Like I said, I don't have shit to say to you."

"You don't have to talk, just listen. I'm sorry. I didn't mean to hurt you; but I knew if we would have stayed together and me not love you the way you needed to be loved; eventually I would have hurt you. You're a wonderful man so don't think it was you that caused our relationship to unravel. It was all me. I needed more and you had already given me so much. I just felt that I couldn't ask you for anything else."

"Fuck that! DeDe I loved you so much, I would have given you the world. You just should have come and talk to me to let me know what was going on. You didn't even give me a chance to change."

"I didn't think you could."

"You didn't want me to, because you were so in love with him. You had it already made up in your mind that you were leaving. You were fucking him all along; and don't even try to tell me you weren't."

"We are not together now."

"So what. I'm happy and I've moved on with my life. You taught me a lot and I'm stupid for making other women and my new love sometimes pay for it. The funny thing is, I thought you loved me just as much as I loved you, Dammit. I'm not about to ever let anyone else shit on me."

"I did love you, I just wasn't happy."

"How could you have not been happy, when I loved you and everything I did was for both of us."

She didn't want to tell him what she was really thinking. She couldn't say, "I was always really in love with Stephan. You Waymon are dull and boring, and I didn't want to spend my life being married to someone that I didn't enjoy and didn't love." So, she decided to use one of the many lies Stephan had told her. "You loved too hard."

"And what in the fuck does that mean?"

She didn't even know, but she gave it a try anyway. "We were always together smothering each other...I guess I loved too hard also."

"That's pure Bullshit, and you know it! The truth of the matter is DeDe, you were bored in the relationship. There wasn't enough drama happening for you. I cared for you, I didn't cheat and we didn't argue. I'm guessing that the sex was okay, but then again, I don't know."

"It was." Yeah, before I met and slept with Stephan and Elliott, she said to herself. But now Elliott tops them all. He was right; she was bored. She didn't want to be like the rest of their friends; so perfect and so routine. "Waymon, I didn't want marriage." At least not with you, she thought. "And I didn't know how to tell you, when your heart was so set on it. I didn't want to hurt you. Stephan was only there because I was confused and as you already know it didn't work out. You were a wonderful boyfriend and a perfect friend. I just wasn't ready for marriage, that's all. I never meant to hurt you. That was never a part of my plan, I just wanted to be happy." She hoped her sincerity had convinced him to let go of his anger.

"Well, I hope you are now," he said and looked away.

"I hope our conversation brought closure to the anger you have."

"I'm not angry, I just didn't understand."

"I hope now you do."

He sighed while still looking away from her. "Somewhat."

She smiled. "It was nice seeing you again."

"Yeah, same here."

DeDe turned and walked back toward the salon. She felt relieved that they had talked. What she had gone through with Stephan was truly a reciprocation of the hurt she had caused Waymon. She felt by her apologizing, she had not only made things right between her and Waymon, but also it righted and paved the way for nothing but good things between she and Elliott also. In her mind, there was nothing else for her to receive pay back for. When she walked back into the beauty salon, the same conversation amongst the women was still going on and Waymon's fiancée was standing at the counter paying.

"Ms. DeDe Wilson, I thought you had left" Roberta said.

His fiancée did a double take, as if she had heard DeDe's name before. DeDe spoke to her and smiled. "Hi."

She rolled her eyes, grabbed her change, left a tip and briskly walked out with an attitude and a huge frown on her face.

"We as Black people can be so hard on one another," Roberta said, as she draped DeDe and rubbed her hands through her hair to feel for new growth. "We have no compassion for other's mistakes unless we think it's a conspiracy from the White man."

"No, it's we as Black women who are very hard and judgmental toward one another," Ginger Shaw added, just before getting under the dryer. "We are so quick to point fingers with malice and judgment, as if our lives are so perfect and we don't make mistakes."

DeDe could agree, but she didn't know what Ginger was talking about. As long as DeDe has known her, she has always acted as if she never made any mistakes. At that instant, DeDe remembered attending a taping, when Charva had her talk show. She recalled how Charva cried out loud, while reading the criticizing letters from Black women who only wrote in to cut her down. They slammed her for mistakenly misusing or mispronouncing a word, wearing too much or not enough makeup, for dressing too flashy or too homely, and they even had the audacity to dog her about her hair. They claimed it looked like she had a bad hair day everyday; even after she had sat in her hairdresser's chair for hours to accomplish the look she thought would make the sistahs proud of her. They also accused her of not being Black enough and not representing Black women. DeDe could count on both of her hands the number of women that wrote in and praised Charva for doing a great job. In order to count the number of critics and slashers; she would need the hands and feet of everyone in the shop, including the fingers and toes of the children in the play area. DeDe wondered if those same vicious women took an equal amount of time out to write nasty letters to their elected city officials to have the streets cleaned and potholes filled in their neighborhoods. She also wondered if they wrote to their state representatives to lodge complaints regarding the impending vote vying to remove affirmative action legislation.

"The craziest thing that I ever heard 'us' blame each other for; is the topic of why Black men date White women. There are some of 'us' that can give a list of reasons why Black men don't want and shouldn't want other Black women. How stupid does that sound?" Ginger asked and chuckled as other women agreed.

"Now that says something about Black women and their judgments of others," another woman said.

"Our problem is; we think every Black woman has to represent us. That's not how it should be. It doesn't make sense." Darinda said. Only Roberta and a couple of other women in the salon agreed, by saying, "I heard that and now that's on point"

"It shouldn't be that way, but it is." Dorothy said. "Black women are still a minority on every ladder that it takes to get to the top. And everything we do has to represent the sistahs who only dream to climb those same heights."

"I disagree," Roberta said. "Oprah doesn't represent me, so if she wants to cater to the Whites, that's on her. Toni Braxton can walk up on those stages completely nude to receive her awards, if she wants to. I don't care. She doesn't represent me, so she's not setting me back as a Black women as I heard plenty of sistahs say when they called in on H-103 to give their view of the good, bad, and ugly of the award show the other night. Li'l Kim, I don't even listen to rap and I don't know who she is, but I heard she can get nasty and she calls herself the "queen bitch". She has a right to live her life as a queen bitch, a slut or any damn thing else she wants to. That's her life and if that's how she wants to be identified, why not allow her that? We need to stop holding everyone else accountable for defining our lives. She's living her life and she didn't ask to be a role model for my daughter and I didn't ask her to be. We need to stop putting people in pedestal-type positions they didn't ask for; whether they're on television or in public office. If we stop doing this, we won't be so quick to judge these other mortal humans, when they don't live up to our lofty expectations."

"Yeah, you're right! But teenage girls listen to the Li'l Kims and Foxy Browns of the world and they espouse through their music that it's okay to use what's between their legs as a bargaining tool," Linda Roper said.

"Some women are going to have sex promiscuously whether someone raps about it or not. Some women are going to contract AIDS no matter who tells them how to protect themselves or not. Why? Because there are some men out there who are bi-sexual and we do not even know about it," Darinda said. "Some women are going to use sex to get their bills paid, because that's what some of them were taught to do. For hundreds and hundreds of years, there have been women; single parents, hell, even some of our mothers who have used what they have between their legs to help get the bills paid and put food on the table. It's a part of life, whether others want to believe it or not. And guess what? Black women are not the only ones doing it. This is something that overlaps all demographic and socio-economic boundaries and has been going on, since the beginning of time."

"So true."

14

MAKING sure the new album release party for Erika St. James had all the top celebrities and full media coverage it needed to put her back at the top of the Billboard charts after her four year hiatus wasn't nearly as stressful as it was for DeDe to sit and listen to Stephan, as he pleaded with her to take him back. She didn't know what to do. She was angry, but she couldn't slam down the phone in his face like she told herself she'd do, if he ever called her begging to come back to him. She felt sympathy for him and as crazy as it may seem, she somewhat believed his apology. For two weeks she hadn't heard from him and she was actually fine with that. She had moved on with her life. She had Elliott and like the saying goes, it always take one man to help get over another. She had no desire to call Stephan crying and begging for him to come back to her. She had no desire to call him period, although he owed her money for all the car notes, child support, after school programs, and pocket money she had loaned him. She was his girlfriend, and hoped to become his wife. Also, she loved him. So to keep his car from being repossessed, and to prevent Shannon having him locked-up if he was one day late in child support, and to subsidize his wages when he had to leave work early to pick up Alexis from school, she gave him money. She figures she would never see any of that again, because they have broken up. She loved him too much to make him sign a contract stating that he would pay her back. At this point, there was no way in hell she was ever going to get her money or television back.

"Hey baby, what's up?" Stephan asked, as if he had just talked to her yesterday.

"Hello, Stephan," she said with a solemn attitude, as she got up from the bed and walked over to the sofa in the lounging area of the hotel suite. Hearing his deep voice caused her heart to pound with nervousness.

"What have you been up to? I thought about calling you, but I didn't think it was a good idea. A brotha didn't think he could handle you cursing 'im out," he chuckled. "You know how you get."

"What do you want Stephan?"

"What do you mean, what do I want? I want you and you want me."

She rolled her eyes and sighed at his assertiveness. This wasn't going to work, not this time.

"So you're in 'the apple' huh, New York? I talked to your sister yesterday at Melvin's and she told me you were going there. All I want to know is do you miss me?"

"Stephan," she whispered while looking around the corner for Elliott. She didn't want him to come out of the shower and catch her whispering in the phone. He had been so wonderful to her; she couldn't possibly hurt him. In thinking about Stephan's question, no, she didn't miss him at all. She didn't have the time or a reason to miss him, since she was with Elliott almost 24/7. "I need to be going."

"Baby," he pleaded. "Please just listen. It's all about you now. I know that I've done some shit in the past, but now baby I'm willing to do right. I ain't been shit, since you've been gone. I can't sleep, eat or damnit think without thinking about you."

His plea could not break through the iron steel bars she had around her emotions and heart. She wasn't hearing him.

"Baby, I'm sorry. Please take my apology. I'll do anything to get your love back DeDe. You were the best woman any man could ask for, and I'm all messed up without you. I'm willing to admit it, I gave you a hard time and I was wrong. I took your love for granted, because I didn't know how to handle it. I was a sorry ass at showing you how much I loved you, but I'll do anything right now to get your love back. Don't turn your back on me right now, baby, please." Stephan pleaded. "He couldn't possible love you as much or the way I do."

"What are you talking about, Stephan?" Not for a second did she believe he believed she had another man.

"Kendra told me, but that's okay. I know he'll never love you like I do. You and I, we've been through too much together."

"That's it. I've been through too much."

"Baby, I'm sorry. Please, I can't stand being here all by myself looking at the walls instead of you. You should be here with me. I don't want any other woman. Shannon doesn't mean shit to me because she's not you. Baby I'm reaching out to you. Baby, please. Do you want me to say it? Okay, I'm the one that fucked up this good thing between us. Baby, please don't marry that muthafucka."

Marry? She thought. Kendra and her lies, but she didn't tell him differently.

"I need you. I love you and you love me. Hell yeah, I admit it, I fucked up."

"Stephan."

"I'm all messed up without you; just ask my mama and my sistah. Baby, you pray— just ask God, he'll tell you how life has been for me without you. There's no women out here for me because they can't make me happy like you do."

"Stephan—"

"Baby, please listen. Why do you want to see a grown man cry and beg you to give him another chance? But I'll do that for you to come back to me. Girl, I know you still care. You're just like me, you can't let this go just like that. We've been together for three years. How in the hell can you just let it go like that? You tell him."

"Tell who what?" She asked.

"You tell him that you don't want him. Tell 'im you're coming back to the man that loves you. Hell yeah, I take the blame. I've messed up. What we had was beautiful. It's all about you baby. I'm doing things on your terms now, anyway you like it. Don't let him come between us."

Elliott walked out of the shower. "Baby, have you seen?"

"Who in the hell is that?" Stephan asked, as DeDe covered the mouthpiece of the phone with her hand. He had succeeded and pried through the iron steel bars surrounding her heart and emotions. She didn't mean to, but listening to him pour his heart out to her made her feel that she had to protect him. If Stephan would have called the first week after they broke up, she wouldn't have given a damn if he had heard another man's voice or saw her holding Elliott's hand in public. "The niggah is in New York with you?" He asked.

"I'll see you when I get back to Houston," she said quickly and hung up the cell phone by pressing "end" and turning off the power, just in case he tried calling her back. She sat there nervously, with her stomach in knots. Damn, Stephan had heard Elliott's voice just when he was thinking about coming back. Just when he was opening up to her about how he really feels, she had caused him pain by Elliott opening his big mouth. All the things she longed for him to say when they were together, he had finally said it. She was a good woman, he loved her and he was miserable without her. Stephan had heard another man call her baby and he probably knew for sure she had slept with him. Now she was sure he was never coming back. DeDe just sat on the sofa shaking her head at the mess she's made. She wanted Stephan to hurt two weeks ago, but now that he was considering coming back and doing right by her; hurting him was the last thing she wanted to do. She wished Elliott would just leave, so she could call him back and make things right. But knowing Stephan, chances were he wouldn't answer the phone. He was through with her. He had never shown his emotions to her before and she hated that about him, but she excused it as a part of him being macho. Kendra had told him several times after they broke up previously that she had found someone else and he never came back groveling and begging for another chance like he had tonight. However, he did realize he had messed up a good thing.

"Baby," he said clapping his hands to wake her out of her daze. "Get out of that daydream." He bucked his sexy bedroom eyes as wide as he could. "You see what time it is. The limo will be here at seven."

She stared at him before smiling. He didn't have a big mouth; she just had a foolish heart that wouldn't let her give up on loving a foolish man. It was Elliott who was responsible for her not hurting and being able to move on with her life.

He really is the perfect man. "Okay," she said and gave him a genuine smile, as she walked over to him and wrapped her arms around his waist. "What were you looking for, baby?" She asked and kissed the center of his wet back, as he stood in the mirror rubbing lotion all over his wet body and face.

"My lotion, but I have it now," he said, as he turned around and kissed her on the forehead.

"That was Kendra and her usual drama." She told him just in case he was wondering. She grabbed her towel and feminine bag from the bed and walked into the bathroom. She couldn't wait to get back to Houston to see if Stephan was for real about wanting them to work things out. Dionne told her she would drop everything and anyone, if Stephan called her begging and she was right no matter how much she tried to tell herself and Dionne she would not. She liked Elliott and she knew he was diggin' on her. They have a great time when they are together, but there's still something missing just as it was with the other men who loved her more than she loved them. She always found herself unhappy and still searching. Elliott is a little different from them, but he still doesn't give her the challenge she needs to stay interested. He doesn't give her the challenge in an argument to prove she's right, when she knows she's wrong. They've never argued and they probably never will, because of his personality. He does what he says, he's always on time, and when he's running late he calls. He's romantic, he listens and he likes spending time with her. He also doesn't show the slightest bit of jealousy, if she puts on a skirt too short. If he sees her talking to another man, he speaks and stands to the side. If that would have been Stephan, an argument would have ensued, then he would have probably punched or cut the fool. She's had three very good men come into her life and she's now beginning to think maybe she's one of those mislead women who doesn't know a damn thing about a good man. If he does not give her a challenge that will leave her heartbroken and crying or he displays sensitivity, caring and understanding; she interprets that as a weakness. Elliott stares at her as if she's the most beautiful woman in the world. Instead of it making her feel beautiful and special, it makes her feel very uncomfortable. She's not used to it and she feels he's searching for imperfections and flaws; which she does have but has not allowed him to see. DeDe felt she was once again wearing the persona of the bright and intelligent woman Daniel and Waymon perceived her to be, because of the conservative look she hides behind. Since she's been seeing Elliott, she has yet to show him who she really is and they've slept together nearly every night. When you sleep with someone and it isn't a one-night-stand, there is always a sense of closeness afterwards. She now wakes up before him so he will not see her hair standing up on her head. Normally, on the weekends she doesn't brush her teeth or take a shower as soon as she gets out of bed, but because he does she feels like she needs to. She uses profanity, she enjoys gossiping with her girlfriends and she uses broken English. But around him, she does none of those things. She's been at his house plenty of nights having to really use the bathroom, but doesn't. She doesn't feel comfortable with the perception he has of her and she doesn't want him to think that her bowel movements may smell worse than his. So, she holds it until the next day when she can go home.

There's nothing more that can be added to the attributes that he already has that will make her more interested. She thinks he's perfect. He's handsome, sophisticated, imposing, strong, ambitious, rich, great in bed, passionate and he's shown her positions she didn't know existed. But she doesn't feel he's the man for her, because she wants to be where her heart is and that's with Stephan. After making love with Elliott; Stephan isn't shit in bed. There is nothing to compare. Stephan could use some lessons, he doesn't make nearly as much money as either of them, and he talks too much. He's broken her heart at least two times too many. He's not polished and he's far from sophisticated, but she loves him. Elliott is a wonderful man for a woman who can appreciate him and love him. But at this juncture, DeDe doesn't feel like she can and she's not going to push herself into trying. The real truth is; no matter how hard she tried to make herself deny it, she will always love Stephan.

DeDe thought by her inviting Elliott to the party with her he would be impressed by the people she knew, but he showed no excitement. She had worked closely with several celebrities and she still glimmered with excitement to be in their presence. She hoped he didn't mistake her excitement for immaturity or the insane groupie worship that had captured her siblings. He looked of class and elegance in his Versace suit and Cartier watch and glasses. Although he had picked out and bought the thousand dollar Versace dress and four hundred dollar Gucci heels that she was wearing, she still didn't feel like she had the prestigious flare he was carrying. She would have settled for a no name after-five beaded dress, but he insisted on her having them both wear something by Versace. He held her hand and they glided into the room with a strut and confidence of a couple of enormous importance, although they were just as pedestrian as some of the fans that screamed for the true stars and whom they were perceived to be.

The large ballroom of the Ritz Carlton was crowded with singers, movie stars and professional athletes. Everyone mingled, ate, drank and laughed as the music of Erika St. James played in the background. The woman of the hour hadn't shown up as of yet. It was customary for an artist to be fashionably late for his or her own album release party. DeDe was pleased at how beautiful the room looked. For four months, she planned for this party and it had turned out to be beautiful. She had the caterer fly crab cakes in from Maryland, fresh flowers and candlelight surrounded the room and a bottle of Cristal and a copy of Cultured Pearl magazine adorned every table. She favored event planning only as a side job but it was being a publicist that she really enjoyed.

She and Elliott stood as they gazed around the room. It truly was beautiful and elegant. DeDe once again had planned another successful event.

"Hey girl," Charva sang as she walked toward her with her arms opened wide. She was beautiful as usual and looked nothing of thirty-three, or the mother of four. Her body was perfect and many thought her life was too, because she was the wife of multimillionaire Jeremiah Williams. "It's beautiful in here and so are you. I love that dress."

"Thank you, my friend," she said, as she placed her hand on Elliott's arm, "picked it out for me."

"Great taste."

"Elliott, this is Charva Williams and Charva this is Elliott Anderson."

"Nice to meet you." They shook hands while smiling.

"Are you in the industry?" Charva asked.

"No," he answered.

"Good."

"He's a former Wall Street investment banker and he owns a restaurant in Houston, ElBuddha's. So, when you are there in a couple of weeks, I'll take you for lunch."

"Cool."

Elliott knew they wanted to talk about him without him standing there, so he excused himself with grace and charm just by asking them, "Would you ladies like a glass of wine?"

Charva looked him over before answering. "No thank you."

"Yes, I would," DeDe told him and watched him until he was out of earshot, before they begin talking.

"He's cute and sexy. Where did you meet him?"

"At a party."

"So where is Stephan? I hope he's history."

"Not really."

"Not really," Charva replied. "But Elliott runs circles around him. He has style and prestige and this is my first time ever meeting him. I don't even know the man and I can tell he's the shit. Look at him. Girl you need that."

"Looks do not make a man and neither does how good he makes me feel in bed."

"Is he that good?"

"It's unspeakable." They both grabbed each other and cringed at the thought. "But he's not a challenge."

"As if Stephan is. He takes you through hell DeDe. Is that the challenge you want?"

"No, but I love him."

Elliott walked back over and handed DeDe a glass.

"Well Elliott, it was nice meeting you," Charva said and patted him on the arm.

"Nice meeting you too." He shook her hand once again, before she walked away.

"You know Charva is the wife of Jeremiah Williams the super-producer and record executive of Element Records."

"I didn't know that." And he didn't seem like he cared.

"She and I went to college together."

"She seems like a nice sistah."

They began walking around the room. DeDe didn't personally know many of the people that were there; just a couple of faces. She waved and they waved back which made her feel important and well known.

"What's up dog?" Jamal said, as he approached them from the side.

DeDe nearly fainted when she saw Kendra and Kendall were with him.

"Hello DeDe, Kendra sang and waved. "Hi Elliott."

"Hello Kendra. Dog, what are you doing here?" He asked Jamal as they gave each other the Blackman's hand-grip.

"Man, Erika and I go way back. I got a personal invitation from her. A phone call," he said, while looking at DeDe up and down.

She smacked her lips and rolled her eyes at him as she grabbed Kendra and Kendall by the arm and walked over to the side with them.

"Why and what are you two doing here?"

"Don't worry about it. You didn't invite us, but we are here now and we are here to party. Kendall don't look now but there goes Jeremiah Williams."

"Where?" He asked as he tried looking through the crowd for him.

"Standing over there talking to Ryan Peoples, Cameron Day of Laser Records and that bitch that sings in 995. I can't stand her; she got pregnant by Beau Wood's on purpose. What's her name?"

"India, but damn he looks good," Kendall said, as he looked at him through the top of his glasses.

"I hope you're not talking about Jeremiah?" DeDe asked him with a disgusted look on her face.

"Hell yes."

"He's married and he has no interest in men."

"Fuck you DeDe," Kendall said, through clenched teeth as he rolled his eyes at her.

"Isn't he handsome?" Kendra asked.

"Yes, he is girllll..."

"I want that." Kendra said with dreamy eyes.

"Go for it." Kendall encouraged her.

"He's married to Charva and you know it," DeDe reminded her.

"She's your friend, not mine."

"Okay…" Kendall agreed, as he and Kendra gave each other a down-low, high-five.

"Didn't you come here with Jamal? Don't start any shit drama queen, because sister or not I will personally have your ass thrown out of here if you decide to show it. Jeremiah is off limits and so is Hezekiah. They are both married men. I was in Charva and Jeremiah's wedding." DeDe told her, as she waved at Jeremiah smiling. He walked over to her.

"DeDe, you look lovely," he said, and gave her a big tight hug. "How are you doing? This place looks so nice."

"Thank you."

He was nice looking, but he wasn't all that. He was shorter in person than he appeared on television. He had a noticeable birthmark on the left side of his face that is never noticeable on magazine covers, because of all the makeup. Also, his right eye seemed smaller than the left. He definitely looked better on television and on the cover of magazines than he does in person. But of course, he has super-producer, CEO of his own record label, Element Records and multimillionaire behind his name. That's enough to make him look good to any woman. Kendra and Kendall stood pining, yearning and hoping that they would get the chance to hug him.

"Don't I know you?" He asked Kendra. "I've seen you somewhere before."

She smiled and flipped her long hair behind her left ear. "I don't think so." She knew where he had seen her. He had seen her on the set of several video shoots and industry parties, but a man always accompanied her.

DeDe knew he was trying to flirt, but she wasn't going to let him do it in her face or with her sister. Charva was like a sister to DeDe and whether Kendra was blood or not, she wasn't going to let her fool around with Charva's husband. "Jeremiah, that is my sister, Kendra," she told him just so he could back off and put his tongue back in his mouth and stop his drooling.

"Oh, really?"

"Yes, you've probably seen her in a couple of your artist's videos."

"No, she didn't just call you out," Kendall mumbled and began to laugh.

Kendra looked at DeDe and rolled her eyes.

"Now that you mention it, I have. You were in Beau Wood's video *'Sweet Baby'* about a year ago?"

She shifted her tall slim body to one side and slightly threw her straight, relaxed hair to the other side. "Yes. I was."

He smiled and she smiled back. "I remember you."

DeDe's cock-blocking tactic did not work. He was still drooling and Kendra's eyes were still flashing dollar signs.

"Well, it was nice seeing you again Jeremiah. Kiss those kids for me," DeDe said.

"I will," he said while staring at Kendra smiling.

"And Kendra did you and Jamal," DeDe said pointing at Jamal, who was a few feet away. "Get a room here or at the Ritz?"

"Jamal," Jeremiah replied.

"Yeah, that's Kendra's boyfriend."

"Who, Jamal Raspberry?" He asked, as he walked over to Jamal and they gripped hands and hugged each other.

"Bitch, I don't like you," Kendra made it a point for her to know.

DeDe smiled and walked over to Elliott.

The way was parted as Erika St. James entered the room wearing a seductive, long, white, floor length, tight fitting, and strapless leather dress with a split stopping an inch away from her crotch. She was beautiful just as always. She glided into the room as if she was on a cloud, as every one cheered and clapped for her return after four years. She stood in the middle of the room intoxicated by all the love shown to her by her close friends and fans. Jeremiah walked out to her took a bow, kissed her hand and led her to the stage. She was one of the top moneymakers on his label.

"Thank you," she said as the cheers continued. "Thank you all for the love." She waited, before trying to speak again but the cheers continued. "You all are about to make me cry and please don't do that. My make-up guy spent quite a bit of time on this face of mine, you know?"

Everyone laughed.

"It feels good to be back and know that my family; all of you who are here tonight, have so much love for me—"

The crowd began to cheer once again.

"Four years I've been gone and I missed all of you like crazy, but I'm back now and I have something great for you. You will not be ashamed. 'Lover By Night' is the bomb."

More cheers from the crowd roared.

"The super-producers Mr. Jeremiah and Mr. Hezekiah Williams and myself devoted precious time into making 'Lover By Night'. This is one of my best albums yet and I'm extremely proud of this project. Not that I haven't been proud of all the other four albums, but this one has a little something extra." The lights on stage dimmed, the band began to play and she began to sing. Through four songs, she hypnotized and mesmerized the audience with her voice. She then walked off the stage through the crowd where she received and gave hugs to everyone she knew.

"Hey girl," she said as she hugged DeDe.

"You sounded great."

"Thank you."

"I know this album is going to be a success like all the others," Elliott told her as he shook her hand.

"Thank you," She looked at him and smiled in a way that made DeDe take notice and wrap her arm around Elliott's arm. She hated to seem so insecure, but she remembered a long talk with Erika some months ago, where she expressed how she craved and needed an ordinary man with no connection to the music industry, or the public. She was staring at Elliott like he was that ordinary man. "But you have to buy at least two copies of the CD in order for it to be a big success."

"I will."

She finally noticed DeDe's arm around his. "Are you two together?" She asked him without giving DeDe a second look.

"Yes."

She then looked at DeDe and chuckled. "He's handsome, how'd you get 'im?"

No the hell she didn't go there, DeDe thought, but forced herself to smile anyway. "Some of us don't have to be Erika St. James to get a man, all we need to do is just be ourselves and we can get any man we want." Although Erika was DeDe's client, she wasn't too crazy about her and she didn't care if Erika knew it. Her contract was with Element and Erika was just one of the many artists she had to handle, under that contract.

They both stood staring at each other with forced smiles that really meant "bitch I can't stand you." Elliott looked around the room eyeing his cousin and the other guests, as one dared the other to pass the first lick to get the catfight rolling. He pretended neither one of them were standing there carrying on like jealous school girls.

Jamal walked over. "Erika baby, you look and sounded good as hell tonight," he said, and kissed her hand.

"Thank you."

"Have you met my cousin? He's the best financial advisor around. So, if you need someone who's trustworthy to count all those millions of yours, he's the man. He used to be a broker on Wall Street."

"Is that so? We are going to have to exchange numbers."

Elliott didn't say a word.

"Yeah, y'all are going to have to do that." Jamal said, while patting his cousin on the back.

DeDe had relaxed her grip on Elliott's hand, when she thought about how childish she was acting by sparring with Erika playing the man is mine game. Erika could have Elliott if she really wanted him, because she was going back to Stephan as soon as she gets back to Houston. "I'm going to get something to nibble on," she interrupted. "Would you like something?" She asked Elliott.

"No thank you."

She walked off towards one of the many lavish food kiosks.

TWO HOURS HAD gone by and DeDe hasn't seen Elliott, since she left him and Erika fawning all over each other. She tried not to let her mind lead her into believing they were somewhere in a corner together, but she couldn't help it. Her mind had led her feet to walk around the room looking in every secluded corner and booth not knowing the first thing she would do if they were together. Jamal was on the dance floor with someone other than Kendra, which was no shocker. She didn't even see her or Kendall. She could only imagine what those two had gotten themselves into. They were probably already in bed with someone whom they just met. DeDe knew she looked cute and she could pass for someone with tons of money, although she didn't have a whole lot. But for some strange reason, the men didn't give her a second glance. She hated being at celebrity functions alone. That was another reason why she invited Elliott on top of trying to impress him. She seems to have gotten what she deserved. It looks like he had run off with her client; the woman she doesn't care for. The male celebrities didn't speak, unless you were a sex crazed groupie or an up-for-anything White woman, because they considered you to be outside their circle. The women in the industry who had been dogged by the high expectations of their superstar male peers only wanted 'ordinary men' whom they didn't mind taking care of. DeDe knew she was beautiful and she looked like money, but a lot of the men weren't looking twice at her. And then it hit her; she realized she was amongst the men of the music industry and professional athletes who might be gay. She didn't see Elliott and she was tired of looking for him, so she said her good-byes to the handful of people that she did know there, and she left. The limo was still outside which meant Elliott had gone with Erika. She couldn't wait for tomorrow to come so she could leave New York and Elliott without looking back.

WHEN SHE GOT to the room, Elliott was coming out of the shower.

"Did I come back too soon? Should I expect Erika to walk out behind you?" She asked sarcastically as she kicked off her shoes and rolled her eyes at him.

He ignored her.

"Why did you leave?" She asked him.

"I didn't know anyone there. You left me standing there saying you were going to get something to eat, and you never returned."

"Well, you and Erika were exchanging numbers and fawning all over each other, so I thought you were going to get to know her better. I didn't think you wanted me to stand there, while you two gushed over each other. I got tired of watching you two, so I excused myself." She slid her dress down and hung it up.

"Why not, you went out of your way to let her know I was with you."

DeDe replied sarcastically and said, "Ha, ha, ha, very funny Elliott. It took this trip for us to see this isn't going to work."

"No, it took him calling and begging you to come back, for us to see this isn't going to work. This trip had nothing to do with this not working. It was your little phone call."

"And he has nothing to do with this," she said, as she grabbed her nightgown out of the drawer.

Elliott calmly stated, "He has a lot to do with it, but if that's where you want to be, I'm not the man to hold you here. I knew it was him on the phone, as soon as I saw Kendra tonight. You lied, because I distinctly remember you ending your conversation by saying, 'I'll see you, when I get back to Houston.' I'm no fool DeDe."

"And neither am I." She walked into the bathroom to take a shower, without looking back at him. She couldn't stand to see the hurt look on his face or for him to see the guilty look on hers.

When she got out of the shower, all the lights were out and he was in bed asleep. She climbed into bed beside him without saying a word. She laid awake wanting to be touched by him one last time, before she goes back to Stephan. Although she was upset with him and he was upset with her, they were in bed together and the loveseat on the far side of the room was not an option. She was attracted to him and her wanting his sex was overpowering. She tossed and she turned, until her foot rested on his leg and her knee was very close to his back. She hoped he'd turn over without her having to touch him first. He didn't move from his fetal position.

"Are you asleep?" She finally whispered.

He turned over and stared into her eyes through the darkness. "No, are you?"

"I can't."

He slid closer and began kissing her lips, while reaching over and gently tweaking her breast.

15

WHEN putting the last time on anything, it makes it difficult for it to be just the last time. Mainly because the last time is always better than the first time and it gives hope for a new beginning, which then confuses things. Making love to Elliott for the last time before going back to Stephan was impossible for DeDe to do, after it was all said and done. With every deep stroke, caress, moan, and kiss, Elliott made her forget why they were doing it for the last time and why she was trying to go back to Stephan. Stephan had broken up with her and he damn sure couldn't work his thang like Elliott's. When she got back to Houston three days ago, she didn't run as fast as she thought she would to call Stephan. Also, he hadn't called her, which she didn't mind either. She had Elliott still. She didn't care if Stephan was upset about hearing another man's voice, when he called her in New York, but when she drove up in her driveway and saw him standing outside his car waiting for her, her heart had changed instantly as the feelings for him had resurfaced. He followed her into the garage.

"I thought you said you were going to call me when you got back from New York," he said as he opened her door. "What's going on DeDe, you've been back for three days now and I haven't heard from you, why not?"

If she understood the expression on his face, the questions he was asking and the tone in his voice correctly, she would think he was groveling and he was worried that she had moved on with her life. If she let the truth be told, she had. Her girlfriends were right; the minute she had moved on with her life he would try to come back, and nine times out of ten she would take him back. She was excited to see him, but she wasn't going to let him know it, because he would automatically think he was in there. Not this time. The ball was in her court now and she had home court advantage, as he tried to find his way back into her heart, and she decided that she was going to play dirty. "I've been busy, Stephan," she told him without looking at him.

"Not that busy where you couldn't call to say you made it back safely, huh?"

"And how are you?" She asked him, as she grabbed her purse and briefcase from the back seat of the car. She unlocked the door and walked into the house and to her bedroom, without inviting him in. But he followed her anyway. He looked around the house, as if it was his first time being in there.

"I'm fine and yourself."

"Couldn't be better."

He glanced around her bedroom looking for anything belonging to another man like a tie, some shoes, underwear or a T-shirt.

"What are you looking for?" She asked him.

"Nothing." He held out his arms for a hug. "So I don't get a hug?"

She hugged him reluctantly as if she didn't want to, but because he asked she did.

"Oh, you don't want to hug me. This other niggah must really got your mind?"

"Stephan what are you talking about?" She was flattered that he was now finally playing the jealousy role and the tables were turned.

"That little hug you just gave me, it was fake. It wasn't a hug to say you missed me and you're glad to see me."

She flopped down on the bed, took off her shoes and discretely reached over to the nightstand and turned off the phone's ringer, just in case Elliott might call. She didn't feel like explaining to Stephan why she wasn't answering her phone and she didn't want him to think he could answer it for her. She was glad Elliott was a neat freak and he had made up the bed the minute his feet touched the floor this morning. If not for that, Stephan might have known she hadn't slept alone last night. While making love, Elliott and her had a way of tearing the sheets off the bed and knocking the pillows to the floor.

"You didn't sleep here last night did you?" he asked.

"What are you talking about," she chuckled. "Of course I did."

"No you didn't, the bed is made up. You don't make up this bed until the weekend."

"I've changed."

"Yeah right. Either you are trying to impress the niggah by trying to make him think you make up your bed everyday or you haven't been home since the week-end."

"Or he likes to make the bed each morning, when he gets out of it. Have you thought of that?" DeDe acted like she was teasing, but she was telling the truth.

"Hell no."

"Then stop it Stephan." She grabbed her lounge clothes and walked into the bathroom to get undressed.

"Where are you going?" he asked. "I've seen you naked before. You don't have to go in the damn bathroom to change."

"We are not together, so why would I change in front of you?"

"We are together. We just split up for a second and it seems like you thought it was forever."

"Wasn't it supposed to be?" She asked.

"Shit no, so don't you tell the niggah that either."

She walked out of the bathroom in her black leggings and sweatshirt too short to cover her ass that seemed to have more roundness to it, since the last time Stephan saw her and it.

"What the hell?" He yelled and followed her, as she walked out of the room to the kitchen.

"What?" She quickly turned around to see what he was talking about.

"Your ass," he said turning her around and touching it. "You have one."

She had even taken notice herself, a couple of days ago. "Stop being silly Stephan."

"No, I'm not. As long as we've been dating, you've never had an ass." He flopped down on the sofa and dropped his head in his hands. He looked as if he was about to cry. "Are you fuckin' this other niggah?" He didn't expect her to answer and he didn't give her time to. He wasn't ready for her answer. "I can't believe this. Three weeks and you are sleeping with someone else already. He must have always been there?"

She could have walked out of the kitchen and torn him to strands by telling him yes and rubbing it in his face. She wanted to say that she was finally being fucked right by another man, who had caused her flat ass to finally develop curves in only three weeks, and he adored her and she adored him. Stephan looked so pitiful and truly hurt, she couldn't make him feel any lower than he already seemed to be, even though he had hurt her worse many times prior.

She quickly flipped the switch on the wall phone and walked out of the kitchen. "Stephan, what are you talking about?"

"I love you and this is the God's honest truth DeDe. I became afraid of us and how close we sometimes get and I shut down and run. You are the woman for me. I can't see life without you as hard as I might try to act like I can, but the truth is I can't."

Her defenses had fallen and her heart surrendered through the pried open steel bars. He was showing his love for her. She had no need for playing hardball anymore. She sat down beside him, embraced him and everything he was saying with her heart.

"You are a good woman and Shannon gets mad, because I let her know that you are. I wouldn't dare disrespect you for her, baby. You don't have to worry about me ever leaving you for her. What we had is over; I'm in love with you. She's the mother of my child so I have to deal with her; but it's nothing for you to worry about. I know she stresses you out, when she calls and comes over to the house acting a fool. I'm putting an end to all of that drama right now. If you tell me you don't want her over to the house while you're there, I won't let her come."

She was speechless. She had been waiting for this day to come around forever. She had also waited for the day that he would take her side over Shannon's "But how would you get Alexis?"

"Either I'll meet her in the grocery store parking lot up the street or I'll just pick Alexis up from school. She will not be allowed at the house. You and I are going to be married one day and I'm not about to let Shannon mess that up. Would you please give me another chance DeDe?"

As they stared into each other's eyes, Elliott popped into her head. What on earth was she going to do about him? They hadn't committed to a relationship yet, but they were working toward one. She felt this way because they spent so much time together; they must be moving in that direction. Then again, he knew she would eventually go back to Stephan. He had even said so himself.

"You don't have to answer right now, but if you just want me to prove to you that I'm worth another chance I will. Please don't just throw what we have away. We click like a lock and key. You can be yourself around me and I can be myself around you. There are some married couples who are still pretending with each other, but you and me are way past that."

And she hated trying to get to that point with Elliott.

Stephan grabbed her hand and kissed it and then kissed her lips again and again, until she opened her month and their tongues met.

DEDE CHECKED HER messages before heading to work and saw where Elliott had called her twice last night and once this morning. She was happy she had turned off her phones when she did. Since Stephan was there and he felt there was another man somewhere in the picture, he would have definitely answered her phone. Knowing Elliott, he would have asked to speak to her and all hell would have broken loose. She wasn't going to call Elliott back, because she didn't know what lie to tell him without being harsh and telling the truth. What? Tell him that she was at home and she had turned off her ringers, because Stephan was there and she didn't want to hurt him by him hearing another man's voice again. And as of last night, she and Stephan are back together and she doesn't want to see him anymore. Her conscience wouldn't allow her to be that harsh. She just figured that if she doesn't return any of his calls he would get the hint and stop calling. That was a tactic sure to work and this way no one will get hurt. She thanked God for the innovative development of caller I.D. She could see his number and not answer. But from time to time, he had called her at work from a number she didn't recognize and she answered the call.

As DeDe sat at her desk organizing her client files and daily agenda, her telephone rang. She answered it by hitting 'speaker', to keep her hands free. "Good morning, DeDe Wilson speaking."

"Hey DeDe, what's up?" Elliott asked.

Her heart sank at the sound of his voice. "Hey." She tried to sound cheerful, but there was no faking it. She didn't want to talk to him.

"I called you twice last night. Where were you? You told me you were coming by after work. What happened?"

"I worked a little later than I had planned. When I had gotten home I poured myself a glass of wine, ate a salad, laid across the bed and dozed off. By the time I woke up, it was four in the morning. I knew it was far too late to call or come by."

"No it wasn't."

"I thought it was. I didn't even hear the phone ring. I was so drained and I didn't get your message until this morning."

He paused as if he was debating on whether he should believe her or not. "Am I going to see you tonight?"

"Sure," she said, knowing he wasn't, because she was going to be with Stephan.

"What are you doing for lunch? Why don't you come down to the restaurant and we can have lunch together?"

"I can't. I'm swamped with reviewing files, press releases I have to send out and phone calls to make and return."

He noticed the sad tone in her voice. She wasn't acting like her usual cheerful self, when she hears his voice. "Baby, is everything okay?"

"Yeah, I'm just overwhelmed by all this work on my desk."

"Well, I know how that can be, I have a lot on my desk also. I'll let you get back to work and I'll meet you at my place around eight tonight."

"Cool. I'll see you then." She hung up the phone not knowing what to do. She didn't want to hurt him, but she didn't want to be with him anymore either. It would be a lot easier for her if she knew how to juggle two men at the same time.

But her heart always loved one guy more than the other and eventually it showed and she would have to choose.

There was a page over the intercom for her to come to the lobby. When she got there, there were twelve huge roses sitting on the desk of the receptionist. She smiled along with everyone else, as they marveled at the beauty and the smell of the red roses in the Lenox crystal vase. Her heart was deeply saddened by how she was doing Elliott and he had cared enough about her to send her roses so beautiful. He was going to be another man she was going to hurt and he's going to hate her like Wayman and Daniel Colwell from college. She was worse than a child opening toys on Christmas, when it comes to a man keeping her attention. As soon as she found someone she really liked, she would drop him and move on to do the same thing with somebody else. Stephan had kept her attention the longest, because she thought of him as a challenge. She read the card, "You are truly special to me, Love, Stephan." Her eyes lit up and she smiled so hard that she began giggling. "You are special to me too baby," she said, as she rushed back to her office with the heavy vase of roses to call him. She had forgotten about Elliott and how she was treating him. The roses weren't from him, like she originally thought.

She and Stephan made arrangements for him to meet her at her place so that she could show him how much she loved him before going out to dinner later that night.

Just before she left work, she called Elliott's voice-mail at home to let him know she wouldn't be able to meet him tonight. She could have called him at the restaurant, but she didn't want to go through the hassle of explaining why she was canceling. And she didn't want him asking her a thousand and one questions and have her lies sound like an excuse to do something she had no business. "Hey baby, I'm sorry, I know you and I had planned to see each other tonight, but something has come up. I have to meet with one of my clients tonight and it's going to be kind of late when we finish. If you and I can get together tomorrow night it will be all better, if you know what I mean," she smiled. "I miss you." She hung up the phone feeling relieved that she was temporarily off the hook. If she were Elliott, she would be convinced that she was telling the truth also.

WHEN SHE GOT home, Stephan was waiting for her just like he said he would. She was excited and her love began to throb, as she desired him to lie inside of her. As she drove into the garage, he got out of his car and followed her. Whatever happened to the key she had given him? She jumped out of the car without bothering to get her briefcase or purse and held her arms open for him. They hugged tightly and he let down the garage door with the automatic door control on her sun visor.

They kissed as they walked to the bedroom and DeDe unbuttoned her blouse, while tearing off his jacket and unbuttoning his shirt and pants. Once they got to the bedroom, she had laid him back on the bed and straddled herself over him. She slid her hand into his underwear while she kissed his neck and chest with passion. She had taken control and he couldn't believe how she was acting. He had noticed her aggressiveness last night, but he didn't say anything. He didn't want to think she had been with another man and he had turned her out to act like a slut, instead of the innocent woman he was used to. She had her hands in his underwear and she was on top of him. "Hold up," he said grabbing her hand from rubbing him. "What are you doing? What in the fuck is all of this?"

"What are you talking about?" She asked, as she began kissing him on his neck.

"Stop it. This shit ain't cute."

"What are you talking about Stephan?" She swung her body away from his and laid beside him.

"If this is the type of shit you did with the other niggah, then you and I—"

"What other man, I told you there was no other man." But she felt he could tell there had been, just by him being inside her last night. She surely could feel the difference, because she couldn't feel him and she became terrified of the myth that he could actually tell the difference himself. So she had gotten up in the middle of the night, while he was asleep to douche just in case he wanted some this morning. Although she really couldn't feel him like she used to, she still had an orgasm, because it was Stephan on top of her and she loved him. Loving someone enough, always outweighed whether he had bad sex or if it was big or small. She didn't want to tell him there had been another man, after he had poured out his heart to her and he was willing to do right. She was afraid that if he knew there had been another, he wouldn't want her. He was sure he had heard a man's voice, while she was in New York and she had lied and told him he was Jeremiah's limo driver. "Kendra just told you there was somebody else, because she thought it would make you jealous."

Although he believed her, he didn't want her to think he did. He got up and walked out of the room knowing she would follow him to try and convince him even more that there wasn't another man, but she didn't budge.

Fuck that. Things have changed. No more will she lie on her back with her knees pushed back to her ears, while he thrush himself inside her as hard and fast as he could and no more was she going to run behind him. She has seen the light, thanks to Elliott.

The doorbell rang and DeDe jumped. She had gotten up from her bed to go answer it, but Stephan had gotten up to answer it before she could tell him not to. She stood at her bedroom door wondering who it could be, because Kendra and Kendall didn't live with her anymore. And they hardly let anyone know they were staying with her, because she didn't live in an expensive high-rise or mansion that all of their friends were accustomed to seeing them in. Her intuition told her it was Elliott at the door. He had called her cell phone, after she left the message on his home voice-mail and she didn't answer. She became nervous and frightened at him finding out about Stephan and Stephan finding out about him, because she was lying to them both. With her heart pounding with fear, she listened.

"Who is it?" Stephan asked. "Elliott," was the reply. Hearing that, Stephan swung the door open with a lot of attitude, as if he knew this guy was there to see DeDe. "What's up?"

"Hi, is Kendra here?"

DeDe could imagine the expression on Elliott's face, but she was happy that he had the sense and decency to play it off.

"No she doesn't live here," Stephan told him. He and Stephan stood staring at each other. "Maybe her sister can tell you how to get in contact with her. DeDe," he screamed.

Her knees buckled as her heart dropped to the pit of her stomach. She felt like she had to shit; she was so nervous. She swallowed and slowly walked up the short hallway that seemed like a long and winding country road.

"Baby, there's someone here trying to get in contact with Kendra."

As she turned the corner, Elliott's eyes met hers. She could see the hurt in them, as he looked her up and down. She dropped her head.

"Hi," he said.

"Hello."

"I didn't know Kendra had moved. If you could give her my number," he handed her one of his cards and she took it and read over it as if it was her first time ever seeing it. "If you could have her call me, I would appreciate it."

"I will."

He turned around and walked out of the door as she stood there wanting to cry and curse Stephan out for answering her damn door.

16

"*WHATS* up girlfriend?" DeDe said, as she cheerfully waltzed into Dionne's office and flopped down in the chair across from her desk. "It's hump day and the weekend is near."

"Good."

"What do you have planned?"

Dionne exhaled and fell back in her black leather swivel chair. "Nothing as of yet."

"Good."

"But I don't know what Byron has cooked up," she said, just in case DeDe was going to ask her to go out someplace with her. She was still angry with her for stealing her account but Brad and Chris had given her a huge house account that pays twice as much in commission to make up for the account DeDe had taken.

"Nothing. Tell him he can't plan anything, because I want you two to go to dinner with Stephan and me on Friday night. I know this nice little jazz café on the other side of town."

"Hold up, you and who?"

She smiled and busted out into laughter. "Stephan."

"Your ex-Stephan?"

She nodded, while smiling and turning red.

"When did this happen? I thought you were going to tell him to go to hell, if he called you back again?"

"I was, but when I saw him it was too hard to say anything like that."

"Yesterday you were so in love with Elliott and now you are talking about Stephan. I don't understand." Dionne shook her head at DeDe's stupidity. She was convinced that DeDe had serious issues and that she enjoyed the drama of being dogged out.

"Well, when I got home he was waiting for me in my driveway. Just seeing him made me fall in love with 'im all over again. I told you about how he called me in New York begging me to take him back? He was doing the same thing last night and it was hard to tell him no. Girl, we belong together. Elliott is a sweet man and all, but he's just not my type. I know you are crazy about 'im and you hate Stephan."

Dionne thought, I could give less than a damn about either one of them. In fact, I could give less than a damn that you are the biggest fool that ever walked. It's women like you that make the sistahs look bad, because you are stupid and you keep going back to this man that doesn't want you for anything but a fool.

"But I love Stephan, he's more my type. That's the man I want to marry. You told me I would go back," she laughed.

But I didn't mean for you to go back dummy, Dionne screamed out in her mind as she sat staring at DeDe as if she had stupid stamped across her forehead.

"We talked for the longest last night and he expressed himself to me. And you can call me stupid, but I fell for it. He sometimes becomes afraid of how close we get and he runs."

And you fell for that? Dummy. Dummy. Dumb. Dionne couldn't wait for her to leave, so she could call Charlotte. She was really going to trip off of this. "Run?" Dionne replied and chuckled. She hoped she was making her feel like an even bigger fool than she already was. "So he goes through this every other month, right?"

"Well, we are close and we're always together and actually it's not every other month, Dionne. It just seems like it."

"I'm sorry, but it sure as hell appears that way to me. But I could be wrong." She was just going off what DeDe had told her and what she had seen, since she's known her. "Girl, I just don't want to see you crying over him anymore."

"I'm not. We talked about Shannon, since she's our main issue you know. He's agreed to not let her come by the house, when I'm there. Also, he's not going to call her either, if I'm around. This should keep the trouble down."

Dionne fell back in her chair with her mouth wide open. She had just heard it all and she couldn't believe what she was hearing. "He's what? How is he going to do that and why?"

"She causes problems and besides, she and I don't get along. I'm his girlfriend and future wife; she's just his damn babymama. I've done more for him than she has ever done. She left him for another man, she gave him a child he didn't want and she wants to act a fool, because he's moved on with his life."

Dionne could have reached over her desk and knocked the hell out of her for sounding so stupid and stealing her account. It's not Shannon you should be worried about. There are other women, but you are just too damn blind to realize it. She wanted to tell her exactly what she felt, but she knew DeDe was too far-gone to accept it.

"He's going to meet her in the convenience store parking lot for Alexis or pick her up from school. We're trying to move our relationship to the next level and she keeps up this damn babymama drama. I believe he's going to propose to me soon. He made the statement of not being able to live without me and I will be the perfect wife."

Dummy, please, she thought. "And what makes you think that? Has he been hinting around or have you?"

"He has, but if he doesn't propose, I will. I want to spend the rest of my life with him and I have no shame in asking him to marry me. Girl we've been together too long and we've been through too much."

Which is all the more reason why you shouldn't want to marry him, Dionne thought. "You are kidding right?"

"No, I'm hearing it more and more each day. I also read it in a magazine. Women are not waiting on the man to ask them, they are now proposing."

"That's desperate."

"No it's not. You mean to tell me, if you had been with Byron for over three years and you know he's the man you want to spend the rest of your life with and he hasn't proposed marriage, that you wouldn't ask him?"

"Hell no, I wouldn't! Don't do that. A man knows when and whom he wants to marry. "

"Us being apart for those weeks made him see things a little differently."

"What, that you have the ability to quickly get another man? Speaking of which."

DeDe looked at her and smiled.

"So you and Stephan are back together? Just like that; and you've dropped Elliott?"

"It's not just like that. I'll talk to Elliott tomorrow night and let 'im know it's just not working."

"Girl, I don't know what to say about you," she said, and chuckled at how stupid DeDe was.

"So, would you like to go with us on Friday night?"

"Girl, I would love to," she said knowing she wouldn't dare. "But knowing Byron he already has something planned."

DeDe nodded her head as if she pretended to understand. "You know you never told me what Byron does for a living."

Dionne felt put on the spot. What does it matter to you what he does for a living she wanted to ask her. "It never came up, but he's a civil engineer for the Houston Transportation Department."

"Oh, he designs the highways?"

"Yeah, why?"

"Just curious." DeDe got up and walked toward the door. It never seems to fail, whenever she asked Dionne to go somewhere outside of work, she always has a thousand and one excuses. DeDe thought to herself, from now on, I'm not going to ask that bitch to go nowhere else, so she doesn't have to lie. If she only wants friendship at work, she should just say so and I'll leave it just at that. She doesn't have to lie about having other things to do. "Maybe some other time I'll get to meet your mystery man," DeDe said, and walked out before Dionne could

KG

respond.

Dionne immediately picked up the phone and called Charlotte. She answered on the second rang. Charlotte, that fool has taken Stephan back and she's going to ask him to marry her."

Charlotte grabbed her pen and pad and began writing as fast as Dionne talked.

ꝏꝏꝏ

"GOOOOOD… MORRRNING Houston on this beautiful, sunny, Friday morning. The temperatures are expected to reach the high nineties to one hundred degrees, so find an air conditioner and keep your radio dial locked in to H for Hot-103. I'm Casey Jenkins."

"And I'm Sylvia Reed and the time is eight o'clock. Ladies if you haven't already gotten your papers this morning you need to, because what some of you expected Angelic to do, she has done. Let's face it, she loves this man and she can't see life without 'im."

"We as men have that affect on women, if we put that thang down right."

"And what would that thang be?" Sylvia asked and chuckled.

"Kicking game and laying it hard, long and deep," Casey said as both of them laughed.

"Your mind is somewhere else this morning. We can tell you had a good night last night."

"And morning too. So if you are not making love, what in the hell are you doing?"

"Let's see." With the usual instrumental music playing in the background, Sylvia began to read. Dionne sat down at her kitchen table with a cup of coffee and read along. She was as addicted to listening to the caller's responses as the people of Houston were to reading the column and Charlotte was to writing it.

Last weekend in Miami things became really hot and rocky for the inseparable couple Angelic and Jasper, and it left her questioning their future together. Tibias called while they were at the hotel begging her to

K4

take him back. Angelic being the fool in love; began considering it and ended what she and Jasper had. I say she used Jasper to keep her mind off of Tibias, until he decided to come back. And once he did she dropped him off at the curb where she picked him up and hasn't bothered to look back. The sad thing about it is, he doesn't even know he's been dropped off. Whatever Tibias told her, he made it seem believable. But when a woman is in love with someone, there isn't too much he can't tell her that she won't believe. When she and Jasper had gone to the birthday party of a well-known female R&B singer, which is one of Angelic's close friends and client's, she had really made her mind up that she was going back.

Dionne thought about how glad she was that DeDe listens to her CD's instead of the radio, because what was just said about the R&B singer and client is a dead give away that Charlotte was talking about her. Dionne was still apprehensive about the column, although she felt it was justifiable for the knife DeDe had placed in her back by stealing her account. She immediately picked up the phone to call Charlotte. "Couldn't you have made the column a little bit more fictitious? R&B singer and client."

"Relax, if she hasn't read it by now, she's not going to."

"She has friends."

"Stop being so nervous, there's no way she can prove this is her. You only know it's her, because I told you."

"Bull, I knew it was her when I first read it."

"I have to go, I'm missing Sylvia read it. I'll call you later."

The birthday girl and Jasper drooling over each other had nothing to do with her decision, yet she blames it on that. What a cop-out. I guess she needs someone other than herself to be the scapegoat. A chart topping R&B singer and a commercial realtor; what are the chances? Senseless drooling and flirting can sometimes mean nothing. But the insecurities of the one on the outside looking in can make it seem like disrespect. Jasper is too handsome for words, yes he is. And the R&B singer did come to her own birthday party alone. But my question still stands; what are the chances of them getting together? Angelic became pissed at both

K6S

of them and she left them standing together to decide on their chances. Her head was back in the clouds for Tibias.

The groupies were at the party, her best friend Rolanda and her brother Reese. What's a party without them? Rolanda was with the basketball player whom her ex-husband nearly killed and whom she nearly got killed over, because she was sitting on top of him in the pool during an orgy. Her swollen lip and blacken eyes had healed from where her ex-husband had beat the hell out of her for disrespecting him. Her brother, Reese the very manly, gay groupie had a choice of whether to leave with a well-known rapper or comedian. Neither of their names can be disclosed for privacy purposes, but let's just say the rapper is very fine and no one would ever suspect him of switch-hitting . But isn't that the description of most bi-sexual brothas? So listen-up women, be careful and maybe invest in a toy that looks the part but runs on batteries and it will surely satisfy your part. The comedian, he's funny alright, but we all suspected him.

"Damn, what comedian do we suspect is gay?" Casey asked and laughed. "Sylvia do you know?"

She continued to laugh.

"This Reese guy gets around doesn't he? Women y'all have some competition out there. He had a choice between a rapper and a comedian?" Casey replied. "He likes them hard and funny but who did he leave with?"

"This is just saying to us women that we need to be careful," Sylvia said and continued to read.

"Well you heard what she advised you women to do?"

"Either that or become celibate."

"No, that's not a good idea. What would the straight men do if all the women decided to become celibate? Don't put that thought in women's heads, continue to read."

Some women just never know when to walk away without looking back, because they always feel they're walking away from an opportunity to have someone love them the way they have always fantasized to be loved, by this person. It's easier for them to walk away from someone that wants to be with them and love them, than it is to walk away from a man who could give less than a damn about them. And why is that? I had expected that Angelic would go back to Tibias sooner or later, because she had done it so many times in the past after he had broken her heart. I was hoping she would fall in love with Jasper and realize love is never worth crying or begging for. But that was just wishful thinking on my part. She loves Tibias and wants him in her life no matter how much pain he has brought her in the past. I understand forgiving someone for hurting you, but being stupid is an entirely different issue. Once someone hurts you, you should always believe they could do it again. Life 101. She had always wanted to hear Tibias cry for her and when he did, that was all she needed to believe he really loved her. He told her that their time apart had shown him she was the best woman any man could hope for and being without her was pure misery. On the surface, it sounds very good. But knowing this man and his past history, playing with her emotions is a joy to him. It will only be a matter of time, before he gets her just where he wants her and drops the bomb that shatters her heart once again? And I'll be the first in line to say, I told you so. Tough love for a blinded girlfriend is the only way to make her open her eyes to see a snake for what it really is. It's my duty to show her that a rattler should not be kept around as a trustworthy house pet.

Hurting women who care for him is Tibias's way of getting an arousal. Believe it or not ladies, there are some men out there that are just like Tibias and some of you might just be in love with one. I believe Tibias only wanted Angelic back, because he realized another man had his fool and he might just treat her like the beautiful queen she really is. If Tibias stood back and let that happen, he might just lose Angelic forever and he couldn't let that happen. Now that they are back together, they've both agreed that their real problem wasn't him wanting to be with another woman, or her hounding him for marriage, but it was the drama with his child's mother. Talking about putting the blame on outside issues. Let me *be the first to say this relationship will never work. They've decided to focus all of their attention on taking the power they had given his child's mother away. Someone's been watching too much Oprah. Power. My question to them both is; what power can they take from this woman if she never had any?*

Angelic is so excited about them being back together; she's thinking about asking Tibias to marry her in a couple of months. Talking about desperate. Marriage is not the answer, but Angelic does everything possible to get a ring. But the one thing I don't like is her pretending she likes his little girl, when she dislikes her as much as she dislikes the babymama. I've met women like her before. They first add their insecurities to the confusion of the child's father and mother and once that relationship is destroyed beyond mending, they attempt to destroy the relationship between the child and the father. Deep down she believes he still loves his babymama, as she calls her and she believes that when he goes to pick up his daughter, they are sleeping together. And she came to this conclusion, because he's never taken her with him to go pick up his daughter. What does that say? Chances are he may still be sleeping with her from time to time. I believe that every man loves his child's mother, if he's a man that ever cared.

I've come to realize by listening to Angelic that it's just in some women's blood to require and want less from a man than they deserve.

"Damn…I think I might like this 'Frustrated Friend', but if she keeps hipping the sistahs on how to deal with us men, I don't know."

"I kinda like her, but I don't think I would want to be friends with her. She is backstabbing, but on the other hand she's also helping other women."

"Like I said before, if you are not making love what in the hell are you doing? The lines are lit up with callers. The time is eight ten and here's *Avant* with 'My First Love'."

Byron walked into the kitchen with shaving cream covering his face and head and a towel draped around his waist. Dionne quickly turned off the radio. "Baby would you like a cup of coffee?"

"No, but could you iron my shirt for me."

"Yes."

The phone rang. It was Charlotte. "How would 'No More LoveMaking' sound as a book?" she asked Dionne.

"Good, if it were ever going to be one."

"I was approached by the Kensington and Bradenberg literary agency and they said they can at least get me a deal for six-hundred thousand with Omega Publishing with a seventy thousand dollar signing bonus. That's a tidy bundle, for turning the lives of Angelic, her best friend and her brother, Tibias, Jasper into a book. What do you think?"

"No, Charlotte."

"Don't say that. This is a deal of a lifetime. It sounds like a good book deal Dionne. I can sell the paper and I can just sit back and write. Don't say no. If the women of Houston, New York, Atlanta, Chicago and Philly love it; what do you think all the women of the world would think?"

"No. A friggin' book Charlotte? This is a woman's life that you are exploiting. Just imagine, if she puts two and two together and realizes someone has written a book about the ins and outs of her life?"

"She doesn't know me Dionne and as far as she knows, I don't know her. There is no risk. The book is covered by the disclaimer clause. I can already smell a bestseller. Kensington and Bradenberg is one of the largest literary agencies in the world. If they believe this book idea will fly so do I!" she screamed with excitement. Charlotte could give less than a damn about Dionne telling her not to and there was no changing her mind. "Seventy thousand just to sign."

"Charlotte, you are talking as if any of that money is going to benefit me."

"What are you talking about, it will. We're in this together, we're friends remember."

"I don't know. I'm kinda getting tired of this anyway."

"Tired of what? You can't be tired, when everything is going so well."

"There's still that question in the back of my mind; what if she finds out?"

"She's not going to find out," Charlotte proclaimed, as she tried to assure her by putting the question out of her mind. "The column has been running for over a month and a half now. Let's not go through this again. It's going to work."

"Dionne, will I be getting that shirt anytime soon?" Byron asked as he entered the kitchen.

"Yes baby. Hey girlie, I got to go." She hung up the phone and dashed into the laundry room to iron the shirt.

17

THE look on Elliott's face when he saw Stephan had DeDe wishing she were dead right then and there. If she could have died last night and bypassed heaven and gone straight to hell for the hurt she had caused Elliott, she would have. He looked so devastated, as he stood eyeballing Stephan, when he answered her door. She never intended to hurt him with her decision to go back to Stephan. She knew he really liked her and she liked him in the beginning, when she thought there was no chance in hell of her and Stephan getting back together. The mistake she made was confiding in him and telling him about the hurt Stephan caused her heart, which made both of them believe she would never go back. She couldn't go back, when she thought Stephan was long gone with whomever he had left her for and Elliott was God sent.

During dinner last night, she couldn't eat and she wasn't up for much of a conversation with Stephan. The thought of Elliott and what he was feeling had her mind. When she and Stephan made love, she just laid there like a dead woman with her legs wide open and he had the nerve to say that was good lovemaking. She hadn't done anything but lie there. Afterwards she didn't bother to cuddle, she just curled-up on her side of the bed. She was awake most the night, staring at the ceiling replaying the look on Elliott's face as he handed her his business card and looked around her to see Stephan lying on her sofa semi-clothed with his shoes off, as if he was at home. Elliott weighed so heavily on her mind, she had dreamed about him last night when she finally dozed-off. She had awakened thinking about him this morning. She didn't know what to say to him, when she thought about calling him from the office. None of her lies seemed convincing enough, but she knew she needed to call him. While sitting at her desk, she had picked up the phone several times to dial his number, but hung it up before even pressing one button. He had heard Stephan call her baby and he looked too damn comfortable to be at her house bringing things to a closure. She became terrified, because she didn't know what to expect from Elliott if she called. Even laid-back guys could go off, if they were pushed and felt used. Then she thought maybe she shouldn't call. Maybe him seeing Stephan said it all. But by her not saying anything meant she was guilty. She waited a couple of minutes, until she thought he was en route to the restaurant and she called his home expecting to get his voice-mail. He answered. "Hello."

She held the phone with her heart pounding and her stomach turning and tightening into thousands of knots.

"Hello," he said again.

"Hi, I thought I would get your voice-mail."

"Well you didn't. I'm running a little late, so I'm still here but I guess you talking to the voice-mail is a lot easier than you being confronted and talking to me."

"About Tuesday night."

"No, DeDe that night spoke for itself. You're back with Stephan. I understand."

"I'm not back with him, he was just over there wanting to talk."

"Wanting to talk, about what?"

She could detect the anger in his tone. She froze.

"You told me that the shit was over, so what did he have to talk about? Furthermore, you lied to me; so that he could come over and talk. So, it's evident you wanted to hear what he had to say and it wasn't all about talking."

"He wanted to bring closure to this."

"Closure," he replied and chuckled. "Look DeDe, I'm not up for your game. You didn't have to call me and explain shit. You are with who you want to be with."

"Elliott, I'm telling you we are not back together. He just wanted to talk."

"I don't give a damn! And we are not together. And I don't want to talk." *Click.*

She sat holding the phone baffled at the fact he had just hung up in her face. "No he didn't just hang up this damn phone in my face." She took a deep breath and called him back but the phone just rang. This time she got his voice-mail.

"I can't believe you just hung up in my face and now you are not going to answer the phone. I never expected you to act so childish, Elliott. Here I am trying to talk to you and you are acting like a kid." She felt this was her chance to put an end to it all without it being any fault of hers. "You don't have to ever worry about me calling you again." And she wasn't, because the man she loved was back in her life and there was no need for another.

σσσσσ

DURING DEDE's LUNCH hour she had gone over to Stephan's house to follow him to Sears to drop his car off for servicing. He was on the phone arguing with Shannon. It had been two weeks, since DeDe and Stephan have been back together and he hasn't mentioned Shannon or Alexis. She hadn't called the house acting a fool like she usually does. DeDe had almost led herself to believe Shannon had found herself a man and she was no longer going to be a problem to them like Stephan said. But now he was on the phone with her arguing. Every other word he screamed was a curse word. It was DeDe's first time ever hearing him carry on in such an outraged screaming match with her. DeDe had walked into the kitchen pretending the argument was none of her concern and she didn't need to hear it, but at the same time she couldn't wait to call Bridget and tell her what was said. It was shocking, but delightful to hear him finally put his foot down and put her in her place. She was no longer going to have any power over him or their relationship. By Stephan's response, DeDe could tell the argument was about something silly. He had told her that he wouldn't be able to pick up Alexis this weekend, because he wouldn't have a car. Her response to that was to borrow DeDe's car. "You don't even like her, why would you ask me to borrow her car?"

Why does she even call here, DeDe thought? She finally got tired of just standing in the kitchen and she walked into the room where Stephan was. "Baby, don't let her get you upset like that, just hang up the phone and lets go," DeDe said loud enough so Shannon could hear her and know that she was there.

"I know baby, but I can't help it, she's a damn bitch."

"Are we having this conversation in front of her?" Shannon asked. "Now you have to really put on a front, but the sad thing about it is, she can hear you and not me. Go ahead."

"Don't worry about who I'm talking in front of," he screamed at Shannon, as he jumped up and walked into the kitchen. "Yeah, she's here and she's gonna always be here."

"I don't care anything about her being there Stephan," she screamed hoping DeDe could hear her. "Why are you trying to step on me to make yourself look big in front of her? I'm the mother of your child. When she's gone I'm going to always be here asshole. We have a child together, you're that ignorant and weak that you're playing into her game."

"You're a bitch Shannon! You give me drama about every damn thing."

"Because you make plans to get her and when that bitch comes around, you drop my child as if she's nothing and she's second to that bitch."

"I won't have a fuckin' car this weekend."

"What happened last weekend and the weekend before that? Tell me Stephan?" She chuckled. "You gave me another excuse. If my child isn't second to DeDe, she's second to your other important plans that don't mean shit to me. Since she wants to sit there and take all this shit in, you let her know the real reason why we are having this conversation. Let her know it's because you don't take care of your child and you don't spend any time with her. I don't want you and I don't care who you're with or who you love."

"I do love her."

"You are really pouring it on thick now. This is just making her day to listen to you curse me out, because she's an insecure bitch and you're playing into it."

"You're a drama queen Shannon."

"And Stephan, you're a bastard and your little game will crumble as soon and she sees you for who you really are. Yeah, I give you drama, because I'm not going to let you run over me or my child. And if that bitch was in my shoes, she would deal with you the same way."

"See Shannon you are so ignorant, because she hasn't said anything about you. She's sitting over here quiet not even paying us any attention, so why would you want to call her a bitch."

When DeDe heard his comment she took offense, because she was sitting back being quiet and she was now tired of it. She had said nothing, while Shannon did all the talking ever since she and Stephan have been together. She stormed out of Stephan's bedroom into the kitchen where he was and screamed, "She's the damn bitch!"

"Both of you are ignorant," Shannon told Stephan. "No wonder you two are still together. Not only are you a pretender and ghetto; so is she."

"You keep up too much drama. It's those lonely girlfriends of yours you listen to. If you think you are going to come between us, think again. Our love is too strong for that. I'm going to marry this woman. We are together, because we love each other. I never loved you—period."

"You need to make a correction to that statement. You love her as long as she's going to keep taking care of you; and she's so stupid she probably will for a long time. Let her not give you another dime, she'll be out of there so fast her head will spin."

"Bitch, you don't know what you are talking about, but you think you do."

"I know you, Stephan. You can call me a bitch all you like in front of her.

And she can gloat at the sound of it, but I'm so happy I'm not in her shoes. Taking care of a niggah while he puts shit up his nose all day and giving him money, is not for me. You sorry ass bastard."

"You are the reason I don't see Alexis. I haven't been by to see her, only because I don't want to see you. When she gets of age to deal with me on her own, then I'll see her. But as long as I have to deal with your bitching ass, I won't see her. I don't want shit to do with you Shannon. You keep up so much drama, you should be on a damn soap opera."

"She doesn't need to call here anymore," DeDe mumbled as she walked out of the kitchen.

"No, we'll never be together, because I got somebody. And if I do get Alexis, you can't bring her to my house."

"What are you talking about?"

"Just like I said. I don't want you over here."

"You won't get her any other way. I'm not going to meet you in the streets with my child. I've never disrespected you for no man. How dare you try to disrespect me for her. You must be crazy. Now let me get off the phone with you because either that bitch or that shit you put up your nose every so often has you strung out and talking crazy or you're just plain crazy. Since you want to act up on me and put on a show, I want my child support today, goddammit! If you don't have it to me by two o'clock, I'll have them come and pick yo' black ass up right where you stand. You think I won't, try me. What you got to say now?"

He paused and sighed slightly, as he thought about how serious she sounded and the way he carried on. She might just send the police to his job to get her point across. "Come and get it Shannon," he told her and hung up the phone.

DeDe jumped up off the sofa. "She's coming where? Didn't you just tell her that she can't come over here? I don't want to see her."

"Well, she's coming to get some money and I figured you have to go back to work, so y'all won't have to see each other."

"Oh, so she knows if it wasn't for her having to come and get this money, she wouldn't be over here, right?"

He nodded as he looked down at the cordless phone waiting for her to call back to have the last say by saying she'll send the police instead.

"I thought you wanted me to take you to drop your car off?"

"I did, but Dedrick came by this morning and followed me over there. Didn't you notice that the car isn't outside?" He flopped down on the sofa.

"How are you getting to work?"

"I'm going to use Melvin's truck, I think," he said sounding unsure. "I need to page 'im."

"Well, I guess I'll head back to work," she said, as she bent down and kissed him.

"Are you going to be here when I get off?"

"I can," she said and smiled.

"With a chicken fried steak dinner cooking I hope."

"Maybe," she said, as she kissed him once again and walked toward the door. "I'll call you later to see if you got in contact with Melvin."

"That's fine." He had told Shannon to come by and get the money he owed her for child support, knowing he didn't have any. But he knew DeDe did. He was skeptical and kind of embarrassed about asking her to borrow money, because he and DeDe had just gotten back together and he owed her money already, but if it kept Shannon from putting him in jail he would have to. "Uh, oh yeah, baby," He said, as he jumped up off the sofa, before she walked out of the door. "Let me hold a couple hundred until next Friday."

Her hand slid from around the gold doorknob, waiting for an explanation without having to ask. She didn't want to give Shannon shit.

"I only got two hundred on me and if I don't give her the full four hundred she'll have the law at my job so fast it wouldn't even be funny."

"I thought you weren't going to tell her that you were working."

"How long was that supposed to go on, before she found out? Baby, I wouldn't ask you if I had it. You see, I had to pay my car note and Alexis' tuition and after school program."

"What, is that a part of the court order? Why are you giving her child support, if you are paying for tuition and the after school program? She's being greedy. You are a wonderful father for her to act so stupid and try to rake you through the coals," she said and rubbed her hand across his face. "I don't want to give her a damn thing." She reached into her purse and pulled out her checkbook.

"I don't either, but if it will keep me out of jail. You know she's just waiting for a reason to have me locked up. She's an angry, bitter bitch. You just write me a check and I'll deposit it into my account on my way to work, and then I'll write her a check. I'll give it back to you next Friday," he told her.

And he damn sure was, because she was going to meet him on his job Friday afternoon. Her plan was to follow him to the bank to cash his check and get her money back right then and there. She wasn't going to start loaning him money again. He hadn't paid her back for all the other money she had loaned him.

As she drove down the street, she began smiling. She now felt a sense of security knowing that Stephan now hated Shannon. She no longer had to take the back seat to her, while wondering if he was still longing for his ex. Today he showed her that she came first, when he cursed Shannon out in front of her. He was right by calling her a bitch, because she really is and he finally sees it. There was no more holding Alexis over his head to draw him back, so that the two of them could get back together, because he doesn't even want to see Alexis. Now he's all hers and she didn't have to share him with Shannon nor Alexis.

She was a block away from work when Stephan called her on her cell phone breathing hard with agitation in his voice.

"Hey."

"Stephan, are you okay? What's going on, baby?"

"It's Shannon, she just came over to the house acting stupid. I left because I didn't want anything to happen. Come and pick me up from the 24 hour store up the street from my house."

"What? I'm on my way." She hung up the phone and turned around in the gas station parking lot and drove as fast as she could. She didn't know why Stephan put up with Shannon's crap. She was messy and angry, because he had moved on with his life. This is exactly the reason she had told him Shannon didn't need to come over anymore. She knew something like this would happen. Anyway she could, she would try to put him in jail. She was bitter, venomous and angry.

DeDe drove to the convenience store and pulled in on the side where the payphone is located, but she didn't see Stephan. After waiting for five minutes and fearful that Shannon had called the police on him; DeDe drove down to his apartment and there was Shannon's car parked at the curb. DeDe ran up the stairs and noticed the door was unlocked. Upon pushing the door open, Shannon jumped up off the sofa. Her clothes were torn. Also, her hair was standing up on her head to the point that it looked like a fright wig. There was broken glass from a couple of picture frames and the pillows from the sofa were scattered on the floor. The room was in total disarray.

"Stephan," DeDe called out, as she stepped over the broken glass.

"The bastard isn't here," Shannon cried. "What are you doing here?"

DeDe walked through the apartment looking for him. "What went on here? Why are you still here, if he's not?"

"What do you think went on? He beat my ass. Is this what you wanted? He took my fuckin' keys, so I couldn't leave."

"No he didn't. I just stepped over a set of keys outside the door. Now leave."

"Bitch, who do you think you are talking to? I'm not going anywhere," she said, as she snatched one of the throw pillows from the floor and threw it at DeDe nearly hitting her.

DeDe looked at her in shock. "He's not here," she yelled and threw the pillow back at Shannon and it landed upside her already messed up head.

Shannon rose up from the sofa again. "No the hell you didn't just hit me," she said, as she picked up a broken CD case and threw it at DeDe but missing her as DeDe jumped out of the way as if she was dodging a flying ball.

"Yes, the hell I did," DeDe said, while picking up a broken candle and throwing it at Shannon and missing her, because Shannon blocked the heavy three wick candle by using a pillow.

"Bitch, I hate you," Shannon screamed, as they both grabbed and picked up everything but the sofa and chair and began throwing things at each other's face and head. Thing were flying all over the room like a scene from The Matrix. The only reason they didn't injure each other was because they both were really poor at throwing. However, they were both very good at ducking and dodging. CD's and cases, pillows, broken glass, picture frames, wooden African sculptures, and what-knots flew across the room like bullets in a war zone.

DeDe ran into the kitchen for cover, as she ran out of things to throw. Shannon ran behind her with an empty beer bottle and a heavy African mask with the intent to throw them as hard as she could, because she wanted to kill DeDe. DeDe frantically looked around the kitchen for something she could use to defend herself with, before Shannon came around the corner. DeDe grabbed the canister of flour and a cutting board and threw them as hard as she could, as Shannon threw the beer bottle and mask. "Ouuuch!" DeDe screamed, as her leg gave-way and she hit the ground. Shannon had hit her in the kneecap. "You bitch, you broke my knee," DeDe cried, as she looked up at Shannon who was covered in flour from her head to her toes.

"Look what you've done," Shannon cried.

"Fuck you very much. Look what you've done. You broke my knee," DeDe cried, as she held her knee trying to massage the pain away and get up off the floor.

Shannon grabbed her purse and stormed out of the apartment.

DeDe's cell phone rang. She pulled herself up by putting all of her weight on the cabinet door and grabbing the countertop. She limped to her purse to answer her phone. It was Stephan.

"What's wrong with you?" He asked, as he heard her breathing hard. "Where are you?"

She sighed. "At your place."

"What? What are you doing there?"

"I came looking for you," she cried. "You weren't at the store."

He ordered her to leave the apartment right away, just in case Shannon decided to come back with the police. He swore on a stack of bibles, that he didn't hit her, so he had no idea why her lip was bleeding. He claimed that the broken glass came from her throwing things at him, but he wouldn't dare hit her back even in self-defense. DeDe didn't care if he had hit her, because she was sure Shannon deserved a slap across the face for just being a colossal bitch.

ANXIOUSLY, DEDE RUSHED back to her office to tell Dionne what had happened. Although DeDe was in pain, she was glowing with excitement, as she thought about Stephan taking her side over Shannon's. She also called her girlfriends Bridget and Marie leaving brief messages on their answering machines.

"Girl, call me when you get this message. Shannon went over to Stephan's acting a fool and he had to knock the hell out of her. That's what she says, but I don't believe he did. That girl is crazy and Stephan said he doesn't want anything else to do with her. It's about time, don't ya' think? Call me when you get in."

She limped around the office looking for Dionne and spotted her coming out of a meeting.

"Hey girl!"

"Hey, what's going on? Why are you limping?"

"Drama."

"With who?"

"Shannon, Stephan's crazy babymama. Shit has hit the fan. I told you she was psycho."

"What did she do?" Dionne asked, as she stood back looking down at DeDe's leg.

"She came over to his house acting a fool and breaking all of his things and she hit me in the leg with a beer bottle."

"She what? Why?"

"But I got her though," she said beaming. "She's loony like I've been trying to tell you and Stephan for the longest. He called me all upset, because she was at his house trying to start a fight with him. But he wouldn't hit her, and to avoid the temptation of knocking her the fuck out, he left. When I got there Shannon was sitting on the sofa looking a mess like she had been crying. Her hair was standing up on her head and her shirt was torn."

"So he beat her ass?"

"No, he left her in the house, because she started hitting him. The bitch is so evil she threw his things all over the place and broke them, so it looked like they had been fighting. But you know what? If he did hit her, she deserved it. I guess now she'll sit her ass down and stop acting so foolish. He also told her that he didn't want to see Alexis or her anymore."

"My God," Dionne said, as she noticed the slight smile and joy on DeDe's face while she told her what had happened.

"That's what I said. She's crazy and then when I told her to leave, she began throwing things at me. Stephan told me to leave, because he felt she would bring the police back."

"And she should have. It's a shame how some men can make some women act so out of control, ignorant and ghetto."

"What are you talking about? She was already ghetto anyway," DeDe said and chuckled.

"Not her, you. You are actually euphoric, because that man put his hands on that woman and called you over to watch. I wonder why he would call you over to see that he had fought her?"

"I didn't see it. When I got there, whatever happened between them was over, but nothing happened. He didn't hit her. He doesn't believe in hitting women. She's just that evil that she would try to make it look like he hit her."

"Well how do you explain her hair looking a mess and the torn shirt?"

DeDe sighed. "I'm trying to tell you, she did it herself. He wasn't even there. She was just sitting on the sofa looking a mess. I had to tell her to leave. If he had beat her up like she said he did, why would she be sitting on his sofa and he wasn't even there?"

"So you don't really know what happened? He just told you she came in acting a fool, correct?"

DeDe rolled her eyes and sighed. "I know he didn't hit her."

"Well, I guess if she couldn't beat him, she beat you because you are limping," Dionne laughed.

"No she didn't beat me either," DeDe chuckled. "Right now, she's at home trying to wash off a whole canister of flour I threw on her," DeDe laughed.

"You did what? Girl, you are ridiculous. DeDe, he called you over there, because he knew you were so insecure about her. On the other hand, there's also a chance he might lose you with you trying to decide on whether it's him or Elliott."

DeDe resented the fact that she was trying to counsel her. "He doesn't know about Elliott and that's been over. And I'm not insecure about that bitch either. He called me over there to pick him up from the convenience store he had gone to, so there wouldn't be theatrics."

"He knew there was another man. Don't act stupid and naïve DeDe."

DeDe was taken aback, by her choice of words. Stupid. Naïve. "I don't think so."

"Every single thing he's done to Shannon, he'll do it to you at a later time and date. That's the type of man he is. He's not going to change his spots for you."

"No, he won't do me like he's done her, because I won't be that stupid to give him a child he didn't want and then hold the child over his head. The difference between she and I is that he loves me. He told her in front of me that he never loved her."

Both of them sat staring at each other, as if the other was some type of moron and had no clue what they were talking about.

"It's over between them and she needs to realize that and move on," DeDe said.

Dionne was thinking, get real bitch, you are thirty-four years old and you are carrying on like a clueless ghetto teenager over a man who ain't shit. If Dionne knew she wouldn't completely shatter her feelings, she would have vocalized those precise words. "So, what is it that y'all have? It seems to me that you're the one always crying and upset. Remember, you thought he was still sleeping with Shannon and that's the reason he was breaking up with you every other week or month? Girl, get a grip, before that man brings you down. I got to go. I have some phone calls to make," She stood up. "Elliott is the best man for you," she told her as she walked down the aisle back to her office.

18

"*HEY* girly, what 'cha got cookin' over there?" Charlotte asked Dionne.

"Fried fish, baked beans and a salad."

"Sounds good. Ian and Iyana went out to dinner without me. That bastard, he could have waited another fifteen minutes for me to get home. He knows Friday traffic in Houston ain't no joke."

"Byron should be on his way." She took the phone away from her ear, thinking she had heard someone at the door. She loved having a man to cook for.

"Why doesn't he just move in?" Charlotte said and chuckled. "He's over there all the time."

"Well, we can't go to his place, because his brother lives with him. Besides, I feel more comfortable in my own house."

"His brother lives with him?" Charlotte replied.

"Yeah, he just graduated from medical school and he owes his first born in student loans. So Byron let him stay with him for awhile."

"Oh okay, because I was about to say, ain't nothing worse than a grown man having a roommate."

They both laughed while agreeing.

"I had completed my column for next week, but when you called and told me that fool had gone over to Stephan's house and fought his babymama; I had to pull it back from the paper's editor, Cynthia, and rewrite it. That DeDe is a natural fool."

"Hell yes. Some women might look classy on the outside, but be all the way ghetto on the inside."

"I believe he did hit her."

"So do I, but DeDe said *he* said he didn't hit Shannon."

"That's her name?"

"Yeah, she's a social worker for Winston County."

Charlotte chuckled. "Do you know I almost named his babymama that in the column?"

"Well, I'm glad you didn't because anyone who knows DeDe would know you are talking about her."

"I hope she presses charges against him and her, because both of them are ridiculous. I'm telling you girl, this will make a great book."

"No it won't either."

There was a knock at Dionne's door. Her face lit up with a smile, because she knew it was Byron. Only he knocked twice with a slight pause, before knocking twice again. "Let me call you back, Byron's at the door."

"Don't let him eat up all the food, because I'm on my way over."

"Over where?" She asked, as she and AJ, her nephew walked to the door to answer it.

"Over there… to eat silly."

Dionne didn't say anything, because she didn't feel like being bothered with Charlotte and having her sitting around with her and Byron for the rest of the night. Why did she have to come over there? Dionne didn't have time to sit and talk to her. At least not while Byron was there. When Byron is at her house, she devotes all of her attention to him. "Hey baby," she said, as she opened the door and he walked in. She greeted him with a kiss and he gave AJ a fist-to-fist knuckle-five.

"Oh, you don't want me to come over? All you had to do was say so, Dionne."

Dionne didn't mean for her to notice. She began to feel guilty. "No it's not that; I just didn't cook enough. But if you're hungry, I can have Byron run to the store to get some more fish."

A 'no the hell you won't' look, came across in his facial expression as he turned around and looked at her and rolled his eyes. He walked into the kitchen and Dionne followed him smiling.

"No need, I'll just page Ian and have him bring me something back. You go ahead and I'll talk to you later." She hung up the phone with much attitude and without giving Dionne a chance to say good-bye. Dionne felt bad, but it didn't last long. Her man was there.

"I just said that because she was trying to make me feel bad, because Ian and Iyana left without her and went to dinner. "Baby, I cooked you some mullet," she said, as she pulled the piled-high plate of hot fish out of the oven and placed it before him. "And some homemade baked beans—"

"Is Clifford coming to pick up AJ anytime soon tonight?" He asked and leaned forward placing his elbows on the table.

"No, he's at work. And there's some salad."

"Damn, then why doesn't he get a babysitter instead of putting him off on you every Friday night," he whispered so AJ, who was in the next room wouldn't hear him. "I can see some Friday nights, but every Friday? On top of that, he doesn't come and pick him up on Saturday, until he wakes up which is four or five o'clock in the evening. The day is almost gone. If I have something planned for us, I might as well hang it up, because your family might have you obligated for their needs."

She stood speechless, as she tried to figure out why he had his ass on his shoulder. He knew she kept AJ every Friday night, when they first started dating. He thought it was sweet that she helped her brother out who was a single parent.

"I didn't say anything before now, because I thought you and Clifford would have sense to realize you are dating now and I don't want to sit around every single Friday night, after a long, hard work week keeping a child that isn't yours or mine."

"He's my nephew and I'm helping his father, which is my brother until he gets back on his feet."

"You told me you've been doing this for a year and half now. He's not on his feet yet? Dionne you are a good person and your family is taking that for granted. How about your mother, why can't she keep AJ on Friday? She's his grandmother. But now that I've given it some thought, she goes out and parties as much as you and I do combined. So what, if she gave up most of her young life to raise five children? What African American mother didn't?"

"Byron, have you been drinking?" She asked.

"No, I haven't and I resent you for asking me if I had, because I'm telling you about your family. Dionne, I like you...no, I love you and you are the woman I want to marry. But I don't think I can standby and let your family run over you. When we do get married it's going to be my money that's going to have to help take care of them. I don't want to take care of grown people that are capable of hustling and busting their asses, just like you and I. That house that you moved out of so your mother and brothers would have a place to stay; is that still in your name?"

She dropped her head and shamefully nodded. When she had told him about that, she never expected he'd use the information against her later.

"That entire situation would have to change, before we get married along with you helping them pay the lights and gas."

Dionne couldn't believe her ears were hearing him correctly. He definitely had a problem with her helping her family. She didn't feel they were taking advantage of her; they were her family. Her brothers were trying to do better. She couldn't blame them, because they didn't have the same drive as she did to make it. Her mother told her there was something about Byron she didn't like. Maybe she knew he was self-centered because he sure as hell was sounding that way now.

"Three grown men and your mother, and they can't make ends meet? They know that they're wrong. One thing I can say about my family, we don't rely on each other to carry our loads."

"Your family is rich."

"Rich," he replied.

"Your mother is a doctor, your father is a lawyer and both of your sisters are attorneys along with their husbands. You're an engineer and your brother just graduated med school. My mother doesn't have a high school education and neither do my brothers. They are working the few factory jobs that are still left in the area. You know Byron, that's very hard labor."

He fell back in his chair as nonchalant as he had sounded. "That shouldn't be your problem."

σσσσσ

THERE WAS NO room for discussion about Shannon and what happened between the three of them, although DeDe felt they needed to talk about it, because of the affect it was having on Stephan. He tried to act as if he was fine, but he looked depressed. He wasn't talking, he wasn't in the mood to make love and that wasn't like him. DeDe had played with him to get it up, she jumped on top of him, grinded her pelvis into his and had even walked around the house naked and he did nothing. He didn't stare at her and he didn't touch her. He just held on to his beer bottle and kept his eyes glued to the television all weekend. The most moving he had done was from the sofa to the refrigerator for another beer and to the bathroom to piss it out. He didn't want to leave the house and they had so much planned for the 4th of July weekend. DeDe wanted to stand by his side, but she was tired of staying in the house doing nothing. She couldn't understand his behavior. However, she didn't take it as him caring for Shannon in a loving way, but rather him hating what had gone on at his house between them. DeDe's heart pained for him, but she knew how Shannon could push someone to the edge with her smart mouth. Anyone would hit her, she had wanted to plenty of times herself.

"Damn!" She heard him yell. She threw her shirt over her head and rushed into the kitchen, where he stood in front of the refrigerator holding the door open.

"What's wrong baby?"

"There's no more damn beer."

"Good, you've been sitting in the house drinking it all weekend, it's gone."

"Shit!" He slammed the door shut and walked back into the den and flopped down on the sofa.

She flopped down beside him. She hoped he was ready to talk. "What's wrong baby? You haven't been talking, your lips have been glued around a green, glass bottle, you don't want to make love and you're just sitting in the house watching television."

"You can go out, I'm not keeping you here. I just want to sit in the house and relax. It's Sunday."

"The 4th of July…you know. Remember, we had a lot planned for this weekend?"

He looked at her and continued to talk. "The baseball game is on and that's what people do on the weekend; relax."

Not the response she expected. She sighed and jumped up off the sofa. "Marie, and Russell invited us to their house for a cookout today."

"Go, I'm not going."

"Fine." She stormed to the bedroom to continue to get dressed. She really didn't want to go by herself. She was tired of having a man and having to do couple things alone, when it came to doing things with her friends. She sighed and walked back into the den. "Russell is watching the game and he has beer."

He looked at her before answering. "Well, I don't want to stay over there too long."

BEFORE THEY GOT out of the car to walk up to Marie's door Stephan grabbed DeDe by the arm. "I understand she's your girlfriend, but I don't think you need to tell her what happened. I don't need her to know my business."

But he was way behind, because she had already told Marie on Friday. She became offended that he felt he had to tell her what she can and cannot say to her friends. "Why do you feel you need to tell me that?" She asked with pure attitude in her tone. She wondered if that was his concern, as they drove there in complete silence. He looked like he was in deep thought, during the entire trip. When she attempted striking up a conversation he would only give her one-word answers.

"Don't act like you don't discuss what goes on between us DeDe. Your friends know all of our business. I don't need them to know any of this, because it's none of their concern. They shouldn't have an opinion on it and it shouldn't be talked about. The shit shouldn't have happened in the first place.

"But nothing happened, right?"

" Let's just keep it between us. "

19

$\mathcal{AT}$ six-thirty a.m. DeDe had gotten up to get dressed for work, while Stephan lie in her bed stretched out from his drunkenness. He drank everything Russell had in the liquor cabinet and then some. DeDe was so embarrassed, after Russell nearly had to carry him out to the car. She hated Shannon even more.

The doorbell rang and Stephan jumped up out of his sleep and whispered. "Don't answer it. Shit." He ran to the guest room across the hall and peeked through the blinds. "Damn, it's the police."

"The police," DeDe replied. "How did she know where I live?"

"Damn, I don't know. She's a social worker and she works for the state. She can get any address she wants. I didn't even think about that."

The doorbell rang again.

"Why don't you go out the back door," DeDe told him as he slipped on his pants and shirt. She threw on a T-shirt and some jeans.

"Hell no! If she put out a warrant for my arrest there's a policemen already standing at the back door. He peeked through the blinds. "What did I tell you? Ain't this a bitch and a half! I don't have any money for an attorney and I damn sure don't have any to post bail. Shit!" He looked worried and nervous. "Ain't this some fucked-up shit?"

"Don't worry, I know the perfect attorney and I'll loan you the money for bail. You won't have to spend a second in jail," she assured him of that.

The doorbell rang again.

"Why don't I just answer the door and tell them that you're not here."

"No, they might search the place."

"They have a warrant for your arrest not a search warrant. They can't search my house without one."

He hoped she was right, as she walked to the front door to answer it.

"Good morning," she said, as she opened the door.

"Good morning. Is Stephan Brown in?"

"No, he doesn't live here."

"I have this address as a second address for him."

"He doesn't live here," she told him once again.

"Are you DeDe Wilson?"

"Yes."

"Ms. Wilson you are under arrest for the simple battery of Shannon Holcomb."

A second officer walked from around the house.

"Excuse me," she bellowed, as the policemen turned her around and placed handcuffs on her, as if she was a criminal. "I don't know what you're talking about."

"On July 2, 2000, Ms. Holcomb claimed you and Mr. Brown attacked her."

"Attacked her," DeDe replied and chuckled. "This is crazy. I don't know what she's talking about. She hit *me* in the knee with a beer bottle! You're making a mistake." Tears came to her eyes. She was being arrested for something she didn't do. She hoped and prayed none of her neighbors were watching.

The arresting officer spotted Stephan's shoes by the sofa. "Now Ms. Wilson, are you sure Mr. Brown isn't here?"

"Yes," she said, as she spotted the same pair of shoes.

"You wouldn't lie to us would you?" The officer nodded for his partner to look at the shoes.

"Well Ms. Wilson, we feel he's here so we are going to look around."

DeDe's heart dropped and she cried. "Not without a warrant you're not."

"We have a warrant for Mr. Brown's arrest and if he's here we are going to take him into custody."

The officer walked to the back of the house and began searching behind all doors that were closed, under the bed and closets. DeDe stood nervously, with her arms behind her back feeling just as ghetto as Dionne tried to make her feel, when she told her about what had happened. A minute later the officer walked out with Stephan in handcuffs.

"Look who I found hiding in the closet. I thought you said he wasn't here?"

DeDe looked at the officer and rolled her eyes.

"I guess if you would fight for him, you damn sure will lie for him." One of the officers remarked, as both of them began to chuckle while walking them both outside.

"Why are you arresting her," Stephan asked. "She did nothing."

"According to Ms. Holcomb, she hit her," The officer said, as he placed Stephan into the backseat of the police car.

"She's lying," Stephan proclaimed. "She's just upset, because I don't want her and I've moved on with my life and she hates the fact DeDe and I are happy."

So, did you hit her?"

Stephan looked at DeDe who was sitting beside him crying. "No. I didn't touch her."

"That's not what she says; but tell it to the judge."

FOR FOUR HOURS, DeDe had to share a holding cell with seven other women who were real criminals as far as she was concerned. There was one who had shoplifted, another who had been charged with possession of drugs with the intent to distribute, a niece and her aunt, who had bounced fifty-thousand dollars in checks in two months, and a woman who had been charged with assault and battery with a deadly weapon. She also was hit with the intent to kill her girlfriend and husband, because she caught them in bed together. DeDe tried not to look terrified but it was written all over her face. She sat on the wooden bench waiting her turn to make a phone call to have Kendra come and bail her out.

"Ms. DeDe Wilson," the female officer called out as she opened the cell looking her up and down. "You can make your phone call now." She pointed her in the direction of the phone in the far corner. DeDe hurried to the phone.

"Kendra," DeDe whispered at the sound of her voice.

"What are you doing in the county jail?" Kendra asked as she glanced at her caller I.D.

"It's a long story."

"You got caught writing bad checks."

"I don't think so. That's your hobby, not mine. Remember? I need you to bring five-hundred dollars to bail me out."

"For what, what did you do?"

"Don't ask questions right now, I'll tell you later. I just need to get out of here. I have a meeting with one of my big clients and I'm late."

"It's the day after the 4th of July; you have to go to work?"

"Yes, because I took the Friday of the Memorial Day weekend off. Please don't ask anymore questions right now."

"I don't have five-hundred dollars."

"Kendra, you just received your child support checks two weeks ago, what do you mean you don't have five-hundred dollars? I have to get out of here. I'll give you the money back ten minutes after I get out of here and get to the bank, if that's what you want."

"Like I said, I don't have it."

She felt like saying, 'bitch you haven't sent mama any money to help her with your kids in five months, so what in the hell do you mean you don't have it', but she didn't want to say anything that might make her not want to post the bail for her.

"I'll call Jamal and get it from him."

"No, don't do that. Because knowing you, you'll tell him that I'm in jail and he'll tell Elliott. What about Melvin?"

"I'm not talking to that bastard. I'll get the money and I'll be there in an hour."

"Hurry." DeDe hung up the phone and just sat there not believing what she had gotten herself into. Maybe she wasn't better than any of the other women who screamed through the jail cell bars for a phone call. At this point, she really hated Shannon, because she felt like she was victorious once again. If DeDe had known she would have to spend four hours in jail for nothing, maybe she would have warmed the grease that was on the stove and poured it on her and really given her something to have her locked up for. She was so steamed; the notion of really hurting Shannon had crossed her mind several times. She had made a vow to herself that if Stephan ever talked to Shannon again, she would have nothing to do with him.

She looked at the phone wanting to call Dionne, to ask her to meet with Bushel and Coleman in her place. She had no idea whether Dionne knew Chris had given her the account and she had already used up her one phone call. She looked at the officer with a pitiful expression. "Excuse me Ma'am, I know that I just made a phone call, but it's imperative that I make another one to my job. I have a huge meeting at stake and I just need to get someone to go in my place."

The officer looked at her and rolled her eyes. "Go ahead."

She picked-up the phone and immediately called Dionne.

"I need your help."

"Where are you? I went by your desk to see what you were doing for lunch, since we are the only two people in the entire downtown area working the day after the fourth."

"Shannon pressed charges on me and Stephan. The police came by my house this morning and picked us up, so I'm in jail waiting for Kendra to come and bail me out."

Dionne felt it was her rightful duty to say, "Didn't I tell you she was going to do that, because he hit her? You and her throwing things at each other was nothing."

DeDe let out a loud sigh. "No Dionne, he didn't hit her. I feel like shit and I hate that bitch right about now, so I don't want to hear you tell me what you really don't know."

There was a slight pause. "Okay, what do you need for me to do?"

DeDe sighed and paused for a second as she prepared herself to be cursed out, after she tells her she was now handling one of her accounts. "I don't know if Chris or Brad told you or not, but Bushel and Coleman requested that I head the QuittersPatch campaign. I refused because I knew it was your account, but Chris told me I would take the account or no longer work for Stein and Stockton. He promised me that he would inform you. I told him when I came up with the campaign idea, it was only a suggestion and I was just helping you out—" DeDe waited for Dionne to respond. "But he still insisted on me overseeing the account."

If Dionne wanted to say something she couldn't. It had been almost a month and a half, since she found out DeDe had the account. She was no longer upset. Also, Brad had given her one of the house accounts and she was making more commission than she made on Bushel and Coleman. But she didn't believe DeDe tried to refuse the account; not for one minute.

"I have a meeting with them and it looks like I'm going to be here for another hour or so. Since you know some of the same people I work with over there, I was wondering if you could go in my place."

Dionne sighed. "Yeah, I can. What time?"

"At a quarter to two. I have all the information on my desk in a folder."

"Will do."

DeDe felt relieved that Dionne didn't react and curse her out.

Finally, two hours after DeDe hung up with Kendra, she and Kendall had posted bail for her and they were standing on the sidewalk waiting for her, when she walked out.

"What's up jailbird?" Kendall teased her.

"Ain't shit funny Kendall."

"Simple assault, who did you assault? Stephan I hope." Kendra asked, as she pressed a button on her key ring to unlock and start her brand new 2001 baby blue, convertible Jaguar.

"So is this why you didn't have any money?"

"Get in the car. So who did you assault?"

"Nobody, but I damn sure should have!"

"Who Shannon?" Kendra asked, as she took a chance at guessing.

"Well, yes, she lied and claimed I hit her. I hit her with a pillow and threw flour on her."

"You are ghettooo…, to the max!"

"And without the fabulous." Kendall chimed in. "I hope you two weren't fighting over Stephan."

"No. And we didn't fight we just threw things at each other. She threw an empty beer bottle at me and hit me in the knee with it and she claimed I hit her."

"Where was Stephan?" Kendra asked.

DeDe sighed as she explained. "At the store. She and Stephan had an argument and she claimed he hit her but he didn't. He called me over—"

"For what?" Kendra and Kendall asked in unison. If they too, thought him calling her over was ghetto, maybe Dionne wasn't being cruel after all.

"To pick him up from the 24 hour store because he left the house so they wouldn't fight. When I got to the house, she was just sitting on the sofa with her shirt torn. She had broken all of his things to make it look like they had fought. I just told her to leave because he wasn't there, and she picked up a pillow and threw it at me."

"Girl, you are the biggest damn gullible fool I've come across in a long time. Are you trying to say he didn't hit her and the torn shirt was self-inflicted? Have you forgotten he's a friend of Melvin's?"

"No, I haven't, but he's nothing like Melvin. He doesn't beat women."

Kendall laughed so hard a tear came to his eye. "DeDe, as much as you don't want to believe it, he hit that girl."

"He must have thought you were really damn insecure and he needed to pull some trick out of the hat to put that demon to rest," Kendra said. "You had to be giving that man hell about that babymama. For him to call you over to see him beat another woman's ass. This doesn't say much for his character or anything else, DeDe. That was a lot of drama. In fact, this is more than that; it's melodrama."

"He didn't call me over there," DeDe said and dropped her head.

"You insecure 'girlfriends' are always causing drama between the babydaddy and mama. Y'all are the blame; and the weak-ass men allow y'all to do it. What are you doing with Stephan anyway? Where is Elliott?" She looked at her out of the rearview mirror waiting on an answer.

"Keep your eyes on the road Kendra. Elliott and I didn't have a commitment."

"Neither do you and Stephan," Kendra told her.

"Why don't you have any money after two weeks," DeDe asked, as she tried to get the spotlight off of her.

"Bitch, get out of my pockets! This is about you and not me. However, we do need to stop by the bank, so that I can get my money back from you. You know that I had to take a Gucci bag back for your jailbird ass?" She quickly spotted and pulled up to the nearest ATM machine and opened the door for DeDe to jump out and go get her money back.

STEPHAN WAS SITTING on the sofa, eating and watching television, when DeDe walked in. Her mouth dropped open along with Kendall and Kendra's. The officer had told her he hadn't made bail yet, so she had gotten an extra thousand dollars out of the bank to go back and bail him out. But there he was, sitting on her sofa.

"No, he ain't."

"Shut the hell up Kendra," Stephan told her, as he got up from the sofa and walked into the kitchen for another beer. "I just got here." He walked over and kissed DeDe on the forehead.

"Who bailed you out?" DeDe asked.

"My father and brother."

"Why couldn't they bail her out too?" Kendra asked.

"Because I was going to bail her out, when I got here to get money, Kendra."

"But you are sitting here eating," Kendra told him. "You weren't in too much of a rush were you?"

"I called and they said she had already been bailed out."

DeDe was pissed. "I'll talk to y'all later," she told Kendra and Kendall and walked to her bedroom and slammed the door behind her.

Stephan sighed and got up off the sofa, to follow behind her. "You two get the hell out of here."

They walked out shaking their heads and laughing.

20

PARADISE was now hell for Charva and DeDe had dropped
everything to come and comfort her. It felt good to be someone else's shoulder to cry on instead of always needing one, DeDe thought as she listen to
Charva cry. When things between her and Stephan were crumbling, DeDe
knew she could call Charva and she would be there for her. Even if she knew
DeDe wasn't paying any attention to her advice to leave whomever and find
her someone new. DeDe couldn't believe Jeremiah was fooling around and it
was hard trying to convince Charva that he wasn't, but she tried. "How do
you know there's another woman?" DeDe asked Charva, as they sat outside
on the patio of DeDe's favorite restaurant having lunch. DeDe had picked her
up from the airport this morning, when she called her and said she was in
town. "Has she been calling the house and hanging up? "Have you seen pictures, did you find a number or have you seen them together?" Answering yes
to any of those questions still didn't mean there was another woman. At least
that's what Stephan had always told her, when she accused him of fooling
around. Someone calling the house hanging up in the middle of the night could
be anyone, not necessarily a woman. The woman on the picture could be an
old friend and not necessarily an ex-girlfriend. The number on the piece of
paper could belong to a friend or a contact for a new job. The woman on the

passenger side of his car could have been a co-worker he was just taking home, because she doesn't have a ride. Stephan always had an answer for everything.

"No, none of that. A woman knows her man and when there is another woman who's trying to take him. You knew when Stephan was fooling around with Shannon didn't you?"

"Yeah, but I don't have to worry about that anymore," she beamed as she wiped the corners of her mouth. "He hates her after what happened. You know I've always hated her, but now more than ever. I spent seven hours in jail four days ago for that bitch. So we had to go out and get us the best attorney out there, because of all her lies and pent-up anger. "

"Because Stephan doesn't want her?" Charva asked.

"Yes."

"I don't want Jeremiah to hate me. Another woman can turn your man against you and his kids. He'll see you out in the streets and act as if y'all never had anything."

"Jeremiah hating you or leaving you for another woman, I can't see it. Stephan left Shannon because she was a bitch. They were never married and they only have one child together; you and Jeremiah have four. He's not going anywhere."

She nodded. "She's already making him disrespect me by staying out with her all night. When I try to talk to him about it, he just goes off. I'm thinking about getting pregnant again."

"For what, especially if you think he's fooling around?"

DeDe understood her reasons for wanting to do so, because she had thought about getting pregnant several times by Stephan, just to get him to marry her. She wanted to have a distinct link to him just as Shannon and Alexis did, as well as prove to Shannon that she could. Having a baby seems like the answer to a lot of problems in a relationship. In actuality, it's just another factor that is added to the already existing problems. It was her girl-friends, who talked her out of making such a foolish mistake, so she needed to convince Charva to think straight.

"Girl I don't want to lose my husband and become the ex-wife who's bitter and angry, because suddenly finding myself single and the mother of four is nothing cute. Another woman has the capabilities of making a man leave everything he has ever loved behind."

Had DeDe made Stephan do that? A couple of months ago, he and Shannon were the best of friends and he always had Alexis in tow. "But Stephan never loved Shannon, that's why it was easy for him to walk away from her. He really loves his daughter. He doesn't want to deal with Shannon, so he doesn't want to see Alexis right now. When Alexis gets of age, he'll contact her then. He told Shannon he doesn't want to see her anymore and especially after the lies she's told. Right now, he doesn't want to have anything to do with either one of them. Do you know we are paying twenty-five hundred dollars a piece for an attorney? I hate that bitch."

"I don't want to go through that. I want my children's father there so that we can raise them together. Whoever this other woman is, she has him wide open. I just packed up and left him and the children there this morning, when he came walking in at seven-thirty this morning. He said he was out in the back of the house in the studio."

"Was he?"

"I don't know. I was asleep. It's funny how some women wish they were in my shoes, because I'm the wife of super-producer Jeremiah Williams, but they have no idea what I go through to keep him and what it's like to be married to him. I never told you or Roberta this, but three years ago he had a baby outside of our marriage."

"He did what?" She asked, as she pushed her plate away.

"A little boy; and the bitch had the nerve to name that bastard after my husband. I stayed with him, although I hated him for cheating on me. But just so she couldn't have him, I accepted it and made him promise he would never bring that child around me and he hasn't. He doesn't have anything to do with the little boy, but he does pay child support and if I could stop that, I would."

That's exactly how DeDe felt at times; she longed to put an end to Shannon's money bank. DeDe believed Stephan was paying way over and above his share of child support. He was helping keep Shannon's rent paid and her electricity and gas on. Who was she going to turn to now? Because DeDe was going to see to it that Stephan only send the four hundred dollars the court ordered him to pay her every month and nothing extra.

Charva checked her cell phone for messages from Jeremiah. "He hasn't even called me. He doesn't care anymore."

DeDe could see that she was really hurting behind him and this other woman, because she hadn't eaten any of her lunch. "He does care. You are the mother of his children and wife. He's not going to leave you for another woman. She means nothing to him, believe that."

"I'm thinking about giving Jeremiah a surprise birthday party in two months and I would like for you to plan it for me."

"Sure." DeDe looked out into the parking lot and nearly stopped breathing. She became nervous and fidgety. "Oh-my-God, there goes Shannon."

"Where?" Charva began turning around trying to find her. "Where is she? What does she look like?"

"She's getting out of the green Honda Accord." They watched her as she walked up to the restaurant door without noticing them. DeDe pulled out her cell phone and called Stephan at work. "Hey, baby," she whispered. "Guess who just walked into the restaurant?" Not giving him time to answer, because of her anxiousness. "Shannon."

"Get up and leave and don't say shit to her," he commanded her.

"I can't believe she's here," she told Charva.

"Just leave, DeDe," Stephan commanded her once again.

"Okay baby. I'll call you when I get back to the office." She hung up the phone and slid it back into her purse.

"What did he say?" Charva asked.

"He told me to leave." She wiped the corners of her mouth took a gulp of her Coke and pushed her plate away.

"Leave where? We are still eating. Don't run from her. She's nobody."

"I know that, but I don't want any additional mess."

"And there's not going to be any. That's the problem; you haven't stood up to her. We are not going anywhere. If we have to, we'll both beat her ass. It's two against one."

"I can't do that. Dionne already called me ghetto for fussing with her and throwing flour on her at Stephan's house. What would I be called, if I fought her?"

"A bad ass bitch. Don't listen to that Dionne; she doesn't know anything. Marie told me about some of the things she tells you and how she never comes to anything you invite her to. Like I was telling Bridget and Marie, I don't think she likes you. I believe she pretends. You need to watch her."

"She's just funny acting and she doesn't trust women; because some women can be messy. She really helped me out by going to one of my meetings with one of my clients on Monday, when I was in jail. I believe she likes me, but she just doesn't want to get close to anyone."

"Girl, women like that are crazy. I'm sure that many men have burned her more than women have and she still allows them to get close to her."

"No… she's the type that doesn't allow men to run over her either."

"Yeah right, that's what she's telling you. DeDe girl, every woman has been a fool for a man at some time in her life."

DeDe refused to believe that about Dionne. She seems to have men figured out.

"I don't trust women like Dionne, because they'll burn you before you even think about burning them. Women who don't trust other women and are so quick to say all my friends are men, they are usually the backstabbing, messy, gossiping vultures they claim other women are."

Shannon had walked out onto the patio and she and DeDe gave each other a long stare before rolling their eyes at one another. "Girl, let's go."

"No, I'm telling you don't run from her or she's going to always give y'all problems. That's how I had to deal with Jeremiah's daughter's mother."

"Daughter? I thought that you said the woman named the child after him. You are talking about the woman he had the child with since y'all have been married, right?"

"No, no, no he had a child before we got married, while we were dating."

DeDe tried not to look so shocked. But it was the first she had ever heard of Jeremiah being some kind of doggy dog. Although he did have a hungry and lustful look in his eyes, when he was checking out Kendra, at Erika's album release party. Charva turned around, looked at Shannon, and rolled her eyes. "Just stare at her, until she leaves. Make her feel uncomfortable. Show her that you're not afraid of her."

DeDe looked up at Shannon but quickly dropped her head, when they made eye contact. She didn't want to cause anymore trouble. She had gone to jail, she had paid for an attorney and Stephan told her to leave and not say anything to her. "I really need to go."

Charva grabbed her by the arm. "Don't."

Shannon got up from her table and walked back into the restaurant.

"She's leaving," DeDe said, as she watched her disappear around the corner.

"No she's not. She's going to the ladies room. Get up and go in behind her."

"No," DeDe said and chuckled. "I've never known you to be such a shit starter. Are you nuts? I'm not going in there behind her."

"DeDe you have to. You have to walk in there with your head up high and show her that you are still here. Show the heifer you still got Stephan and her lies didn't stop anything. She's expecting you to call him and go running to him, because she's not. I know her type. Being married to Jeremiah Williams, I run into them all the time. They don't break and neither can you."

She was right, Shannon didn't bend for anyone and she always won the fights. She had come between her and Stephan too many times. DeDe couldn't get over the fact she lied and had them both thrown in jail. Also, she dangled Alexis over Stephan's head like a carrot. DeDe felt she was always the one to acquiesce. She always held her tongue, when it came to Shannon. The times when she should have lashed out at her, she refrained. She felt that if she had fought her, she would have had something real to go to jail for. DeDe jumped up out of her seat. "I'll be back."

When she walked into the ladies room, Shannon was standing in the mirror fluffing her hair. They looked each other up and down, before DeDe chuckled and rolled her eyes.

"Bitch, haven't you had enough," Shannon asked her.

"Have you?" DeDe retorted and stepped back out of the stall. Her heart began to race. It was just the two of them once again, without Stephan or the telephone wire to separate them. "You're just mad, because I got Stephan and you want 'im. He doesn't want you Shannon, so you had to make up some lie about him hitting you."

"Honey, please, don't nobody want him but you. I've been there; done that."

"Well, you have to stop being so angry and bitter about him moving on with his life."

"Angry and bitter. Where do you get off trying to tell me how I feel? Is that what he's telling you? Girl, you haven't the slightest clue. It's just like you insecure types to keep up trouble. Stephan and I have a child together and you are too insecure and void to even realize that. I don't want him. I just want him to do right by my child and to respect me."

"I know he didn't hit you."

"Maybe he did and maybe he didn't. You weren't there, so you don't know what happened now do you?"

"I know you are a lying bitch."

"Whatever," she said just before she walked out of the ladies room.

DeDe was so happy she stood up to her and sent her running. Charva rushed into the ladies room toward DeDe and began attacking her head. "What are you doing?" DeDe cried.

"Just go along with whatever I say."

"But what are you doing?"

"You'll see. She's going to get hers." She tore the sleeve of DeDe's shirt and without warning hauled off and swiped her thin skinny hand across DeDe's peachy tan face as hard as she could. DeDe screamed and held her face tight to stop the burning sensation. Charva looked her over and snatched her out of the ladies room by the arm, just before the two policemen and the manager of the restaurant approached them. "Ma'am, are you okay?" The Hispanic policemen asked.

DeDe didn't know what to say. She was trying to figure out what was going on. "She's in shock officer, but there's the lady out there who attacked her."

"Do you know her Miss?" The White policemen asked DeDe, but she stood holding her face not knowing whether or what to answer. She couldn't believe what was going on and Charva had her in the middle of this mess.

"Yes, they know each other officer. She's the jealous ex-girlfriend of my sister's fiancé. I'm Charva Williams, Jeremiah Williams, the super-producer's wife. I flew in from L.A. today and my sister and I were here celebrating my birthday. My sister had gotten up to go to the ladies room and that woman followed her in there and began screaming at her. When my sister tried to get away from her and walk out of the ladies room, she jumped her and began hitting her." Charva sighed through her outpour of drama. "I don't want any trouble officer, because my husband—"

"I understand Ma'am…Miss is that true? Is that what happened?"

DeDe looked at Charva and then the officer and nodded. By then, the White policeman was walking back into the restaurant leading Shannon in, by the arm as she yelled and screamed. "What the hell is going on?"

"She's an animal officer. I've never seen anything like it," Charva said.

"Ma'am, did you attack this young lady?" The Hispanic officer asked.

"No, she's a lying bitch."

Charva placed her arm around DeDe to comfort her. "You are a vicious animal! You could have made her lose her child. She's three months pregnant."

"I'm sorry Miss, we're going to have to take you down to the precinct."

"I am not going anywhere, because I don't know what you're talking about." She tried snatching herself away from the officer, but to no avail.

"Do you want to resist arrest and get in even more trouble?" The White officer turned her around and placed handcuffs on her.

"I can't believe this. That bitch is lying," Shannon bellowed, as the officer walked her to the door.

"Baby, what's going on?" A tall, light-skinned man asked Shannon and the officer, as he met them at the door.

"Baby, this is crazy," Shannon cried.

The man walked back toward DeDe, Charva and the Hispanic officer. "Officer, what's going on here?"

"Do you know the suspect?"

"Suspect," he replied. "She's my girlfriend."

"She's been charged with committing assault and battery on this young lady. Miss, you will have to come down to the station to file charges."

DeDe nodded.

"That's ridiculous." He ran out the door behind Shannon and the White policemen.

Charva left DeDe standing in the middle of the lobby, while she had gone to pay their bill. After the police car drove off with Shannon sitting in the back of it crying and her boyfriend tailing behind, DeDe walked out to her car and sat there in a daze and disbelief, at the drama that had just happened. Stephan and what she was going to tell him was all that was on her mind. She couldn't scream with joy for finally putting her foot down and getting even with Shannon, because she was afraid of how Stephan was going to react. Charva jumped into the car and began screaming. "She won't mess with you anymore."

"I can't believe what just happened."

"When you went into the ladies room, I called the police."

They both busted out laughing. "Girl you are crazy."

"It'll show her that two can play at that lying game."

"And you're damn right," DeDe said and they gave each other a high-five.

She later dropped Charva off at Roberta's house and she went back to work elated. She ran into Dionne and as bad as she wanted to tell her what she and Charva had done, she didn't. She didn't need to know. Also, DeDe didn't want to hear her damn 'Miss Righteous' mouth talk about what she wouldn't have done. DeDe was still upset with her for calling her ghetto, for standing by her man and arguing with Shannon. Sometimes acting ghetto is needed, when it comes to someone like Shannon, who is the essence of ghetto on a daily basis. Dionne is so quick to talk about Starla and everybody else acting so high-and-mighty, she does the same thing herself. She often gives good advice, DeDe must admit. But sometimes a sistah doesn't want the advice to leave her man, just because he's acting up a little. How about saying, 'Girl, hang in there. He'll realize how good you are, and straighten himself up.' And when it comes to dealing with Shannon, she doesn't need for Dionne to tell her to try understanding what Shannon is going through. She could give less than a damn about her hurting. How about saying, 'You go girl, and be a better bitch than the one you are dealing with.'

STEPHAN SHOULD HAVE been at work, but his car was parked in DeDe's driveway. She became nervous as hell. She felt he knew what she had done and all hell was about to break loose. She walked into the house and he was sitting on her sofa.

"What's up, what are you doing here? I thought you would be at work."

"What in the hell happened today? I thought I told you to leave!"

"What are you talking about?" DeDe's heart began racing as fast as it was, when she stood face to face with Shannon in the ladies room. How did he find out?

"Today at the restaurant."

DeDe dropped her keys on the console in the foyer and began explaining as if she was trying to talk her way out of an ass whipping. "Well, I was trying to leave, but she started calling me bitches and I had gone to the ladies room and she followed me in there."

"She said you followed her in there."

"I know you are not going to believe that lying bitch. We both spent time in jail, because of her lies. I went to the ladies room, she followed me in there, she began laughing and telling me I got what I deserved. She was still calling me out of my name, Stephan. So, I got tired of it and I called her a bitch back and she pushed me as hard as she could into the wall, which hurt my back, because that wall was solid brick. I told her I didn't want any trouble and I didn't want to fight her. Then she said, "Well Stephan isn't here to protect you now bitch", and she came at me. Evidently, the manager of the restaurant heard me screaming in the bathroom and he called the police. When the police got there, they saw me looking a mess with this bruise on my face and my hair going every which way. I tried to fight her back, but she was a damn wild woman. Baby, if you did hit her, I see why. I didn't have to tell the police anything. They knew she had attacked me, because she looked like she hadn't even been in a fight."

"Where was Charva, during all of this bullshit."

"She was waiting for me in the lobby, when she saw the police come to the bathroom. That's when she walked in."

"Shannon tells a whole different story."

"Yeah, because she's a liar."

"I am not going to be put in the middle of this shit with you and Shannon anymore."

"You're definitely not. It seems that with her going to jail, she's had a change of heart. I received a call from our attorney saying she dropped the charges against us."

"She was dropping them anyway."

"How do you know?" DeDe hoped he hadn't been talking to her. Not after what she's done to them. "You've been talking to her?"

"No, her mother called me yesterday at work and she made her drop them."

"I don't care. She should have never filed them in the first place, because she was lying. I didn't hit her and neither did you."

"She works for the state. If they find out she's in jail, she could lose her job."

"So what, I could have lost mine and you could have lost yours also, when she had the police come and pick us up. So what are you saying Stephan; what do you want me to do?"

He looked at her long and hard before answering. "Nothing."

21

WITH the radio blasting, Dionne ran around the room trying to get dressed while she listened to Sylvia and the response of the callers, as they read the new drama of Angelic and Tibias. Dionne didn't have time to sit and read along like she normally does, because she had a meeting with one of her new clients and she was running late.

A man that hits a woman whether she provoked him to or not is a weak, empty hearted, malicious fisted coward, who's insecure in his manhood." Sylvia read and paused for an Amen from her studio guest and Casey. *For those men who get their rocks off by hitting a woman they claim to have so much love and respect for; just imagine that woman being your grandmother, mother or sister. Someone you should truly love, and then imagine some man off the street puts his hard heavy fists to their heads, because they mouthed off to him and she was too helpless to fight him back. Let that marinade in the hearts of the men who have raised their fists to a woman. But to beat another woman in front of his insecure girlfriend, is his way of trying to prove to himself that he has extreme power over something in life, if it's not his own life."* "Tell it girl," Sylvia screamed. *"Angelic gleamed with excitement as she told me about the fight between Tibias and his child's mother the other day. I could have thrown up, but I did something better than that. I let her know how stupid and ghetto she really was for dealing with Tibias. It wasn't really much of a fight. It was more like an ass whipping from Tibias to his child's mother. Angelic stood by in the next room listing to this woman plead for Tibias to stop hitting her. At that very moment, she felt she could lay her insecurities to rest about him sleeping with his child's mother. He finally hated the woman she had so much envy toward. After all the grief this woman had caused her, when she had the power to keep Tibias wanting her, Angelic wouldn't dare try to stop him from hitting her. That whole ordeal means that he is a coward. If he would batter his child's mother, what makes her think one of these days he won't beat her too. She thinks he'll never do any of the things he's done to his child's mother to her, because he tells her that he loves her and he's never loved his child's mother; so she feels she's different. How different could she be, since he makes her cry and breaks-up with her every two weeks or so, because he wants to be with other women. She's too blind to see any of that. But like I told her before, it's not the child's mother she should be worried about. I have no doubt in my mind that his child's mother doesn't want him, but Angelic believes she does. She has formed her opinion based on what he keeps telling her. I believe he's the one that still loves his child's mother, most men do. But with Angelic being the woman who can help him when he gets into a financial bind, he'll do anything to keep her and his pockets secure. He had come close to losing her before, because he didn't take sides when she and his child's mother had gotten into an argument on the phone. Previously, he would say 'I'm not getting involved in any of this mess'. Right now, I'm sure he will tell Angelic anything that she wants to hear because he realizes that she's a first class fool. He's not going to upset the fool that helps pay his bills and child support. So, he ran a game on her and she fell for it, but under one condition. The condition is that he turn his back on his child and show her that he has absolutely no love for the woman that carried that child. He had told his child's mother that she wasn't welcome at his house and* that he didn't want to see the child, until the child was old enough to deal with him on her own. Angelic thought he had done it for her, because he loved her and only her.

I've always thought most men to be strong. But for any man to allow a woman to come in and destroy his relationship with his child and the woman that gave birth to his child isn't strong. My father and mother were never married, but there was no woman that could tell my father she didn't want my mother calling the house or me coming over to my father's house; whenever I wanted him or my father wanted to see me. He would not be manipulated, because I had his blood running through my veins and my mother was the woman who had given him the joy of fatherhood, whether they were together or not. But I understand it has to take a mature, unselfish man with unconditional love for his child to not be put in a situation to have to choose between his child and his insecure girlfriend. A real man in this sort of situation keeps everything in check, to assure that his relationship with his child doesn't suffer. Yes, there are some babymamas who don't make it easy to deal with a man with a child. She's extremely difficult, because she's a woman who had no intention of being a part of the rapidly growing statistic of Black women who are finding themselves single parents. And I say that to state, there is no such thing as babymama drama. However, there is such a thing as a woman watching a man walk away and leaving her to be a mother and father, while he starts his life over; as if he didn't just leave one behind. A woman coming to that reality will hurt and act out her pain, hoping someone can give her the help she needs to heal. I know men are scarce, so a lot of women have to put on their insecurity suits. Some women are threatened by another woman who is just innocently walking on the same side of the street that she and her man are walking on; so forget about what happens when they have to deal with a babymama or the child. These insecurities must stop. Because a man that turns his back on his child, will eventually angrily turn his back on the insecure woman that did everything possible to come between him and the woman that brought *that child into this world. But it's only a very secure, confident, unselfish woman that knows when he says 'it's over' between he and the ex; that it's over. Therefore, there's no need for the insecure girlfriend drama. And to the men who have fallen prey to the jealous, insecure girlfriend drama and have turned their backs on their child; don't be surprised if you are not welcomed back into that child's life, when you finally realize you've been bamboozled.*

Sylvia sighed. "I got to give it to her, she did it."

"Damnnn... If you're not making love, what in the hell are you doing at 8:30a.m. this Friday morning? My God. She has hit the nail on the head and all hell has broken loose. Look at those phone lines light up. People have something to say about this one," Casey said.

Dionne hoped one of those people wasn't DeDe or one of her friends, because Charlotte had done it again. She hadn't made the column fictitious enough. It hit too close to home. Dionne was happy she didn't tell Charlotte about the arrests or jail episodes.

"But what does she mean there's no such thing as babymama drama?" Casey asked.

"And she's right. When I was growing up, there was no such thing. My mama and daddy weren't together either and my dad's wife couldn't tell him anything about me or my brothers and sisters. She tried to start with him about my mother, but she was quickly put back in check. The woman that took the man away from his family was always looked at as the one in the wrong, not the babymama," Sylvia said.

"No one has sympathy for mothers who are single parents anymore, they just think they should just move on. Caller, what do you think?"

"I think that Angelic deserves everything that's coming to her in the future. She's crazy and she better think again, if she believes that low life won't beat her up one day and let his new woman watch. My child's father doesn't even talk to my child right now, because his girlfriend and he won't accept any of my phone calls. When his girlfriend is at his house, he will look at the caller I.D. and see that it's me, and ignore the call."

"What are you calling for? For the child or just to talk?" Casey asked.

"For the child. But if I did just call to talk, why would he not answer the phone anyway? I'm not a woman who's trying to get with him; I'm his child's mother."

Sylvia chuckled. "What would you have to talk to him about if it's not about the child? Y'all are not like that anymore, it's over and he has a girl-friend."

"So what. He and I are not enemies and we have a child together. It's his girlfriend who feels insecure. When we do try to talk like civilized adults, she messes-up the ability for us to be friends; just like that damn Angelic does with Tibias and his child's mother. It's the girlfriends and the weak babydaddys who give babymamas such a bad name."

"The 'Frustrated Friend' has struck the nerves of some men as well as the women. WHEE, caller, you're on the line."

"There *is* such a thing as babymama drama. I got one and she flattens my tires, if I'm late one day with child support. She sends the authorities on my job and she calls me and curses me out, whenever she feels like it. She tells me I can't see my son, if I'm going to have him around another woman and I respect her wishes, so I don't."

"Now I ask you, is that taking it a little too far?" Casey asked and chuck-led. "I have a friend who's going through the same thing right now. Because he doesn't agree with all of his child's mother's demands, she doesn't allow him to see the child."

"And I would rather see my child than not too." Sylvia said.

"So would I. But how long is that supposed to go on; until she finds some-one else?" Casey asked and chuckled.

"My girlfriend doesn't like it, but of course she's not a mother. And my girlfriend tells me that I'm taking my child's mother's side, but I don't think I am. I feel I'm doing what's right for my child. I don't think just because I have a girlfriend that she has to be with my child every minute that I'm with my child. I know a lot of men don't think like that, but I'm also aware of those women that change after marriage. My dad married one like that. We, his own children were not allowed at his house, because his new wife felt we were too bad and she also didn't like my mother calling the house. When they were dating, she loved us, but it was after she got the ring, when she began tripping," the caller said.

"And that's how DeDe is playing it," Dionne said, as she stood in the mirror putting on mascara.

"She caused all the drama between my mom and dad, but my dad was too blind to see that. In a sense, it is the girlfriend that causes drama also. But then again, it could be the babymama in some cases as well," the caller said.

"WHEE caller, you're on the air."

"I don't care what that article says. My boyfriend has a crazy babymama and she and I can't stand each other. She's always trying to put the kids off on him to take care of every single weekend. She's their mother and they should be with her, but she's out there in the clubs or running the streets trying to find them a daddy to help her take care of them. I can't wait until she does, because my boyfriend and I can't do anything because we always have the kids. I'm tired of it."

"Do you have children?" Sylvia asked.

"No."

"So who are you to say the children should be with the mother most of the time just because you and their father can't do anything? Start doing things that include the children."

"Okay," Dionne agreed, as she buttoned up her suit jacket and pants. She felt that Byron needed to start planning things that included AJ since he says there's so much for the two of them to do on Friday nights.

"He has children and he's supposed to have as much responsibility for them as their mother. No one should have the child more than the other, if they are both active parents in the child's life," Sylvia told the caller.

"Is he complaining?" Casey asked.

"No, but I told him he better do something, before I take my ass out of there."

"See that's a girlfriend interfering with the relationship of a father and his child," Sylvia said, as she disconnected the call.

Dionne was excited about the response.

"Because she's self-centered. WHEE, caller you are on the line," Casey said.

"My situation is different from what y'all are talking about. My child's mother's husband is the insecure one in my situation. He was so afraid that my child's mother and me might get back together that he packed her and my son up and moved them to another state six years ago, and I have no way of knowing where they are. I haven't seen my son in six years."

"Damn. Now that's wrong; but like we can't place all the blame on the insecure girlfriends or the babymamas, you can't place all of the blame on your child's mother's husband."

"And I don't. She knows where I live. She could at least send me a picture or a letter just to let me know how my son is doing, but she's angry."

"About what?"

"She's still upset because I wasn't there during her pregnancy with my son; only because I didn't believe the child was mine. And when I finally realized he was mine after a blood test three years later, I was ready to take on my responsibility and be a father, but her husband said, 'No you are not needed.' I had even gone to the courts to start paying child support and she refused it. She told the courts she didn't want my money. A month later they moved out of the state."

"Damn. She doesn't want your child support, bro she's beyond angry. I don't know too many sistahs that will turn down child support. WHEE, caller you are on the line."

"My child's mother and I are not together. I'm dating and she's not. We have a wonderful relationship. We both take equal responsibility in raising the child, because we laid down and had a child together and that child didn't ask to come into this world. My child's mother is more than welcome to call my house and my girlfriend can be sitting right next to me, when I answer the phone. I have nothing to hide. I would never tell her she couldn't come to my house. I don't give a damn if it's my girlfriend's house, she's welcome. And to put my hands on her; I would never think to stoop so low. My girlfriend got me hooked on this 'No More LoveMaking' thing. This Tibias; he can't be real, because I don't know any brotha like 'im. If a man is not going to be with his child's mother, he should at least respect her. My girlfriend has no opinion about my child or her mother, because we are not married. Even if we were, I'm too much of a man to allow her to say what type of relationship I should have with my child or her mother."

"What are you listening to?" Byron asked, as Dionne jumped at the sound of his voice, while he stood in the doorway of her bedroom. She didn't hear him walk up the stairs.

Her heart began racing; she was busted and knowing him he was about to go off. "I thought you were at the gym?" She asked and looked at her watch.

"I just decided to go running around the block a couple of times." He wiped the dripping sweat from his face with his t-shirt. "I was downstairs listening to Casey and Sylvia talk about Charlotte's column. That is *her* column they're talking about isn't it?" He didn't give her time to answer. "I thought you told her to pull it?"

"I did, but she refused," Dionne said, as she pretended to be in a heavy mental debate on which black pumps to wear.

"And you're still telling her DeDe's business?" Byron asked with a smug look on his face.

"No, that stuff's all made up," she said, as she tried to look him in the eyes.

"Didn't Stephan and his child's mother fight the other week and DeDe was there?"

She skeptically answered while nodding her head and looking at him. "Yeah."

"So you're still telling her."

His disappointed stare tore into Dionne like a knife. She wished the floor would just swallow her up to keep her from having to go through his integration.

"Dionne, don't you think that you are being two-faced and stabbing DeDe in the back?" he asked her just before he walked off shaking his head.

Actually I don't, she thought as she rolled her eyes and she stood up from the bed to slide her foot into the size eleven Prada pumps.

"WHEE, caller you're on the air."

"I agree with Tibias. My babymama can't call my house, she can't come by my house and she doesn't know where I live. I also know it might sound ghetto and wrong."

"We didn't say that, but you must know that it's ghetto and wrong; otherwise why are you doing it?"

"She's crazy. She has a boyfriend, but he's not the man that she wants to be with so she still gives me hell. She wants us to be together and I don't want to be with her, just to raise a child in a two-parent home. I got to be happy and I have to love a woman, before I marry her. Right now, she doesn't allow me to see my children but that's okay, because my fiancé has two children and I'm helping her raise them, because their father isn't around.'"

"Now what's wrong with that picture?" Casey asked. "Here's R. Kelly with one of my favorites '*I Wish*'."

Dionne grabbed her purse and briefcase from behind her bedroom door, turned off the radio, rushed down the stairs, and dashed out of the house, before Byron could come back out of the bathroom to scold her some more.

22

*TECHNO.*com is a black owned technology and internet company that advertises for job openings all over the world. Derwin Edwards, a multi-millionaire out of the Silicon Valley is the owner with several successful .com companies under his belt. DeDe had called on this account for months, before she received a call back to meet with him and several board members. The purpose of the gathering was to introduce the company to the public and promote their efforts to become one of the largest IT career placement .com companies in the world. DeDe was thirty minutes early, so she sat in the lobby reviewing her press release, as she waited for Renee Collier, the human resources director to escort her to the conference room. She sat nervously watching everyone who walked through the door. She nearly fainted as she and Dionne glared into each other's eyes, when she walked through the door. Techno.com was her client.

"What are you doing here?" Dionne asked DeDe, while trying to catch her breath from rushing from the parking deck, to the elevator through the office doors.

"I have a meeting," DeDe told her, as she waited for Dionne's explanation for being there.

"I have a meeting with Latrice Baker in marketing."

"I have a meeting with Renee Collier and Derwin Edwards," DeDe told her.

"There must be some type of mistake. Brad has been working on this account for me. He arranged this meeting."

DeDe didn't give a damn, although she felt there was some modicum of truth to what she was hearing, because Dionne and Brad were friends. He always gave her accounts, but she had called on the account also and as far as she was concerned, it was hers and she was going to keep her scheduled meeting with Renee and Derwin.

Renee Collier walked around the corner. "Hi I'm Renee Collier." She extended her hand between both of them, waiting to see who would reach and speak first.

"Hi, I'm DeDe Wilson," DeDe said and shook her hand.

"And I'm Dionne Scales. There seems to be some type of misunderstanding. DeDe and I are both from Stein and Stockton."

"Yes," Renee said with a confused look on her face, while attempting to figure out the misunderstanding.

"Brad Michaels spoke with Latrice Baker, your marketing coordinator and she scheduled a meeting with me this morning."

"Yes, I see," she answered skeptically while pondering her point. "Do you need me to get her for you?"

"Yes…No," Dionne took a deep breath and smiled through her frustration. "Ms. Wilson and I are here from the same company to offer you and Ms. Baker the same services."

"Oh, I'm very sorry for the misunderstanding," Renee apologized.

"But Mrs. Collier, I've been leaving messages for you on a daily basis and I scheduled this time to meet with you and Derwin Edward," DeDe told Renee.

"Yes, I remember but if she's already met with Latrice—"

"She hasn't."

"Well, I'm ready to meet when you are."

"DeDe, can I speak to you for a brief moment?" Dionne asked her.

222

"Sure." They walked off to the corner.

"It's obvious there has been some type of misunderstanding. Like I told you before, Brad did arrange this meeting and this is my account. I know you went behind my back and stole the Bushel and Coleman account. I'll let you have that, but this one is mine."

"I didn't steal anything. I explained to you before, Chris Shultz gave me that account, because they asked for me. Stealing is not even a part of my character. I don't care how much the commission is," DeDe told her.

They both looked over at Renee', who was getting impatient as she cleared her throat and checked her watch.

"What time were you scheduled to have your meeting?" DeDe asked Dionne.

"Eight-thirty."

DeDe looked at her watch and smiled, but she was dead serious. "You are twenty minutes late and since I was here first, I'll just go in and have the meeting with her." DeDe walked off before Dionne could object; not giving a damn how mad she was.

As Derwin walked into the room, she expected him to look like a nerd with a lot of money and nothing to do with it. In other words, she expected him to look like a black version of Bill Gates. But instead, in strides a well-groomed, extremely polished, professional man with no wedding band. All of his success and no one to share it with; she thought, as she stood at the front of the room. She waited for everyone to be seated, before she introduced herself and present her ideas outside the realm of their normal marketing procedures that would introduce the company to the public along with flooding all media outlets. Her intent was to encourage them to hire her as their PR spokesperson. DeDe finally got a chance to utilize what she learned as a marketing major, during the presentation. She had suggested that they have the largest three-day job fair in the world. If it's promoted correctly, which it will be; the company should expect to draw 1.5 million in attendance. She spoke with a vibrant smile on her face and exuded the enthusiasm of an energetic, young, White cheerleader who loved her job and was good at it. She gave each of them the press release she would be sending to the media and universities to publicize the event. The meeting lasted for an hour, which included questions and answers. She won them over with her innovative ideas and they welcomed her aboard.

After the meeting, each of them came up to introduce themselves and shake her hand. Derwin didn't ask any questions and remained seated, while looking over the press release and the Stein and Stockton portfolio. He approached her after everyone had left the room.

"Hello Ms. Wilson, I'm Derwin Edwards." He extended his hand out to her. His voice was deep, yet pleasant to DeDe's ears.

"Nice to meet you." She became nervous as she looked up into his round dark brown steel-like eyes.

"Where do you get all of your energy?" He smiled.

DeDe smiled and shrugged her shoulders feeling like she should say something, but she was too nervous to speak. His mannerism and demeanor had her speechless.

"You look very young to have as many connections as you say you do. How long have you been with Stein and Stockton? You failed to inform us of that."

No, I didn't. I just didn't think it was important, she thought, and answered. "Six months."

"What were you doing before then, college?"

"No, I've been out of college for fourteen years now." But she cared not to mention that she didn't graduate. She prayed that he wouldn't ask her what college she had attended. She would have said, Howard University but she dropped out during her junior year, after going to L.A. to visit Charva. She had gained her experience as an events planner by lying her way through the doors of a company that planned celebrity and entertainment weddings and parties. She worked there for six years before she grew tired of being overlooked for promotions and raises.

"So you're not twenty-three years old?" He asked with what seemed like a disappointed tone.

"No, but thank you for the compliment," she said and smiled anyway.

"It was nice meeting you Ms. Wilson." He extended his hand out to her again and walked out of the room.

She packed up all of her belongings, disbelieving how abrupt the conversation ended. Was he trying to hit on her and decided not to, because she wasn't twenty-three years old? What nerve. She didn't look a day over twenty-five and he didn't look a day over thirty-five. She mouthed to herself, "Humph, men and their standards. I guess I'm old-enough to have my own mind, so he can't control me with his money."

As she rushed down the hall to the elevator, she bumped into him.

"Are you in a rush Ms. Wilson?" He asked as he held the door open for her to get onto the elevator. "I guess with it being Friday, you have a lot planned for tonight."

"No, I'm going to the beauty salon."

"On a Friday night?"

"Every Friday night as a matter of fact," she chuckled. "But I have to get back to work right now to make some phone calls."

He didn't respond. The elevator stopped on the second floor and both of them got off heading their separate ways. "Have a nice weekend Ms. Wilson," he said, as he ambled over to his black Bentley coup that was parked a couple of feet away from the elevator bank, in a corner all by itself. He didn't even look at her, as she walked down ten spaces to her car.

She threw her briefcase and laptop in the backseat. She saw him out of the corner of her eye driving slowly toward her, as she pretended looking for something in her trunk, all the while hoping he would stop and strike up a conversation. As he drove closer, she was afraid he would drive past her so she stopped him by nearly jumping in front of his car. She couldn't believe she had done that, but then again she could. She was sexy and she believed he really wanted her to stop him. Elliott had given her the confidence to know that she was sexy and beautiful and it was okay to initiate a conversation with a man, as well as take the lead role, when engaging in sex. He assured her that it was a turn-on; if she didn't show any man the emotional baggage she carried after being hurt and scarred time after time by Stephan. Men would believe she was a woman that would not misconstrue or mistake love with an orgasm. Elliott didn't say it in those exact words, but she could read into what he was trying to say, during one of their men are from Mars and women are from Venus conversations. With Derwin she wouldn't show any type of emotion or love, because she was sure women came a dime a dozen for him and she would not be one of them. She just wanted to let loose on him sexually and show him all the tricks she knew as a thirty-four year old, that a twenty-three year old has yet to learn.

"Hi," he said, as he stopped.

"Hi." Just before she leaned into his car, she turned her back to him and undid the top three buttons of her shirt to show a little cleavage, which might entice his imagination of what her peachy-tan body looked like nude. "You never told me if you liked the idea. Everyone else told me that they did."

"Yeah, I like it. If I didn't, we wouldn't be going through with it."

She smiled extra sexy, while feeling relieved at the same time. "I was worried."

He looked straight ahead, as if he was fighting himself not to look at her. Was he gay or just in a rush? She took it that he was just in a rush, because he was far too handsome to be gay. But flashing back to the men Kendall has been with, he could be.

"So, I guess because I'm not twenty-three was the reason you ended our conversation so abruptly."

When he looked up into her eyes, it did something to her. She could have jumped into his car, sat on his lap and kissed him. Since Elliott, she now had a hot and aggressive side.

"Excuse me?"

"In our brief conversation in the conference room, you asked if I was twenty-three years old. When I told you I was thirty-four, you basically told me to have a nice day."

"Oh, you seemed like you were trying to get out of there and I didn't want to take up anymore of your time."

"You weren't."

He sighed while looking at his expensive looking watch. DeDe was sure that it was, because of the overall classy, polished, well-manicured, expensive; money is no object look that he possesses. "Okay, well… I need to be going, traffic is hell on Fridays in Houston."

"Yes, it is." But it was only eleven thirty in the morning and there was no traffic. She was beginning to feel that either he really wasn't interested in her, because she wasn't twenty-three or her looking him straight in his dark brown eyes was making him nervous. She felt she was making him nervous.

"You have a nice weekend Ms. Wilson."

"The same to you Mr. Edwards." She stood watching him, as he drove off. She couldn't help but embrace his challenge for her to go after him. Not that she wasn't happy with Stephan, but Derwin was intriguing, a new challenge and rich.

WHEN DEDE GOT back to the office, there was a message on her voicemail for her to come to Brad's office. She knew Dionne had told him about the situation with the Techno.com account and she was pissed. Brad's secretary wasn't at her normal 'guard dog' post, so she reluctantly walked into his office without having to exchange pleasantries. She did not want to give up her account, but Dionne's years of friendship was thicker than the phone calls and hard work it took DeDe to obtain the account. DeDe walked into his office and sat down. He began to go into some off the wall spiel about what Stein and Stockton stood for and DeDe wanted to get to the real reason why she was there.

"Brad, I know why you called me in here and it's not to tell me the history of the company. I called on that account without the knowledge you were doing the same thing for Dionne. That account is mine."

"Dionne has been with the company for ten years and I've never known her to give up an account; but she gave you the Bushel and Coleman account to help you enhance your portfolio."

"She didn't give me anything. They asked for me and you know it."

No More LoveMaking

He sighed. "Well, I have the authority to make all final decisions on any account I choose and the Techno.com account belongs to Dionne," was the way he simply put it, with no room for any objections from DeDe.

"Fine." It was time she started looking for another job and she was going to start the first thing Monday morning.

She jumped out of the chair and stormed out of his office. She had to give up her account. She grabbed the Techno.com folder from her desk, stormed into Dionne's office and threw the folder on her desk. "You can have the account."

"Hold on. No, let me call you back," Dionne said and hung up the phone. "Don't come in here like you are giving me something. That account was mine in the first place."

"How do you figure? We both called on it, but since you are good friends with Brad it's yours, right? Here is the signed contract, the press release I gave to them and the media line-up for their job fair."

Dionne didn't bother to look through the folder, she was still angry and she wanted DeDe to just get the hell out of her face and take her folder with her. Once again, she was not to be trusted.

"There are no hard feelings Dionne, just a misunderstanding. You called on the account and so did I."

"I have a lot of work to do."

DeDe turned around and walked out of her office. Before she could close the door behind her, she was already thinking that there was absolutely no chance of her ever seeing Derwin again.

23

$\mathcal{I}$ $\mathcal{T}$ was DeDe's fifth week retouch appointment, at the beauty salon. She was thirty minutes late, due to traffic. But being a long-time customer and the best friend to her beautician's sister, Roberta held her spot. She drank her glass of wine, as she sat in the chair listening to the conversations going on around her while Boo, Roberta's assistant, based her head with thick grease. Her scalp burned so easily. Just because she was getting her scalp based didn't mean she was going to be the next one in Roberta's chair. There were two ladies ahead of her. But with the hot conversation and the bonding amongst sistahs, there was no need for wanting to rush. The women were loud as usual, during their Friday night 'KiKi sessions'. They were relaxing in the salon's lounge, speaking openly to one another; as if they've known each other for years or as if they were family. There were several conversations going on at once and DeDe tried to listen in on each of them, because each topic had some component that she could relate to.

"Well, my husband left me for another woman two years ago and I let him leave without a fight," a woman sitting across from DeDe said. She had seen her many times in the beauty salon, but she didn't know her name. She wore a huge platinum princess cut diamond wedding ring; so DeDe assumed she was married.

The woman handed her beautician pieces of rolling paper. "I knew of this other woman for months; before she began calling the house asking for him and hanging up in my face, when I would answer. But I never said anything. You see, I made him think I was blind to the fact of knowing something was going on, while hoping he would realize what he was doing was wrong. I thought that he would stop it, but he never did."

"They never do. They are too weak and caught up to realize that what they are doing is wrong," Dorothy Phillips said, as she walked over to the dryer and sat down.

"When he came home one morning after being with her all night; he packed his things and told me he was leaving. I didn't cry like I thought I would and I didn't beg him for God's sake, the children's or mine. I just let him walk. And all the clothes he left behind, I neatly packed them into a box and put them in the garage for him."

All of the women stared at her like she was crazy. He left her for another woman; she neatly packed his things and did not burn them, when she had every right.

"You are a good one, because I would have killed his ass." Dorothy said, just before she pulled the hood of the dryer down over her head.

She chuckled. "I couldn't kill him, he was the father of my children and we were still legally married. He just left me for another woman, that's all. He wasn't worth going to jail for and ruining my children's or my life."

"I guess you're right, but when he left, didn't you feel like your life had ended anyway?" Kimber Patton asked. DeDe looked at her and rolled her eyes, because she didn't like her. She hated to hear her talk, because of her annoying lisp and her mouth full of bulky braces that seemed like they were always covered with saliva. She was forty years old with braces; and there was nothing worse than an older woman with a mouth full of silver tracks going across her teeth. DeDe didn't like her ever since she put up a fuss about Roberta allowing DeDe to leap-frog over everyone else that had been waiting to have their hair done. DeDe had an important meeting she couldn't be late for and she had asked everyone if they would mind if she could go before them. They all allowed her to go ahead, except big-hipped, tinsel teeth Kimber, who got up and walked out.

"My life had ended in a sense, but then again it was reborn."

Everyone was with her, until she started talking about that reborn shit. When a man breaks a woman's heart, there's no optimistic way of looking at it. Maybe it should be, but placing the blame and allowing the heart to be filled with bitterness is a lot easier and more human. Being reborn is the last phase of the healing process and it takes every day of two to three years, before that point is reached.

DeDe's number was called for her turn to have her nail fill-ins and pedicure done. She grabbed another glass of wine and walked to the rear of the beauty salon, which was the spa. There was a conversation going on back there also, and once again DeDe became all ears. She didn't know any of the women by name, but she had seen them once or twice.

"A woman that asks a man to marry her is hard up," one of the pedicurist said, as she scrapped away at dead skin from the bottom of her client's foot.

"That's not true, especially if she's been with the brotha for some years. It ain't nothing wrong with her asking him to marry her," a woman getting a manicure said.

"It's hard up, when she knows he doesn't want her and she ask him any-way and months later he turns around and throws it back in her face," the second pedicurist added. "That's the part that I don't think I could handle. If a man said to me 'you are the one who asked me to marry you. Hell, we could have just stayed the way we were as far as I'm concerned.' Girl, I would have to kill him, because he knows I was hard up in the first place. When a woman asks a man to marry her, she's sort of taking away from him being a man."

Some women agreed by shaking their heads.

"I'll never ask a man to marry me," a woman said, as she walked over to the sink to wash the acrylic from her hands.

"Neither would I," another agreed.

"I don't find anything wrong with it. I asked my husband and he accepted and he didn't look at me like I was crazy. We've been married for four years now and not once has he thrown it back in my face," Brienna Monroe, the flight attendant said, as she got up and strolled over to the massage table. She has a bad case of vitiligo. Just two years ago, she had the prettiest chestnut brown complexion. Now she's nearly as transparent as Michael Jackson. The only visible areas that are still brown are her hands and feet. As she stretched out in a prone position on the table, she sighed and retorted, "We are now living in the new millennium and men are open to women taking control."

"Did you get down on one knee?" A woman asked and everyone laughed with her.

"No, I asked him over an elegant dinner."

DeDe didn't find anything wrong with asking a man to marry. As a matter of fact, she was seriously thinking about asking Stephan, if he didn't move his ass to ask her first. She wasn't going to wait another second, minute, hour, day, week, month or year for him to ask. They've been together for three years, and she knows that he loves her and he wants to be with her the rest of his life as much as she wants to be with him. So, they should be married, whether he asks her or she asks him. His fear and not having the money for the huge ring he believes she deserves, is what's holding him back. But she's in no real rush to ask him tonight to marry her. She's waited this long, she can wait another three months. If he doesn't ask her by then, she's asking him with no problem.

ROBERTA ALWAYS HOOKED DeDe up just right and she was always satisfied, when she got up out of her chair. She never cut her hair too short and she never styled it in a way DeDe had to go behind her with a comb and style it differently. DeDe glanced at herself in the rearview mirror, as she drove home and raked her fingers through her short flips and bangs. She looked beautiful. She wished she had some place to go besides home. It was a Friday night, all of her bills were paid and she still had money to burn. She received more money than she had anticipated on her commission check. Stephan was at work and if she goes home, she would be bored and twiddling her thumbs, while waiting for him. She was looking too pretty to do that, and besides she was tired of sitting at home on Friday nights waiting for Stephan to come over, if his friends didn't persuade him to go out for drinks after work first. She didn't want to go over to her girlfriends' houses and sit up and do nothing. She might as well sit at her own house and do little of nothing. She felt like doing something she doesn't normally do. She felt like wearing that thousand-dollar Versace dress Elliott bought her and going to a club dancing all night long, but she didn't want to go by herself. All of her girlfriends were married and they no longer found the clubs or anything that was not couple oriented interesting. Before DeDe thought about it twice, she grabbed her cell phone out of her purse and called Elliott. She had been thinking about him, but never had the nerve to call again. She didn't know what she would say other than 'hello'. Being that the two of them almost had a thang goin' and then he stopped by her house and her ex-boyfriend answered the door; something more than just 'hello' needed to be said. It had been eight weeks, since she last spoke to him. She figured enough time had passed. With no doubt in her mind, she knew he had thought about her, but his pride wouldn't let him call her. He was too crazy about her to totally put her out of his mind. He must have thought about her once or twice. Men are men. They can tell a woman a thousand times in one day that they do not want to get involved in a relationship, then they knock themselves out wining and dining the same woman. They will have the best sex of their lives with this woman, enjoy having her around every second of every day, and still fool around. Regardless of what happens, they find time to think about the one they didn't want a relationship with, but was with her nearly all the time. Elliott had to have thought about her, she just hoped he wouldn't play the machismo role and hang up on her, like he had before.

He answered. "Hello."

"Hi. What's up? What do you have planned for tonight?" She asked him in a chipper mood, but surprised he answered.

"Nothing really. What's up with you?"

"Oh, not much. I was expecting to get your voice-mail."

"So why did you call?"

"I was going to leave a message. You're not at the restaurant working tonight?"

"No. The budget allowed us to hire someone to work weekends."

"I guess that's good. I was wondering if you wanted to go out tonight? I'm in the mood to dance."

"I don't club."

"Oh sorry, I forgot. You did tell me that. What about dinner my treat?"

"I've already eaten."

"Bowling then…meet me at Victory Lanes in thirty minutes. I'm going to go home and change into some jeans and I'll meet you there. You owe me a game, since you beat me last time. Let me redeem myself by showing you that I'm truly a near pro-bowler."

He paused and let out a short sigh, before giving her an answer. "Fine… but I would rather pick you up. I don't want to get there and have to wait. Thirty minutes for you is actually an hour and thirty minutes."

She chuckled. "You think you know me don't you?"

"I thought I did," he said sarcastically.

She didn't respond. A response would only give him a reason to be more sarcastic and to begin asking questions, to which she had no answers, only lies. She and Stephan were back together and she does love him. But no, she did not use him to get over Stephan. Although she didn't think it was a great idea for him to pick her up at her house, she said "Okay" anyway. She would make sure they were back before twelve. She will also call Stephan on his cell phone just before she leaves to go home, to make sure he wasn't en route to her house as well. "Meet me at my house in thirty minutes." She hung up the phone smiling, because he was over it and they were friends again. She said to herself, 'although everything isn't totally cool with me and Elliott, I wonder if we're going to sleep together tonight.' She wouldn't stop him, if he tried to get some. But they would have to go to his house.

HER HEART SANK and her stomach divided into several knots, when Stephan greeted her at the door. She tried to smile through the puzzled look on her face, as she tried to figure out how in the hell did·he get a key. He told her after they had broken up that he had thrown the key away.

"Hey baby," he said, and kissed her. He led her through the hall to the candle lit living room. Joe's CD was playing in the background and a bottle of Cristal was sitting in a champagne bucket on the coffee table. She remembered Kendra saying how expensive this champagne was. What was the occasion, she wondered. She hoped he wasn't up to one of his schemes for money from her. She didn't have any extra money; and what she had; she wasn't going to give it to him. She had doled out the twenty- five hundred dollars for the attorney for both of them that they didn't need, because Shannon dropped the charges.

He sat her down on the sofa and positioned himself beside her. She was nervous. In fifteen minutes Elliott would be ringing the doorbell, if not sooner.

"Baby," she said, as she anxiously jumped up off the sofa. "Why don't we go to the club tonight. I'm in the mood to dance."

He smiled and pulled her back down. "Baby, we'll have time for that later." She nervously looked at her watch and the front door.

"You know I love you," he said turning her face toward him. "And I care so much about you. When you had gone, I thought I had lost you forever. I prayed to God that if he would bring you back to me, I would do right by you. You are the perfect woman and because of that, you are the woman I want to know the secret tours of my heart, to wake up beside you for the next fifty years, and to share my name and have my children. You are the woman I want to marry and make my wife."

Her eyes filled with tears and she trembled with joy, as he got down on one knee and pulled out a small black ring size box out of his pocket. He was going to ask her to marry him and take the ring back in the same sentence, as soon as Elliott rings the doorbell. She couldn't let that happen.

"Yes," she sang anxiously.

"Calm down baby." He swallowed his nervousness, took her hand and placed the princess cut six-karat diamond on her finger. "Will you marry me?"

"Yes, yes I will marry you."

He took a deep breath relieved that she had said yes. They hugged and kissed. "Let's celebrate." He reached for the champagne.

DeDe looked at her watch. It had been thirty-two minutes, since she spoke with Elliott. "Baby, let's get out of the house and celebrate. We'll bring the champagne with us. I'm just too excited to sit around the house with this big rock on my finger."

He had never seen her so excited. "Cool, but I need to call Melvin and Dedrick and tell them."

"We'll call them in the car." She grabbed her purse and ran around the room blowing out the candles. "I'm so excited. I'm going to be Mrs. Stephan Brown. We have to stop by Bridget's and Marie's." She pulled him out of the door, handed him the keys to drive, and opened the garage door. She did everything but place her foot on top of his, as she told him to go and he sped out of the driveway. They left just in time. As they turned out of her subdivision, she spotted Elliott's grey Lexus turning in. She became even more excited.

Once she was in the car, she decided against going over to her girlfriends, she would call them tomorrow. They made reservations at Houston's restaurant and told Melvin and Dedrick to meet them there. As their waiter led them to their seats, DeDe spotted Dionne. She couldn't believe it; she was finally going to see Byron. "Baby, there's Dionne," she whispered. She was no longer angry about the incident that had happened in the office, earlier that day. She was over it; she was engaged and happy. DeDe grabbed Stephan's hand and they walked over to her table. "Hey girl," DeDe said. She had startled Dionne. "It's just me." DeDe reached down and hugged her.

Dionne had to hug her back, although she was still angry. She was even angrier that they would run into each other in this restaurant. "Hello Stephan," Dionne said.

"Hi."

"Byron, this is DeDe and her boyfriend Stephan."

Byron stood up to shake both of their hands. "Nice to meet you."

"So how are you?" Dionne asked, while trying to keep a smile on her face.

"Great," DeDe said, as she threw her hand out for Dionne to see her ring.

"Congratulations!" Dionne got up to hug her again. "So have you set a date yet?"

"No, but it will probably be next spring."

"Or sooner," Stephan said.

The three of them looked at him smiling.

"Well, congratulations to you once again."

"Thank you. We'll talk on Monday," DeDe said, as she and Stephan walked over to their table.

Stephan couldn't wait to begin talking. "No wonder she didn't want you to meet that niggah. He's gay just like she is and he's more feminine than she is too. Did you see the way he was holding that glass? Just like a bitch. He seems more feminine than Kendall and we know how much of a sissy his ass is."

DeDe felt embarrassed for Dionne and even more embarrassed for wishing she had a man just like she had. It was all coming to light why Dionne didn't want her to meet Byron. Maybe she felt he was effeminate and she knew others would think it also. But Charlotte met him and she would be the first to tell her if she thought he was flaming or not, because she was her best friend. DeDe didn't believe Dionne was gay. Although she couldn't understand why she was with Byron who looked like he was. She was attractive enough to get a more masculine man. DeDe had already created a mental picture in her mind of what she thought Byron looked like, as much as Dionne bragged about him. She imagined that he would be a tall, light-skinned, masculine brother with a low haircut, thick mustache, beautiful smile and a drop-dead body. He looked nothing like she thought. Byron wasn't bad looking, but he didn't seem like he was all man either.

"From now on, when she comes to work bragging about how great of a weekend they had and how well he treats her; don't come home telling me about that shit, because I will never be like him. It's obvious he's more in touch with his feminine side than I will ever be," Stephan said and laughed.

DeDe looked over her shoulder at Dionne and Byron.

The waitress walked Melvin and his date over as Dedrick and Carla followed.

"What's up Dog?" Stephan asked, as he jumped up to hug Melvin, Dedrick and Carla.

"Congratulations," Carla said, as she hugged DeDe's neck.

"Thank you." DeDe knew she was going to give Dedrick hell tonight. DeDe's ring was bigger than hers and she and Stephan would be getting married a lot sooner than five years from now.

"So we're family again after all," Melvin chuckled and hugged her.

DeDe just smiled with no comment.

"So Dog, you did it huh?"

"I had to," he said, as he and DeDe looked at each other smiling. She showed off her ring to Carla and Melvin's date, whom he hadn't yet introduced. It was just like Melvin, he was disrespectful and ignorant like that.

"So what does your sister think?" Melvin asked DeDe.

"Who Kendra? I haven't told her or anyone else yet."

Melvin replied, "She wouldn't care, even though she hates my niggah's guts." DeDe noticed his whole calm demeanor had changed into an angry bull the minute he began talking about Kendra. They had fallen out once again. "Normally, she would go crazy and tell you anything for you to give Stephan that ring back. But right now, she won't even care, because her head is so far up Jeremiah Williams ass—"

DeDe broke out into a sweat and prayed they were talking about someone else with the same name as her best friend Charva's, husband, whom she suspects is fooling around.

"Jeremiah Williams, the super-producer, Dog?" Dedrick asked.

"Isn't he married?" Carla asked.

"Yeah, to DeDe's best friend Charva Williams," Stephan said, while shaking his head.

"What? She's trifling. She's fucking your best friend's husband," Melvin said, as if he cared anything about the fact it was DeDe's best friend's husband. He was far more upset at the fact that she was fucking another man, and that man had more money and power than himself.

"I don't think so. She's trying to get a job with Element Records and since I know Jeremiah and Charva, she's been talking to both of them."

"A job," Melvin replied. That bitch ain't worked a day in her life. She's fucking the niggah, I tell you that."

And DeDe knew it also, but she didn't want anyone else to know.

24

THE minute DeDe woke up at one o'clock in the afternoon, she stared at her ring then looked over and smiled at Stephan, who was asleep beside her. She remembered showing him the twelve-thousand dollar platinum ring and the Vera Wang wedding dress in a wedding magazine a year ago. That was back when she threw hints at him, about them getting married and now she had it on her finger. She reached over, kissed him on his left shoulder blade and jumped out of bed, to go cook him breakfast. She could get used to him lying there for the next fifty years or longer. Finally, she was marrying the man she wanted to marry. This time there weren't any doubts in her heart like she had during her three other engagements, regarding the person she would be spending the rest of her life with.

Last night they had truly celebrated. Melvin had used his NFL status to get them through the line of The Roxy, one of Houston's liveliest clubs. He also bought them several bottles of Cristal champagne. They danced until their feet hurt and afterwards they came home and consummated their engagement, by making love non-stop and it was all good. He allowed her to have her way with him, by being on top and rocking her knees backwards and forward. The motion of her body had him screaming out he loved her. He couldn't stop telling her how good she was making him feel. She had finally perfected the ability to please the one man she loved so much, thanks to another man, Elliott. She wasn't going to bother to call him about last night, as he hadn't called her. She didn't know how to apologize and there was no need of lying and trying to keep Elliott as a friend anymore. She was engaged to be married to the man she really loved.

There were several people DeDe needed to call and tell the good news to, so she grabbed the cordless off its base and tucked it between her chin and shoulder. She first called her mother in Ohio.

"Hey, Mama."

"Hey, baby. Your daddy and I were just about to take the boys to Boy Scouts."

"Guess what? I'm engaged."

"Engaged? Congratulations! Honey, DeDe is getting married," she yelled outside to DeDe's father. "When is the date baby?"

"We haven't set it yet, but Stephan wants to do it New Years Eve." She said, while dicing up the potatoes and onions.

"New Years Eve," her mother replied.

"Yeah, it falls on a Saturday this year."

"It's the middle of July now, so that gives you only five months to plan. I don't know baby."

"The date is not etched in stone. What did daddy say?"

"You know your daddy, he doesn't think anyone is good enough for his daughters. He hasn't said anything. I can't wait to call and tell your Aunts Jessie and Viola. They are going to be so happy. What is the boy's name again?"

"Stephan," DeDe said, annoyed that her mother didn't already know.

"You didn't expect me to know that did you? I only met him twice. Did you call the twins and tell them?"

"No."

"How are they doing anyway? You know we don't hear from them, until they need something. God bless their hearts.

"I guess they're doing fine." DeDe didn't want to tell her mother what

Kendra was really up to.

"You know, I received a call from someone about a month or two ago asking for Kendall. He was pretty upset. How he got this number; I just don't know; but he said something very awful about Kendall. I didn't dare tell your dad. Bless his heart. He thought he was getting a son; but so did I. I also thought I had a daughter who would have some respect for herself, but I got Kendra. How could she have left these children behind? Every time I think about it, I just get sick to my stomach."

DeDe was use to her mother rambling from subject to subject and forgetting what she initially meant to talk about. "Mama, who called the house looking for Kendall?"

"He didn't tell me his name. He cursed me out so bad I had to hang the phone up on 'im. The words that man used were awful. He said, if he ever found Kendall he would kill 'im. God, please protect my children. I pray for y'all every night and that's something I should have done, when you were little. Maybe those two would have turned out better."

"Why did he curse you?" DeDe asked, as she poured a cup of grits into a pot of boiling water.

"He said, I'm the mother of the," she hesitated before saying the curse word; "muthafucka that gave him AIDS."

DeDe became silent to the point where, she didn't breathe for about five seconds. She held the boneless chicken breast under the warm water and fell into a daze, as she tried to swallow the lump of sickness that had enlarged in her throat. She had never known anyone with AIDS. And she damn sure didn't want to believe her brother had it and had given it to someone. "I saw Kendall about two weeks ago and he looked fine. As a matter of fact, he had gained weight," she said, as she patted the chicken dry and seasoned it, just as Stephan liked it. "He didn't give that person AIDS, Mama. The next time he calls you, just hang up on 'im."

Her mother sighed. "We have one gem out of three. You are perfect, and your father and I are so proud of you. Kendra's boys are our second chance; and we won't fail again. Will you wait," she yelled outside to her husband, who was rushing her to get off the phone. "I'm talking to our daughter on this very happy day for her. Baby, let me get out of here. Your daddy is so impatient, but I still love 'im anyway. Please do not exclude your mother from assisting the planning of your wedding. I know this is the new millennium and you think I'm a woman of yesteryear, but if any of my money has to go into this wedding, I will have some say-so."

"Yes mother."

"You take care."

DeDe felt sorry for her mother and father and their efforts to raise twins they could be proud of; instead they turned out to be huge and often embarrassing disappointments. DeDe called Kendra, right after she hung up from talking to her mother, but got her voice-mail. "Bitch, you call me the minute you get this message. I know what you're up to."

All of DeDe's girlfriends seemed like they were happy for her, although she knew they weren't. But they still accepted her invitation to be bridesmaids. They didn't want her to marry Stephan, because all the tears he had made her cry in the past. As soon as she had hung up with each of them, she knew they had called each other voicing their opinion about the mistake they thought she was making. They had asked her several times, if she was sure she was ready for marriage. This was their way of asking, if she was sure she wanted to marry Stephan. They knew she was ready to be married, because she had talked about it several times prior. She was thirty-four years old, no children, and she had been a bridesmaid in all of their weddings. She was sure about marrying him in spite of the past. Marrying him was all she ever wanted.

"Damn, how did I sleep this late?" Stephan said, as he came behind her and kissed her on the neck. "It was how you worked it on me last night that made me sleep like a baby. Girl, if I didn't know better, I would swear that you hit me with some voodoo love from that magic box of yours."

She giggled, while continuing to flip the golden brown chicken.

"Okay baby, tell a brotha why you've been holding back, for the past three years that we were dating?"

She giggled again. "What are you talking about?"

"You weren't doing tricks like you been layin' on me lately. You made a brotha feel like a bitch and I slept like a baby. Promise me that when we get married, you are going to continue to please yo' man, like you did last night." Stephan said, and patted her on the butt, before going to sit at the table.

"I promise." She placed his plate in front of him and straddled across his lap. "I promise to be a wonderful wife, friend and lover," she said and licked him from his top lip to the tip of his nose.

He smiled. "I would pick you up and carry you to that bed back there, but a brotha is hungry for this food you just put in front of him."

They both laughed and kissed. They were pulled apart, by the ringing of the phone. It was Charva. DeDe became nervous.

"Why-didn't-you-tell-me," Charva asked in very slow motion.

"Tell you what? I didn't even know," DeDe sighed. "It was a shock to me. Did you see them together?"

"Did I see who? What are you talking about? I'm talking about why you didn't tell me you're getting married? Why wasn't I the first person you called?"

DeDe busted out laughing; trying to play it off, while she pulled her foot out of her mouth. "Girl, I thought you were somebody else. I'm still hung over from last night. I knew that talking Marie and Bridget would call you and save me the long distance charges. That's why I didn't tell you. Hell they probably didn't give me time to hang up the phone, before they called you. Is that how you found out?"

"Hell yeah! You're a special type of bitch, but you ain't that special or important where it was announced on ET or Oprah."

"I'm too through with them, for not letting me tell my good news myself."

They both screamed with excitement. "Congratulations girlfriend, welcome to the 'now I's married' club. I'm coming there and I'm going to throw you the badest bachelorette party ever in bachelorette party history. When is the date?"

"New Years Eve."

"Five months away. Girlfriend, I know you can plan some elegant events, because that's what you do. But this time you are going to sit back and let someone else do this extravaganza of a wedding for you. I know the badest chick."

"I don't know if I want to spend ten thousand, for someone to plan my wedding. I think I would want to take that money and put it into the wedding."

"Cool, I don't care what you do, as long as you tell the other two, Bridget and Marie that I'm the maid of honor."

DeDe began to laugh. She hadn't even thought about it.

"I tried telling them, but they got mad at me and we cursed each other out and hung up the phone."

"Girl, y'all are crazy."

"You tell 'em."

Stephan walked into the den where she was sitting and began kissing her on her neck, to try to get her off the phone. She felt tingly and in the mood. "I got to go. My baby needs me."

"Well, the wedding is only five months away; so try not to walk down the aisle with a swollen belly."

DeDe chuckled. "Girrrl, bye."

AFTER THREE DAYS of calling and leaving messages, DeDe decided to stop by Kendra's house right before going to work. She had missed her favorite television show last night, Alley McBeal while she patiently listened to Charva cry and sniffle for two hours, about this other woman whom she believed Jeremiah was about to leave her for. She didn't want any advice, which made it impossible for DeDe to console her. But it still goes to show you, how some women will be damned and determined. Although she knows that her man is cheating, she still wants to go out of her way to throw him a huge surprise birthday party and consider giving him a child, during the height of this storm.

DeDe knocked on Kendra's door.

"Hello," Kendra, nonchalantly said, as she opened the door.

"I know you got my messages," DeDe said, as she walked in pushing Kendra out of her way.

"Yes, I did and I was going to return your call at my earliest convenience and not a minute sooner." Kendra said and closed the door.

"You are ridiculous."

Kendra rolled her eyes at DeDe, as she walked back to her bedroom and got back into bed.

DeDe pushed away from the sofa and stormed down the hall behind her. "Bitch, how dare you? That is my best friend; and you got the nerve to be fucking her husband."

"Like you said, she's *your* friend and not mine, so I could give less than a damn. He's her husband and not yours, so you should give less than a damn about who I'm fucking. He's her husband and he doesn't care, so why should I? She knows he's fooling around and she's not going to leave 'im and I know you don't think I'm going to leave 'im, just because she's your best friend; so you brought your ass over here huffing and puffing to confront me about it."

"You're just a money hungry bitch, who doesn't care about anyone. She loves him."

Kendra's head spun around and her eyes cut over to DeDe, as if she was demon possessed and she spoke in a very deep voice. "And so do I."

"You what?" DeDe screamed. "You can't love him. Child, you hardly know him, and plus he's married. He's not going to leave Charva for someone like you. Someone who has slept with every man who pulls his dick out to piss, because he has money and he's the popular niggah of the season or flavor of the month."

"Get out of my house," Kendra screamed, as she jumped out of her bed and stood toe-to-toe with DeDe, while looking down in her eyes. "I'm your sistah, your blood and you are coming in here talking to me about some bitch and her husband? I don't give a damn about her or you. Get the hell out!" Kendra screamed, as she slung DeDe's small petite body to the other side of the room.

DeDe caught her balance, turned around and looked at her, as if she was crazy. She had never seen her act so outraged.

"You want to fight me?" She asked DeDe, as she approached her. "If so, you better be sure about that honey, because I won't be throwing nothing at you but hard licks. And, as mad as I am with you for coming in my house taking sides with some other bitch, I'll probably beat you down and leave you for dead."

DeDe wondered if drugs were the reason for how she was acting. As mad as DeDe was, she would fight her too. They've fought before being sisters; but that was when they were much younger, not grown women. What difference would it make anyway, she wasn't going to leave Jeremiah alone. DeDe rolled her eyes at Kendra and walked out of the room. "What if she finds out it's you?" DeDe said, just before she opened the front door to leave.

"Then the bitch just finds out, because I'm not leaving him."

"Mama didn't raise you to act like this Kendra."

"And she didn't raise you to act like the bitch you are either," she said, and slammed the door in DeDe's face.

THE EPISODE WITH Kendra stayed on DeDe's mind the entire morning. She tried blocking it out, as she met with a reporter from the Houston Times, the local television stations and the executives of Bushel and Coleman for their kick-off campaign for the QuittersPatch; but Kendra's demonic behavior dominated her thoughts. Kendra had acted like a total bitch, without reasoning or caring. DeDe was terrified of Charva finding out and ending the friendship they've had since college. She was sure she would think DeDe knew all along about Kendra and Jeremiah. To keep her from thinking that, a part of DeDe felt she needed to tell Charva, before she found out on her own. But she just didn't know how to tell her. After all, Kendra was her sister.

DURING LUNCH, DeDe and Dionne had gone shopping. Dionne was going to meet Byron's parents this weekend. Dionne thought that wearing the sharpest outfit she could find was the best way of making a great impression on them. DeDe really wanted to tell her the best way was for her to keep her loud, smart, bragging, opinionated mouth closed, but she was in no mood to get into it with Dionne. This just wasn't the time, especially since she had other things on her mind. Her advice to her probably would not have been as effective as she'd like. For some reason, DeDe felt obligated to lie to her and tell her that she thought Byron was cute. He wasn't bad looking, and he wasn't all that either. But with Dionne asking her a thousand times, "What did you think about my Byron"; the truth would only crush her. She also wanted to ask her if she had checked out or had any concerns regarding his mannerisms lately. Dionne was delighted that DeDe would say that he was cute and she somewhat felt relieved. She couldn't dare date a man that no one thought was nice looking.

Now DeDe felt it was a mistake that she had told her he was cute, because she hasn't stopped talking about him since. Today, DeDe wasn't up for much conversation. She just came along for the ride, but Dionne's every word was Byron this and Byron that.

"Byron said his family just can't wait to meet me. We're leaving Friday night to drive to Dallas. I can't wait. Charlotte is so jealous that I have someone like Byron and she's stuck with Ian."

DeDe hoped not. She wondered if Charlotte had seen Byron before, because any woman in her right mind would say he looks fruity. She needed to ask Kendall, since he had the gift of recognizing his own kind and he seemingly knew and or slept with everyone gay in Houston. "Has she met him before?"

"Yes, and every time she sees him, he's all over me. I'm not the skinniest person in the world, but he likes me just the way I am. Ian is always trying to change Charlotte and she's slightly thicker than you are. He doesn't want her to cut her hair and she can't wear much make-up. I've told you about him and his controlling her. She's got it bad and she knows it, but hell can't pull her away from him."

"What is it that she does again?" DeDe asked, as she tried to conjure a mental picture in her mind.

Dionne pretended to not have heard her question, as she examined the fabric of a pair of pants.

"What does she do?"

"She's a writer."

"Yeah, for the newspaper. That's right, you told me that."

Dionne had to change the subject. "Girly, you've been looking like you have a lot on your mind today, what's up?"

"Nothing."

"You're not acting your normal talkative self, you should be smiling. You're getting married in five months. Something is definitely up with you."

"My sister is fucking my best friend's husband," DeDe blurted out, before she even knew it. "When I confronted her about it, she went crazy. I don't know what to do."

"Does your best friend suspect her husband is fooling around?"

"Hell yeah! But what she doesn't know is, it's with my sister."

Dionne wanted to ask her which girlfriend was it. She had heard her talk about several and she felt like she knew them.

"What am I going to do? A part of me feels like I need to tell her; and then another part of me feels like, I just need to stay out of it. Stephan, told me to stay out of it."

"I say the same thing. If and when your girlfriend finds out, just tell her you knew nothing about it, but you dislike your sister for being disgusting and trifling."

"Aren't all gold-diggers? She had the nerve to tell me that she loved him. Charva and Jeremiah have been married for ten years with four kids—"

"Charva ... Jeremiah, isn't he the super-producer of Element Records?" Dionne couldn't wait to get back to the office to call Charlotte. This was going to be juicy for the column. "Girl, don't let it get to you. It'll work itself out before Charva even gets a clue that the other woman is your low-life sister."

"I sure hope you're right."

"It will...now what do you think about me in this olive green?"

25

JUST before it was time for the alarm clock to go off for DeDe to get up and go to work, Stephan woke up in the same horny mood he had gone to sleep with last night; when he kept begging her for sex. She kept telling him no, all because he had talked to Shannon for about fifteen minutes last night. He was as hard as the times were in 1929 and being inside of her was the only way he was going to get some relief from the pressure. Playing pussy games was DeDe's only way of getting back at him, during an argument. And this was a war she won every time. Right now was no exception; because he was willing to apologize and promise to never talk to Shannon ever again, so he could get some. The reason he called her was, he missed Alexis and he desperately wanted to see her. It's been a month and a half and Shannon hadn't called him to tell him how Alexis was doing or anything. He's been too angry with her, to call before now. He thought he could wait until Alexis is of legal age to call him on her own; but he was crazy for thinking so. His life was missing a very crucial component, and he was becoming more miserable day by day.

Making love to DeDe was Stephan's pleasure. He knew if he was going to get some before she leaves; he'd better wake her with something more than his usual pat on the ass, which usually meant for her to roll over and open up. He went under the covers and under her gown instead and gave her the one thing she couldn't say no to.

"Stephan, what are you doing?" She asked through her moans. She didn't expect him to answer, but to keep on giving her hot spot that feeling of sheer bliss. "Baby I'm going to be late." She said, as she looked at the clock while squirming away from him. She then pushed her body into his face and his face into her body. That was Stephan's cue to realize that she would rather have his manhood inside her, instead of his tongue. Stephan rose up on his knees, pulled down his pajama pants, and placed her hand on his hard love-stick to guide him inside of her. Once he was finally in, he slowly gyrated his hips, as he felt her vagina walls embrace his love with tautness and wetness. The feeling was raw and pure pleasure. Stephan tried to hold back his cum as long as he could. But with DeDe whispering in his ear those nasty things she wants him to do to her, he was sure to release very soon. He hated to seem so greedy and try to get a month of lovemaking in thirty minutes, but DeDe had a hectic work schedule and she was always tired. Who knows when the next time he might get some? He was going to have to be greedy and selfish, for another fifteen minutes at least. She grabbed him by his ass, pushed him deep inside her, and screamed the one thing that is always sure to make him explode. "Fuck me."

He pulled her close to him and took off like a track star as he long stroked her while probing deep into her wet tunnel of love. They both exploded and collapsed into their juices simultaneously.

"Damn, why did you say that?" He asked and kissed her bare, sweaty, peach shoulder.

"Say what?"

"You know." He rolled over on his side of the bed and propped his hands up under his head, while trying to catch his breath.

She jumped up to go take a shower. "Stephan, you know I have a client to meet first thing this morning."

"You could have at least given me another ten minutes."

"If I didn't have to beat the media there, I'd give you longer than that," she said, leaning over the bed and kissing him, before she walked into the bathroom.

He began kicking up his legs with excitement. If she would let him, he would make love to her every day, because the loving between the two of them was surely all that, and so was she. She was beautiful and he was in love with her. Before now, he just loved her. But now, he was in love with her. He could definitely stand being married to her. She was perfect for him. She had always been by his side. Out of all the women he's dated, he couldn't have chosen a better woman to spend the rest of his life with. They were connected spiritually and emotionally. At one point, he was torn between her, his child's mother and living the single life. Losing DeDe to another man like what happened with Shannon; he couldn't bear the thought of a repeat performance. The pain he felt when he found out Shannon was dating someone else six months after she walked out on him was shocking. A year later, she was married. Those two events were both debilitating and devastating. She had pleaded with him to marry her, since they had a child and they had been dating for five years. But to Stephan, giving up his life to become responsible for a wife and a child scared the living shit out of him. He didn't want the same thing to happen between he and DeDe. So, when Melvin told him he had seen her talking to another man at a party and Kendra told him she was seeing someone else, he had to straighten up. If not, he was going to lose her for good and he couldn't let that happen. She was a good woman and he had realized it way before he knew she was seeing someone else, but he had taken her love for granted. They've broken up and gotten back together several times a year. This situation had become a routine ritual, whenever he felt he needed his space and he thought she loved him too much to want another man. His father and friends tried to tell him that they would have issues and problems, because she made more money than him. Also because of that, she would try to be the man and the 'shot-caller' of the relationship. Stephan took their concerns and somewhat made them his fears, as well as his number one reason for not committing to her. He couldn't handle a woman that he couldn't dominate; be it related to their careers, financially, sexually, or mentally. Although DeDe has never held the fact that she makes more money than him over his head, he wouldn't allow himself to become close to her. No matter what, she's always had his back and at the same time allowed him to be a man.

DeDe walked out of the shower with the towel wrapped around her body. "So when are you supposed to get Alexis?" She asked.

"This weekend."

"Is she bringing her by your place or what?"

"No, she's going to drop her off at my mother's." He sat up in bed and reached for the remote on the nightstand, to turn on the television.

"Just when I think we are getting her out of our lives," DeDe said in frustration, as she rolled her eyes back in her head.

"What do you mean? I have to see Alexis; she's my daughter. Shannon isn't coming anywhere around me. I made that clear to her, when I spoke with her yesterday."

"Has she been calling you and bugging you about seeing Alexis?" DeDe flopped her naked body on the bed and began to lotion her legs. "I tell you Stephan, it's not about Alexis, it's about her. She just wants to stay in your life. I bet she's not messing with Harvey, and she was married to him and had a child with him too."

"I'm not thinking about Shannon. I just want to see Alexis. She has a birthday coming up and I would like to be with her that day."

"I understand that, but Shannon is using her to keep you two in the loop. You know that. I tell you, if you do what you said you were going to do and not see Alexis, until she's old enough to deal with you on her own; Shannon would stop acting so damn foolish." DeDe was angry and she hoped that it showed and didn't care how he was taking it. DeDe thought, 'Well, if it's a child he wants, I'll have it for him. I've been thinking about having one anyway, and then all this Shannon crap will stop.'

"I knew I couldn't do that when I said it; but I was angry. You are not holding me to that are you?"

"No," she said. But she thought that he would hold himself to it. "What about when Alexis is over your house and Shannon has to call?"

"I just won't answer the phone. I don't want to deal with Shannon and I don't have to."

"I don't think she needs to call there, when Alexis is there anyway. It's not like you're not a good father and you are going to allow something to happen to Alexis. So what, she dropped the charges. I paid three-thousand dollars for our attorney and that's money I can't get back. Even though she dropped the charges, there isn't any such thing as a refund, because the attorney filed some paperwork for us. That bitch doesn't need to be calling over there and she's damn sure not going to call over here, if Alexis is here with you."

Stephan could understand DeDe's anger with Shannon, but he couldn't understand it enough for him to turn his back on Alexis. She didn't come right out and say it, but that's what it seemed like she was asking him to do. After Shannon had come over to his house acting a fool and she had filed a warrant against him, he was angry with her and wanted nothing to do with her or Alexis. But in the overall scheme of things, how long could he ignore Shannon and neglect his little girl? They had a child together. By no means was he innocent, in what went on between them on the night in question. He was cruel to Shannon. He hadn't been the best father, and he had hit her. Now that DeDe had done so much for him, she was going to be his wife. He felt totally obligated to stand in the position she was putting him in. DeDe wanted him to forever be angry with Shannon and take her emotions and insecurities into consideration. Maybe it was true; that he didn't need a friendship with Shannon now. He was quite sure Shannon didn't want to ever be his friend again— period. He tried to keep a friendship with her for Alexis's sake. Also, just in case he was ever late with the child support, she wouldn't call the men in blue on him.

"Do you understand what I'm saying Stephan? I understand that you two have a child together; but I don't want that bitch thrown in my face anymore than she already has been."

"I understand." He felt he had no other choice, but to understand and agree or he might just lose her, when he needs DeDe the most.

26

"SHIT," Stephan mumbled, as he looked around to make sure no one saw the neon pink eviction notice stapled to his door, as he snatched it down, balled it up and threw it on the ground. He didn't have fourteen hundred dollars for two months past due rent, before the scheduled court date. He wasn't going to court without it and he wasn't going to sit around and let the marshals come and throw his shit out on the corner either. He didn't exactly know where he was going to stay, but he knew he couldn't stay there. He drove around the corner to the liquor store, grabbed several boxes next to the dumpster and a six pack of Heineken and came back and began packing. Life had brought on a string of bad luck and he felt like he deserved it. He was finally reaping the shit for the bad seeds he had sewn for years. It was hitting him hard and all at once. It didn't come in the form of a woman breaking his heart as he had done to many of them. His big payback was coming in the form of his life falling apart and him feeling like there was nothing he could do to bring it back together. He was behind on all of his bills. He was about to lose his car. He was being kicked out of his apartment. He had just lost his job over some bullshit and he couldn't pay child support, even if he really wanted to. Everything seems to be unraveling. All of his dirt had pushed him into a hole that he could not find his way out of. He could easily get the money, if he called a couple of women and made them think and feel like they were the only ones. But that's the kind of stuff that put him in this shit to begin with. Never thinking it would come back on him; he recklessly hurt and lied to everyone who cared for him. As he looked around his living room, Stephan gazed into the mirror that Shannon cracked and said, "I am really in a deep hole this time." He smiled, as he remembered what Miss Evans, his favorite high school teacher told him about the 'first rule of holes', "once you're in there, stop digging!"

There were several angry messages left on Stephan's cell phone, from women who couldn't get the hint that he was now a one-woman man.

"You knew you wanted to be a one-woman man, when you came over here and slept with me last month. But that's okay, that shit ain't gonna work. Once a low-down dog; always a low-down dog. Stephan, you muthafucka!" He deleted the message and pressed the number one for the next one.

"I haven't heard from you in a while. What's up? I miss you and I would like to see you in spite of what you told me last week. You having a woman ain't got shit to do with me. You really don't love her. If you did, you wouldn't be over here all the time." He deleted the message and went to the next.

"I heard you proposed to that bitch. I just hope she knows you got a—" He didn't bother to listen to all of the lecture before he deleted it.

He knew he'd better change his pager and cell phone number, before DeDe came across some of the messages. With her now zero tolerance for bullshit from him; she might just throw him back his ring and keep walking. As tempted as he was, he didn't bother to return any of the phone calls. Including the one from his ex-girlfriend, Charniese Richardson from eleven years ago. She called to say she was in town to see her sister and to attend a T.D. Jakes Convention. She also wanted to see him to apologize to him in person. He really didn't need her apology. He had gone on with his life and it was best if he not see her, since hearing her voice brought his anger back to the forefront. She told him her life had changed. She was now living a wonderful life for the Lord. God had put it on her heart to apologize, for the hurt she had caused him. Stephan didn't believe a word of her so-called changed life and didn't give damn about it. What about the hell she had caused in his life?

For five years, he had raised a child that wasn't his. He had given up his teenage life to be a father to a child he would have to turn his back on. He enjoyed being a father; although it was hard and caused him to become more responsible, than any fifteen year-old tenth grader should have been. It was joy for him knowing he was working to put food in his own son's mouth, just as his father had done for him. He enjoyed having him and his son's hair cut alike and wearing the same sneakers and basketball jersey. He thrilled at having his son scream out 'daddy' in the stands of his high school and college basketball games; to later find out he wasn't his biological son.

Stephan had just gotten home from college for the Thanksgiving break, when a man he had never seen before approached him; while he was outside his parents' house raking up the autumn leaves from the ground.

"What's up," he said, extending his hand out to Stephan. "My name is Jeffery Mathis."

"Stephan Brown. Do I know you?"

"Naw, but whatcha' know about that?" He asked, while noticing the ring on Stephan's finger.

"What do you know about it?"

"I'm spring '84 Beta Phi."

"Damn, fall '87 Sigma Tau."

"You just went over. What's up frat?" They embraced each other with a brotherhood handshake and hug by locking their forearms together pulling each other close and wrapping their leg around one another.

"What's going on?" Stephan asked.

"Damn, I didn't know you were frat. You and I need to talk bro. We got issues."

"Issues like what?"

"Charniese."

"Charniese is my girl, bro, that's not an issue. She's the mother of my child and we've been together, since our freshman year in high school. I'm gonna marry her.

So what you talking about…issues?"

"Darnell."

"Darnell," Stephan repeated. "That's my son. What issues do you and I have with him, man?

"He's not your son, he's my son.""

"What the hell—man, are you out of your damn mind? Darnell looks like me, he has my last name, and I was there when he was born. This is a joke right? Big Brother Leo sent you didn't he? He doesn't stop does he? You tell that niggah, I crossed, and I made it. The pledging is over." Stephan laughed out loud and clapped his hands. "He's good. He used to mess with me when I was on line, but it doesn't work now."

"Bro, I'm serious. She was a freshman and I was a senior in high school. We met at this party and ended up doing it in the back seat of my boy's car. When she called me a month later and told me she might be pregnant, I wasn't tryin' to hear any of that. I cussed her out and told her I didn't want anything to do with her. I was young getting ready to go off to college, and I really didn't know her. It was a one-night stand and I already had a steady girl. I never heard from Charniese again. I knew she had had the baby and you thought you were the father. I'm now a commissioned officer in the U.S. Army. I'll give you everything back that you gave my son."

"What? Darnell is my son!" Stephan yelled.

"I've tried contacting Charniese for a blood test, but she hangs up on me. So, I had to get me an attorney. I want to be a part of my son's life. I want him to have my last name, instead of yours."

"Frat or no frat, niggah, you betta get the hell out of my yard, before I bust a cap in your ass. I'm a step away from popping my trunk and killin' yo' ass."

"Do what you have to do, bro." He opened his arms and took a couple of steps backwards.

"Stephan, what is going on?" His mother asked, as she ran out of the house with his father behind her.

"This niggah here is crazy. I oughta kill 'im."

"Stephan," his mother said trying to calm him.

"Son, what's going on?" His father asked.

"This niggah is talking about he's Darnell's father," Stephan yelled.

"Ma'am, I didn't come over here to start anything. I just came over here to tell him, because I knew he didn't know."

"To tell him what?" His mother asked.

"That Darnell is my son."

"How do you figure?" His father asked.

It was evident, now that Stephan was looking at Jeffery. Darnell didn't look a damn thing like him; he looked the spitting image of his real father. He couldn't understand what he and everyone else saw. He guessed the sayings were true; "If you feed a child long enough, they will begin to look like you" and "Mama's baby, Papa's maybe." Maybe everyone else knew Darnell didn't look like Stephan, but they just didn't want to hurt his feelings. He surmised that if someone said something, it might have put suspicion in his heart that Darnell probably wasn't his child. But he never would have thought that, because as far as he knew, he was the first and only one Charneise had slept with. Stephan had a cocoa brown complexion with nappy hair that had to be cut every week, just to get it to lie down and not roll up into little beads. Stephan had large marble eyes, with one dimple in his right cheek instead of his chin, small ears that were close to his head. But for some reason, he thought he and Darnell favored. So Jeffery is where Darnell got his curly hair and his dark chocolate complexion from and not Charneise's great-grandfather, as she had told Stephan. The small resemblances he thought he and Darnell had didn't seem so acute anymore. Now that he was looking at Jeffery who also had thin arched eyebrows, eyes that are recessed in his head, pointy ears that stick out from his head, and a dimple in his chin. Stephan was so hurt, he felt like falling to his knees crying out to God and simply asking why. But his pride had conquered his emotions and doubt.

"Get your attorney. We'll take your blood test. Just be ready to hear them say that Darnell is mine."

"Fine."

Stephan turned around and walked into the house thinking; what if Jeffery was telling the truth and Darnell really wasn't his son? That means he's given up his life for nothing and Charneise is as good as dead. He called her at home and asked her to come over without giving her a clue as to what was going on. His laid-back reserved mannerism had transformed into a person of rage and anger. Thoughts of killing her raced through his mind. He didn't give a damn about jail or anything else. His life had been ruined, because of her lies. He met her outside.

"Hey, baby what are you doing out here standing on the sidewalk, it's kinda nippy?" She asked him; as she stepped out of the car wearing his college sweat shirt and his baseball cap. "Are you okay?"

"I'm fine what about you? Guess what, I had this niggah Jeffery come by here, this house, earlier today and tell me he wants to see his son."

"His son," she replied, and leaned up against her car. "Who is Jeffery and who is his son?"

"You tell me. Y'all had the one-night stand. He tells me that he's Darnell's daddy."

"I don't know what you are talking about, Stephan. You are Darnell's daddy. Look at 'im. He looks just like you, crazy."

"No he doesn't! Not after I saw Jeffery. He wants a blood test. Now who is he and don't lie to me or I'll kill you," he said, grabbing her by the neck and squeezing it lightly but tight enough for her not to get away. "Who is he? Why did you do this to me?"

She began to cry, because she knew Jeffery was telling the truth.

"He hasn't been there. He's not his father, you are."

"You lied to me," he said, releasing her neck. "You lied to my family and you lied to Darnell. How could you?"

Crying uncontrollably and trying to catch her breath, Charneise said, "I didn't mean to. I was scared. I love you."

"You love me. Man, look here... I can't take this."

"Stephan we can work this thing out. It's not as bad as it seems."

"It's not? The damn son I've been raising for five years; I find out today he's not even mine. What's not bad about this situation? Go straight to hell Charneise! I want you out of my life and out of my damn sight! I don't want to see you or Darnell ever again!"

"Why? He's your child, Stephan."

"Dammit!" He yelled, while hitting the hood of her car and putting a dent in it. "He's not my child. That's the worst possible lie that you could ever tell me. When I get back here, I want you gone. I never want to see you again do you understand?"

"Stephan don't do this." She cried, while grabbing his shirt.

"Get off of me." He said, snatching himself away while pushing her away from him. "When I get back, be gone."

She sat on the ground screaming for him to come back as he walked down the street. He never looked at her once. Eleven years later, he still doesn't want to look at her. He wished that she would get the hint that he did not want to see or talk to her and stop calling. He hated her so much. He felt if she were on fire, he wouldn't even piss on her to put it out. She lived a lie that caused him a portion of his life. He now wished he had choked her to death for it.

After snapping out of his flashback, he found old newspaper to pack all of his dishes, pictures and whatnots. There were far fewer things to pack; Shannon took care of that. He labeled all the boxes. He was on his second beer with the music blasting, as he ran up and down the stairs loading his clothes into his trunk. He was comforted somewhat in thinking that he was at least a step ahead of the leasing office. No one was going to throw his shit out on the sidewalk. He called Melvin and asked to use his truck to move his bed, sofa, loveseat, dinette set and entertainment center.

"Going some place?" Charneise asked him, smiling as she approached him, as he bent over the trunk of his car.

His mouth dropped open at both the sound of her voice and the sight of her. He stood speechless, trying to figure out how in the hell she found out where he lived." What in the hell are you doing here? How did you know where I live?

"I was going to look your address up through the internet, but I called your sister and she told me."

"She what? She had no damn right." He slammed his trunk down and stormed up the stairs to call his sister and curse her just for living and breathing.

"Stephan, don't blame her." She said, as she stormed up the stairs behind him.

"I begged and cried for your address, so she felt sorry for me and gave it to me."

He turned around, looked her dead in the face, and rolled his big marble eyes. The sight of her was making him sick and angry. He busted through the door and picked up the phone to call his sister and realized his phone was turned off, due to not paying the bill. He then called her from his cell phone. There was no answer, so he left a message.

"What in the hell are you doing giving out my damn address? I wouldn't give a damn if she was dying!" He hung up the phone and flopped down on the sofa. Charneise walked past him and sat on the love seat.

She didn't look anything like he had imagined her to look. After eleven years, she had gained weight in her hips and butt. She still had a small waistline, but her hips and butt were wide and huge. To some men that might be sexy, but to Stephan it was nasty and unattractive. Her butt shook as she walked and she didn't even bother to put on a girdle. He liked a woman with a butt and hips, but not with a butt that needed to be contained by a harness and the thickness that was only a meal away from being overweight and gross. How did she gain so much weight, he wondered. If they would have been married, there's no way in hell she would have gained that much weight. Even if he had to lock up all the cabinets with chains and make her eat celery and carrots for a month; he would have before letting her get fat. He remembers when she used to weigh a buck-o-five soaking wet; and complain about him being too heavy, as he lay on top of her. Now she probably wouldn't even feel his small lean body on top of hers. He didn't expect for her to look so different. Just by one glance at her, he noticed she was no longer the attractive woman he had loved at one point in his life. Her face was still beautiful, but her body did nothing for him. Not that he was hoping that it would. He was happy with DeDe and he would never tell her Charneise had come by. He had never told her, Shannon or any of his others about Charneise. That's how much he despised her, for all the lies she told. That was a part of his life he regretted and he had blocked it out, as if it never happened. His friends that had grown up with him knew about it. But he felt that they would never tell anyone of consequence.

He was proud that he hadn't let himself go and he knew she was thinking the same; by the way she looked him up and down, as he sat with his legs wide open looking straight ahead. He still looked the same with maybe about ten pounds of extra chest and arm muscles, and now sporting a baldhead. His round face hadn't gotten any wider, his smile was still sexy and his shoulders were broad and round. He was sexy and he damn sure thought he was cute.

"Can't I get a hug?" She asked, as she stood up with her arms open wide.

"You didn't come here to get a hug, Charneise. What do you want to talk about? You've left me several messages, with your number for me to call you back. So what do you want? We don't have shit to talk about. I thought you would have gotten the hint, when I didn't call you back."

"I understand your anger Stephan."

"You don't understand shit. What I can't understand is why my sister gave you my number, or my address. Look here Charneise, Don't call my mother, don't call my father, and don't call my dilly-ass sister. Don't call anyone in my family. Nobody wants to talk to you. Why you called me, I don't know."

"Why do you hate me so much Stephan?"

"As if you don't know." He said and let out a sarcastic chuckle. "You intentionally lied to me and you knew you were. I gave up several years of my fuckin' life for you and a son that wasn't mine."

"I heard you were engaged and you have a six-year old daughter. Congratulations."

Stephan didn't say a word. He stared at her with the same hate and anger he did eleven years ago, when she told him it was true that Darnell wasn't his son, after devoting his life to him and her. He was so angry for her being there; he hasn't even offered her a drink of water or a seat.

She looked down at her hands, as she twisted them in knots and took a deep breath. "Stephan I've paid for the lies I told you and your family. My life hasn't been anything without you. For eleven years, I've wished every time my phone rings that it would be you and you would be willing to listen to me explain about why I lied. I prayed you would ask about Darnell, because he asks about you almost everyday. Have you been that angry with me that you haven't even bothered to call him and say hello? Six years we were together, how could you just walk away, as if you never loved me or Darnell?"

"Don't you dare come here putting that shit on me. You lied, not me! And the scary thing about it is, you weren't going to even tell me; if that bastard didn't show up in my yard and tell me and my family his damn self. I shouldn't have been mad at him. I should have sent him a thank you card, because he sure did me a gigantic favor."

"I apologized to your family. Now, I'm here to apologize to you."

"We don't want your apology!" He yelled before realizing it. "I tell you what... apologize just like you've been doing... by staying the hell out of our lives. Five years I took care of a child that wasn't mine, because of your lies and deception. I didn't even go to the Atlantic 10 College I had gotten a scholarship from; because it was too far away from helping you raise Darnell. I worked during high school and college when I didn't have to, because you had me thinking somebody else's child was mine. What you took from me, I can't fuckin' get back."

"What did I take from you Stephan?"

"My life, dammit!"

"I didn't mean to. I loved you. I thought you would make the better father. I couldn't hurt you, by telling you I had slept with a boy I had just met at a party and I was pregnant by him. You are right, I'm wrong and I've paid for the pain I've caused you."

"To hell with that shit!" He said, fanning his hand at her. "I wish you would have hurt me a lot sooner than you did. Trust me, I would have gotten over it."

She didn't know what to say. "You are still as handsome as you where eleven years ago."

"Charneise, don't even try it." He hoped she didn't think anything like them getting together for old time sake was going to happen, because he wouldn't touch her if she lay naked with her legs spread-eagle.

"Darnell, asks about you almost every other day."

"Why? Didn't you tell him I wasn't his daddy?"

She nodded. "He still remembers you and as far as he's concerned, you're the only father he has."

"Don't let him think that. I don't want to be the one that hurts him. Where is Jeffery?"

She sighed and took a deep breath. "Married. He stayed in Darnell's life three months, after he told you. His wife thinks Darnell is bad; at least she thought so eleven years ago. She was upset at the fact Jeffery had a child. So for eleven years, Darnell hasn't had a man in his life and neither have I. My brother has been too busy with his family to spend time with him. And I think you know my daddy died a year after you and I split."

"So he's in the tenth grade now, how are his grades?"

"Ridiculous. He's a smart kid, but it's the company that he keeps. He's giving me a little bit of trouble from time to time. The threat of putting my foot on his neck isn't working anymore."

"Because you haven't done it yet. I told you when he was five not to make threats you weren't going to keep. I can only imagine how he's running over you."

She smiled. "He's my little boy."

"Where is he now?"

"In California. We live with my mother. I couldn't afford living on my own, once I lost my job. Can't you just call him and let him hear your voice?" She wrote down her number and handed it to him. "Hearing your voice would make him much happier."

He looked at the slip of paper, put it on the table and then looked at her. "I think about him a lot, but me calling him will only give him mixed signals. I'm not his father. Besides, I have another life now and I don't think she'll understand."

Charniese nodded her head. "I understand, but what does she have to do with Darnell. I know you think about him quite often, so why don't you call him. He's asking me a thousand questions about girls and sex and I don't have the answers. Believe it or not Stephan, you are his father. You took care of him for five years. Those were important years, because he still remembers you. I know you hate me, but don't make him pay any longer for what I did."

Stephan didn't say a word. His anger toward her and his stupidity for not asking for a blood test like his mother had told him to in the beginning had him speechless. Deep in his heart, he felt he had an obligation to Darnell. After all, he had been his father for five years, but his anger wouldn't allow him to acknowledge the fact. "What time does the convention start?" He asked her, as he looked at the time on his watch. He was now ready for her to leave.

"Well," she said, smiling. "I need to be getting back to the hotel now. The first meeting starts at 5:30p.m. and I was told the bus will be getting there early."

Stephan looked her up and down and asked her a question he just had to have the answer to. "So what's up with the weight?"

"You never did bite your tongue did you?" He had embarrassed her to the point of no return. "The years and food. Mama cooks for Darnell and me every day. I didn't gain this weight, until we moved back with her," she chuckled.

"You better push away from that table. Those hips are too, too big." He said, while giving her the most repulsive look.

"I forgot, you like 'em skinny and anorexic."

"No, I just don't like 'em—"

She looked at him with a daring stare. "You better not say it."

He shrugged his shoulders and sighed.

She noticed DeDe's picture lying on the coffee table. "Is that your fiancé?"

"Yes," he said proudly, as he swelled up his chest knowing that inside she wept with envy.

"She's pretty." She had to admit, as much as she didn't want to.

"Yes, she is." Speaking as a matter of fact, while intentionally rubbing it in Charneise's face hoping he was making her feel like shit.

She nodded, while trying to keep her self-esteem from shattering into millions of pieces. He was still angry, after eleven years no matter how much she prayed that he wouldn't be. The purpose for her trip was defeated. "Well, I guess I better be going," she said, as she stood up and pulled her skirt down over her hips and butt and rubbed her hand over the short hair tapered to the back of her neck.

"I was wondering when you were, or was I gonna have to throw your big ass out. But before I'd be able to do that, I'd have to take some steroids and go to the gym for about a month first."

"Must you be so mean Stephan?" She asked, as she walked toward the door.

"To you, hell yes! Because I want nothing to do with you ever. Please,

Charneise don't call me ever again. When Darnell is eighteen, you can have him contact me and I'll be more than happy to explain to him what a deceiving, lying bitch he has for a mother."

She felt like putting her religion on the shelf for five minutes, to spew the words that brewed in the pit of her stomach out of her mouth at him. But then again she felt she had no right to say them to him, because she was the one who had lied. "Bye Stephan."

He rolled his eyes and slammed the door shut in her face.

27

THERE was more drama, rhythm and spice happening in 'No More LoveMaking' than there really was in DeDe and Stephan's life. Since everything has been going so well between them for the last month and a half, Charlotte had only taken bits and pieces from their saga and added her own made-up drama to keep the readers wanting more of her semi-creation column. Because of Angelic and Tibias, the advertising space in the paper was now selling at top dollar. The column was the talk of the town in every city it was circulating in. Charlotte was truly contemplating turning it into a book, with or without Dionne's approval.

"Gooood....Morrrning Houston." Casey chimed. "If you are not making love on this beautiful, sunny Friday morning, what in the hell are you doing at 8:30am? Everybody get your papers, and if you don't have one you're... *Bleep*... out of luck. Parents, I know it's summer time and little Kaleb and Ashley might be up running around the house instead of outside at this early hour. I need for you to get them out of the room or you need to put on some headphones, because we need to have a grown-up conversation. Do you feel me? What I'm about to say, they don't need to hear. I'm mad and I'm about to go off. I had to read the article before getting on the air. I did that because I didn't want to be stumbling over any words or passing stop on the periods and have the article not make any sense," he chuckled. "I'm angry. I want you to know that right off the bat. My phone lines are already starting to light up. People don't tie up the lines, if you are trying to get a request in for *R. Kelly, Erika St. James, or Jill Scott,* because we aren't taking requests right now. Some things need to be discussed and this column is at the top of the list." He began to read.

Angelic has finally gotten the three things she's always wanted from Tibias and they are his undivided attention, a ring and a wedding date. She seems happy and I'm happy for her, although I don't think the marriage will last. I find it strange that after six or seven weeks of them being back together; Tibias suddenly decided he wants to marry her. No, she's not pregnant. But what brotha marries a woman these days, because she's having his child? Shotgun weddings are definitely a thing of the past.

"Who says a man has got to marry a woman, just because she's having his child?" Casey blurted out. "In a perfect world that would be great, but this world is far from perfect sistah. This sistah is a trip, she's trying to take cheap shots and think people are too dumb to notice." Casey continued to read.

Maybe it was her pressuring him or he had a change of heart. I'm not saying men can't have a change of heart and turn from their doggish ways, but most of them don't.

"No the hell she did not. Is she trying to male bash or what? If so, I'll throw on some rap that can tear a hole in a woman. A man can have a change of heart. We are human, not heartless. I tell you what; their marriage won't last, if Angelic keeps confiding in her." Casey said and continued to read.

She called up all of her male friends to tell them the good news of her getting married. She told them she would like it if they do not call the house anymore. In other words, lose her number, because she and Tibias were now living together. The men congratulated her and respected her wishes. When she got around to calling Jasper, it wasn't that easy. He finally exploded and went off on her for how she had used him on the rebound, until Tibias decided to come back into her life. His outrage left her speechless, but she felt she deserved it, because she knew she had hurt him. He didn't want her apology. Instead, he asked if he could see her for one last time.

"This brotha thinks just like I do. We tried it and it didn't work. We don't have to be friends and I don't have to ever call you again, but just let me see you for one last time, before we go our separate ways." Casey said and continued to read.

Angelic, being the faithful one-man woman, good girl she had been portraying herself to be; I thought she would have hung up the phone in his face. I say that because, it was obvious he wanted sex with her one last time. She tried to act as naïve as she wanted me to believe she was. She actually convinced herself to think that sex was the last thing on his mind. He just wanted to see her, that's all. She had told Tibias she and I were going to our book club meeting, as her excuse to get out of the house. She and Jasper met for dinner and afterwards they went back to his place and made mad, lusty, passionate love. When she told me, I nearly fell out of my chair in shock. Miss Goody-Goody cheated on the man she claimed to have loved so much, when he broke up with her every other month. Before, she couldn't pay enough of his bills to get him to love her back. Now that he does, and she has the ring, a commitment and his child's mother is out of the picture, she's sneaking off to see the man she should have stayed with in the first place. Because Jasper wasn't much of a challenge, she kicked him to the curb the minute Tibias came running back. My question to women is this; why do you need a challenge and heartache from a man to know if he's the right man or not? When Angelic had gotten home around midnight from her evening of passion, Tibias was up waiting for her. He was in the mood for exactly the same thing that she had just given to Jasper and he wasn't taking no for an answer. I'm not a goody-goody myself, but I'm not a slut either. Only a slut would share herself between two men the way that she did, and I told her just that!

"Ladies what are your opinions on this? It sounds to me like she's trying to condemn women, for getting their swerve on. The lines are open, come get her ladies." Casey chuckled and continued to read.

Women need to realize they are not men and they cannot do what men do; as far as jumping in and out of bed with multiple partners is concerned. AIDS is out there, and it doesn't discriminate.

I guess now Tibias is about to get his payback, so lets see if he handles it like Angelic has for all these years. I don't feel sorry for him, but I am mad at him for giving up his relationship with his child's mother and his child for Angelic. She's now about to take Tibias through the ringer, because she said she's going to continue to see Jasper up until she's married. They've been meeting almost every other night since their 'last time'. When I asked her why she was fooling around now that Tibias is showing her the love she fought so hard to get from him, she said because Tibias had lost the ability to make her desire him. That was another shocker for me and I knew then she was stone-cold crazy! I think she's quite confused and doesn't know what she truly wants from a man. So I asked her, since her desire for him has waned, if she was still going to marry him. She said yes, because she didn't want to give the ring back and the invitations were already being printed up. What dumb reasons to marry someone that you have no desire for, but I guess people do it all the time. I also asked her since she was losing desire for him now, what did she think would happen once they got married. She shrugged her shoulders and laughed. "I'll deal with that, when I get to it," is what she said. And that left me to say life is funny and so are the people who try to live it.

But my hat goes off to her, because she hung in there. She did like most women do; come hell, high water or near death experiences, they will put up with anything for the man they love. No matter how bad men dog them, they will not leave, unless he leaves them first. Then they cry and beg for him to come back, as if that's all they are used to and they can't ever get another man.

"She has done it now. She's trying to say sistah's are desperate. The lines are lit up like a Christmas tree. This 'Frustrated Friend' has gotten some people very upset. The women are about to tear into her and I'm going to let 'em."

Dionne stopped putting on her make-up and rushed into her bedroom to call Charlotte. "What in the hell did you do?" She asked her, when Charlotte answered the phone.

"Keeping it going. It was getting boring to me, so I added the drama of her *not* being happy and her cheating with Jasper."

"Damn your drama, why did you make me sound so cynical? People are angry at me."

"This is good material for the book. That's what we need. Hey baby, are you listing?" She yelled away from the phone to Ian.

"Who are you talking to?"

"Ian."

"You told him?"

"Yeah, I had to. I need him to be there with me, when I sign the contract later today."

Dionne thought, is this fool crazy? He hasn't been there for you since you started the damn paper a year and a half ago. He told you what a big mistake you had made for starting the paper. He also took his money out of the joint account; so you wouldn't use any of it to start the flop as he called it, remember? And now you need him to be there with you to sign some damn contract? It was me who gave you the story to write in the first place; and you want Ian to go with you to sign a damn contract? Dionne pondered and knew she should have voiced it, because it was obvious Charlotte had forgotten.

"But yeah, that's what we want to keep this story going; anger from our readers. They love it girl. I heard in Chicago and New York they're asking for the book and I'm going to give it to them. I'm signing with Omega Publishing House today. HBO wants the movie rights."

Dionne didn't bother to try and talk her out of it. Charlotte had her mind already made up to do exactly what she's wanted to do. She was going to write a book because Ian approved of it, and she was happy. Now, all is right with the world.

"WHEE, caller you're on the air."

"Casey, I knew from the beginning the 'Frustrated Friend' was crazy. Anybody that put their so-called friend's business in the streets the way she's put Angelic's, is demented. On top of that, she thinks that everybody else is beneath her. Who died and made her queen? I don't try to act like a man, but I have needs. If my boyfriend, whom I live with can't satisfy me to my liking, I need someone on the side who can."

"Damnnn… I hear you girlfriend," Casey chuckled. "WHEE, caller you're on the line."

"Some of y'all women are just like White folks. You always want to put the brothas in the same category. I'm not a dog and a couple of my partners aren't either. I don't cheat. I don't hit my woman and we got married two years after we started dating. I know for a fact that I'm a good man."

"My hat goes off to you brotha. Although I must admit, in my college days I was a real bow-wow. WHEE, caller you're on the line."

"I love this column. I look forward to reading it every week. When are they going to come out with the book and why can't they print the column twice a week?"

"The Rapture and the 'Frustrated Friend' is responsible for answering that question. Are you a desperate sistah? How much would you put up with to get a ring?" Casey asked.

"I'm married and I didn't have to put up with nothing. The first time my husband saw me, he knew I was going to be his wife."

"The first time he saw you…yeah right," Casey said, as he disconnected the call. WHEE, caller you're on the air."

"Casey there are some women that put up with a lot of sh*t."

Bleeeppp… "Ma'am this is live radio and you are on the air. Thank God for the seven-second delay. If it happens again, I'm gonna have to cut you off."

"I'm sorry Casey."

"Okay; are you trying to tell me women will put up with a man dogging them just for a ring?"

"Yeah, because they are in love. But I don't think Angelic needs to keep that ring though."

"Why?"

"She doesn't love him like a real woman should, who's going to be married in a few months. She's sleeping with another man. I agree with the friend, I think she should have stayed with that Jasper guy in the first place."

"Remember, he was drooling over her client not too long ago."

"And? Men drool over other women all the time, but it doesn't mean they want them."

"Damnnn... I wish more sistah's would think like you," Casey said. "WHEE, caller you're on the line."

"My hat goes off to Angelic also because she got Tibias right where she wants him now. It's apparent, she's going to break him down and hurt him like he's hurt her."

"What is your response to the friend calling women who sleep with two men at the same time sluts?"

"I guess I'm a slut then, because me and a whole lot of other women have done it. I like the column because I think I know who she's talking about; but I don't like the 'Frustrated Friend' though. She does think she's better than everybody else. She may be a one-man woman, but that doesn't mean everyone else in the world has to be."

"Sistah's are not like they used to be, that's for sure." He chuckled. "But if Angelic isn't a one-man woman, here's Dave Holister telling the world he's a *'One-Woman Man'*. Call us up people and talk to us on your breakfast with jam station. "

28

$\mathcal{A}$ wave of fear had come over DeDe, when she thought she had left the iron on from this morning. She clutched her chest, and took a step towards the door to rush back home. She couldn't rush home, because Stephan used her car to drive to work. She immediately called him at work, to see if he had noticed the iron and shut it off. When she called his job, the receptionist told her that Stephan was no longer employed with the company. She hung up the phone and tried paging and calling his cell phone. She even tried reaching him at her house. There was no answer. She hoped he was working somewhere else or looking for another job. She couldn't understand why he didn't tell her he was no longer working at the bank. She called the receptionist back to make sure she was speaking of Stephan Brown. The lady on the other end assured her that Stephan hadn't been employed with the company for nearly a month and a half. DeDe was now even more pissed with him than she was before. First of all, he moved his things into her place without discussing it with her. Secondly, he lost his job and didn't bother telling her.

It's funny because at one point in their relationship, she felt she wanted them to move in together so that they could get closer. Back then, of course he didn't think it was a good idea. Now that he has proposed, it's a good idea. 'A man should live with a woman for at least eight menstrual cycles, before getting married', he now says. DeDe thought it to be a crock! They could have gotten married without living together first. It's been four weeks since they've been living together and she never thought she would feel this way; but he was getting on her nerves and she wanted him out of her house. By them living together, they were made to face their differences daily. They were even forced to take off their masks every now and again to show each other who they really were. As a result, DeDe didn't like Stephan. Stephan had a way of going into a shell more than ever, now that they were living together. She had known about him keeping his guard up whenever he thought they were getting too close, but they were going to be married. Holy matrimony meant they were going to get even closer. He had put up countless communication barriers between them, until it was time for bed and he wanted to make love. He expected her to jump right into place and when she didn't, there was an argument. He was also messy. She wasn't the most meticulous person in the world, but she did clean up. He let dishes pile up in the sink and put empty ice trays back into the freezer. She had to tell him more than twice to take the trash out. He uses up all the toilet paper and never has the decency to replace it with a new roll. He expects her to cook every night and make love to him on demand. And to make the cake batter blander, he hasn't given her so much as ten dollars toward groceries, let alone assist in paying any bills. She looked down at her ring. If he lost his job, how was he paying for this ring? She pondered, while watching the light dance through the magnificent stone. I know he didn't have twelve-thousand lying around to pay cash for it. Also, how is his seven-hundred-fifty dollar a month car note getting paid? He hasn't even had the money to get it out of the repair shop. It's been there for a month, while he's being charged a storage fee. She was glad he hadn't fixed his lips to ask her for any money, because she would just have to tell him no. She tried calling him again. When she didn't get an answer, she just left a message for him to check the iron; she didn't want to let him know she knew he didn't have a job. She felt somewhat at ease after realizing he always runs an iron over all of his clothes, whether he was going to work or otherwise.

276

SHE HAD GOTTEN Dionne to drop her off at the salon and Roberta was going to take her home. She walked in, spoke to everyone she knew and took a glass of wine and a couple of crackers and waited her turn, while getting a manicure. She would be one of the last to be waited on, since Roberta was going to take her home. She felt kind of nervous about being around Roberta lately, knowing her sister Kendra was sleeping with her sister Charva's husband. And DeDe is Charva's best friend to boot. She's been praying that Kendra would find someone else or Jeremiah would get tired of her money-grubbing ass and leave her alone altogether. Charva's been calling DeDe like every other day and she talks to her as if she doesn't know anything. They've set Jeremiah's three day surprise birthday bash for a month from today and the three hundred invitations will be going out on Monday.

"Single women want to be married and married women want to be single. If I had it to do over again, I swear I would stay single." Felicia Freeman said, as she hung up her cell phone and took a sip of her wine. "If the single women know what I know, they would enjoy the single life while they can. Marriage isn't all it's hyped-up to be." She said, and rolled her eyes up in her head.

"Ain't that the truth, girl?" Tangala, said, as she and her sister Debra laughed, while staring at each other. Both of them were housewives, married to prominent doctors who were also brothers. DeDe had met them a few years ago at a Christmas party she had gone to with Waymon.

"Why are you downing marriage? I'm happily married." Katina, their beautician said. She was the only one out of the six beauticians in the salon that was married. Everyone else either had live-ins or boyfriends. No one was engaged and seemed happy about it.

"So am I." Dawn said, as she gloated. "My husband and I are the best of friends." DeDe expected all of the other women in the shop with huge rocks on their fingers to agree with her, but they continued to stare out in space or flip through their magazines without looking at her once.

"You can't tell me he's your everyday best friend, like a girlfriend would be?" Debra asked her. "A husband and wife are not meant to be best friends." She laughed, only wishing she and her husband were that close.

Dawn nodded. "I can talk to my husband about any and everything."

"You need to get a life outside of him." Tangala chuckled. "That's what's wrong with us women when we get married; nobody outside our husbands and children exists."

DeDe knew that to be true, because of her girlfriends Bridget and Marie who will not do anything without their husbands. Their lives mainly consist of their husbands and their children.

"I have friends, but we are all so into our lives we don't have time to sit and talk on the phone, as much as we did when we didn't have families. Having a husband is a lot within itself. " Dawn said and chuckled. She seemed so happily married. DeDe hoped that when she got married, she could speak so highly of it.

"That's the type of marriage that's very boring, when your only life is your husband." Laverne said, as she popped a cracker in her mouth. DeDe knew by her husband being a Major in the army and spending most of his time overseas, it's impossible for her to make him her life. "You don't have any friends besides your husband?"

Dawn nodded. "Yes, but he's my best friend. My husband and I have been married for eleven years and we still have fun together," she said. "We go to the movies and we might have dinner over candlelight, when the children are at his mother's. Also, our communication is great. We lived together before getting married."

DeDe looked up, but dared not to say how miserable she was with Stephan living with her. Shacking-up isn't for everybody.

"My husband and I wanted to move in together, but his mother and my mother told us if we did there would be no wedding. They said we might as well go to the courthouse, if we were going to shack-up and pretend to be married," Laura Banks said. Her husband was a quarterback for the Dallas Wranglers. Everyone knew it, because she made a point to broadcast it on more than one occasion.

"I lived with my husband before we got married. We had problems then and we have problems now." Her girlfriend Vicki said, and rolled her eyes at the thought of her own many problems. DeDe could only imagine what their many problems were. Her husband was a basketball player for the Houston Scorchers and everyone knew he fooled around on her. He didn't care who saw him with his many women.

Although DeDe felt her problems with Stephan were annoying, but things weren't nearly as bad as him fooling around with another woman, like Vicki had. However, she still felt if they didn't sit down and have a long talk before getting married, she was going to be even more miserable.

"I feel sorry for the single women that are out there trying to find a man to marry them. They don't know what they're getting." Roberta said.

"That's the problem; they're looking for the man, when he should be looking for them." Tanisha said.

"To each his own," Vicki said. "We're now living in the new millennium and it's alright to pursue a man."

"Yes indeed it is," Yolanda said, as five other women in her Amen Corner agreed with her.

"Women who are single should be thankful they are, and learn to live their lives alone." Felicia said, and other women agreed with her. It was mostly the married ones.

"Living alone is not as easy as you put it Felicia. It's hard out here with one income," Yolanda whined.

"Not for today's black woman, it isn't," Dorothy said.

"All of us are not Superwomen and those that are, still want to be married. I don't know too many women that can willingly conceive the thought of not getting married or just being alone and lonely, for the rest of their lives." Darinda said.

"But they are not alone." Yolanda said. "There isn't a woman out there that's alone. She might feel lonely on some days, when she wishes she had a man. But hell, there are some married women that will tell you they sometimes feel alone, and they're married."

"So very true." Laverne and Vicki said in unison.

"I want to marry the man I'm in love with and plan our wedding." Candace said. "I want my daddy to walk with me down the aisle, in my beautiful white dress and I want to say that's my child's father instead of my baby's daddy."

"Married women were once single, so they know the joys of being single, Yolanda said. "However, single women have never been married and they can only idolize those who are."

"Like I said, marriage isn't for everybody. And if you know like I know, you'll stay single as long as God allows you to." Felicia said, while applying some lip-gloss.

DeDe listened to the conversation, as she flipped through one of her many wedding magazines for ideas. She wasn't sure about her colors or what she was looking for in bridesmaid dresses. Whatever she chose, she wanted them to be sexy. She hoped her going to the wedding expo tomorrow would help her, because she had no idea what she wanted, after planning hundreds of weddings for other people. The planning of her own wedding was much more stressful than any she had planned for others. She felt angst; mainly due to the fear and doubt she now had about marrying Stephan. Her doubts were beginning to weigh heavily on her mind. One minute she was excited about finally getting married. A few seconds later, she was questioning herself about whether she was ready to marry Stephan or anybody else for that matter. She loved him. She had always thought that she wanted to spend the rest of her life with him, since they began dating. But now things seemed different because she's looking at the situation with a clearer pair of lenses. He's not working, and as long as they've been dating he's been in and out of work whether he was fired or just quit. She doesn't want to always have the stress of carrying the load of their finances by herself. He has child support and bills and she doesn't want to pay his debts. She has bills and responsibilities of her own. Needless to say, with only one income it would be like robbing Peter to pay Paul. Stephan has got to help. When she gets married, she wants to take off the Superwoman suit she's worn for so long and rely on her husband to handle their life plans. That's what Waymon wanted to do, but she didn't want him.

Second doubts are the same thing that caused her to call off her other two engagements. Lately, she's thought about telling Stephan to take that damn ring and get the hell out of her house. But she is thirty-four, her mother has told everyone in her family, she's told everyone and Bridget has told Waymon and Stephan has told Shannon. If they were not married, Shannon would try to put her claws back into him for the family she's always wanted. And DeDe would just die, if they ever got back together.

"Marriage ain't for everybody, it's okay to still be single," Felicia said, once again.

WHEN DEDE GOT home from the beauty salon Stephan wasn't there. She was not upset, but happy. She didn't want to see his face or hear his lies about why he didn't answer his cell phone or return any of her pages. She went to the laundry room to check the iron and Stephan had put it away on the shelf. She walked to the kitchen, opened a bottle of wine and poured herself a glass. She walked to the bedroom and got undressed into her sweats and a t-shirt, walked back into the den and flopped down on the sofa. The room looked a mess from where Stephan had been eating in there. There were wrappers scattered about and crumbs everywhere. She wasn't going to vacuum up any of his mess, this time. For four weeks, she's been cleaning up behind him. There were several water rings on the coffee table. He was too lazy to grab a coaster that was only inches away from his fingertips, and place the glass on it. Three pairs of his shoes sat under the coffee table from three straight nights of him leaving them there. Also, there was a random bedroom pillow on the sofa. His stereo system sat in the corner, because hers was in the entertainment center. His furniture cluttered her garage, because he didn't want to put it in storage. She became infuriated, because she felt like he was taking advantage of her. He walked into the house dressed in a suit and tie, in a very chipper mood, as he usually is after he gets off work. She cut her eyes behind her.

"What's up baby? Did you cook?" He asked, as he walked into the house and made a quick left turn to the kitchen.

She didn't say anything, as she continued to sip on her wine and watch television. The phone rang and she answered it on the first ring, hoping it was someone for her. He had given her number out to all of his boys and family, as if it was his place. Well, he was living there. He slept, ate and showered there and he had all of his clothes hanging in her closets. It was Bridget on the phone and DeDe began talking to her, as if they hadn't talked in years.

"We can get together tomorrow. I've already picked out my invitations and Mama knows this lady in Ohio who makes cakes that are the absolute bomb. So, I put her in charge of the cake. Girl, there's so much to do, when it comes to a wedding. My dress….no, I'm not getting married in white," she chuckled. "The Vera Wang dress that I'm so crazy about comes in white, but I'm ordering it in a champagne color. It should be here in about a month." She noticed Stephan sitting on the sofa waiting for her to acknowledge him and perhaps tell whomever she was talking to that she had to go. She had done precisely that so many times before. She jumped from subject to subject laughing and gossiping, not looking at Stephan once. She got up and poured herself another glass of wine. She turned the television from ESPN that Stephan had flipped it to, back to the Lifetime channel she loved so much. She thought about just going in her bedroom and closing the door, but she was getting a kick out of the annoyed look on his face.

"I'm so ashamed of myself, I've been talking to you about everything else, but I haven't asked you how those babies are doing. You know they are in the wedding, along with my nephews. How is Jerome? Is he at home? He must not be, because I don't hear him trying to put his two and a half cents into our conversation."

"No, he and the girls are out and about. I think he took them to McDonald's, since I didn't cook." Bridget said.

"Why not? You're at home all damn day."

"Girl, you sound like Jerome. Just because I agreed to sit at home and be a full-time mother didn't mean I was going to cook everyday or get pregnant every year. After this baby, I'm going to have me a nice glass of wine, a giant Hershey Bar and get my tubes either tied, clipped or burned. All three if I have to. I don't want no more babies. I'm going to leave populating the world up to you. So have y'all discussed when that first blessed event will occur?"

"No," DeDe said, as she cut her eyes over at Stephan, who was staring at her. He looked like he was getting ready to snap, if she didn't get off the phone. "Well girl, I'm going to get off this phone. I need to go do some grocery shopping; but we'll get together tomorrow okay?"

Once she hung up the phone, Stephan sat slouched down in the chair with his tie loosen and his shirt open. "Not that I was listening to your conversation, but I heard you name everyone else that was going to be in the wedding except Alexis. Am I wrong?"

DeDe turned and looked at him. "No."

"So are you saying, she's not in the wedding?" He didn't give her time to answer before he went into a rage. "You have everybody else's damn kid in it, except for my child. Are you out of your goddamn mind?"

"No. Are you out of yours? I didn't put her in the wedding, because I know that bitch Shannon isn't going to let her."

"How do you know that?"

"She won't even let her come over here. How do you think she's going to feel about letting her be in our damn wedding?"

"Hell no, she's not going to allow her to come to a place she can't even call or come herself."

"Well, she's not coming to the wedding, so I guess Alexis isn't going to be in it. Therein lies the answer to your question."

"No, that's not the answer to my question, because it's not the right answer. Shannon not being able to come to the wedding is neither here nor there. But what's getting me is that you didn't even discuss with me that you didn't want my daughter in it. That's a special day for me also. I would like to have some say-so in it."

DeDe said to herself, 'Oh no he's not talking about discussing things. He didn't discuss quitting his job and he didn't discuss moving in with me.' "Discuss," she replied. "You do have some say-so in the planning of this wedding. But since we're talking about discussing things with one another; why haven't you discussed with me the fact that you no longer work at the bank, huh?"

He dramatically let out a long sigh with his eyes rolling to the back of his head. "Aw man, I didn't think I had to let you know when I decided to change jobs."

Yes the hell you do. You are staying in my house, rent-free. You need to let me know something, she thought. "So where are you working now?"

"I'm temping." He walked into the kitchen and poured himself a glass of wine.

"Temping?" she responded as she jumped up from the sofa and walked into the kitchen behind him. "What about a full-time job; something that's stable? Bills need to be paid around here Stephan." And if you are going to be living here; you are going to pay some bills, is what she wanted to say. But she knew that would be a completely new argument.

"And I know this DeDe, but right now I can't pay shit. I have child support I have to catch up on, before Shannon wakes up one morning and decides to put the law on me."

DeDe thought, is this the man I want to marry? Am I going to be saddled with someone who puts everything second to child support; a man who has to kiss the ass of his child's mother, because he's behind in support payments, and a person who can quit his job, just because he feels like it. "Why did you leave the bank anyway? That was a good job."

"I don't want to talk about it. I'm working now and I'll give you some money next week, when I get paid." He said, as he walked to the bedroom to undress and take a shower.

She looked at him and rolled her eyes. "Why don't you take that money and go get your own place. I don't remember asking you to move in here either," she mumbled and walked back into the den and flopped down on the sofa. Him quitting his job needs to be discussed, whether he wants to talk about it or not. And where was he all damn day, when I was paging him about turning off the iron? She jumped up off the sofa and stormed toward the bathroom, for some answers. He was just stepping out of the shower. "Where is your car right now and how are you paying the seven-hundred dollar note on it?"

"DeDe, have I asked you for any money?"

"No, because you already owe me money."

"And I'm going to pay that to you...right now, I have the whole fuckin' world on my shoulders and I don't need you to add to the pressure. Get off my back!" He yelled and walked out of the room leaving her feeling like she was the bad guy, for wanting answers. As she let out a sigh, all the anger and power she had to stop him from running over her had left her body, within a second of her exhaling. Maybe he did have the world on his shoulders. She was sure he felt emasculated with that bitch Shannon not letting him see his child, him trying to find another job, and his finances being in disarray. She was ashamed of herself for not being supportive enough to understand. After all, this was the man she claimed to love and wanted to marry. She walked into the kitchen where he was loading dishes into the dishwasher. "Stephan."

He cut his eyes over at her, as he continued to load the dishes. She looked a lot differently than she did a couple of minutes ago. She looked much softer right now. He could see the caring and understanding of what he was going through in her eyes.

"The last thing I want to do is add more pressure to the load you already have on your back. I'm here for you and I want to help you relieve some of that pressure if you would just talk to me. I had no idea you were under so much duress. We hardly talk anymore."

"I've noticed," he said, starting the dishwasher and wiping down the countertops. "And mainly it's been all my fault."

She couldn't believe her ears. He had never taken the blame for anything that has gone wrong between them. Except for his behavior that led to the last break-up, when she met Elliott. She felt it was all her fault, because she was angry with him for moving in and she displayed her anger by snapping and not talking to him. She walked over to him with her arms open wide. "I love you, baby."

They hugged each other tightly for two minutes; and then Stephan's hands began to travel south.

29

INSTEAD of DeDe getting together with Bridget like they had planned and confirmed last night, she and Stephan had gotten up early this morning to go to the wedding expo and pick out bridesmaids dresses. They had a great time talking, laughing, viewing wedding dresses, tuxedos, sampling foods for their menu, meeting photographers, and meeting other happy engaged couples, who were trying to get ideas for their weddings also. Everyone they met admired DeDe's ring, which made she and Stephan feel great. DeDe still wondered how he was paying for it, since he didn't have a full-time job. She walked around the convention center proudly with Stephan by her side; giving his input as she planned the wedding. Since their talk last night, things seemed like they were headed back to normal between them. They spent four hours at the expo, afterwards they went bowling, grabbed some fast food and went home and made love for the rest of the day and night.

THIS SUNDAY MORNING DeDe had gotten up to go to church, and she was very glad she did. Stephan who has never stepped a foot in church; since the last time his mother made him go on Easter Sunday when he was fourteen, tried to talk her into staying in bed with him for the morning. She figured she better show her face, if she wanted Bishop Blake to counsel and marry them in the church for no charge. She could hire a preacher and get married in a rose garden, but so many of her friends had done that. She felt it was becoming repetitious and tired. DeDe used to attend church every Sunday, before she met Stephan but she stopped going. Not because he talked her out of not going, but when Sunday came around, she just couldn't pull herself away from him. Although he probably would have been there when she got back, she just didn't want him out of her sight.

She was in a good mood, as she sang all the songs the choir had sung. She was ready to go through the week holding on to the good word the Bishop had taught. 'God is always with her and He will never forsake her. His mercy and grace does endure forever'. Her spirit had been fed and her soul was nourished. She was going to start attending church regularly, even after the Bishop marries them. Also, Stephan was going to begin attending, starting next Sunday whether he wanted to or not.

But when she got home, her anger overcame her uplifted spirits and a thousand curse words raced through her mind; but not one parted through her lips. She wasn't the type of woman to cause a scene and show-out, but Stephan and three of his friends were sitting in the den on her nice cream and peach colored sofa and chairs, drinking beer and watching baseball. She could have fainted. It wasn't enough that he had it looking twenty years old from him lounging all over it; and now his friends. It was starting to look grayish already. When she chose those colors, she didn't think anyone would be sitting on them, because she hardly sat in her den. She rarely entertained and she doesn't have any children; therefore, she didn't have to choose darker colors. Everyone said hello to her. She waved, even though she was in no mood to speak. She and Stephan were supposed to go look at some flowers and go look-over a guest menu, for their sit-down dinner reception. They were also supposed to go out to dinner, his treat. But she figured they weren't going to do any of that, since he had company. His boys were so important to him. She was going to spend the rest of her day in her bedroom, watching the Lifetime channel. She walked to her bedroom, changed into her sweats and walked into the kitchen for a glass of water. The refrigerator was fully stocked with bottled Budweiser and Michelob. Over in the sink were two family-size packs of chicken wings, and sitting on the countertop were two heads of cabbage. Attitude immediately presented itself. Her eyes began to roll, and her lips began to smack. "I'm not cooking anything, so he can just hang that up. I'm going to fix me something to eat and go get in my bed and watch television, for the rest of the day. So, if he wants anything cooked, he'll do it himself," she mumbled.

Stephan walked into the kitchen and walked up behind her wrapping his arms around her waist. "Baby, Dedrick and Stewart brought over some wings and cabbage and we were wondering, if you didn't mind cooking the cabbage and seasoning up those wings and dumping 'em in some hot grease for a brotha," he asked her and kissed her on her neck. He walked out of the kitchen, before she could tell him, hell no. Why can't Dedrick's fiancée, who he's been engaged to for five years do it? Or why can't whoever the hell Stewart's woman is, season up this shit and dump 'em in some hot grease for a brotha?

For an hour and a half, she walked back and forth from her bedroom to the kitchen frying both packs of chicken wings. All they left her were two pieces of chicken, which was the equivalent of one wing! Stephan and his friends had feasted on over eighty-four pieces and the whole pot of cabbages. She couldn't believe it, but then again she could. They didn't have to slave over a hot stove; all they had to do was chew. She threw the two pieces of chicken into the garbage, fixed herself a salad and walked back into her room while watching them lick their fingers and drink ice-cold beer. If they didn't have the decency to leave her more than two pieces of chicken, after she had taken her time to cook it, she didn't want it and they damn sure weren't going to have it.

The clock read 12:30am when Stephan climbed into bed smelling like stale beer. He began patting and rubbing on DeDe, for round two of the lovemaking they had last night.

"No, I'm asleep," she slightly yelled through her sleepiness.

"Baby, roll over," he slurred, while running his hand up her nightgown to discover she had on panties. "Why do you have on panties?"

"Leave me alone, I said I'm asleep."

He reached over and turned on the lamp. "If we are playing this hold-back-the-sex game before we get married, what in the hell will I have to deal with when we do get married?"

"Change," she said, and pulled the covers over her head.

σσσσσ

SEEING STEPHAN LIE in bed, while she dressed for work really ate away at her. They had a wedding to pay for. He claimed to have the pressure of the world on his shoulders, so why wasn't he up looking for a job? She called his name several times to see if he needed to use her car to go to his temp job or go to an interview, but he didn't move. She began slamming the drawers and the closet door shut, hoping to wake him. Nothing she did got him to move from his comatose, deep sleep and stretched out position. She stormed out of the room slamming the door behind her, and went to start a pot of coffee. As she walked back to her room, she ran into Dedrick coming out of the guest bathroom. "Oh my God," She jumped behind the wall, while trying to cover up, with her arms and hands.

"Damn, DeDe," Dedrick grunted, as he turned his head after catching a quick glimpse of her in her pink lace panties and bra set.

"Stephan," she screamed. "Bring me my robe!"

Dedrick rushed back into the guest bedroom and closed the door. After realizing Stephan wasn't coming with her robe anytime soon, she flew past the closed door, as if Dedrick was trying to get one last peek. She busted through her bedroom door and began to yell. "Dammit, Stephan!"

He jumped out of his sleep and sat upright.

"Why didn't you tell me Dedrick was sleeping in the other room? I walked out there in my panties and bra and he saw me."

"Damn baby, I forgot. But it ain't nothing he's never seen before."

"He's never seen me Stephan," she said, as she snatched her pants off the hanger that was hooked on the doorknob.

"Well, he needs a place to stay for a couple of days, until he works things out with Carla. She put him out."

"A couple of days," she swallowed, as she hastily got dressed. "Dammit Stephan, what's wrong with you?" She walked into the bathroom and began putting on lipstick, and a little of her new Tyra Banks makeup.

"What's wrong now? DeDe, he's my boy."

"Do you have to work today?" She asked, as she walked out of the bathroom and grabbed her purse and briefcase.

"Yeah, and I also have an interview for a permanent position with Conaco Financial, as a manager in their credit card department. Dedrick is going to let me borrow his car, while he's at work."

"Good." She walked out of her room to go to her car and bumped into Dedrick sitting on the sofa.

"I'm sorry about that DeDe."

"It's fine. It's nothing you haven't seen before," she said, as she walked out of the house feeling embarrassed.

THINGS HAD SLOWED down for DeDe, since her work for the Bushel and Coleman campaign had been completed. She was now able to concentrate on some of her smaller accounts and drum-up some new business. She took out her hot market list and began calling some of the new .com companies that had moved to the San Antonio, Austin, Dallas and Houston area. She was feeling happy, because she was successful in setting-up an appointment for later on in the day with one of them.

She got up from her desk and walked down to Dionne's office. She wanted to know how her weekend had gone, with her soon to be in-laws. She softly knocked on the door before entering.

"Good morning girly," DeDe sang, while trying to sound as cheerful as possible to cover up her anger with Stephan.

"Good morning," Dionne said, sounding nonchalant and dry. DeDe figured her weekend didn't go as well as she expected.

"How is everything?" She asked, as she walked in and sat down.

"Busy. The Wynnhill Clinic is conducting free mammograms and AIDS test screenings for low-income, single women, head of household families to raise breast cancer and AIDS awareness. So, I've been sending out press releases on that. So far I've received three phone calls from the radio and television stations. I've been working on that since I got here this morning and I'm already tired."

"I just thought I would stop by and say good morning, and see how your weekend at your in-laws-to-be went."

"It was fine," she said, and left it at that.

"Stephan and I spent the entire day at the wedding expo on Saturday and we went bowling and rented some movies afterwards."

"Sounds like y'all had a good time."

"It was cool in spite of me being mad with him yesterday."

Dionne didn't even need to ask her why, before she began talking.

"First of all, he got upset because I'm not putting Alexis in the wedding."

"Why not? That's his day also, and his little girl."

"It's her mother who's not going to let her be in it. So, I'm not going to give her the satisfaction of telling us no, if we request that she be in the wedding. I'm just not going to put her in it."

Dionne had always thought that DeDe was a bitch, but now she was truly acting like one. "I think you should put her in it," she said with her elbows on her desk and her face plastered in her hands.

DeDe sighed, and rolled her eyes. "Secondly, he let his friend move in with us, without discussing it with me first. And thirdly." She couldn't possibly tell Dionne or anyone else Stephan wasn't working and she was footing all the bills. She felt they would think of her as stupid and hard up. People never seem to think that if a woman helps a man out financially, she might just love him enough to not want to see him in a bind. She had given him money, helped him pay his bills, child support and had even paid for his attorney, after Shannon had pressed charges on them although he was fully employed at that time. But he just didn't have that much money. To her, there was a difference between being a fool and helping him out. "Ain't no more lovemaking going on between us."

Dionne tensed-up with nervousness and began fidgeting with her thumbs. She didn't dare tell DeDe that there was a column in The Rapture with the same thing that she just uttered, in the title. Dionne kind of held her breath and prayed that DeDe was still oblivious to everything; because there was no way that she would ever mention it to her.

30

WHILE Charlotte was in such a cheerful mood, Dionne sat miserably upset over lunch, as she's been since she came back from Dallas from meeting Byron's family.

"Girly, why are you picking over that food? Eat up and be happy. I truly am. Ian and I made love all weekend."

Dionne looked at her in shock and for an explanation.

"I know girl you are looking just as shocked as I was, when he began touching me. We had gone out Friday night to celebrate me signing the contract with Omega Publishing House. He told me how proud he was of me and happy that I found something I enjoyed doing. We drove around the town and went home and got it on like two dogs in heat," she said, gleaming with excitement and laughter.

"What?"

"Yes. Since we hadn't slept together in five months, a sistah had forgotten why she loved her husband so much. He put it down!"

"Are you sure he's not fooling around?"

"Yes, did you not hear me, we made love. He called one of his attorney friends to read over my contract and he called his family bragging about me being a signed author. Girl, he's just being very supportive.

I wonder why, Dionne thought.

"So what happened between you and Byron this weekend?"

"He's changed."

"Girl all men do. They don't stay the same. I thought you knew. The thrill is gone. When that happens, you are faced to see whom you're really dealing with afterwards. But I tell you, if he doesn't want you to do anything for your family, you need to leave him alone."

"He thinks his family is better than mine, and I believe they think so too. Do you know that he told his family that I moved out of my house into a condo, so that my mother and brothers could have some place to stay? His brother-in-law brought it up to me, while we were at dinner. Can you believe the likes of him questioning me about it? Byron had also told them that my mother loves to party, so she can't be a grandmother to AJ and that she dates younger men. He also told them one of my brothers is on drugs and he always calls me asking me for money. And since I'm in denial that he's doing drugs, I give him the money. My brother has been clean for two years. He just told his family all of my business. And then, there I was thinking I looked good, and his sister made jokes by calling me the green giant and he just laughed, as if that was the funniest thing he had ever heard."

"Green giant," Charlotte chuckled. "What were you wearing?"

"The olive green suit I was telling you about. When I told him about it, all he had to say was 'you got to have a sense of humor, to deal with my family'," she said and folded her arms and fell back into her chair fuming.

WHEN DEDE GOT off the elevator in the Quantum Place office building, after visiting one of her new clients, she noticed a gray Lexus with tinted windows and shiny silver rims parked out front. It looked familiar and if she could see the license plate that read 'ELBUDA', she would know for sure, if it was Elliott's or not. She became nervous. Her heart sank and her stomach developed knots the size of golf balls and Tiger Woods was teeing off. She looked over her shoulder, before stepping into the revolving door and pushing it open.

She didn't have to check out the license plate, because out of nowhere Elliott appeared behind her. She did a double take wondering and looking to see where he had come from. "Hey," she said, smiling through her nervousness.

"Hi."

When he stepped through the door behind her, the early autumn breezes of late August whirled his cologne through the air, causing her to reminisce about the lovemaking they had shared. CHROME by Azzaro was her favorite. They walked down the stairs in complete silence, not knowing what to say or how to say it. Elliott was walking slightly behind her. When they got to the bottom of the stairs and he walked over to his car, she realized he wasn't going to say anything else to her. This just may be the last time they see each other for a long time, so she asked him, "What are you doing on this side of town?"

"One of my customers decided to entertain their clients in the office, so we catered their lunch."

"I guess that's one of the perks of knowing the owner," she chuckled, as she tried to make small talk.

"I guess," he said, and continued to load hot oven bags out of his trunk.

She rushed over to her car and threw her briefcase over the seat. She felt like a fool for even trying to talk to him. It was obvious that he was bitter and angry with her, and no matter what she said or did could change that.

He looked over the hood of his trunk at her, and sighed. Of all people, he had to run into her. It was evident he was still attracted to her; in spite of the games she had played. How could she even be thinking about getting married to that niggah, let alone actually going through with it? Just before she jumped into her car, he asked her. "I hear you're getting married?" Kendra had told him, but he wanted to hear it come from her. It wasn't too long ago that she called him to go out, and now she was getting married.

What if I told you I was having second thoughts would you believe me, she wished she could ask him. But instead, she said, "Yes... I am."

He looked her straight in the eye, while nodding his head. "Congratulations."

"Thank you." She jumped into the car, with her heart racing and drove as fast as she could through the 15mph parking lot. She took one deep breath, as she waited at the stop sign and began screaming, as soon as she got completely out of Elliott's view. "Kendra and her big damn mouth. Who told her to be telling my business anyway?"

"Damn, DeDe thought, and rolled her eyes, as she looked at the caller I.D. of her cell phone, just before answering it. It was Charva. She sounded as if she had been crying, and DeDe really wasn't in the mood to talk about Jeremiah or hear her cry. She had her own issues to deal with, and she felt like crying herself. She is engaged to be married, but she isn't happy. She didn't think she loved Stephan like she used to. The only reason she was still going to marry him was, because she had told so many people and her mother was so excited. And now to top everything off, after seeing Elliott, she wanted him. She wasn't listening to a damn thing Charva was saying.

"Charva, what is it?" DeDe blurted out, before going into a rage. "I know he's your husband, but he's broken the vows. Why are you holding on and crying every damn day about something you can't change. You haven't even confronted him with this fooling around business, because you're afraid of him telling you the truth; that yes, there is another woman. If in fact there is another woman." DeDe knew for a fact that there was, and who it was. "What are you going to do about it? You're not going to leave him, because he's already had at least one bastard child, during y'alls marriage. All you're worried about is who's going to be the next damn Mrs. Jeremiah Williams, while he's out there fooling around doing whatever he wants to do. You're no better than any of those other sistahs you call me talking about. You call them stupid, because they don't know how to let go of those high-powered niggahs, with deep pockets. Divorce is not just a word, it's an option."

Click.

"Charva," DeDe called out, after hearing a clicking sound, then the dial tone. "I know she didn't just hang up on me." She pressed the end button on the cell phone and began shaking her head. "I guess I struck a nerve. The truth does hurt."

She sat at the traffic light only a couple of minutes away from her house.

During the time it took for the light to change, DeDe decided she would rather be at home than back sitting in that office with nothing to do. All the press releases had been sent out and all the phone calls she needed to make were completed this morning. She was going to go home to spend some quality time by herself and regroup and relax for tomorrow, before Stephan and their new roommate Dedrick gets home. Those were the benefits of not punching a clock and having the flexibility to go out and visit clients. She would check her voice-mail throughout the day, just in case Brad Michaels decided to check up on her.

When she got home ten minutes later, her cell phone rang again. It was Charva.

"Hello."

"Bitch, I had to hang up on your ass. It took me a while to call you back, because you had my blood boiling. I take it I called you at the wrong time, because that mess you were talking to me wasn't even right. I've been an ear plenty of times to you, when you thought that niggah you're about to marry was cheating with his babymama. I've also taken up for your raggedy-ass, when Bridget and Marie thought you were stupid for dealing with 'im, and now you're on the verge of marrying 'im. If you weren't in the mood to be bothered, you should have told me. Then I would have left your ass alone and called you back some other time. And as far as your last comment is concerned, divorce is never an option in my marriage. Okay? Even if he was broke-as-a-joke with no power or money, it's simply not an option. That is my husband and I love 'im. Now you go deal with your issues and we'll talk later. I just had to call you back and get that off my little chest, since you got so many heavy things off yours."

They both hung up without saying good-bye. Hearing that Bridget and Marie thought that she was stupid for marrying Stephan was nothing new to her. She always knew they felt that way. That's the main reason why she stopped talking to them about her and Stephan. She just hoped their marriages and men were as wonderful as they believed them to be. DeDe also caught Charva's dig regarding her large breasts. She smiled and said out loud,

"That's okay, but they'll never be mistaken for two mosquito bites like yours."

DeDe got undressed, put on her leggings and t-shirt, and turned on the television to watch one of the many judges with their own court television shows. She laid across her bed and dozed off, into a deep sleep. She was awakened by Stephan calling her name, as he stood over her with a dozen of red roses. She looked over at the clock. It was six-thirty in the evening. She had slept for four hours.

"What are you doing here?" Stephan asked. "I had gone by your job to take you to lunch and they said you were out in the field visiting a client."

"I was, but I was tired from the sun. So, I just came home and laid across the bed." She looked at the roses. "What are those for?"

"You." He handed them to her and kissed her on the forehead. "I got the job, so tomorrow all I got to do is take the drug test and I start the day after. A brotha will be starting out at forty-five a year."

"Are you serious?" she asked, as she placed the roses on the nightstand. "That's great, baby."

He climbed on top of her and said, "That's more than great, that's wonderful. With your hundred and my forty-five with a three-thousand raise after my first year, we can move out of here into something bigger."

"Wait a minute there's nothing wrong with living here. What we need to do is pay everything off for the wedding. And that's going to cost us an estimated twenty."

"Hundred?" He asked.

"No, silly. Thousand."

"Damn." He began kissing her neck and breasts while getting them both aroused. "Can a fiancée get a little."

She looked into his eyes. The roses, and he got a job; why not. "I guess since we're celebrating the fact that you have a new job and all."

He tore off his and her clothes and wasted no time in making love to her.

DEDE WAS IN a very chipper and satisfied mood. She had taken out a bottle of wine out of the fridge, and defrosted some hamburger meat in the microwave for some spaghetti. She was in the kitchen cooking, while talking about the wedding with Stephan, who was sitting in the next room watching television. His pager went off.

"Damn, why didn't he just call the house?" He asked out loud, as he checked the number on his pager.

"Who is that, baby?"

"Dedrick, I need to go pick him up. Damn." He got up and walked to the bedroom to get dressed into his dry-cleaned Sean John T-shirt and jeans and his Timberlands. He looked like he was going someplace other than to just pick Dedrick up from work. But DeDe was used to him dressing nicely, even just going on a trip to the grocery store. His sometimes roughneck look turned her on. "Baby do you need me to stop by the store for anything?" He asked her, as he fastened his watch and silver nugget chain-link bracelet.

"No."

"I'll be back in a few." He kissed her on the forehead and walked out of the door. She dashed into the den, turned off the television and put on her new TP-2 CD by R Kelly and turned it up as loud as possible and began to groove and vibe off of each song. In her mind, it was only R Kelly's voice who had the ability to make a woman moist, and ready to give it up to whomever she was with; be it an attractive man or not. She grooved down the hallway to the bathroom popping her fingers and shaking her hips, when she heard her cell phone ringing in her purse. She rushed over to her purse and checked the caller ID before answering it. The number was private.

"Hello," she said, while trying to catch her breath.

"Hi."

"Elliott." His voice sent chills through her body and her racing heart sank to her feet. She sat down on the edge of her messy bed. "What's up?"

"Can you get out?" He asked.

DeDe really wanted to see him, but what excuse would she give Stephan for leaving the house at eight-thirty on a Monday night. She thought about it, he wasn't there so she didn't have to give him an excuse if she left him a note and finished preparing dinner before he got back? "Yes."

"Why don't you meet me at my place."

"Right now?"

"Yes, of course."

She hung up the phone ran into the kitchen poured the jar of spaghetti sauce into a pot, cut up some green, yellow and red peppers, onions and mushrooms and dumped them into the sauce. She wanted to be out of there, before Stephan got home. She poured the water off the noodles, took the garlic bread out of the oven and rushed into the shower lathered her body in lavender and vanilla body-wash, rinsed off, grabbed her towel and jumped out of the shower. She turned on her curling iron, just to bump a couple of curls in her hair. She put on her CK jeans and matching t-shirt and mules, and she was ready. She wanted to wear the Versace jeans and matching shirt Elliott had given her, as a gift. She knew trying to explain to Stephan why she wore tight painted on Versace jeans over to Bridget's wouldn't be easy. She called Bridget and told her not to call her house and lied and said that she would explain later. Next she called Stephan's cell phone and left the message. She stated that Bridget wanted to bounce something very important off her and they were headed to Starbucks to talk over a cup of ridiculously expensive coffee. She then dashed out of the house headed straight for Elliott's. Him seeing her today must have made him forget about being angry with her. She had to admit; she was looking mighty good. But then it dawned on her that he might still be angry and he wants some payback. He wants her to drive all the way over to his house and he's probably not there, just like she did him. "No the hell he's not going to do me like that." She reached into her purse for her cell phone and called him.

"Hello," he answered.

"Hey there, I forgot, do I make a left or right on Morrison?"

"It's a left."

Although men are men, they can also be boys who still like to play childish tit for tat games.

She hung up the phone and within ten minutes, she pulled into his driveway. She looked into the rearview mirror to make sure she had no lipstick on her teeth. She also checked that her hair was in place, and that there weren't any little foreign things dangling from the hairs of her nose. She popped a piece of gum into her mouth and walked to the door. He answered the door smiling and looking as handsome as he was earlier that day.

"Hello sexy," he said.

And she walked right into his open arms as he wrapped them around her. They looked into each other's eyes, before allowing their lips to touch once and then twice. A third time would not be a peck, so they stepped away from one another. He led her over to the sofa where he poured her a glass of the Zinfandel that he knew she loved. They began talking non-stop like they did back when they were hot and heavy. They both had so much to say about what had been going on in their lives for the last past couple of months. She waited nervously for him to bring up her going back to Stephan and her standing him up; the night they were supposed to go bowling, but he didn't say anything.

He noticed her ring. And to show her he wasn't bothered about her going back to Stephan; even though she had sworn up and down to him she wouldn't, he complimented Stephan's great taste in rings. Just as he expected, she didn't know how to respond. He immediately jumped to another subject. He wouldn't dare allow the conversation to be about her and Stephan, because he would have to relive how she had jerked him around for someone he considered less than a man.

After them telling each other how much they had missed one another, she still didn't feel comfortable with telling him she was having doubts about marrying Stephan. She had done Elliott wrong, by going back to him. She felt that would be his opening and opportunity to rub the shit in her face, and she was not about to let that happen.

"Why are you sitting over there? Come," she said, while patting the sofa cushion next to her. "And sit by me."

He smiled. "I would love to, but I know myself. If I sit next to you, I would not be able to contain myself. I respect the fact that you're getting married; but I had to see you one last time, other than in passing, like what happened earlier today."

She knew this game. He wanted to see if she would come, if he called her. She showed up, so now the ball was in his court. If she had come with expectations of things picking-up where they had left off, before she went back to Stephan, he would object. If she hadn't come with expectations, he would be all over her right now. She also knew that if he thought she was really as happy as that huge rock on her finger indicated she was, she wouldn't be there right now. She flicked her short hair behind her ears. "What makes you think this is the last time?"

"Because I can't see you anymore, after tonight."

Her mouth dropped and her face grew very tight. She was taken aback by his response. She didn't want the surprised look on her face to seem so obvious, but she couldn't smile without her face cracking. "I understand," she said, although she didn't.

"DeDe, being in your company like this, or in public would just be complete hell. I would want to hold you, kiss you, make love to you and have you for myself. It seems to me that things are pretty much, you know, settled. From where I'm sitting things look cut and dried, said and done. You got the ring and you're about to be married. As much as I desire you and could give less than a damn about this man you are about to marry, I still can't allow my instincts and heart to prevail. I don't want to watch you get up and go home to him, after being with you. I don't want to know that he's making love to you." He wasn't about to share her and he didn't think she cared enough about him to make a choice.

I'm not happy and I don't want to marry him. We made love today and I didn't enjoy it. Those were all the things she wished she could tell Elliott. But nevertheless she said, "I think I understand," and left it at that.

WHEN SHE GOT home last night at eleven o'clock Stephan was asleep. She tiptoed around the room to get undressed, so she wouldn't wake him. She wasn't good at telling a boldface lie face to face. The next morning, she was ready for questioning about what time she had come in and where she had gone, but he said nothing. As they both got dressed, they laughed, and joked. He complimented her on how well the spaghetti tasted last night, and how nice she looked for work this morning. He was excited about taking his drug test and starting work and she was happy for him, but she still wondered if she would be making a mistake if she married him.

31

ALEXIS was in the car with Stephan when he picked DeDe up from work this evening. How did this happen? She thought. Attitude had come over her demeanor, as she placed her briefcase on the backseat floor. Seeing Alexis meant he had been talking to Shannon, and her insecurities of them sleeping together behind her back resurfaced.

"Hey baby," Stephan said, as she got in the car and sat down.

"Hello," she mumbled. "Hello Alexis." DeDe said, as she turned around and looked at her noticing she looked just like Shannon. "Aren't you getting to be a big, pretty girl?"

Alexis didn't look at her; she continued to eat her cookies. More attitude came over DeDe, because Stephan was letting her eat in her car, the same way he and his friends slouched all over her sofa, while drinking and eating. It was obvious he didn't give a damn about any of her shit.

"What do you say Alexis?" Stephan asked her, as he looked at her through the rearview mirror smiling.

"Thank you."

"Baby, are you going to cook tonight?"

"No," she said, while shaking her head.

"Then let's go for pizza. I promised Alexis pizza, because she got all A's on her progress report."

"That's good, but take me home."

"Why," he whispered, while again glancing in the rearview mirror at Alexis and turning up the radio.

"I'm tired. And you didn't tell me you were going to pick her up." He looked at DeDe trying to figure out why he would have to tell her he was going to pick up his daughter. "You did pick her up, didn't you?" She asked, to make sure Shannon didn't come to her house.

"Yeah, I did. Alexis don't you want DeDe to go with us for pizza?"

"Yeah."

"See. You're not that tired and we won't be out that long."

When they got through the doors of Coyote's Pizza World, Alexis took off running for the indoor rides and games. Stephan and DeDe were shown to their table by the host, and Stephan couldn't help but notice her foul attitude.

"What's wrong with you? You've been trippin' with an attitude, since I picked you up."

"So now y'all are buddy-buddy, huh?"

"Who?"

She sighed, and rolled her eyes. "Do you have to take Alexis home tonight?"

"No, she's spending the night."

"Why? Doesn't Shannon know you don't have a car, to take her to school?"

"No she doesn't. But, is it a problem if I use your car to take her? Because if it is; I'll just catch the bus to drop her off at school and then go to work. Are you thinking that just because I have my daughter, Shannon and I are the best of friends now? DeDe, please don't take the hate you have for Shannon, out on Alexis. I want to see her. I'm her daddy and if you and I are going to get married, you have to understand that and trust me, when I say Shannon and I are ancient history."

"Well, if you are going to be picking her up, I think you should let me know in advance."

"And why?"

She couldn't give him the reason she was thinking, without him blaming it on her insecurities.

"That's what I thought," he said, as he got up from the table to go find Alexis.

SHE FELT USED and dammit she was angry. No wonder he insisted on her going, she thought, as she looked at him out of the corner of her eye, as they drove home. He knew he didn't have any money, when he promised the child pizza. When the bill came, he looked at me with a sheepish grin on his face, silently wanting me to pay. She sat in the car, as quiet as a church mouse with anger throbbing in her head and at the base of her heart. He tried to talk to her, but she was paying him no attention. If he knew any better, he would leave her alone, before all the anger she had bottled up inside of her makes her go completely off! She was feeling somewhat 'postal'; due to all the money he borrowed from her and never paid back, him moving in with her without asking, her paying the money for their attorney, him letting Dedrick stay with them, and him quitting his job without discussing it with her first. And now, he and Shannon are back being friends. If he continued to talk as if everything was fine, she was going to explod on him and show him just how fine things are.

When they got home, she stormed to her bedroom and slammed the door. She did not feel like being bothered. She got undressed and jumped into the shower.

"Damn, I need to go pick-up some money I let my man Thomas borrow. Can you watch Alexis for me, until I get back?"

She pulled her t-shirt over her head. "Can't you pick it up in the morning? I'm about to get into bed, and she hasn't had her bath."

"Give it to her for me baby. Her night clothes are in her bag." He rushed out of the bedroom, with DeDe following him.

"Stephan."

"Alexis, baby, daddy will be back. Get ready to take your bath and get into bed."

"Okay daddy."

"Stephan." DeDe called out, as he closed the door in her face.

She let out a frustrated sigh, as she leaned up against the door. "Alexis let's take your bath and get ready for bed."

"What time is it?" Alexis asked.

DeDe looked around the room for a clock. "I don't know, why?"

"Because, I don't go to bed until nine-thirty."

"Well, I'm sleepy and I have to give you your bath."

"Can't I wait until the PowerPuff Girls go off?"

"Yeah, and get your feet off of that sofa. If you want to sit on it, please sit like a lady."

She went to her bedroom grabbed a magazine and waited fifteen minutes before going back out to give Alexis a bath.

"What are you doing!" she screamed, as Alexis jumped up and down on her sofa.

"Nothing," Alexis said, as she quickly sat down and gave her an innocent look of sorrow.

"Do you jump on your mother's furniture?"

Alexis shook her head and said, "No."

"Then don't jump on mine. You're not outside or still on the moon bounce at Coyote's Pizza. You know better."

"I wasn't doing anything, stop being mean to me," Alexis cried.

"You were. You were jumping on my sofa. I saw you."

"My mommy said that you were mean, and you are. I want to go home."

"As soon as your dad gets here tell 'im that. Until then, you will take a bath."

"No," she said, and folded her arms. "You are mean. You put my mommy in jail and you made my daddy not come and see me."

"Your mother put me and your daddy in jail."

"No she didn't. I want to go home. I want to call my mommy to tell her to pick me up."

"Your daddy will take you to your mother, as soon as he gets back." DeDe rushed into the kitchen, grabbed the phone and paged Stephan to get home ASAP. "I just paged him and he should be here soon."

Alexis laid on the sofa crying. "I want my mommy, I want my mommy."

DeDe looked at her and rolled her eyes with no obligation to comfort her. Like DeDe said all along, she was too damn grown for her own good.

AN HOUR AFTER DeDe paged Stephan, he stood over her as she slept.

"DeDe," he said, as he tried to wake her. "DeDe."

She looked up at him and then at the clock. "Where have you been?"

"Why is Alexis asleep in her clothes on the sofa with no cover on her? She hasn't taken a bath or changed into her pajamas. I thought I asked you to give her a bath?"

"Why didn't you return my page?" She asked him, as she sat up in bed. "She was crying about wanting to go home."

"Why?"

"Because she's too damn grown," She blurted out. "Shannon has her brain-washed. She called me mean, because I put her mother in jail. How did she know that, if Shannon didn't tell her? Of course she didn't tell her that she put us in jail also. She was in there jumping up and down on my sofa like some child who ain't never had nothing."

He exhaled and went into a rage. "Damn DeDe, I leave her here with you one minute and you —"

"Oh no; you are not going to turn this around on me."

"I guess Shannon was right. You don't want me to deal with my daughter, because you think Shannon and I might get back together. And you don't want me to have shit to do with Alexis, because you have something against her mother. You didn't want her here from the jump. When you first spoke to her in the car, I saw then that you were being fake."

"Fuck you Stephan!"

"Yeah, that's what you've been doing and I've been allowing it, by letting you control this whole situation."

"What about her?" DeDe yelled.

"Shannon too, but not anymore. This is about me and my daughter now. And I'm not going to fuss and cuss with Shannon, so you will feel more secure."

"Secure," she replied. "You fuss with her, because she's a bitch. It has nothing to do with me."

"Never again am I going to sneak and call my daughter to see how she's doing, so you won't think that Shannon and I are being the best of friends and we're screwing. There has to be some trust somewhere between us, and this bullshit has to stop. You've made it quite clear; this is your house. So no, I won't let Shannon drop Alexis off here, because this is your house. However, when and if we get married we are moving the fuck out of here. We are going to get a house with my name on it. And as long as I have a house with my name on it, I will not meet my child or her mother in the street. They both will be more than welcome to come to my house. You don't want to see Shannon and she doesn't want to see you either. That crazy shit has got to stop because I want to see my child. You will be my wife; and you will go to her house with me to pick up Alexis, if need be. Now I'm going to take care of my daughter." He walked out the room, without giving her a chance to say a word.

THE NEXT MORNING Stephan and Alexis played around the house making DeDe late for work. She didn't say anything; fearful that it would be taken the wrong way. Stephan knew what time she had to be at work, but he pretended to not notice. As he drove her to work and Alexis to school, he talked to Alexis instead of her, as if she wasn't even there. She refused to become upset or jealous of their relationship even if she did feel left out. She didn't want anything she might say or do this morning to be a misunderstood or a sign of insecurity.

He dropped Alexis off at school. DeDe did tell her goodbye, trying to sound as sincere and genuine as possible; so that Stephan wouldn't later tell her he detected her phoniness.

"Why aren't you talking?" He asked, once he got back into the car.

"Because, you're not talking to me. Also, I don't want to come between you and your daughter anymore than I already have."

He looked at her and rolled his eyes at her sarcasms.

DEDE SAT LEANING back in her chair drinking a cup of coffee, when Dionne came moping over to her desk with her head hung low.

"Hey girly," Dionne said, as she sighed and flopped down in the chair. "You look like I feel."

"How do you feel, because I'm sad and you might be happy?" DeDe asked her, as she forced herself to smile.

"Girl, you can look at me and tell I'm sad."

"About what? I know it's not about a man."

"Surprise. I haven't heard from Byron since Sunday, when we came back from Dallas."

"Why, what happened?"

"I don't know. We were happy, when we left here on Friday. When we got there, his family double-teamed me and he sat back and laughed. He had told his family everything I told him about my family. They had the nerve to make judgments about my family; and think they are superior to us. On our way back, I cursed him out something awful; and I haven't heard from him since."

"Maybe he's angry at some of the things you said."

"He has no right to be. And Charlotte is so high up in seventh-heaven, because of her big time book deal."

"Book deal, you're going to have to let me know when that comes out so I can pick it up. I love to read books by Black authors.

"Yeah, I will," Dionne said, with anger, honesty and promise. "Ian finally approves of something that she's doing and is now showing her some damn attention. She is much too busy to comfort me, when I've been there for her gullible ass so many times in the past."

"Are you hurting?" DeDe asked.

"Hell yeah! I really liked him and I know he liked me... No, he loved me; at least that's what he said."

DeDe couldn't believe her ears. Dionne always claimed to be very tough, demanding and hard, when it comes to men. DeDe couldn't believe she was that naïve and stupid to believe a man could love her after only six months. It was rather shocking to see her hurt, because it didn't work out between them. But DeDe knew even the hardest of women needed to be picked up, when they were let down. DeDe rolled her chair over to where Dionne was sitting and reached over and hugged her. Without warning, the woman that DeDe thought was the strongest female that ever lived began to cry. With the advent of tears cascading from Dionne's face, DeDe became weepy herself. However, she wasn't sure whether she was feeling sorry for Dionne or herself and her own predicament.

32

IF you are not making love, what in the hell are you doing on this beautiful, hot Friday morning? I know a lot of you rushed to the newsstands yesterday with hopes of finding out the latest about Tibias and Angelic. But it's over folks. The column has run its course; only to be turned into a book, that I hear will be released the first of the year. I know a lot of you are upset, by the way the lines are lighting up. Give us a call and we'll try to help you through this," he said and chuckled. "555-WHEE. Your breakfast, toast and jam station."

STEPHAN HAD A new job and Dedrick was still living with them. It was four weeks after he was only supposed to be staying with them for a couple of days. DeDe hardly saw Stephan lately. He worked twelve-hour days. Four days out of the week, from Thursday to Sunday, he ran the streets with Dedrick. DeDe was upset and she made sure he knew it, by starting arguments and walking around the house with a major attitude. She was somewhat hoping the arguments would push him away, like they had done in the past. He claimed to be a person who doesn't like to argue, but he always did things that would cause an argument. DeDe not only wanted to push him away; she was hoping he would be the first to verbalize that they shouldn't get married, before she had to call it off.

"Do I have to look forward to your attitude and arguing everyday, when we get married?" He asked her.

"You don't have to."

If Elliott would just return one of her phone calls, so they could meet someplace. She could give less than a damn that Stephan would rather be with his friends than with her. Elliott meant what he said, about him not wanting to see her after that night.

Stephan had given her money for bills like he promised, after receiving his first paycheck. But he still hadn't gotten his car out of the shop and she still has to share hers with him; which she hated but he had no other way to work. Having him drop her off at work every morning was very inconvenient. This was especially a problem, when she needed to visit with one of her clients or on Fridays, when she had to go to the beauty salon. She was tired of asking Dionne to take her home, because she knew how people can get. Although they don't mind helping out in the beginning, they get really tired after about three weeks.

It was imperative that DeDe visit with her new clients today, instead of communicating with them via phone, fax and e-mail. Stephan claimed Dedrick would not allow him to drive his car, and since Melvin was in Chicago playing football, he couldn't borrow one of his many vehicles. But sometimes he's so selfish. DeDe knew he probably wouldn't let him borrow one of them, even if he was in town. DeDe couldn't understand why Dedrick was acting this way. It really wasn't like him to act selfish. Besides, he was practically staying with them rent-free. She borrowed Bridget's car so she was able to see all of her clients today, and go to the beauty salon on time. This week, she would not be the last one to leave.

WHEN SHE GOT home, Dedrick was sitting on her sofa with the music blasting, flipping the channels on the television and drinking. His round glassy eyes were halfway closed and blood-shot red.

"Hey DeDe," he slurred, and turned down the volume on the radio and television with the remote.

She spoke; half mumbling, while she flipped through her mail. She was wondering why was he lounging all over her furniture and not out somewhere else? Also, why in the hell didn't he let Stephan use his car? She had an attitude. She walked into the kitchen and turned around and walked out. "Dedrick." The sternness in her voice startled him. His eyes were naturally brown. But today they're red and brown from the alcohol, she believed. He didn't seem like the type to cry. "Why wouldn't you let my man use your car this morning?" She asked, and folded her arms.

"De, I've been offering my car to Sporty everyday. He's the one who says he'll use yours."

DeDe knew Stephan to be full of pride, so she couldn't say Dedrick was lying.

"Sporty and I go way back. Anything I got is his. Y'all helping me out by letting me stay here; why wouldn't I let him use my car?"

DeDe unfolded her arms and leaned up against the sofa. Dedrick was the nicest out of all of Stephan's friends, and the only one she liked. He sat at the edge of the sofa and placed his glass on the table. "De, I'm ready to go back home, baby." He sounded pitiful, which was the same way he looked since he's been there. Maybe he had been crying, she thought. DeDe felt sorry for him, but she knew whatever pain he was going through, he deserved it. He had done Carla the same way Stephan had done her, but they had two kids together and she was pregnant with the third. "I love Carla and I miss her and my little girls. I knew when she started going to that damn holiness church, it was a big mistake. The preacher told her it was a sin for us to be living together. Also, if I didn't marry her within a week, I wasn't ever going to marry her and God wouldn't want us living together in sin another day. So, she put me out and started dating the preacher's brother-in-law. He's an ex-convict, who just got out of jail two months ago," he said, as hurt whispered through his slurring speech. "The preacher said, "God showed him in a dream that Carla and this ex-convict were to be together." She's going to marry him, I just know it." As fast as the prolonged tear fell from his eyes, he wiped it away. "She's finally going to have a little boy and I'm afraid that if she marries this man I might not be able to see him. Do you think you can call her and talk to her for me? She'll listen to you, if nobody else."

DeDe couldn't understand why Carla would listen to her, since they were not friends at all. They never talked on the phone and they hardly saw each other, unless they were with Stephan or Dedrick. As bad as she was ready for him to leave, she didn't know what to say to Carla to convince her to let him come back.

"And Sporty giving you that ring and y'all sitting there at the restaurant planning the wedding in front of her didn't make it any better. She's the woman I want to marry, DeDe. We have two children together but this brotha is scared of marriage; that's why I haven't let her set a date. All I ever heard about marriage was horror stories. But that is no excuse why I had her holding on as long as I did. Marriage ain't easy, DeDe," he said, while shaking his head from side to side. "Sporty had to propose to you after knowing you were serious about that guy you had taken to New York with you. He couldn't let another man get you. You're a good woman; you're smart and you got your shit together. We don't know how Sporty got you, but he did."

Lately, DeDe had been wondering the same thing. "Who are we?"

"Melvin and me. Sporty gets some good women. I got to give it to 'im and y'all love the hell out of 'im too."

DeDe was now embarrassed to be one of those women.

"I know you love 'im too, because after all has been said and done, you're still here." He chuckled.

"After what's been said and done?" She asked, as if she didn't know. After Stephan had all of his fun and broke her heart for the hell of it, she stayed with him for a damn ring and his last name that she doesn't even think she wants anymore.

He chuckled and fell back into the sofa, as he ran his hand over his short wooly hair. "The women. The cheating."

She didn't want to react or ask any questions that might stop him from telling it all in his drunkenness. She wanted to hear it come from him that

Stephan had cheated. "I knew he was fooling around with Shannon but that's over now," she said with confidence.

"Shannon, his babymama? Hell nawh! Shannon don't want him and he says he doesn't want her. That's old. What they had is in the past. Sporty took Shannon through hell and I know for sure, she doesn't want him back."

"What makes you so sure? She's always acting a fool on him like she wants him back. She doesn't allow him to see his daughter without drama."

"I don't know anything about that. But what I do know is she was good to him like you are, and just like me he didn't appreciate it, until the woman gets fed up."

"What makes you think she was so good to him? She left him for another man."

"Because she got tired of him fooling around and not wanting to marry her. But you're getting marriage out of him, because he didn't want to make the same mistake twice and I don't want to make that mistake with Carla either. I guess I better let her set a date, if I don't want to lose her to that ex-convict, because I know there's no way that God meant for them to be together. The niggah was in jail eight years for robbery, and she got him around my daughters."

"She loves you too much to marry—"

"She, loves me? It's been over three weeks. She's changed the locks and she hasn't so much as called me, and she knows I'm staying here. I hurt her DeDe and she's now in love with another man. She doesn't want me back."

"Yes she does. She just needs time. You two have children together."

He smiled at her comforting words, although he knew she felt he was getting what he deserved. "I like you DeDe. I hated to see you hurt, when he would break-up with you and you would call him crying. But you know, I couldn't say anything, because he was my boy and I was doing it myself. Commitment to one woman is hard."

DeDe turned up her lips and rolled her eyes.

"You would have to be a man to understand."

"Is Stephan cheating now?"

"No, he's dedicated like I am. There comes a time in a man's life where the cheating game plays itself out. The women get crazy, once they realize you're not going to leave the one you love for them. Like that crazy Tawanda scratching up Sporty's car, after she found out about you."

"Tawanda?" DeDe snarled.

Dedrick then realized he had just stuck his foot in his month, and hell may have just broken loose. He was now getting sober, as he tried to figure out a way to clean up the mess he had just made. "Damn, DeDe," he got up and walked toward her. "I didn't mean that. This alcohol got me talking about things I don't know anything about. My mind is all screwed around. I want Carla back and ain't shit going right for me in my life without her. Just forget you heard me mention that name."

"No Dedrick, she scratched up what car and when?" DeDe had seen the words "HIV Positive" carved into the black paint of Stephan's BMW one morning. When she asked him about it, he swore up and down he didn't know who and why someone would choose to engrave those words in the door of his car. DeDe didn't believe him, but she still had given him the money to paint the car. "A woman just doesn't scratch up a man's car for nothing Dedrick. Who is she, were they sleeping together?"

He sighed. "I don't know, but it's in the past now."

"Eight months ago is not the past."

"All you need to know is that it's over now. You got him and y'all are about to be married."

"And that ain't shit!" She rolled her eyes at him, stormed to her room, and slammed the door just as Stephan walked into the house.

KEEPING HER PROMISE to Dedrick to not say anything to Stephan about their conversation last night had her boiling with anger inside. Something needed to be said, just so he'd know he had not gotten away with anything. Now she knew that all the times he broke up with her for his so-called space, it was because of at least one other woman, maybe more. If she had to keep her mouth closed about all she knew and not confront him, she couldn't stand being around him. She didn't want to see or talk to him. She jumped out of bed before he woke, got dressed and planned to stay gone the entire day, until she thought he was gone or asleep. She had even thought about checking into a hotel for the night and not coming home at all; that's how pissed she was. She was angry with herself for allowing him to make love to her, even if she did just lie there. She couldn't understand how and why she let it happen. In the past, he's begged her, kissed on her neck, and rubbed between her legs when she's been angry with him, and she's still said no. She grabbed her keys and threw them in the bottom of her handbag, just so he wouldn't drive her car today. She went outside, hopped into Bridget's car, went and filled the gas tank and then drove around town trying very hard not to think about Tawanda or Shannon. She still believed Shannon wanted him, in spite of what Dedrick believed. After driving around town spending hours at the mall and sitting at the bar of Houston's restaurant; she then drove over to her girlfriend Marie's house and joined in with their family night of playing Monopoly, Sorry and Scrabble. She finally checked her messages on her cell phone and Stephan had left several messages asking her why she had taken her keys. Around eight-thirty after feeling as if she had worn out her welcome there, she had gone over to Bridget's to take her car back. She made herself comfortable while bathing her goddaughters, putting them into bed and watching a movie. As bad as she wanted to, she wouldn't dare tell Bridget or Marie what was going on between her and Stephan. Especially not after Charva told her they considered her stupid for even being with Stephan. With Bridget being pregnant, she began yawning and falling asleep on DeDe; so she finally asked Jerome to take her home. He talked at his usual 100mph about nothing she was interested in knowing, but it did pass the time. For some reason, he hadn't mastered keeping his foot on the gas and talking at the same time. It was twelve-thirty when she got home. She would have asked Jerome to drop her off at a hotel, if he wasn't going to ask her a thousand questions and tell Bridget.

THERE WERE THREE other cars besides hers parked in her driveway, which meant Stephan was home and he had company. She silently sighed and rolled her eyes to the point of no return, as she dreaded walking into the house and seeing him. It was sad that she had fought so hard to keep him, because she thought her life would be hell without him. Ironically, now she's feeling like her life will be hell with him, because the love she once had for him is gone and she can't explain how.

"I see Stephan is home," Jerome said. "You know, if he's going to be a part of the family now, he and I need to go out for a couple of beers and get to know each other better. We haven't had a one on one conversation, since you two have been together. And I think since he's about to marry my lil' sistah, I need to lay down some rules in a straightforward way. If he hits you, I'm going to hit him." He threw his car in park. "Let me go in and invite him over tomorrow after church, to watch the game."

DeDe quickly grabbed his arm, the minute he opened the door. If she wasn't talking to Stephan, she didn't want any of her friends talking to him as if everything was okay. The way she's been feeling lately, Jerome getting to know Stephan might just be a little too late. "No, he's going to be working tomorrow."

"Working on a Sunday?" Jerome asked, as if he never heard of people working on Sundays.

"He's the manager of credit and collections at the bank. You know they work everyday of the week, and then some."

"Well I'll just leave the invitation open for anytime." He jumped out of the car and DeDe jumped out behind him.

"Don't bother I'll tell 'im and we'll make plans for next Sunday."

He gave her a weird look, but he didn't press the issue. "That'll be great."

She said goodnight and slowly walked toward the door. When she got up to the front door, she turned around and gave him a final good-bye, took one deep breath and placed her key into the lock. She stood aghast, as her eyes met Stephan's just as he lowered the plate of five straight white powdered lines and a rolled up dollar bill from his nose. Her knees buckled and her stomach turned with sickness, witnessing him doing drugs. The same man she is supposed to be marrying, drugs? The same man she thought she knew.

He could see the shaken look on her face. "What's up baby," he said, as he twitched his nose and joined in the conversation with the other two men she had never seen before.

Without saying a word, she stormed to her bedroom and began pacing the floor, waiting for him to walk in, so she could go off on him.

"Did you get my messages?" He asked, as he walked into the bedroom, as if he had no obligation to give her an explanation to what she had just seen. "You took the keys today and I had some things I needed to do."

"What in the hell are you doing out there?" Tears had swelled up in her eyes and her bottom lip and hands began to tremble. Just think; if Jerome's persistent ass would have come in behind her... "When did you start doing cocaine, Stephan?"

He sighed. "It's nothing DeDe. I only do it every now and then, when I'm under pressure."

"What pressure are you under now?"

"What do you mean under now," he responded. "My job is on my back. Shannon is driving me crazy, because of how you treated Alexis the other week, now I can't see her again. And it seems like we are falling apart. We don't talk anymore and we damn sure don't fuck anymore, without me Bogarting it."

Maybe she didn't give it to him, and she just laid there, because he had taken it. He did plead with her not to tell him no, then snatched down her panties. But then he was as limp as an over-cooked hotdog. No wonder, he's been putting shit up his nose.

"Give me the keys."

"Hell no!" She said, while clutching them tight against her chest.

"Give me the damn keys," he ordered her, just before he snatched them out of her hand and walked out of the bedroom and slammed the door behind him.

She threw herself across the bed and cried, until she had fallen asleep.

33

$\mathcal{DeDe}$ and Stephan sat in complete silence and anger, as they drove to work. DeDe tried to keep her silence as long as she could while he drove bumper to bumper with the car in front of them. She was terrified that he was going to create an accident. Maybe he was still high, she thought.

"Why don't you slow down?"

"Don't tell me how to drive."

"This is my car," DeDe reminded him.

"I don't give a damn."

Just like he hasn't given a damn about anything except himself, she thought.

"I'm not driving fast, DeDe. Haven't you thought that maybe the asshole in front of me might just be driving slow as hell?"

"Then get from behind him, Stephan."

He flipped on the blinker and gave her the scare of her life, as he switched lanes at a heart racing speed. He nearly sent them into the concrete wall that divided the east and west sides of the highway. She grabbed the door handle, to brace herself for the impact.

She screamed, "What are you doing! Pull over and give me my damn car, before you kill me on top of all the other things you've done to me."

He glanced over at her wondering what she was talking about, and where she was coming from. What had he done to her? Whatever it was, he has surely made it up to her over the last past couple of months.

"Don't look at me like you don't know what I'm talking about; the lies and the cheating."

"What lies? What cheating?"

"Your job, the cocaine habit you just so happen to have every time you're under pressure. And who in the hell is Tawanda?"

He looked at her wondering how she had found out. For two years she had no clue about Tawanda; and she had no clue about DeDe. Tawanda doesn't know the number to the house and she doesn't know where they live. Maybe she decided to finally act on her threats and she contacted DeDe. Shit.

"Yeah, I know about her. You took her to Miami with the damn tickets I paid for. All that inane talk about you needing space; because we argue too much, or we were getting too close and me wanting marriage and you didn't, and Shannon and I were running you crazy and you'd rather not deal with either of us, was pure bullshit! All those lies were created, so you could be with Tawanda. She scratched up your car, and you told me you didn't know who in the hell had done it. I paid for that car to be painted, remember?"

He stopped her before she could say anything else. "What in the hell are you talking about?"

"Don't play dumb. Dedrick told me everything."

The strength of the seatbelt threw her back into the seat, as he slammed his foot onto the break pedal, in the middle of morning rush hour traffic. Horns began to blow.

"He told you everything about what?"

She looked at him and rolled her eyes, because she was angry with herself for opening her big mouth. She really didn't intend to tell on Dedrick, but she had done it out of anger. And now there was no way of her taking it back. "People are blowing at us. Could you please go?"

He turned on his left blinker and switched over four lanes of traffic, to get to the shoulder of the highway.

"What are you doing?" She asked him.

There was no way he could talk his way out of this mess. His own boy had sold him out. He reached into his jacket for his cell phone.

"Don't call him."

"Don't tell me not to call him. The nerve of that lousy niggah! Just because his shit is fucked up and raggedy, he's trying to mess up mine. He's going to get the hell out of that house, if I have to pack his things and throw him out myself."

"No he's not. You have no right to put him out. That's my house."

"Oh yeah, I don't care whose house it is! He's getting out. And I would advise you to shut the hell up talking to me right now about what's yours."

And she did just that, as she sat with her arms folded and fuming.

He dialed the number with his temper boiling. He couldn't believe that his boy since elementary school had sold him out. That wasn't like Dedrick, he thought. DeDe had to have been prying, but that's still no excuse for Dedrick to have fallen prey to her game and opened his big mouth. "Dog, you're still there...good. Pack your shit and get the hell out of my crib ASAP. Don't ask me what I'm talking about. You know damn well what you told DeDe about Tawanda. Drunk my ass," he replied. "You know that shit with Tawanda was a mistake. DeDe and I are engaged man. How could you be so stupid to tell her shit? Even if she was being nosey and asking questions; that's no excuse."

"I was not asking questions, Stephan."

"Dog, I want you out of there. Your shit is messed up and now you want to mess up mine. Shit, I guess it's true what they say about niggahs like you; 'when miserable muthafuckas are miserable, they want the whole world to wear their shoe size'." If there was anything to be saved between DeDe and Stephan, this was his opportunity. "You didn't want me to marry her in the first place, but we are still going to be married. That shit with Tawanda has been over and you know it, Dog. I love DeDe. I'm not about to lose her, just because you are miserable and don't have nobody."

Stephan was working hard to try to get her to play into his sick, twisted game. DeDe wasn't falling for any of it. She knew how Dedrick felt about her, and he did not object to Stephan asking her to marry him. Stephan professing his love for her to Dedrick over the phone after he's been flat busted, was just a ploy. He thought that he could once again make her out to be the fool that he took her to be.

"You had no right," DeDe told him as soon as he hung up.

"DeDe, shut up," he retorted. "This sort of thing has always been a problem and it's going to continue to be a problem. You believe everything anyone tells you about me."

She couldn't believe that he was trying to plant the knife that had stabbed him in the back on her. "Dedrick is your boy why would he lie?"

He couldn't say anything. He pressed his foot on the accelerator, merged into traffic and drove as fast as he could, to get her out of the car.

When they got to the front door of her office building, she jumped out of the car. DeDe grabbed her open folders and loose papers, along with her briefcase that had fallen on the floor, when Stephan turned into the driveway like a crazy man. She stuffed them into a plastic grocery bag that was under her seat and slammed the door without saying good-bye.

She stormed through the office to her cubical, without saying good morning to anyone. She was having issues. She threw her briefcase under her desk, and dumped the open files and documents out of the grocery bag onto the top of her desk. As she sorted through the stack, there was a grocery receipt mixed in with the pile of papers. She snatched it up with the plastic bag and balled it up and threw it in the trash. As always, her unconscious habit forced her to retrieve the receipt from the receptacle. She opened the crumpled receipt and read it; just in case it was a receipt she cared to keep.

Printed on the receipt were Pampers, three cans of Similac, and Huggies baby wipes. She hadn't purchased any of those things. Bridget has a child still in diapers, but she hadn't gone to the store for her. In fact, she hadn't gone to the store in about a week. She looked at the date and time on the receipt and it matched very close to the time Stephan had snatched her keys from her last night. She didn't overreact by speculating. Maybe the guys that were with him have children and he had taken them to the store for those things. Instead of throwing the piece of paper back in the wastebasket next to her, she stuffed it in the inside pocket of her jacket.

ALTHOUGH A WOMAN will be a woman, but when she finally gets to the point in the relationship where enough is enough; she doesn't want it anymore, she will take some sort of action. A woman still can't give the ring back; send a man walking with all of his shit and call her mother to tell her there isn't going to be a wedding and leave it at that. She needs someone to make her feel like she's doing the right thing, and encouragement from her girlfriends isn't what she really requires. She needs a man's verification. Because no one likes to be lonely after ending it with the only man she ever really wanted to wed. She decided to take an early lunch and walked down to Elbuddah's. She needed to see Elliott, to find out why he hadn't returned any of her calls. It was him who had taken her mind off Stephan, when they had broken up the last time. She was stupid for ending it with Elliott in the first place. But she loved Stephan so much; she thought she was going to finally get the love she had always craved from him. She sure as hell got the ring.

She sat at her table eating her steamed vegetables and bourbon-baked chicken, hoping Elliott would pull away from his busy host station to come and talk to her. She ate slowly, while trying to give him eye contact, but he didn't look her way. She couldn't understand what was going on with him. He hadn't returned any of her calls and now he was trying to act like she didn't exist. He didn't show her to her table. He got someone else to do it, while he ran to the kitchen. She finally gave up on getting his attention and ate her lunch. By the time she finished, she was sure he would come over and take care of the check, but he still didn't look her way. She wanted to tell her waiter that she was a friend of Elliott's and he was going to take care of the bill. But she refrained, because she felt he would have her pay it anyway. Although he had told her how things were going to be, she was surprised at how he was acting. Maybe seeing her today made him think about how she mistreated him, by going back to Stephan and he was angry all over again. She was now ready to tell him that she wasn't happy and she was thinking about calling off the wedding. He knew she was still sitting there waiting for him to come over, but he pretended that she wasn't even in the restaurant. She waited a short while, paid her bill, then got up and walked out of the restaurant without saying good-bye.

SHE SLOWLY WALKED back to her office, while enjoying the beautiful, sunny day and light breezes of mid-September. It wasn't as hot as it had been in May, June, July and August, but it was quite warm. She thought about how Elliott had acted and she couldn't blame him. There was no need of her getting mad with him. She deserved the cold shoulder he had given her. After all, he explained it to her very nicely, when she went to his house. Elliott could have taken her to bed that night, and he knew it. But being the gentleman that he is, he let her know that he wasn't interested in just fucking her to fuck her. She had hurt him for a man she wasn't sure she loved. She wasn't to be trusted with his heart again, and he wasn't going to let her near him. She was the fool for letting Stephan come back into her heart. Especially when she knew she shouldn't have, and she had someone that was better in every way. What was she going to do now? Stephan was the so-called challenge she wanted. He was now professing his love for her. They were to be married in less than three months. She just found out he does drugs and he had cheated on her many times in the past. Now that she didn't have another man to fall back on, she didn't know what decision to make based on the fact she didn't want to be alone. She and Stephan were going to have to have a long talk, before going another day forward. When she got back from lunch and walked through the reception area, Kaleigh, the receptionist stopped her and told her she had a guest. By the time DeDe could turn around to follow the direction of Kaleigh's eyes, there was a pecan-brown complexioned woman with a long layered cut in her mid-twenties holding an infant, standing behind DeDe. She had what appeared to be a relieved look on her face. The child looked familiar, with the round marble eyes and dark lips. But DeDe didn't know where she'd seen this baby before. The woman didn't introduce herself before asking, if they could talk in private. DeDe led her to the conference room across the hall. They both sat in juxtapose lounge chairs, separated by a small round coffee table.

"Hello DeDe."

"Hi, do I know you?"

"No, my name is Tawanda."

DeDe's heart sank to the depths of the Titanic. The grocery receipt DeDe had in her pocket, the marble eyes of the child, and the name Tawanda; explained it all. If DeDe knew she wouldn't regret it later and be taken as crazy; she would allow her emotions to take control and perhaps send this woman running down the hallway screaming with pain. But instead, she looked Tawanda in her eyes and asked, "What are you doing here?"

Tawanda did not blink once and remained just as calm as DeDe looked. She said, "I felt you needed to know."

"Why? You've been a secret this long. We're about to be married." DeDe threw up her hand to show her the ring.

"I know, he told me. But he's also a fantastic liar."

DeDe knew this, but as a woman who wasn't about to be shaken or taken without a fight, she wasn't about to agree with Tawanda. "He lied about what? We *are* about to be married." DeDe raked her hair behind her ear, to show her the gleaming ring once again.

"Believe me when I say that I didn't know about you, until after I became pregnant."

"And. So, what am I supposed to do, be like Mary J. Blige and go to him singing '*Your Child*' and leave him now? Let's be realistic honey, you have the child and I have the man. I guess you want him so that you two can raise this child together and live happily ever after, is that it? Right now, that's not going to happen, because I don't want it to happen. I'm not leaving him." At that point, DeDe wasn't. Not because she loved Stephan, but because she didn't want to see Tawanda accomplish what she believed she had set out to do. DeDe thought, the nerve of this chick, coming to her damn job with a child that looks just like Stephan. She must have seen this crap work on one of those daytime soaps.

"I didn't come here hoping you would leave him, DeDe."

No, she wasn't cursing like an angry bitter woman who had every right to, after being betrayed by a lying bastard, but it didn't mean she didn't come with hopes of getting a better grip on Stephan. DeDe felt like showing her anger with curse words that brewed in the pit of her stomach. But with Tawanda acting so calm and dignified, she felt she needed to respond in kindness. Maybe if they were somewhere else other than her job and the circumstances were different she would break fool and show-out. "So why are you here?"

" I just thought you should know."

She sighed, and rolled her eyes to the top of her head. "Now I do and I'm not leaving him. If that's what you expected, girlfriend, you need to think again. I know about you. In fact, I found out some days ago and we discussed it this morning. From what he's saying, it's over."

"Did you know about his child?"

From what DeDe could tell, the child seemed like the same age that Dedrick claimed Stephan had ended the relationship with her; eight months ago. DeDe couldn't stop thinking how much she looked like Stephan. "Yeah, I know about her, he bought her Pampers and Similac last night didn't he?"

"Yes he did. We've been together for two years off and on; and from my understanding you two have also."

"Off and on," DeDe replied, resenting Tawanda for wanting her to be in the same situation as she had been. But just then she began to count the number of times he had broken up with her and she'd gone back to him. It was a strange relationship. It had been an off and on relationship from the start.

Tawanda had told DeDe everything and DeDe fought to keep her composure from breaking down in tears. It was Tawanda who picked him up from the store when he and Shannon had it out, it was her who had bailed Stephan out of jail and not his brother and father when Shannon pressed charges against them. His car was repossessed and it wasn't at the mechanic's in storage. DeDe couldn't understand why his car was repossessed when she had given him so much money to help pay the note. What had he done with the money?

Maybe he had always had a habit of putting things up his nose, and she was too blinded with her obsession of him to notice it. Moreover, it was her money that helped him. He didn't quit his job; he was fired after fooling around with one of his employees. When she found out about Tawanda, she filed sexual harassment charges against him. He had used another woman's credit card to purchase DeDe's ring. He led her to believe it was for her and he would pay the monthly bill for it. After he bought the ring, he broke the relationship off with her and stuck her with the bill. She now has no way of getting in contact with him, after he changed his cell phone and pager numbers and moved out of his apartment. He was using and sleeping with three different women, while he slept with DeDe. She was almost certain he didn't wear a condom with any of them. As far as Tawanda was concerned, she knew for sure, because she had a child to prove it. With the others, he had made them feel comfortable enough to allow him to sleep with them without one, because he hated condoms. He also believed if a woman looked like she didn't have anything, it was okay to skip the condom. DeDe had become sick at the thought of her going down on him, and he had been all up inside of other women with his raw unsheathed dick. It was Tawanda he had taken to Miami and it was she who scratched up his car, after finding out about DeDe. They had been together for an entire year then, and she had no idea he was involved with DeDe. DeDe was curious how she had found out where she worked. Three weeks ago, while she was in DeDe's car, she had found a check stub belonging to DeDe in the glove compartment, which clearly stated: Stein & Stockton Public Relations.

DeDe sat at her desk sobbing with hurt and shame while trying not to draw attention to herself, but her hyperventilating scared Starla and Rosetta, who sat in the cubical in front of her. Starla skeptically walked over and placed her arm around DeDe's shoulder. Without asking any questions she already knew from listening to DeDe's phone conversations with Bridget, that she was crying over Stephan. DeDe turned away from Starla, as if she did not want to be bothered. Starla walked back over to her desk and called Dionne on the phone. Dionne rushed out of her office down the aisle of cubicles to DeDe's desk. There was concern in her voice. She helped DeDe to the ladies room.

Between blowing her nose, sudden out burst of tears, gasping for air, and profanity DeDe told Dionne everything Tawanda had told her.

AT FIVE-THIRTY, Stephan was sitting in the lobby waiting to pick up DeDe, to go home. They didn't even look at each other or speak. DeDe had just stopped crying thirty minutes before he arrived. She fought to hold her tears back, when she saw him. They drove home in complete silence for what seemed like hours. With anger and animosity brewing in her entire body and heart, she watched him out of the corner of her eye wishing she could gouge his eyes and pull his heart out, because it was obvious he never used his heart to care for anyone but himself.

When they got home, Stephan checked the guest room to make sure all of Dedrick's things were gone. DeDe looked at him and rolled her eyes. How dare he. She wished his things were gone and him along with them. But if everything goes according to plan, they will be. He's hurt her for the last time and it's not worth it anymore. She hated to admit it, but Shannon had told her he would hurt her badly. But she truly thought it would be different. She got undressed and put on her lounging clothes, turned on the television and grabbed the Essence Magazine that had come in today's mail and jumped into bed. He stood looking at her, as if she had done something wrong. "Are you going to cook or what?" He asked her.

She rolled her eyes, while clucking her teeth. "Hell no…you cook," she told him and continued to flip through the magazine.

He threw on his large saggy jeans and t-shirt and grabbed her keys. "I'm going to get me something to eat."

DeDe threw her magazine down and jumped off the bed. "You don't have to do that. I'm hungry too; I'll just cook. You don't need to spend any unnecessary money." She walked into the kitchen searching for something quick and fast to cook. She thawed out some chicken to fry, boiled some rice in a bag and reheated some canned string beans. She finished cooking by a quarter to seven. He walked into the kitchen grabbed himself a plate and began piling food on it. She was too nervous and upset to eat, so she watched him while drinking a glass of wine. She wanted to say something about what she had found out today, but she had another way of confronting him and she hoped Tawanda didn't back out. She nervously kept watch of the time, while praying she would hear the doorbell, when it rang. She paced back and forth between her bedroom and the kitchen; trying to make sure she's the one to open the door.

When he finished his dinner, he sat on the sofa like a stuffed well-feed pig with his hand halfway down his pants, and a beer in the other, while watching the sports highlights on ESPN. He had no clue that his cover was blown. DeDe began cleaning the kitchen. It was becoming more obvious that, Tawanda was leaving the outcome of this fucked up situation totally for DeDe to resolve on her own. Tears began to stream down her face, as she slammed pots and plates into the dishwasher. She contemplated ways to confront him. Regardless of how she was going to do it, she wasn't going to give him back that ring, but she was going to put him out and change her locks.

"DeDe," Stephan yelled into the kitchen. "Before you put up the food, put me some aside for my lunch tomorrow."

She stopped in her tracks and snapped with much attitude. "I'm not fixing you shit."

"Fine," he mumbled.

The kitchen was clean and she was going to bed. She headed for her room when the doorbell rang. The heaviness of her heart sank to her feet and halted her steps. She took a deep breath and turned around. Stephan looked at her and rolled his eyes and she did the same. She walked to the door and looked through the peephole and she nearly fell to her knees. It was Tawanda. She slowly opened the door as Stephan leaned forward and looked to see Tawanda walk in with his daughter.

"What in the fuck is this?" He asked, as he removed his hand from his pants, put the beer down on the coffee table and stood up. "Tawanda what in the hell are you doing here?"

"To bust your ass!" DeDe screamed. "Is this or is it not your child? You've been dating her as long as you've been dating me, and who in the hell is

Tiffany? I thought you quit your job, but you were fired for sexual harassment. Your car is not in storage, it was repoed and I had given your raggedy-ass money to pay the car note. It was her who scratched up your car after she found out about me—"

"DeDe shut the hell up," he yelled. "Tawanda what are you doing here?"

"She asked me to come."

DeDe looked at her in shock. "Because you came to my job with this child."

"Because I thought you should know," Tawanda retorted "This is his child, isn't it Stephan?"

"Get out of here Tawanda." He stormed toward her and began pushing her out of the door.

"That is your child," DeDe said, as she used her small petite body as a barricade between Tawanda and the door.

"It happened when you and I broke up."

"Broke up," she replied. "The longest we where apart was three months ago and that was for three weeks."

"And we were together then," Tawanda said.

"I don't want you. I never did," Stephan said, as he pointed at Tawanda, while the child remained sleeping.

"And you don't want me, because I don't want you." DeDe said, while looking directly into his eyes. She didn't care if he and Tawanda walked out of the door that very minute, holding hands singing, '*We Are Family*' by Sister Sledge. She wasn't going to play the fool any longer. She couldn't express her love to him anymore than she already had over the past three years; and this is how he repaid her with lies and a child. She had seen Stephan for who he really was, and she was no longer in love with him. For Tawanda to have him; DeDe knew deep down in her heart, she didn't have much of a man. "Stephan you've hurt me for the last time."

"DeDe," he said, moving Tawanda over to the side and pulling DeDe close to him.

"No," she yelled.

"She doesn't mean shit to me. I love you and I know you love me too. Don't let her come in here missing up what we have. This is what she wants to do, but don't let her succeed."

"DeDe, you can keep this liar. I don't want him." She pushed him out of her way and stormed out of the door slamming it behind her.

A liar he was, DeDe thought, as she stood staring at him and he at her. She looked at the beautiful ring and thought about the third engagement that was not going to be carried out as planned. But it was okay.

"For three years I loved you enough to let you break-up with me whenever you felt you needed space. I saw no wrong in you. I used to place your last name at the end of my first name and I prayed for the day you would commit. I understood that I wouldn't be the first woman to give you a child, because of your past with Shannon. But knowing I wouldn't be the first to give you the second, is a pill too big for me to swallow."

"DeDe."

"No, let me finish. I chose not to see a lot of things in you; although you had told and shown me several times before this night, and before she walked into my office and told me again." She slid the ring off her finger and handed it to him, because it didn't belong to her. It belonged to the woman he had manipulated and lied to in order to charge it on her credit card. DeDe didn't feel right or justified in keeping it. "I don't want this anymore. I don't want you anymore, because it's just not right."

"DeDe, baby, she means nothing to me. I wasn't even there during the pregnancy nor was I there during the birth of the child —"

"And Stephan, am I supposed to jump up and down and act like this thing never happened because you weren't? What fool do you take me for?"

"Baby."

"Pack your things and get out."

34

IT was over, just like that. And as she thought she would, she sat sadly in disbelief, as the locksmith placed new locks on all of the doors. She had no plans of ever loving Stephan again; not after measuring the love and the hurt he caused her. And the hurt far outweighed the love. All the love she had for him; she sent with him, and she wouldn't need it anymore. She felt a sense of freedom and strength for finally setting herself free from him, but she didn't need to tell the world as of yet. She was in no mood to be talking on the phone. He was able to pack all of his clothes in suitcases and bags. He still had to come back for his stereo and his furniture that was in the garage. She hoped he would come and get those things soon, because she was ready to close the Stephan chapter in her life.

The locksmith finished with all the locks and he gave her new keys to the doors, as she wrote him out a check. After letting him out, she poured herself a glass of Beringer Zinfandel, then turned off the sound to the constant ringing of the phone that was driving her crazy. It was her mother and girlfriends calling to check on her, after she called them crying about what she had found out. She walked to her bedroom, climbed back into bed, and began reading her magazine. She noticed Stephan had left a couple of t-shirts of his laying on the bed that she liked wearing. She burst-out crying, for all the time she had wasted that she couldn't get back. She also mourned all the hurt she was feeling and there was nothing but time that could heal her. As she wiped away her tears, she had promised herself that the next thirty minutes would be the only time that she would allow herself to live in regret, and cry about it. She had gotten up to get more tissue, when she heard her cell phone ring. She reached into her bag to check the caller I.D. It was Elliott. On the fourth ring, she answered it.

"I thought I was going to get your voice-mail."

"So why did you call?"

He chuckled. "You know you make it very difficult for a man to stick to his guns, when you are so damn attractive and you keep yourself in view for him to notice you, when he tries not to."

"What are you talking about Elliott, you practically ignored me today and you haven't returned any of my phone calls. How is it so difficult to stick to your guns? What guns are you trying to stick to anyway?"

"To not be a part of your game."

"Game," she replied. "I don't have any game. If I did, I wouldn't be in the situation I'm in now." She hoped he didn't ask any questions, about the statement she just made. She really didn't feel at liberty to tell him she and Stephan were no longer together. He probably wouldn't believe her anyway and he wouldn't put himself in the same position to again be used on the rebound. "I just came to the restaurant so we could talk."

"During lunch time? I'm not able to talk, during that time we're very busy. You know that."

"All I know is that you ignored me."

"If a woman protects herself from being hurt twice, what's the saying, 'You go sistahgirl!' If a man does it, he's wrong. Why don't you come by now?"

DeDe looked at her clock. It was ten-thirty. By it being late, as well as how she was feeling, and the vibe she was getting from him, they weren't going to just talk. That wouldn't be all bad, but she didn't feel like putting on clothes. Also, she was tired from crying all day and she had to get up for work tomorrow morning. "Not tonight."

"Okay," he said with disappointment in his voice.

After hanging up the phone she sat back and contemplated what she should do, as her desire to be held in Elliott's arms overpowered everything else she was feeling. She couldn't invite him to her place. Not with her fear of Stephan hiding in the shrubs or him trying to sneak around to see if his key still fit the locks. She picked up the phone and called him back. "I'm on my way."

"Okay, now that's much better."

She packed her clothes for work and her overnight bag. She then jumped into the shower, oiled her body with lavender scented oil, and threw on a dress and some mules. Before heading out the door, she looked through the peephole to make sure she didn't see Stephan, or an unfamiliar car parked near her house. The coast was clear. She dashed out to her car, as fast as the speed of lightning.

Elliott answered the door in his satin blue pajama pants wearing no shirt. DeDe's intuitions were correct and she wasn't mad.

"Hey," he said, and gave her a quick peck on the lips.

"Hi."

"Oh, you're spending the night?" He asked, as he took her overnight and garment bag and placed them in the foyer closet. She watched him, as she burned with the desire to finally feel him inside her again. The wetness from her desire had already begun to flow. He walked back over to her and picked her up and she wrapped her short legs around his waist, as he carried her to his bedroom and laid her on his bed, and himself on top of her.

DEDE WAS IN such a deep, relaxing infant-like sleep, and the man that had provided her such good rest, was lying beside her. She thought she was dreaming, when she was awakening out of her sleep, by the ringing of her cell phone. It must have rung several times, before she realized it wasn't a dream. It was three o'clock in the morning. She reached for her purse to answer it, and it had stopped. She assumed it was Stephan; after he had come by and didn't see her car, and he tried placing his key into the lock and discovered they were changed. There were several messages. She wasn't going to listen to them, but her curiosity had gotten the best of her. She had to listen, so she activated the replay. She couldn't make out the first two messages, because of static and what seemed like Stephan crying. Her phone began to ring again while she was trying to make out the messages he had left. She immediately answered the phone, it was Stephan, and he was crying. She had never heard him cry before. Her heart broke with sorrow although she felt he deserved to feel pain. She didn't want to wake Elliot, so she eased out of bed and walked out into the hall. Dedrick was rushed to the hospital after being shot by Carla's boyfriend, while trying to climb through a window to get in the house. The doctors didn't think he was going to make it, because the bullet was inches away from his heart and he had lost a lot of blood. Stephan didn't have to ask for DeDe to come to the hospital; she was going anyway.

She rushed back into the room and flipped on the light screaming. "I need to go."

Elliott jumped out of his sleep and sat up in the bed. "Is everything okay."

"I just need to go." She searched for her panties with frantic haste and threw them on.

"Baby, what's going on?"

"I need to go to the hospital," she began to cry. "A friend of Stephan's was shot tonight."

If she had mentioned anyone else's name, he would have asked her, if she needed him to drive her. Since Stephan was somewhere in the drama, he knew that wouldn't be a good idea. He got up, put on his robe, and walked her to the door. He reached to hug her good-bye, but she rushed out of the house without even noticing. He yelled behind her, "DeDe, be careful."

WHEN SHE RUSHED to the waiting area of the emergency room; Stephan was there huddled together with a group of others that consisted of Dedrick's family and friends stricken with grief, as they tried to console one another. Dedrick was dead. Stephan ran over to her screaming. "He's gone, DeDe…he's gone!" They held each other tightly, while crying for Dedrick and themselves.

As everyone began to leave the hospital, Stephan jumped into the car with DeDe. She didn't want him anymore, but she wasn't cold hearted. He had just lost one of his best friends and he needed someone to be there for him. She drove him back to her place, so that he could get some rest. He stood in the middle of the vestibule, as if he needed permission to go any further.

"So, you changed the locks?"

She looked at him without answering.

"Where were you tonight, when I came by?"

"At Kendra's." Which was a very necessary lie, she thought. With all the pain he was feeling with Dedrick's death and their recent break-up; the truth had no place emerging here and now.

He said that he needed a glass of cognac, so that he could sleep. She fixed him a glass of Hennessey and sat beside him on the sofa, although she really didn't think that he needed it, since he and some of Dedrick's people had been drinking at the hospital. He reminisced about Dedrick and for the first time, blamed himself. He began to cry, as he laid his head on DeDe's lap. She became nervous. She hoped he couldn't smell the fresh sex between her legs, so she closed them tightly. As he sobbed, he began kissing her thigh, with small wet kisses.

"No, Stephan."

He looked up at her. "Baby, I'm not doing anything." He said, and laid his head back down on her lap and continued to kiss her thighs and knees, while trying to slide his hand between her legs.

"Stephan, stop it."

He sat up and looked into her eyes, as he tried to decide on whether to kiss her on her lips or neck. "Baby, I'm so sorry." He muttered, and kissed her on her neck and lips. "I'm sorry I hurt you. Please forgive me? I love you."

"Stephan, no." She didn't care anything about him loving her. She had no desire for him and she had just hours ago laid with Elliott. DeDe was sure the scent of him was still between her legs. Since she didn't shower before she left, there was no doubt.

"Don't tell me no, not tonight. Not when I need you baby," he said, as he continued to kiss her, while holding her breasts in his hands. "I need you DeDe."

Even if she wasn't in the mood, she felt she could fake it, just so he would leave her alone. "Just let me take a shower."

"For what? No, that'll take too long." His weight forced her back on the sofa, as he slid down to her thighs, while lifting her dress and kissing the inner part of her thigh. She kept telling him no, while trying to move his head. He slid her panties to the side and caressed her wet lips with his.

"Just let me take a shower," she groaned.

He snatched down her panties and threw her legs over his shoulders and indulged himself in tasting her love and it's sweet juices that came sporadically; once his fingers began to massage her inner walls. She was almost there, but instead of screaming the same words she had to Elliott last night; she screamed, "No!" and pushed his head away from her and jumped up.

"What in the hell is this?" He asked, as he looked at her and the condom he had extracted from her vagina, when she snatched away from him.

She could have fainted. It was Elliott's condom. It obviously had slid off, while they were making love, and neither one of them realized it.

"DeDe, what in the fuck is this?"

There was no explanation, because she and Stephan hadn't had sex before she put him out and he never wore condoms with her. He flicked the condom from his fingers onto the floor.

"If you weren't at Kendra's," he said, as he grabbed the flower vase from the coffee table as if he was going to throw it at her.

"No, Stephan. I'll call the police."

"Then where in the fuck were you?" He threw the vase up against the wall. "Fuck! How could you do this to me? I wasn't gone a full ten hours and you were already sleeping with someone else? My DeDe." He began screaming and crying, while holding his stomach. "Aw shit! How could you?" He asked, just before he released the cognac and everything he had eaten and drank onto her peaches n' cream carpet and sofa. She cried for him to try to make it to the bathroom, as he continued to regurgitate all over her floor. By the time he had made it to the bathroom, there was what seemed like at least ten gallons of vomit covering her, her furniture, floors and walls.

She stood in disbelief trying not to inhale the stench of the regurgitated liquor, food and bile. She stormed to the bathroom, where he knelt over the toilet with nothing else to throw-up. "I want you out of my fuckin' house now."

σσσσσ

THREE DAYS HAD gone by, after Stephan intentionally threw up on DeDe's things. She was still angry. It cost her a hundred and fifty dollars to clean her carpets, a hundred for her sofa, seventy-five for the loveseat, and time on her knees to clean the walls. She could have strangled him and let him lie dead in his own throw-up, as mad as she was. When he finally pulled himself up from around the toilet, he called her every bitch and whore he could think of, and he cried out in tears and more expletives how much he hated her. He even called her a skanky, flat-ass cunt! DeDe didn't care, because she felt the same about him and she let him know it. He began throwing up once again on the clean parts of the carpet and then her loveseat. He even puked all over the delicate Japanese lamp that Elliott had given her, because she admired it so much. She cried for him to stop, but he paid her no attention. He stopped when she threatened to call the police. With him being so afraid of the law, he left before she could dial 911. She hadn't heard from him since then, and she hoped to never ever hear from him again. She had made up in her mind not to give him his stereo or furniture, until he paid her back some of her money. She finally called her mother and everyone she had asked to be in the wedding, to let them know it was called off. Everyone except for her mother let out a sigh of relief. Her mother didn't know much about her past with Stephan. Therefore, she didn't understand, until DeDe told her about Tawanda and the child.

DEDE SAT OVER in the corner watching the front door of Dedrick's mother's house, praying that Stephan would not walk through the torn screen door. But if and when he does, she's walking out. She didn't want to come to the wake, for the fear of running into Stephan but Kendra begged her to come with her. She felt she owed Dedrick much respect for stopping Melvin from beating her to death on several occasions in the past. DeDe believed Dedrick was the furthest from Kendra's mind. She was there to see Melvin. She kept talking about him and watching the door for him. DeDe had to use every opportunity she had to convince her to leave Jeremiah alone. This was no exception, but Kendra refused. She still insisted on being in love with him and was convinced that he was going to leave Charva. But until then, they were going to continue to see and screw each other, without skipping a beat. Kendra informed DeDe that he was going to fly in on Saturday to take her furniture shopping.

Melvin walked through the door and immediately spotted Kendra, as if he knew she would be sitting in the corner waiting for him. Everyone welcomed him with cheers, handshakes and hugs. He was paying for Dedrick's funeral, since neither he nor his family had any insurance. He walked over to DeDe and Kendra. DeDe stood up to hug him.

"Hello DeDe," he said, and kissed her on the cheek. He looked at Kendra, who sat with her arms folded trying to pretend that she could care less if he spoke to her or not. "I hate your guts," he told her, while staring at her as if he could kill her.

"And I hate yours too," she told him, in a nonchalant, matter of fact fashion.

They continued staring at each other, until Melvin cried, "Baby, he's gone!" She stood up to comfort him with a hug. For the life of her, DeDe would never understand those two. She would not have that type of love-hate, backwards and forwards relationship with Stephan, because it was finally over.

The burial was scheduled for Saturday, but DeDe didn't think she was going to make it. She didn't like funerals. She liked to remember the person as they were, before they died. She wanted memories of the person being alive and vibrant, not dead, dressed-up in a casket, to be laid in the ground forever. Dedrick had a lot of friends and family to crowd his mother's small house.

Carla wasn't allowed to show her face around there. Not after the man she had put Dedrick out for had killed him.

DeDe was now ready to go. If she didn't want to see Stephan, she sure as hell didn't want to see Shannon. But she now had no choice when she walked through the door with Alexis. DeDe didn't think that Shannon would be there. DeDe moved down two seats and tapped Kendra on the shoulder to tell her that she was ready to go, but Kendra was in la-la land with Melvin. DeDe got up to go wait in the car. Just as she walked toward the door, Stephan walked in holding his little girl, Celine with Tawanda trailing behind him. DeDe wasn't surprised to see them together. Stephan was the type of man who couldn't be alone. Although Tawanda said that she didn't want Stephan, she seemed like she would take him back regardless. Even after he had told her he didn't want her, she would take him anyway that she could get him. DeDe didn't react to the happy family, she walked past them without saying a word or even acknowledging their presence, or them being together. DeDe didn't know whether to feel sorry for them or whether they deserved each other.

35

"*NOW* that he's given her AIDS she wants a divorce, or so she says," Dorothy uttered after she stuffed two crackers into her mouth and took a gulp of wine. "He should give her that divorce, and let her walk out of that court-room with nothing. I don't feel sorry for her, and I will not fall into her pity party. Like they say, she can't prove that he gave it to her. Putting that man's business out in the streets like that."

"He was fooling around in her face and she wouldn't leave him then but now," Tangala said and chuckled. "Eventually he had to bring something like AIDS home, with as many woman as he was fooling with."

"That was her husband, it wasn't that easy to leave him," Candace told her.

"He was fooling around in her face; how come it wasn't easy to get out?" A heavyset woman in about her late thirties asked, as she grabbed a handful of crackers and a big chunk of cheese from the tray. DeDe had never seen her there before but she seemed to know all of the beauticians.

"It takes some women forever to leave a boyfriend, who they aren't legally tied to." Candace told her. "So, how easy is it to leave your husband?"

"Damn easy," Laverne Butler said in a loud and definitive way. "Especially if you thought he was gay all along. She's saying that he was gay."

"Now she's trying to mess up his life and career with rumors," A pregnant woman with swollen ankles, hands, nose, and face said, as she wobbled to the spa area for a pedicure. DeDe thought if she had to swell up and look like that she would never get pregnant. "All because she's angry that he doesn't want her. He doesn't have AIDS."

"He could be just a carrier," Darinda said. "But, why won't he go get a test to find out if he is or not? There's something very suspicious about that. She's his wife, she's been diagnosed with AIDS, and he's talking about his rights to privacy."

DeDe had caught the tail end of the conversation, as she came from underneath the dryer. She wanted to know who they were talking about, but she didn't want to seem nosey and ask. Today's newspaper with the article and the picture of the couple when they were happy was being passed around the salon held the answer to all of her questions. When the paper finally got to her, she recognized the masculine football player right off the bat, without looking at his name. She had remembered standing in shock when Mr. Rick Tatum approached Kendall the night of Jamal's party, and they had gone outside. Rick was gay and there was a possibility that he did have AIDS, if he slept with Kendall, and Kendall is infected. A while ago, when she had asked Kendall whether he knew Byron, she should have come right out and asked him if he had ever been tested for AIDS. And if he said no he hadn't, then why not? Kendall did tell her that he didn't know anybody and never met anybody named Byron, but he would put his feelers out.

"How can you show no sympathy for her, she just found out she has AIDS?" Darinda asked the ladies who seemed like they could care one way or another about Rick's wife.

"No one has sympathy for fools and their hearts." Some of the women nearly fainted, when Tangla said that. But she was right, DeDe thought. No one cares about a fool who's been a fool twice. When she called her girlfriends crying, after finding out Stephan had another child, not one of them showed her any sympathy or even said a comforting word. Their main concern and question was, 'When are you going to leave him?' They were tired of her crying to them after Stephan hurt her. There was no more sympathy for her and now she understood. She was now feeling that way about Charva, after finding out the drama she had been through with Jeremiah and the scarlet disease he had left on her life.

She had called DeDe yesterday very excited about hiring a private investigator to follow Jeremiah. DeDe didn't understand why she was wasting money or what's the point of getting an investigator, when she wasn't going to leave him. Nevertheless, the investigator had given her confirmation that her intuitions were true. He told her that Jeremiah was definitely seeing another woman. Charva also learned that his concubine lived in Houston, and he had bought her a new car. DeDe became nervous. She knew it would only be a matter of days before Charva found out that the other woman was Kendra. DeDe thought she better tell her before she finds out from the investigator and all hell breaks loose. No matter how wide she pried her mouth open to say 'My sister is sleeping with Jeremiah', nothing would come out. Knowing how Charva is, telling her wasn't going to be that easy.

Through all of Charva's excitement of knowing, she wasn't crazy. She began to cry. DeDe didn't feel sorry for her. Her heart had turned hard toward her over the last month; only after finding out how much drama she had put up with from Jeremiah. "Why are you crying," She asked, in a nonchalant way, because Charva's sobbing was running up the airtime on her cell phone.

"Girl, my life is shot to hell."

"Why would you say that? He's only cheating, and if it's a man you are worried about being without, you could get another man."

"It's not that easy. I don't want to go through the process of becoming close to anyone else and explain to them—"

"Explain to them what?" DeDe asked, not knowing what she could be talking about.

"You have to promise me that you won't tell anyone," she said, and waited for DeDe to confirm.

"Okay."

Charva sighed and said. "Jeremiah gave me herpes."

"Oh my God, I'm so sorry." Kendra came to the forefront of DeDe's mind and heart.

"He gave it to me eight years ago. Don't no man want a woman with herpes. I don't care how beautiful I am. I hope he's using protection with this new woman, because with the other woman who recently had his bastard child, he obviously didn't."

DeDe had to soften her heart toward her, and cried out for the pain she was feeling. Charva wasn't only staying with him for the children, power, fame and money. She felt trapped to him, and now DeDe understood.

For the entire day, DeDe tried calling Kendra to inform her of the health risk she was facing. She also wanted to curse her out for being a backstabbing, gold-digging bitch. Knowing Kendra's love for men with money and her penchant for getting pregnant to get a child support check; she didn't require Jeremiah to wear condoms. DeDe wished there was a way she could help Delphinine Tatum.

DEDE HEADED OUT of the salon looking beautiful with no place to go, as usual. She had called Elliott with hopes of stopping by to see him and pick up her things, but there was no answer. They've been playing phone tag, since she rushed out of his house in the middle of the night to go to the hospital. Since she was out, she decided to go by Kendra's to plead with her to end it with Jeremiah, because he was nasty and Charva had hired a private investigator. She had left several messages on her voice-mail outlining details of what she's learned. She expected to hear from her by now, but she had not. She knocked on the door and Kendall answered, which was a surprise in itself, because DeDe rarely saw him anymore. As she stood in the hallway, and he in the doorway, Delphinine Tatum and AIDS came rushing to her mind. She quickly looked him over for external symptoms she associated with AIDS: frailness, sunken face and facial lesions. She didn't see anything.

"What's up? Kendra isn't here."

That was okay, because she could talk to him about Rick Tatum. "Can I come in?" She asked, as she pushed him to the side and walked in anyway. She walked down the hall and around the corner to the sunken den. Her eyes met Hezekiah's, as he sat on the sofa with his pants unbuckled. Her mouth dropped wide-open in shock and she spun and pivoted back to the door, where Kendall was still standing.

"Close your mouth bitch. I told you she wasn't here."

"You two are going to get enough of messing with people's husbands."

"No we won't, not until they get enough of messing with us."

DEDE HAD CLOSED one chapter in her life, after she sent Stephan packing. Now she was beginning a new one. She was stuck in a quandary trying to figure out where her obligations rested. She wrestled with the moral of the various stories and the potential outcomes. She kind of knew what most of the consequences were going to be. She has a sister who is sleeping with her best friend's husband, and there's a possibility she might contract herpes, if she already hasn't. She believed her brother has AIDS or is HIV positive and he was sleeping with married men who already had or eventually will take some form of the dreaded disease home to their wives. Damn! Only in her family, could this type of insane mess happen. Thinking about all of it, was a bit too much for her to try and figure out alone in one night. She could use Elliott's company and bounce things off of him. He was intelligent, good at giving advice and problem solving. He was also good at other things she was defi- nitely in the mood for, besides talking. Since she was on his side of town, she just figured she'd just stop by and say hello. It was nine o'clock on a Friday night, and there was no doubt in her mind that he wasn't home.

She didn't see his car but she knocked on his door anyway. He answered, with a surprised look on his face and the aroma of food behind him.

"What's up?" DeDe asked.

"Hey."

"Am I just in time for dinner?"

He didn't answer. He stood in the doorway looking at her, holding the doorknob, which kept her from making another step into his house.

His actions seemed strange, yet familiar. She couldn't just push him aside and walk in because, he wasn't her brother and he wasn't her man. "Do you have company?" She asked, not really wanting to hear the answer. She had already assumed so, because of his body language and how he was acting.

"Yeah."

"Well, I can come back at another time. I just thought that, since I was on this side of town, I would just stop by and pick up my things; since we've been playing phone tag all week."

"Yeah, come on in." DeDe walked in and stood in the foyer, looking around for the woman, her purse, or an overnight bag; something, anything that said she was there to stay for the night. DeDe jerked her head toward the kitchen, where she heard a somewhat familiar melody being hummed. Just when DeDe began to move in the direction of the sound, the woman who was humming came out of the kitchen carrying two glasses and a bottle of Moet.

"Baby...Oh, hello DeDe."

DeDe forced herself to speak. "Hello Erika."

They stood staring at each other.

"I moved your things to the back, because I had to use this closet. I'll be right back."

DeDe didn't pay any attention to what Elliott had said. She wondered how fast it would take her to snatch the knife out of her back, that Erika had jabbed in it, and go jab it right through her heart. She felt she had a right to show her ass. He had just slept with her on Monday and Erika knew they used to be an item.

He came back with her things in a box, which meant he tried to hide the fact she had been there. It had to be somewhat serious between he and Erika.

"Why didn't you tell me?" DeDe asked, as she took the box.

"Because you didn't call before you came by, and you didn't ask."

"What an answer."

She walked out to her car carrying her box, not allowing herself to feel the pain associated with betrayal and being used. She had been there and done that with Stephan. DeDe knew from experience that the crying and the anger never made her pain feel any better. She turned the ignition, put her foot on the gas and said aloud, "DeDe girl, just chalk it up as another one of life's many learning experiences."

WHEN SHE GOT home, she dropped her box in the hallway, flipped on the television and her CD player. She wanted a glass of Zinfandel, but she wasn't going to have a glass just yet. She was already relaxed and her state of mind was calm. She wanted to be sure she was doing the right thing. She flopped down on her sofa, picked up her phone and dialed Charva's number nervously, with her hands trembling and her heart pounding. Charva answered, in a very cheerful mood, because she saw DeDe's name on her caller I.D.

"What are you doing in the house on a Friday night? You're now single, shouldn't you be out trying to find someone to replace that jerk Stephan?"

DeDe chuckled. "I'm just going to spend some time by myself, for a while. Until I figure out and totally understand what the lesson was that I should have learned, from all of this."

"I hear you girl, because believe it or not; there's a lesson to learn in everything we go through."

DeDe heard the children and Jeremiah in the background. Her heart sank. Right now wasn't the best time to tell her. "Baby, tell DeDe I said hey." Jeremiah yelled.

"Did you hear my husband? He's over here as old as he is, letting these oversized children ride on his back. Tomorrow he'll be singin' the blues, when he tries to get up to fly to New York," she laughed. "I'm making pizza and virgin daiquiris for them. I wish you were here in Phoenix with us instead of sitting in that house all alone."

"Girl, I'm fine. I'm alone, but I'm not lonely."

Her doorbell rang. She wasn't expecting anyone. Elliott was with Erika, Stephan was with Tawanda, and her girlfriends never got out of the house to just drop by. She looked through the curtain of her sidelight window. It was Kendra.

"Why in the hell are you coming by my house looking for me, and calling me like you got a damn problem," she yelled, as DeDe opened the door and she walked into the house slamming the door behind her. "Stay out of my damn business."

DeDe looked at her, while shaking her head and walking back into the den.

"Who is that?" Charva asked.

"Kendra, which brings me to the reason that I called you."

"What?"

"I know the hell you are not," Kendra whispered. "DeDe, who are you talking to?"

"Charva, I think you need to sit down."

"No the hell you're not?"

DeDe looked up at Kendra and rolled her eyes, because yes the hell she was. Kendra recognized the seriousness in her face and she flopped down on the sofa and folded her arms. Kendra was in shock that DeDe, her own sister, was actually about to tell Charva what was going on. "There's no need for you to keep that private investigator to learn who Jeremiah is seeing, because I know who he's seeing."

"You have no goddam right," Kendra snapped at her, through clenched teeth.

"Who is it DeDe?"

"Kendra and Jeremiah are seeing each other."

Kendra could not believe what she was hearing.

"And they have been for some time now. He's not flying to New York, he's coming here to see her tomorrow."

"You evil unhappy bitch!" Kendra jumped up and screamed. "I hate you!"
And stormed into the kitchen.

"I've known for awhile, but I didn't know how to tell you. I tried to get her to stop but she wouldn't. I understand if you're upset with me."

"Nope."

"Well, since you are telling her everything," Kendra said, as she walked back out of the kitchen and flopped back down on the sofa. "Why don't you tell her I'm pregnant, and I'm keeping my damn baby!"

"Here, why don't you?" DeDe told her, as she threw her the cordless phone. Kendra picked up the phone from her lap and hung it up.

"DeDe, you had no right!"

"Getting pregnant for a check every month; was it worth it?" DeDe looked her over hoping she was lying because she wasn't showing. "He has herpes, Kendra! Did you know that?"

Kendra looked at her and rolled her eyes. She knew, but she didn't find out until it was a bit too late. During one of their early screwing sessions right after Erika's release party, while in the throwes of passion, Jeremiah moaned, "Oh baby, you are so good. I'm cummin';" she snatched off his condom and flopped back down on him and waited for him to ejaculate what she thought was her guaranteed ticket to mega-wealth and the big time. Afterwards, Jeremiah told her that he had herpes and she might be sorry that she had done that. She felt she would deal with the problem if and when it arose. She just hoped that she was pregnant.

"That's something you have to live with the rest of your life. Who's going to take care of this unborn child, when you don't even take care of the two you already have?"

"Don't you worry your little short-ass about it."

There was a heavy knock at the door. DeDe looked at Kendra, before going to the door because she wasn't expecting anyone.

"Hello Melvin," DeDe said, looking back at Kendra.

"What's up DeDe? Baby, why were you driving so damn fast?"

"I'm sorry," she said, smiling as she walked over to hug and kiss him.

"Are we going to my place or yours?" Melvin asked her.

"Wherever," she said and kissed him again.

"Kendra," DeDe called, just before she walked out of the door.

"Baby, I'll meet you outside." She walked over to DeDe.

"What are you doing?" DeDe asked her. "Don't mess up his life."

"DeDe get you some business and stay the hell out of mine," she advised her and stormed out of the door, slamming it behind her.

The phone rang, she rushed to answer it thinking it was Charva, but it was Kendall. She answered with annoyance in her voice.

"Hello. What do you want Kendall? I guess now the mission is accomplished once again by the dynamic groupie duo. Hurray," she sarcastically said, as she began clapping her hands. "Did you know your big sluty-ass twin is about to have a baby by Mr. Jeremiah Williams the rich, super-producer with herpes? But what do you care, you might have AIDS?"

"Bitch, I don't have AIDS for your info." Since you like to keep your nosey ass in everybody's business, talk to your girlfriend Dionne and stay out of my shit!"

36

DIONNE prayed for relief from the pain she was feeling from the broken heart Byron had left her to mend on her own. She had promised herself to never let any man take her through what she had seen many other women like DeDe go through. But without warning and no consideration of her age, maturity, mental capacity and the lessons learned from being broken hearted in the past; she was now experiencing it yet again.

"I broke down and called him," Dionne confessed. "Leaving several messages, but he hasn't called me back." She gazed out of the window with a despondent look of woe on her face, as she caught glimpses of the ground as Charlotte flew down the street of her subdivision doing 60mph. "I know I said I wouldn't call him, but I couldn't help it. I really did like 'im; I was hooked. Now I see how love sneaks in, when you least expect it and crushes you just like that," she said, as she snapped her fingers. "I don't know who was the first to say it, but love does hurt! It takes all of your strength, causing you to doubt what you've always been told and believed; that you're not as strong and invincible as you think you are. You also realize that you too can be played for a fool, no matter how careful you try to be. I was that rock of Gibraltar type of person, and now look at me. I'm hurting and dying inside;

with no strength to take the first step to heal myself."

Charlotte gave no comforting words, before she began talking about her own problems. There Dionne was trying to wallow in her own pool of self-pity, while trying to figure out what had gone wrong between she and Byron; and Charlotte jumps in the same pool alongside her beginning to flounder, giving Dionne no room to sink to the bottom and call upon her best friend for rescue.

"Girl, I just knew I was on my way to fame and fortune. So where do I go from here, now that I'm not?" Charlotte asked herself and Dionne, as they reached in the backseat of her car for their shopping bags. "I think we should tell DeDe."

"*We* are not going to do anything of the sort," Dionne said, as she rolled her eyes and jumped out of the car. She was tired of hearing Charlotte talk about a book that never should have been written in the first place. At least she got a hundred thousand dollars out of the deal. Dionne had gotten nothing from Byron, but a shattered heart." Why tell her now, so she and the publishing company can sue you? Are you out of your cotton-pickin' mind?" Dionne asked her, as they entered the house.

"Yes, because I have nothing now. That was my book and my idea, but not anymore. Since I signed the rights over to them, they took it from me and put someone else's name on it. I was on my way to the top and wham! Just like that, I was halted...pushed and left rolling down an endless hill." she said, as she threw her keys in the crystal bowl sitting on the mahogany table in the foyer and called out for Iyana. With speed and purpose, Dionne rushed into the kitchen, sat down at the table, flipped open the Styrofoam container of Chinese take-out they had gotten on their way home, and inhaled the steamy aroma of ginger and garlic. She was starved, since she had been too hurt to have an appetite or even think about eating before now.

"They felt my book would be a best-seller, if and only if it had the right name on it. So, since Euleith Gordon is a well renown author with an established audience base, they gave her my book." Charlotte said, as she grabbed two glasses and a bottle of merlot from the wine closet. She poured a glass taking a sip, before pouring a glass for Dionne and handing it to her. "I had never heard of such nonsense, until they showed me the contract where I had actually signed to be a ghost writer." She took another sip of her wine, while leaning up against the purple marble counter flipping through her mail. "There I was thinking Ian's so-called attorney friend had thoroughly read over the contract, and come to find out he was a damn real estate attorney. He knew nothing about the technical verbiage, fine print or details of a literary contract. Bastard!" she called him, just before she threw the mail down and picked up her bags and went upstairs to her bedroom.

Dionne enjoyed every bite, as she chewed slowly to savor the taste of the garlic chicken and cashews with rice.

"Dionne," Charlotte yelled. "Come and tell me what you think?"

She got up from the table, stuffed one more spoonful of food into her mouth, grabbed her wine and walked up the stairs to the second floor. When she arrived at the threshold of the bedroom door, Dionne's mouth dropped open and her eyes bugged out, and said "What the fuck?" Charlotte stood wearing a feather-covered mask, six-inch heels, dressed in a black leather crotchless, breastless, dominatrix outfit holding a long whip. "My God," Dionne said, as she took two steps backwards.

"So what do you think?" She asked her, as she twirled around.

"Who are you supposed to be?"

"A dominatrix silly. I'm giving myself the name Madame Ooh-la-lick-me."

"For who, for what?" Dionne asked, as she sat down in the chair watching her parade around the room in the stiletto heels with no problem.

"My hubby."

"Well, I need to be going, because I don't want to stay here and watch you beat his ass or him beat yours 'cause he thinks that you have lost your damn mind."

"You don't have to worry about that. I'm kinda kinky, but I ain't no freak. But now that I see the time, he should have been home by now." She ran over to the phone to call him, but noticed the red light on the answering machine blinking. She pressed the 'play' button, and asked, "Dionne, did you leave me any food?" Dionne nodded her head and said, "Of course. What else would I say with you standing there with that damn whip in your hand?"

"Message one," the digital voice on the answering machine said, before playing the message.

"Hi mom or dad," Iyana said. "Raven's mom is taking us to the movies later, so I'm just going to stay the night at her house. I hope it's okay. You guys have been really happy lately; so I figured you two would probably use this time with me out of the house to catch-up on your reading or work on a crossword puzzle together. Bye," as she laughed.

"Good. Did you hear that child, trying to be funny?" Charlotte giggled as she shook her breast and erased the message.

"Aren't you going to check to make sure she's spending the night at Raven's house?"

"No," she said, as if her teenage daughter couldn't lie. "I trust my daughter."

"Those are precisely the ones who lie."

"Let me change out of this get-up, before Ian comes home. I'm saving this for a special occasion." Charlotte said, as she went into her closet and took off her 'take no prisoners' clothes and slipped into a teal, one piece, Anthony Mark Hankins silk jumper.

Message two.

"Charlotte this is your mother call me."

"Not tonight," she said, and erased the message.

Message three.

"Hey Ian, when you get this—"

"That's Byron," Dionne said, as she somewhat lit up at the sound of his sexy baritone voice, which had always soothed her.

"Hello, hello." Ian answered out of breath, as he picked up the phone.

"Hey, what's up? I thought I was getting the machine."

"No, you got me in the flesh; literal and figuratively. I just stepped out of the shower."

"Don't say that too loudly, you might cause a riot."

"Yeah, yeah; what do you want?"

"I was wondering if you wanted to meet me for drinks," Byron asked him.

"Oh, I like his nerve," Dionne chimed in. "He has time to go out for drinks with my best friend's husband, but he can't call me back."

"Girl, that's what I'm talking about," Charlotte agreed. "You're over here hurting and he's out drinking. Men."

"Not tonight." Ian told him.

"Why not, please?"

"I have things to do," he snapped.

"Things, like what? Pretty please?"

Charlotte looked over at Dionne with a puzzled, confused, and perplexed look. She wondered if Charlotte noticed the agitation and gruffness in Ian's voice and the meek passive voice of Byron pleading and looking for an explanation, from her husband.

"I haven't seen you in a couple of nights. I paged you and you have yet to return any of my phone calls. I come by your office and you're too damn busy to talk to me. What's going on, Ian? Come on out for drinks, and I'll make whatever's wrong, all better."

Oh-my-God, Charlotte thought. This wasn't the normal conversation of two guys just meeting for drinks to shoot the breeze. It seemed like something more.

"There's nothing going on. What did I tell you about calling here?" Ian asked him.

"Well, if you don't return my calls, what am I supposed to do?"

Dionne stared down at the floor as the words of their conversation and tone of their voices entered her like a keen knife. They're gay; no they can't be, she thought. Her mother thought Byron was a sissy and so did her brothers, because of his effeminate mannerisms, which she just didn't see. She had always thought that Ian was fooling around and cheating with someone, but not with the man she was so crazy about. Damn, this simply cannot be.

"Leave me the hell alone," Ian told him. "I'm not the one you need. I'm married and I love my wife."

"Yeah, right. You are as unhappy with her, as you are with coming to grips about being gay."

"I'm not gay, dammit!"

He sighed. "How many times do we have to go through this Ian, every other month? You know, it's been two whole years—"

Charlotte had known him for twenty-two whole years, then again, she didn't. She had always joked with Dionne about him being gay, because of their sketchy sex life, which wasn't normal. Although she frequently thought it, she never for once believed that he really was gay. He was her damn husband, and her daughter's father. He was the only man she had ever laid with in her entire life. She had her reservations about Byron from the beginning, but she never said anything to Dionne or Ian. There were so many questions that needed to be answered. How? When? Where? Why?

"Charlotte!" Ian yelled out, as he walked up the stairs to their bedroom. "How many times do I have to tell you to park your car— " His words faded to a whisper as he stood in the doorway knowing he had been found out. He heard the same words and conversation that he and Byron had spoken coming from the answering machine, that Dionne and his wife were listening to. After listening for another few seconds, Charlotte said, "Straight happily married men don't do what's being talked about on that tape. Two men don't go away for the weekend together and sleep in the same bed, and not be gay. You don't let a man suck your dick, and you suck his, and not be gay. I guess if we listen a little more, we'll find out if you two take turns fucking each other in the ass. Which one are you, the fucker or the fuckee? Dionne and Charlotte's eyes traveled over him from head to his feet, in disgust.

Ian said, "Look here, y'all got it all wrong. The two women began walking towards him. What's wrong with you two?" He said, as he tried to back out of the bedroom. While backing up and keeping his eyes on Dionne and Charlotte, he tripped over one of the other surprise-filled shopping bags that Charlotte had brought upstairs with her. With him already on the floor, scared to death and scrambling to get out of there; they both pounced on him and beat him to within an inch of his life. They didn't hear any of the words coming out of his mouth, as he asked for mercy. All they heard was what was coming from the answering machine. They didn't stop pounding Ian, until the tape stopped.

Message four.

"Hello, this message is for Charlotte. Charlotte, my name is DeDe, DeDe Wilson. I work with your best friend Dionne at Stein & Stockton; she may have mentioned me to you. I need to speak to both of you right away. I've been trying Dionne's number, but I haven't had any luck there either. If you speak to Dionne before I do, tell her that I have just found out some information from my brother Kendall and this cannot wait. My number is 555-1506."

They both looked at each other, already imagining what they were going to hear and commenced to hitting Ian all over again, as he was just regaining consciousness.

"When we're through here, Byron's next."

Sonia Renee Caulton the critically acclaimed author of **The Man Hunt** and **VooDoo Love**, enjoys writing realistic romance for the realistic woman. She currently lives in Conyers, Georgia while working on her fourth novel, **When Love Comes Knocking**.

Photograph by Kilven Radford
CoverDesign by Orlando Lewis

www.sistahgirl.com